My Big Fat
Supernatural Wedding

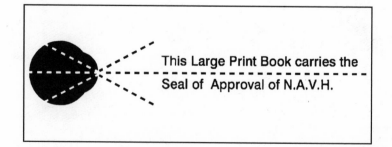

This Large Print Book carries the
Seal of Approval of N.A.V.H.

MY BIG FAT
SUPERNATURAL WEDDING

P. N. ELROD, EDITOR

WHEELER PUBLISHING

An imprint of Thomson Gale, a part of The Thomson Corporation

THOMSON

GALE

Detroit • New York • San Francisco • New Haven, Conn. • Waterville, Maine • London

LIBRARY OF CONGRESS CATALOGING-IN-PUBLICATION DATA

My big fat supernatural wedding / edited by P. N. Elrod.
  p. cm.
ISBN-13: 978-1-59722-528-1 (hardcover : alk. paper)
ISBN-10: 1-59722-528-2 (hardcover : alk. paper)
  1. Weddings — Fiction. 2. Horror tales, American. 3. Large type books. I.
Elrod, P. N. (Patricia Nead)
PS648.H6M9 2007
813'.087380806—dc22   2007009975

Published in 2007 by arrangement with St. Martin's Press, LLC.

Printed in the United States of America on permanent paper
10 9 8 7 6 5 4 3 2 1

TABLE OF CONTENTS

Spellbound

L. A. Banks

PROLOGUE

South Carolina, in the Glen

Hattie McCoy smoothed the front of her flowing white dress and sat down by an adjacent tree. Her gaze fondly drifted over to the pair of young lovers, and she sighed with contentment.

"Now, Hattie," a warm, familiar voice said before the apparition that came with it appeared. "We ain't supposed to be spying on kin like that, specially when they in delicate situations. Just because we spirits, and can, don't mean that we should."

"I know," Hattie said. She watched her friend of many years fully materialize to sit beside her. "But just look at 'em. So young, and so in love."

Ethel Hatfield smiled. "If them two don't watch out, they gonna make a baby this afternoon, if you ask me."

"I know," Hattie crooned, clasping her

hands in joy. "Wouldn't that just be divine?"

Ethel nodded and then frowned. "But that danged celibacy spell both our families cast is gonna get in the way." She glanced up. "Gonna storm, too. Them Hatfields and McCoys is at it again! Don't make sense — always thirteen women aunts conjurin' on one side against them thirteen uncles on the other . . . chile, you know how it goes through the genes on each side, but why can't folks just stop and let sleepin' dogs lie?"

"That's why I came here," Hattie whispered, standing and putting both hands on her disappearing hips. "All these years and our families are still feudin'? Don't make no kinda sense. Working roots on each other, casting evil spells, dabblin' in hoodoo — humph!"

Ethel floated toward the tree near the two lovers. "Girl, you block that tree limb and try to shoo them off the blanket 'fore it falls. I'll try to whisper some sense into these two lovebirds to try make 'em hold off until we can get this all straightened out."

Hattie covered her mouth and giggled, loving that they'd both been allowed to take on their old girlish forms once they'd crossed over to the other side as ancestors. "Chile, I don't think they'd mind right now if lightning *did* hit 'em. Gonna be mighty hard to get in between them two."

Ethel laughed. "Not sure that I want to, given how they's rubbing and bumping and grinding all up on each other. Have mercy!"

"Aw, girl, don't act like you don't remember those days. Love is a mighty powerful thing, magic all by itself," Hattie said with a mischievous wink.

Both ghosts laughed and danced about in the shards of sunlight, becoming shining pollen motes.

"Oooh, honey!" Ethel exclaimed. "What you think they'll make first — a boy or a girl?"

South Carolina, Present Day

He pulled out of their kiss like a man drowning. Odelia's sweet breath washed his lips in warm temptation, her mouth so close to his that he could still taste the mint iced tea she'd had only minutes ago. His hands slid down her shoulders, his eyes coveting every inch of her dark, satiny skin, wanting to lower the thin straps of her yellow tank top.

"I know it's hard to wait, but we can't," she whispered. "We shouldn't."

He searched her face, rendered mute for a moment by the plea within her beautiful

9

brown eyes. But the conflict he saw in them, the passion they belied, while her body against his created a hot seal that rivaled the muggy afternoon, it was more than a man could bear.

"But we're gonna be married soon," he said quietly, his thumbs lazily stroking her upper arms. "We're engaged." He swept up her hand and kissed the back of it, then the center of her palm, as his other hand stroked her long, velvety braids.

She hesitated, glanced at the two-karat stone that picked up sunlight and splashed prism-sent color against his cheek while she gently brushed it, and then stared into his eyes. What could she say to this man?

A yearlong whirlwind college romance in their senior year had turned into an engagement. A whole year of trying to abstain, like Minister had said, had been the toughest thing she'd had to endure in her life. A year of them both mysteriously neglecting to inform their families of this new development was torture. She knew why she'd omitted Jeff's existence from her family's purview, and also knew why he'd never taken her home to meet his people.

She could only pray that Jeff's folks weren't still carrying the generational grudge that was legendary between their families, and that they didn't conjure, too. According to her family's crazy view, his folks were wicked spell-casters and so was everyone in his extended family. No. Couldn't be. Jeff seemed so logical, so levelheaded, and so removed from the old superstitious ways, it was impossible that his people were like hers.

As she stared up into Jefferson McCoy's intense brown eyes, she knew there was no way to explain the insanity she'd grown up with. Once married, they'd be his kin, too. Maybe she'd break it to him gently after the wedding. Yet, how did one explain that her daddy was as close to a Dr. Buzzard-root-master as one could get, or that her aunties all worked roots, with serious, inexplicable consequences befalling the unfortunate individuals who'd dared to cross them? She'd escaped to college to get away from all of that backwoods stuff. Intellectual pursuits and the campus church had been a cloak and a shield against the kitchen conjuring her folks could do. If her family spooked this man, she'd die a natural death.

"Jeff," she said quietly, unable to draw her body away from his, "I don't want anything to mess up what we have. I don't want to tempt fate, or draw down The Wrath. If we

11

just get married quickly, privately, me and you . . . I —"

"You want to elope?" he asked in a ragged murmur, bringing his lips to her neck and breathing out the words. The more he thought about it while caressing her, the more her idea had merit. It was stupid to think that two weeks before graduation they could just drop this announcement on their families and turn what were initially supposed to be individual graduation parties into a combined, surprise wedding. At the time, it had seemed like a reasonable concept; there would already be a cake, food, people gathered, and a minister present — all that would be needed was a license, a few flowers, and a dress. He already had a good suit.

"Okay," Jeff finally choked out, unable to stop kissing her. "I can't stand a long engagement and all the drama of a wedding, anyway."

His ardent attention to her earlobe under the private canopy of trees, where they were just supposed to be having a picnic lunch, was making her forget everything Minister had said, and about the family dangers of going too far. The way Jeff's hot breath scored her ear sent tiny shivers along her spine. He smelled so good . . . deep, rich, male, and earthy . . . and felt divine; his tall, six-foot frame was like solid oak. Lawd. She couldn't help but allow her lips to taste his Hershey-toned skin, and before she knew it, her fingertips began to tingle as they grazed his short-cropped, thick hair.

"You'd do that for me?" she whispered, as he made her breath hitch with a slow kiss on her shoulder.

"I'd do anything for you," he said into her ear hotly. "Anything. I love you, girl."

It was almost too good to be true. She'd escaped. They might be able to have a life together. He'd be fresh out of law school and practicing at his first big job with his new degree in Seattle. She'd have her master's, could go there as his wife, and could pursue social work, far, far away from home. They could make love day and night, without fear of reprisal, because the union would be under the protective cloak of the Almighty; even her folks couldn't mess with that — or could they? she wondered. Maybe her children with Jeff might even be born "normal," and not have the conjurer gene or the proclivity.

When his kiss became more aggressive, she returned it in kind, knowing full well this was foolhardy. All the nights that they'd come close to breaking their vow to wait began to come crashing down on her. The ache he'd produced within her was a fire that hadn't burned out since the day they'd met.

Each near miss had only made it worse. Each chaperoned get-together, dating in a church group from campus, now made her ready to shriek. Each time they'd gone to either his or her apartment, supposedly to watch movies, they had ended up in a passionate tussle of way-too-heavy petting on the sofa, the movie neglected. The past two months, they'd both agreed not to tempt fate by doing that, citing church tenets as the reason — but there was more to it than that. Then he'd messed up and given her a ring during a quiet, unplanned dinner for two. That had almost broken them down. But today . . . she couldn't take it. Her willpower was gone.

"Jefferson, we can't," she gasped, stopping the next kiss and leaning her forehead on his chest. She could feel his heart thudding against her skull and connecting to the thud of desire between her legs. His USC T-shirt clung to his hard torso, dampened.

"Baby, I don't know how much more of this I can take. . . ."

The fact that Odelia had used his full given

14

name made him nervous. That was a no, for sure. Right now, he couldn't hear that word. He didn't care what his momma and her brothers promised would happen if he ever, in his life, hooked up with a Hatfield woman.

"You know there's no sense in us getting ourselves all worked up," she said breathlessly. "That's why I stood up and got off the darned blanket."

"I can't help it," he said, kissing the crown of Odelia's head, panting. "Ain't nobody gonna see us. Won't nobody know. We could fly to Vegas and get married tonight."

"The woods have eyes," she said, resting both hands on his shoulders.

"Then let's go back to your place," he said, hugging her to him hard, still unable to stop touching her. He had to make love to Odelia or heart failure was probable. It was already nearly impossible to breathe, he wanted her so badly. His family could conjure all they wanted, but this woman was *the one.* He refused to let them throw bones and chase her away like all the others before her.

"We can't fly to Vegas . . . I know you spent everything you had on this ring."

"Don't worry about it," he murmured as his hands slid down her back and began to caress her bottom.

Just feeling the rise of her firm behind beneath his palms made him shudder and close his eyes when her tight butt muscles clenched to the rhythm of his touch. Who cared if he was two months late in his rent and had used the last of his book money, food money, and student loan living expenses to put a rock on her hand — she was worth it. It didn't matter that he was currently flat busted. The condition was temporary, any ole way. She didn't need to worry. When he turned twenty-five in a couple of months, he'd come into a little inheritance money that had been put in trust for him by his dearly departed father. He'd use that to start their lives, buy their first home. Never in a million years would he take that home to plow it into a conjuring business with his uncles. Odelia Hatfield was worth every penny he had to his name.

His better judgment in shreds, his body continued to move against her softness, stoking the ache that swept through his groin and radiated sheer agony through his abdomen. They were *not* gonna force him to come back home and join the family conjuring business, in exchange for them lifting the celibacy spell.

Try as he might to forget the threat, the

16

more Odelia moaned and yielded to his affection, the more his mother's words rang in his ears: *You're young, baby, and sooner or later you gonna need to get that spell lifted or lose yo' natchel mind. It was your uncles' idea, not mine. Don't shoot the messenger. Your uncles was jus' angling for a compromise, suga'. So, meet 'em halfway; go on to school, and then why don't you jus' stop fighting your birthright and come on back to us after college and work with the family, like family should. Marry a nice girl from down home who understands our ways.*

It was extortion, pure and simple.

Jefferson tried to push it all out of his mind as he deepened the tender kisses that Odelia's lush mouth demanded. So what if the clan claimed he was the strongest conjurer that had been born into their family in generations? How in the world could he bring a soft, gentle creature like her home to his insane kin? She'd bolt for the hills, and he couldn't live without her. Odelia promised a normal, ordinary life, with normal, happy children. He'd be a big attorney one day and would figure out how to get a restraining order on his entire family. He'd sue them for criminal trespass! Paranormal home invasion.

His hands soon found Odelia's face, and

he cradled it as he stared into her eyes, speaking in a low, urgent tone and lobbying hard for his cause. "You and me are meant to be, 'Delia. What are the chances that we're both only children? You lost your momma on the same day and year I lost my daddy, we're even born on the same day, July twenty-first, and just so happened to be at the same university at the same time from the same part of the world, graduating the same year, and both feeling things the way we do? We practically breathe the same breath . . . can finish each other's sentences. Girl, we have the same favorite color, sky blue, and like the same music, believe the same things, and both want to be together like nobody's business; what are the odds? Tell me this ain't meant to be."

His argument was hard to deny as she stared into his eyes. They had a hypnotic quality to them that she'd seen before but just couldn't place. And the things his touch did to her body just didn't make any kinda sense. She opened her mouth to speak, but only a rush of breath exited where words failed. He pulled that same air into his mouth through his barely parted lips. Just seeing him do that made her nipples sting so sharply that she crushed her breasts against him, forcing him to wince and close his eyes.

"I know," she finally said, swallowing thickly as the ache sent slingshot spasms of desire between her thighs. "We're a perfect match."

He nodded. "That's what I've been trying to tell you. Can't nothing break us up."

"My people got funny ways," she said, practically swooning as his palms slid up her arms until his fingers were able to tease the edge of her tank top. She could barely catch her breath while his fingertips danced beneath the straps and across the swell of breasts, but not daring to go beyond the fabric border.

"Mine do, too," he admitted in a rough whisper. "You wanna go to my place? It's gonna rain."

She could only nod and gently stroke his cheek. He had no idea how serious funny ways could be. Her folks took the meaning to a whole new level. Yet he'd made the statement about the weather without even looking at the sky, just like her daddy always did. Heavy-laden clouds had indeed formed, now pregnant with pending doom. Yes, it was gonna thunder and lightning and rain cats and dogs, and all hell was gonna break loose, once her family found out she was dating a McCoy. But marry one?

Odelia almost cringed at the thought but kept her expression serene as she stared at him with love. They'd put the hoodoo on her Jefferson, would throw every conjure in the mojo book at him, just to get back at his family for possessing the wrong gene pool and because of an old Hatfield versus McCoy land score unsettled. If she slept with him, they'd *know*.

"We can't go back to your place. . . . You know what's likely to happen if we do." It was all a conjangled web of spell versus counterspell. Her aunties had cast a conjure that only a legit marriage could shield. They'd promised her that they had from the moment she'd begun to bud with puberty . . . and the insidious roots that had been worked promised that if any boy went too far, he'd fall dead away. It was their insurance policy that she'd return to the fold, bring her dead momma's inheritance with her to add to the Hatfield larder, and work alongside them one day. She believed them; her aunties didn't play. She'd never tested the theory, until Jefferson McCoy made it hard not to. The way he was looking at her now made it next to impossible to hold the line, even for his own safety.

He kissed her again and didn't answer the

charge. What could she do but kiss him back? There was no way to explain this nightmare. Determined to get away from all of that family drama, she'd up and gone to college, hoping that root conjures had distance limits. But her daddy told her he'd redoubled his efforts and gone in with his sisters on that front — to supposedly protect her virtue. She couldn't chance it, not the way she loved her Jeff.

"We're gonna get wet if we stay out here." Jefferson's voice was a quiet rumble, his gaze penetrating.

"I know," she whispered, already wetter than he could imagine. The slow trail his fingers made along the edge of her tank top was maddening. But she couldn't stop thinking about the few times they'd been alone, had come close, and the mysterious things that would always happen to break the mood and give them pause. A stove popping on — flames on high — a window slamming shut, pictures falling off the wall . . . yeah, Jefferson had ultimately come up with plausible explanations to calm her nerves, but to her mind, the virtue spell was in full effect.

"I love you," she finally said, and tried to put a bit more distance between their bodies, even while still in his embrace.

21

For a moment, he didn't answer. The look on his face was that of a tortured man. She expected the kiss that was coming, but instead he only swept her mouth, bent his neck, and spilled a series of hot, wet kisses along the edge of her tank top until she writhed.

"I love you, too," he said against her breast, and then captured a nipple between his lips and suckled it through her shirt.

He'd never touched her there before, had only held her arms, stroked her back, or caressed her face. No man had ever touched her secret places. The closest they'd gotten to that was hot friction on a sofa, their hands afraid to explore further. The sensation was exquisite; the gasp that escaped her was immediate. It made her fit herself against the hard length in his jeans and grind against it to staunch the sweet pain, even though her mind screamed for her not to.

But she couldn't pull away as his free hand cupped one tender, swollen lobe and then began to roll the distended tip of it between his fingers while his mouth played havoc with her will, wetting her tank top as it attended the other. Before she knew it, her top had been lifted to expose her bare flesh, and the sensation of his mouth against her skin put tears in her eyes. The word "don't" formed and fled on a whimper as he nuzzled the ache within her to fever pitch. Somehow her hand slipped between them on its own volition, touching a part of him she'd dared not before, and the sound that escaped him nearly buckled her knees.

Harsh kisses pelted her face as rain began to fall. A spell be damned, she couldn't hold out for a minister or a judge, nor could Jeff. They had all they needed — each other, privacy, a blanket, and a vow to marry. The intent was clear; today would be the day. Storm clouds would be their witness. There was no stopping love. She began unfastening his jeans.

A bright flash of lightning, followed by an instantaneous loud crack and heavy thunder, made them both stop, look at each other, and then jerk their attention toward the huge pine tree a hundred yards away that had been split clean in two.

"Shit . . . ," Jefferson murmured, and stepped back from her.

Odelia nodded, and fixed her top. "It's a sign."

He nodded. "Baby, listen . . . there's something I need to talk to you about."

"I know," she said, her gaze flitting between him and the angry sky. It had eerily stopped raining, but the overhead threat was still very real. "I've gotta talk to you, too."

"How about if we talk about it in my hoopty on the way home?" he said, gathering up the blanket as she snatched up the basket of abandoned food.

"Ya think?"

Racing to the car, they both jumped into his rusted-out white '87 Ford Tempo jalopy at the same time. They simultaneously turned to look at each other when Jefferson gunned the motor and another bolt of lightning struck the spot under the tree they'd just fled from.

"My family," they both said in unison.

"You first," he said, peeling down the small gravel and dirt road.

"Uh-uh. Not out here," she said, wiping her face with both palms.

"Yours, too? That's all you gotta say."

She stared at him as he drove. *"Yours?"*

"Yeah. Mine."

"They . . ."

"Yeah — they do all of that. Baby, I was hoping that all this stuff they always told us was really just a bunch of superstitious hocus-pocus, but now I don't know. . . ."

Odelia glanced up at the sky again with Jefferson as he stepped on the accelerator. The sun had mysteriously come out. Their

24

words were a quiet, unified confirmation embedded in a terrified whisper.

"Family roots."

To Odelia's mind, there was only one solution: call Nana Robinson. Her mother's mother wasn't a Hatfield and was a powerful woman in her own right. She had never accepted her youngest girl marrying a Hatfield and then dying way too young from a mysterious fever that claimed her the night of a horrible storm. Odelia had only been a crib baby then, but the family oral history on the event was cloaked in whispers and murmurs.

Odelia sat in the car outside her apartment and kept a close watch on Jefferson's expression as she told him about her kin. To her surprise, the man only rubbed his palms down his face and sighed, seeming weary, and then confessed the most outrageous set of circumstances, which eerily paralleled her own.

"So what are we gonna do?" she finally asked, relieved that her fiancé didn't think she was crazy. She'd been fully prepared to slip the engagement ring off her finger and return it.

"I need to go on ahead and meet your daddy, and do this the way men gotta do."

Odelia sat back in her seat. "Are you nuts? With *your* last name, you wanna go into Hatfield territory to meet *my* daddy *before* we get married?" She shook her head no.

"It's the only way. Can't stand another minute not being with you, girl. We gonna have to try to reason with our folks, and you're eventually gonna have to meet my momma, too. That's all there is to it — she ain't no real McCoy, just upholds the traditions on account of the fact that I got thirteen uncles that ain't to be trifled with."

Odelia closed her eyes and slumped back in the passenger's seat. "Can you see it now, Jefferson? My thirteen angry Hatfield aunts squaring off with your thirteen uncles, and all our cousins by blood at the same wedding? My daddy just goes along with the git along to keep the peace and to probably stay alive. But my aunt Effie ain't no joke."

"My uncle Rupert is the McCoy ringleader on my side. But we'll have all the Robinsons from your momma's side and all the Jones clan from my momma's side as a buffer. They'll all be there, since both me and you are the first ones graduating beyond high school on all four sides. So, the way I see it, if I can get my momma's momma, Grandma Jo, to help us out — 'cause she ain't no McCoy but ain't no slouch, either

— maybe we can get through the ceremony. Who knows? Don't worry. My grandma still ain't square with the way my momma, her daughter, ran off to marry my daddy, a McCoy. We still don't know how or why lightning struck a tree that fell on his car and killed him when I was two. I'm half scared to speculate, girl. Just trust me when I say, though, Grandma Jo got some juice, too."

This was a shaky plan; Odelia could feel it in her bones. But there was no denying how badly she wanted to be with this man. Despite the fear, her body still burned for him. It was all over his face, too. Passion denied was a powerful lure.

"We do this together," he said, pressing his point when she'd taken too long to respond. "We go up to your apartment, and make the heads-up calls . . . get a temporary truce in effect, so we can safely drive down home together. All right?"

"Okay," she said, hedging, "but how about if we don't drive down there, have them come up here to campus, and throw the graduation party–wedding reception right at the church on campus?"

"You got a point, 'Delia," he said, nodding. "Might be prudent to let Reverend Mitchell from down home co-officiate with Pastor Wise from up here, just to be on the safe side."

"Yup. You remember how it was back home: Hatfields on one side of that little church, and McCoys on the other. But if you cut out Reverend Mitchell, who knows how to deal with our kin, then that poor local pastor won't know what hit him."

"See, girl, we're on the same page," Jefferson said, opening his car door.

Odelia got out of the car, glancing around and wondering if she was missing her mind.

"What!" Nana Robinson shouted, forcing Odelia to briefly remove the telephone receiver from her ear.

"Nana, I love him, and need —"

"Chile, you go on and get that marriage license straightaway and book the church," her grandmother fussed. "You let me deal with one Ezekiel Hatfield, ornery SOB, even if he is yo' daddy. Serves him right; that ain't nuthin' but the Lord setting the record straight. Probably yo' momma up in heaven orchestrating yo' daddy's payback. So, don't you fret. We's having us a wedding, baby! I'll marshal up Opal Kay, you hear me? My sister can go up against all them Hatfield heifers who think they can conjure. My grandbaby girl done us all proud, gots her education, ain't brung us no babies home, ain't been out in the worl' fornicatin', and snagged herself a lawya — I don't care what his last name is. Humph! Plus, any monies due you by way of your momma's soul going on to glory by rights is *supposed* to stay with her chile, not them!"

"Thank you, Nana. I love you," was all Odelia could say as she watched Jefferson shift from foot to foot close by.

"I love you, too, baby," her nana said. "Stay strong. I'm calling in reinforcements. Bye-bye."

When the call disconnected, Odelia and Jefferson just stared at each other for a moment.

She handed him the cordless phone. "It's started. Nana just mounted up a war party."

He sighed and accepted the receiver from Odelia and then punched in the number he knew by heart. Growing impatient, he waited for the tenth ring, knowing that his grandmother didn't believe in technology, by way of an answering machine.

"Who dis here?" a surly elderly voice finally said once the call connected.

"Grandma Jo, it's your boy, Jefferson."

"Oh, my Lawd in heaven! Chile, whatchu doing calling this ole lady on the phone out of the blue, my favorite grandbaby?"

Jefferson hesitated. "Grandma, I've got a

29

problem."

Quiet filled the line.

"Now, baby," the old woman said slowly, "you know Gawd don't put nuthin' more on you than you can bear. Tell Grandma what's wrong."

"I met this girl; she's real nice, real —"

"She pregnant, son?"

"No, no, it ain't like that," Jefferson said in a rush, glancing at Odelia, embarrassed by the charge. "She's real sweet, a church girl I met at college, and I wanna marry her, now that I'm fixin' to graduate, but . . ."

"Then go on and do the right thing by her, boy. Marry that girl; if she passes yo' inspection, I know she'll pass mine. That ain't no problem. You grown, and did mighty right by yo'self. We's all proud of you."

He let out an exasperated sigh. "She's a Hatfield, Grandma. I fell in love with her before I actually knew that this spell stuff was real." It wasn't the complete truth, but explaining the whole thing in excruciating detail was just too much to deal with.

Again, silence filled the line, and Jefferson closed his eyes, waiting.

"Well, that does create a sticky wicket now, don't it?" his grandmother said, letting out a huff of breath.

"Grandma . . . I can't have nothin' happen to her; you know what I'm saying?"

" 'Deed I do," his grandmother said angrily. "I can't countenance them McCoys worth a damn! Not that I'm casting aspersions on you, suga', but you know how I feel about yo' daddy's people. I ain't two-faced about it; they all knows how us Joneses feel, especially yo' momma. She know it — so I ain't talking behind no backs. When you fittin' to marry this chile?"

"I wanted to marry Odelia when everybody came up here for my graduation, to save everybody a double trip and the double expense . . . since we were all gonna be up here at one time. She's graduating that day, too, so —"

"You was trying to kill two birds with one stone, like it would make sense to do. I hear you, chile. You ain't gotta go into no deep explanations for yo' ole grandma. I know how them McCoys act. Figured up in a public setting, they might jus' mind they p's and q's. But I wouldn't count on it." His grandmother sighed and let out a grunt. "We needs insurance."

Jefferson's shoulders slumped and Odelia went to him to hold his hand for support. "Grandma, I can't have nothing crazy happen to her, and I'm trying my best to do the right thing . . . we wanna be together, and every time . . ."

"They still got that mess on you, son, so you can't even half kiss her? No wonder you half crazy and ready to jump the broom like a fugitive," his grandmother practically shouted. "Lack-a-nookie at your age ain't healthy, boy."

"Grandma!" He dropped Odelia's hand, ashamed, and walked across the room.

"Don't you 'grandma' me," the elderly lady said, becoming indignant. "I know all about the birds and the bees, and been young once. That don't make no sense. Besides, I heard all about it from your momma, who's been worried sick about it ever since your money-grubbing uncles put it on ya! Now you hear me and hear me good, chile. You go on and get the day booked at the church. We Joneses is coming up there, and we bringing plenty to eat with us. They betta not start. I'ma call Reverend Mitchell and tell him all about it, and how them McCoys is at it again! He'll put up a prayer line round you chil'ren, jus' like he did when you all was jus' babies on the tit. Then I'ma get my sister, Idell, and your uncle Roy on the case. While I don't dabble myself, I know people who gots a powerful conjure to go up against a McCoy root any day. They ain't the only ones who can git into a pot and stir it — and you *know* I must be mad as a wet hen, ifn' I'ma go there, as your grandma. Fit to be tied, is what I am! Might even call Mrs. Robinson so we Joneses and Robinsons can form an alliance."

"Now, Grandma," Jefferson said, his voice quavering at the thought, "there's no call for an all-out family —"

"It's settled," his grandmother said flatly. "The dawgs of war have been called, and so help me Jesus, war it is. If we Jonses stand with the Robinson clan, with the Hatfields going up against the McCoys, their numbers will be less than ours. Weaker. Our mojo will prevail, have mercy!"

He stared helplessly at Odelia, as she gestured wildly with her hands for a translation of the part of the conversation she couldn't hear.

"Grandma, please," he said, his voice quiet.

"Naw, baby. I got this. Now you jus' git off the tely-phone, and try your best to reserve yourself from laying a hand on your betrothed for at least twenty-four hours. Give Grandma some time to work it all out . . . jus' as a precautionary measure. I ain't dealt with this in a few years and might be kinda rusty. So, let's stay on the safe side fer now. But we's having us a wedding."

"Thanks, Grandma. I love you." What else was there to say?

"That's right, baby. Now you c'mon and give Grand some suga' through the phone, and I'll be up there directly to git one in person."

Jefferson kissed the receiver and simply shook his head.

"Bye-bye, baby. It'll all work out." Then she was gone.

The couple stood in the middle of the apartment floor, saying nothing as Jefferson clutched the cordless unit in his hand.

"She called out the big guns, didn't she?" Odelia finally whispered.

He nodded. "Yep. It's on, now. The Joneses are forming an alliance with the Robinsons against the Hatfields and the McCoys. Grandma is talking strength in numbers, given that the Hatfields and McCoys are splintered against each other."

Odelia closed her eyes and held on to the dinette table. "It was a really bad idea to call them, wasn't it?"

"Yep. My bad."

He and Odelia stared at each other for a moment and then burst out laughing.

Ester McCoy stood on her front porch with

her brothers-in-law, Rupert and Melville, watching Reverend Mitchell huff up the walkway. Her momma had put out an all-points family bulletin, and Ester hadn't seen Pastor look so upset since her late husband had passed away. Somehow she knew her dead husband had to be doing cartwheels in his grave. Her boy was gonna marry a Hatfield? More important, her son hadn't even told her about it himself and her child was now in harm's way? Oh yeah, the die had been cast and the dragon's teeth sown. After it was all said and done, she was a Jones, and would side with real blood over married blood any day of the week.

She cut a withering glance toward her husband's kin. This had all gone too far — now the church was involved? But she pasted on her most mannerly smile as the elderly pastor tipped his hat and proceeded up her porch steps.

"Afternoon, Pastor. What brings you out on this lovely afternoon?"

Reverend Mitchell set his jaw hard. "Ma'am," he said in a tight voice, and looked at her brothers-in-law. "You know I don't have no foolishness up in my church, right?"

Rupert and Melville returned innocent, astonished gazes at the pastor.

"Why, Rev," Rupert said with a sly smile, "we don't know what would make you draw such a conclusion, that —"

"I ain't drew no conclusion!" the reverend said, stomping his foot. "Don't tes' me, Rupert. I'm a man of the cloth, but I know these backwoods like the back of my own hand. Now you leave them children be so they can get married."

"We's all for holy matrimony, Pastor," Melville said sheepishly. "Ain't we, Ester?"

"The rat bastards is trying to root my boy!" Ester wailed, rushing over to Reverend Mitchell and burying her face against his shoulder. Her composure had fractured like a sudden storm. "They conjures is about to backfire, jus' like it took my husband, Jeb! I wanted my son to come home, but all in one piece and alive — which is the onliest reason I didn't come to you before. But if the boy is set on moving away and marrying, I want him to do well, and to give me some grands!"

"Now, see," Reverend Mitchell said, stroking Ester's back while he set his furious gaze on Rupert and Melville. "Y'all needs ta cut it out, 'fore somebody gits hurt. Both sides been going at it for years, all over money and land, but now we got innocent kids in the middle."

"You needs ta go tell the Hatfields to lay low. My brother died 'cause them Hatfields sent a lightning bolt at him, then claimed it was only supposed to be a warning shot over the bow," Melville protested. "Zeek Hatfield *lied* on my brother. Theys the ones who started it up again."

"And Zeek Hatfield's wife just so happened to die of fever that same night," the reverend argued, "when the way I recollect it, the woman had come out in the rain on a mission of peace!"

"That's right, she died, caught a cold, but we didn't have nuthin' to do with that, contrary to pop'lar opinions," Rupert said with a tight smile. "And ole lady Jones needs to stay out of family bizness and stop spreading mistruths."

"Now you calling my momma a liar?" Ester pulled away from the reverend's protective hug and squared her shoulders.

"Don't start with me, Ester," Rupert warned. "You don't want none-a this."

"You talking ill of my momma and put my boy in harm's way — whatchu think I got for your old ass, huh! If ya hadn't a went up to Zeek at the store and tried to rub his nose in it about his wife, which was a lie, then he wouldn't have tol' his sisters the rumor you-all had started to get his goat!

Don't you forget, I'm a Jones, and —"

"I ain't scairt of no Idell and Roy!" Rupert yelled, even though Melville had backed up a step. "Wasn't our fault that Zeek took things that far."

"It was *his wife.* Whatchu think the man was gonna do? Stand around and let her have an affair with my Jeb?"

"Now, listen to me, all of y'all!" Reverend Mitchell shouted. "We's gonna have us a wedding that might just, for once in history, bring both of these families tagetha. And y'all needs to know this — I done called out the *old* prayer warriors in the church to put a hard line around anybody conjuring, spell-casting, or dabbling in hoodoo over these young folks. If ya send so much as a chicken foot to each other, it'll jump up and backfire on the sender. Oh, we's vigilant on this one. Grandma Jones and Nana Robinson done tol' on both sides!"

With that, the reverend straightened his lapels, tipped his hat, turned on his heels, and walked back down the front steps to the dusty yard path.

Someone was pounding on his door so hard that he and his sister, Effie, thought it was the police. Ezekiel Hatfield rushed with his sister through the small clapboard house and did a double take when he spied Nana Robinson through the screen.

"I know that cow ain't on our porch," Effie grumbled under her breath as Ezekiel opened the door.

He stared at the rotund old woman who had her fleshy arms folded over her huge breasts and who had come out in such a rush that she still had on pink bedroom slippers and a flower-printed housecoat, with her hair tied up in a sheer scarf. Mostly, that wasn't Nana Robinson's style. Under normal conditions, even he had to admit that the old bat wore a very fine church hat and was dressed accordingly, which was the only time he ever saw her. Worry creased his brow. The one and only thing that could have brought old lady Robinson to his door had to be something related to his baby girl.

With that in mind, Ezekiel shushed his sister. "Nana Robinson, you at my front door for a good reason?"

"You know I am, Zeek. So, I ain't gonna mince no words. Your daughter's in trouble. Powerful trouble. And it's in your hands now."

He felt his body slump against the door frame as his sister's palm slid to his shoulder in support.

"My daughter Maylene, rest her soul in

39

heaven, must be spinnin' in her grave."

"What happened to my baby girl?" Ezekiel whispered. "Just tell me, Nana. Please." Before the elderly woman could answer, he spun on his sister. "I thought you said you-all had something to keep that girl from getting knocked up, so she could get her education?"

"We did," Effie said, wringing her hands. "Aw, Lawd . . . who's the daddy? We can strike his ass dead, if —"

"She gittin' married, and the girl ain't done all-a that."

"Married?" both Hatfield siblings said at once, incredulous.

"When?" Effie asked, putting both hands on her hips.

"More important — to who? Ain't nobody ask me could they steal my baby," Ezekiel said, his voice becoming loud as he walked out onto the porch.

Nana Robinson smiled. "Ester McCoy's boy, who's just about to graduate from law school in two weeks."

"Aw, *hell* no!" Ezekiel roared, walking in a circle.

"That ain't gonna happen," Effie spat, and stepped out onto the porch, letting the door slam loudly shut behind her.

"It's outta your hands," Nana Robinson

warned. "I done called both Reverend and Opal Kay — Rev will be by here directly, after he breaks the news to Ester . . . but Opal Kay gots somethin' fer ya, if y'all Hatfields start some mess."

"Opal Kay ain't got *nothin'* to do with this," Effie yelled as she hurried back into the house and closed the screen door behind her and then glared at Nana Robinson through the flimsy divide.

"My baby ain't marrying no McCoy!" Ezekiel raged. "Over my dead body."

"That's a promise," Nana Robinson said, pointing a crocked finger at him. "That's my grandbaby, too — don't you fergit it. Just 'cause I got arthuritis don't mean I'm rusty. Plus, we done formed an alliance — Joneses stand with Robinsons!"

"You threatening me, old lady?"

He leaned down in her face but backed up as her eyes narrowed.

"I ain't threatening you; I'm tellin' ya what Jesus knows." Before Ezekiel could step back farther, Nana Robinson whipped out a little black satchel from her ample cleavage. "This from both alliance clans," she said with a tight smile.

"Uhmmm-hmmm, ain't ready is ya, caught ya by surprise attack," the old woman said, triumphant. "So, don't make

41

me drop this on your porch, fool, because we can do this the old-fashioned way, or keep some civilities. But ya best tell your sister and all the rest of them Hatfield heifers, they done come up against the entire Robinson-Jones coclans — plus we gots Ester McCoy standing with us, and one in the grave, my daughter, who will help us for *her daughter* — she one-a *ours*. All the mothers, dead or alive, is united. Don't you fergit how this all works and be dumb enough to let insurance money make y'all stupid. Speak now, or forever hold your peace. We's having a wedding."

"Them McCoys sent fever over to my wife, your daughter. How you gonna let that go?" Although Ezekiel Hatfield's tone was angry, his voice had lowered a bit in fearful respect.

"I ain't forgot. But that was only 'cause your sisters started up the feud again by sending a lightning bolt over there to kill Ester's husband, thinking my daughter was low-life enough to be runnin' on you, Zeek. She wasn't messin' with Jeb, and you know it. Then you was all weeping and a-wailing up in church at my child's funeral, when ya found out the girl had only gone over there to try to strike a peace bond, given both families had little babies and it was time for the nonsense to stop. Them kids was a matched pair since birth; ev'ybody knows it. So, I'll blame you for listening to rumors, and for your false accusations, as well as your sisters for that misjudgment, till the end of time!" The old woman walked in a hot circle, tears rising in her cataract-stricken eyes. "Enough is enough! Why . . . you know I oughta jus' drop this bag any ole way, and —"

"Naw, naw, naw, now, Nana Robinson, we all remember full well how thangs got outta hand before."

"Uhmmm-hmmm," Nana muttered, and begrudgingly stashed her bag back between her breasts in a huff. "Ester's son is jus' a baby, like our Odelia. They's kids in love, so you-all best quit it. Don't test me."

"What hurts so bad is that my baby girl didn't come to her daddy with the news, first. I shouldn'ta found out like this."

"Well, if you-all wasn't acting such a fool, mayhaps the girl woulda came home and told you to your face, rather than called her nana crying her eyes out on the phone. She's scairt something gonna happen to that boy, and rightly so, 'cause she knows how y'all do. Call a truce, Zeek — right here and right now. She been a good girl, and ought'na have to have a heavy heart while she's about to graduate from college like that. If her momma was still alive, she'd have someone to help her buy her dress, and all the things a bride is supposed to have. Really, you should go on and send that girl her momma's old dress, just out of kindness. But you're as ornery as an old rattlesnake, and even with that, your daughter wants your blessing." Nana Robinson stomped her feet as her hands went to her wide hips. "I *cannot* believe you'd do your own child this way; even for you, Ezekiel Hatfield, this is above and beyond."

The two combatants stared at each other.

"Truce," Ezekiel finally said, looking away, his tone a contrite grumble.

"Truce? Truce! You crazy, Zeekie?" Effie screeched from where she stood inside the screen door. "There ain't no way —"

"My baby girl's involved," Ezekiel said, coming between both women. "Might git her or a grandbaby hurt. We call off the dogs, Effie."

"Like I said," Nana Robinson stated as she gave Effie the evil eye and then turned on the porch ready to leave. "We's having a wedding, pure and simple, and y'all are gonna act right."

Jefferson and Odelia stayed together, wide-eyed, nervous, and under extremely platonic circumstances, practically joined at the hip, each half-afraid to let the other go to the bathroom alone. Every errand that needed to be run was done in partnership, because who knew what could befall one of them if he or she even went to the store independently? The trip to the courthouse to file for a marriage license was viewed as a dangerous mission.

Both parents had called that first night, their voices distraught. Jefferson's mother had broken down and openly wept. Any libido Jefferson and Odelia had was killed. Her father's voice was strained and punctuated with long, disappointed silences, but word that a truce had been activated, slowly, let Odelia and Jefferson breathe.

"You think it's all right if we sleep together on your couch?" Jefferson asked, still jumpy, after she hung up the telephone.

"As long as we don't get into anything, I think we might be all right," she said, sounding unsure.

"Tell you what," he offered. "How about if I sleep in the chair, you take the couch, but at least that way, we can both stay in the same room?"

"Yo, man — you getting married and you

45

wanna bring your fiancée to the bachelor party? Have you lost your mind?" His best friend laughed hard.

Jefferson steadied himself as he held his cell phone close to his ear. "Man, listen, it's complicated. I can't go into it right now."

"She's still at your apartment? Or you still over at hers? Ever since you dropped the rock on a sister, you've been in prison. All the campus parties, you been there with her . . . And dude, for real, like, this might be your last hoorah as a free man."

"Hugh, you're supposed to be my best man. The one who's gonna keep me straight until I —"

"That's what I'm trying to do, partner. A few hours away won't hurt none."

Jefferson watched Odelia as she buzzed around the kitchen in his tiny apartment. A sense of claustrophobia had him in its grip. Two weeks of being together, finding ways to entertain themselves without kissing too much or laying a hand on each other, was driving him nuts. "My folks are coming in later tonight for everything. I can't be going out, getting tore up, plus that goes against everything Minister said, and —"

"C'mon, man. We'll have you back at a decent hour. You know me, right?"

"Yeah, I know you. That's what I'm wor-

46

ried about."

"But ain't it bad luck to be with or see the bride the night before the wedding?"

Jefferson paused. His homeboy did have a point. "Yeah. . . ."

"Well, how about if we take a brother out for a few, and deliver you to the Motel 6 where your people will be, and then you can hang out with your uncles till it's time to put on your cap and gown over your suit. Then, you lose the robes, I pin on your boutonnière, and we roll over to the church so you can get hitched — then we all eat, party . . . everything will be copasetic."

"That might be able to work," Jefferson said. "But I gotta talk to 'Delia about that, first."

"Awww, maaaan. Do you hear yourself? What did the girl do, works roots on your ass, or something?"

Odelia looked up from the stove and met Jefferson's eyes.

"That ain't funny, brother. Don't even joke like that."

It was the first real argument they'd had since the day they met. She couldn't fathom how men could be so stupid! Carlah had been right. Maybe it was better that she got away from Jefferson for a few hours to connect with her girls, to do what she had to do, namely, get her hair beat, feet did, nails did, and spend quality female time without a male appendage.

Carlah was waiting for her on the front steps of her apartment building holding a FedEx box when Jefferson dropped her off. The sly smile on her best girlfriend's face made Odelia smile, despite her foul mood.

"Yo, my sister, my sister — you finally broke free!" Carlah laughed and rushed up to Odelia to hug her the moment Jefferson's car pulled away. "Dayum. I know the brother put a rock on your hand, and I can appreciate being in a love jones with a fine man like that, but ya gotta come up for air, baby."

"It wasn't like that," Odelia said laughing.

"Oh, pullease," Carlah fussed, grabbing Odelia's hand and holding it up to the sunlight. "The man puts two cold karats on you, practically locks you away in y'all's apartments for two weeks, and you want me to believe he slept on the couch?" Carlah thrust the FedEx box at Odelia. "Give up the tapes. Details. Is he worth marrying, doing the till-death-do-you-part thing?"

"He's worth marrying," Odelia said, shaking her head and chuckling as she snatched the box from her friend, but refusing to say more.

"Hot-damn, I knew it. I'm too jealous, but it's all good. Tomorrow, we turn our tassels, throw our hats, and then you go out in white."

The statement ran through Odelia like ice water — the part about going out in white. Rather than focus on that as a possibility, she tore open the box and stood very still.

"What is it?" Carlah peered over the edge of the box as Odelia carefully extracted white fabric wrapped in plastic.

She would know her father's scrawl anywhere, and as soon as she saw white and not feathers, she knew he'd finally given his blessing. As gingerly as possible, she pulled the dress out and held it to her body, while Carlah snatched away the box and rooted within it for a note that didn't exist.

"Whoa . . . ," Carlah said, amazed. "Your *dad* sent your *mom's* dress?"

"Yeah," Odelia whispered, gazing at the dress. The fabric suddenly became blurry as she smoothed the plastic-ensconced gown against her body. "Something really crazy had to go down."

"Girl," Carlah said, slinging an arm over her shoulder. "You're so paranoid. Just put it upstairs, we go eat, and go get ourselves beautiful for tomorrow. What could go wrong?"

Odelia simply nodded and took out her keys, too afraid to hazard a guess.

"Oh, shit!" Hugh hollered, and kicked his tire. "Brand-new truck jacked, right before graduation? Man, how am I gonna tell my people about this?"

Jefferson kept trying his cell phone that oddly didn't work.

"A black cat runs outta nowhere, I swerve, and now my beautiful candy red baby has no front end? Look at her, man! I shoulda run over that freaking thing and made it road pizza!"

True enough; the front of Hugh's new ride was folded in on itself like an accordion, radiator smoking.

"We're lucky to be alive, man. Let's focus on that. Your cell phone working? I can't get reception."

Hugh sighed and flipped open his cellular. "Damn. I can't get none either."

"All right, so we walk till we can find a store or something, and then call for a tow."

"Are you crazy?" Carlah screamed, making all heads in the salon turn in unison. "My hair is green! I'm graduating tomorrow! I'm in a wedding! My maid-of-honor dress is sky blue! This won't work!"

Odelia flung the dryer hood back and stood up. Her girlfriend, who was normally a sandy almond brunette, looked like a punk rocker. "They can fix it; they can fix it," she said, rushing over to Carlah to try to console her as shrieks gave way to sobs. Oh, Lord, it was starting.

"Tell me again why we are sitting in the back of a police car? I'm still trying to wrap my brain around this, man," Hugh said quietly.

"Because you decided to go up to a house, against my warning, and the old lady in there thought it was about to be a home invasion," Jefferson replied evenly while he stared out the window.

"My hair is now hideous, doo-doo brown," Carlah said picking at her salad, her eyes puffy. "With my complexion, *dog poop brown* does not work."

Odelia hadn't touched her meal; all she could do was look at Carlah's once gorgeous tresses that were now redyed to a garish color that made her very pale café au lait skin seem cadaverous. The greenish tinge beneath the layered-on color was still very noticeable in the light. "It'll be all right, sweetie," Odelia said, guilt lacerating her. "It just has to —"

"I'm suing them. I promise you. Feel the texture of it; they turned it into straw with overprocessing." New tears filled Carlah's eyes and fell into her salad.

Odelia handed Carlah a tissue and grasped her hand. "As soon as I can get ahold of Jeff, we'll figure out what you have to do to sue them, all right."

"I don't feel good," Carlah said. "I need to go lie down."

"Okay, okay, we can do that," Odelia said quickly, and tried to hail a very slow-coming waitress.

But before Odelia could get their server's attention, Carlah was out of her chair, screaming. All heads turned in the restaurant, and several waiters rushed over. To everyone's horror, beneath the top lettuce leaves, fat, black beetles had begun to emerge from Carlah's plate. Odelia almost fell over her chair in the scramble to get away from the toxic table. Her girlfriend dry-heaved and then lost her lunch in the middle of an aisle. Nearby patrons shrieked and stood. Odelia crossed herself and ran to her friend's side, hurrying her from the establishment so she could get air, ignoring the apologies and the commotion that ensued behind them. When a crow flew by and crapped on Carlah's head, Odelia just hustled her shrieking girlfriend to the car.

It was all she could do to get Carlah settled down enough to drive her back to campus. Once she and Carlah's sorority sister, Gwen, had gotten Carlah to lie down with a cold wet compress over her face, Odelia headed for the Red Roof Inn, where her people were holed up. The only way she'd been able to get Carlah to let go of her hand was to promise to call the media and get Jefferson to make both the offending salon and the filthy restaurant his first legal cases.

During the entire short drive to the motel, Odelia could feel rage strangling her. By the time she made it to the lobby, she could barely speak into the house phone.

"Aunt Effie," she demanded, "where's —"

"Hi, baby! Congratulations! We all so proud, and just —"

"Where's Daddy? What room are y'all in?"

"Room three twenty-five, honey. C'mon up. We got plenty of food."

"Momma, they only let us go because we had student ID and they drove down the road to check out our story and found our crashed car — which had all the tags, license, insurance, and registration straight, like we'd said. Put Uncle Rupert on the phone!"

"Baby, now you watch your tone, especially when you call your uncles' and them's room. He ain't in here, and we ain't exactly on speaking terms, neither. Don't start no mess you can't finish. So you tread light, Son."

"Tread light? Tread light, Momma! I thought I was playing it safe by moving all my wedding and graduation stuff to my boy's apartment — but noooo. Here I'm about to graduate and get married in less than twenty-four hours and a black cat crossed my path, I've been in a car accident with my best man, we've been arrested, he can't find the ring, and I'm now standing in his apartment that's been flooded by *a toilet* that was in the one above us, and my suit is ruined!"

"Now that's what family's for, suga'. I know you can borrow a suit from one of your uncles, if need be," his mother soothed. "And —"

"I'm not wearing nothing from *them*. Do I sound like I'm crazy, Momma? In the middle of a hoodoo war, wearing their clothes would be like putting a bull's-eye on my forehead!"

"Well . . . perhaps you have a point, Son." His mother sighed into the receiver.

"Hugh just threw me his apartment keys and left to go stay with his family in the hotel — the poor man couldn't take no more tonight, even if we are homeboys."

"Baby, that's such a shame," his mother said quietly. "He'll be all right. His family is prayed up, ain't they? Besides, I don't think your uncles aimed to kill . . . uhmmm, just to deter."

"I ain't got no shoes, no drawers, no clean shirts, and all the good stores are closed. My best man is four inches shorter than me, so scratch me borrowing a suit from him. His car is totaled; my car battery mysteriously just died; how am I gonna get to the mall? Ain't no buses running out here. Not to mention, I can't get hold of Odelia — since for some reason, my cell phone, and any other phone I touch, won't connect with her number. Now you tell my uncles for me, if they don't wanna see Jeb's son really lose his temper, then they'd better stop throwing *whatever* it is that they're hurling over the fence toward the Hatfields! Y'all gonna make me lose my mind and conjure myself!"

"Oh, Lord . . . don't tell 'em that. It'll jus'

get their hopes up."

"Baby girl!"

Odelia stood stock-still as her father waltzed into the motel lobby with a bag of ice. Reluctantly, she hugged him, hoping he wasn't involved in the fray.

"Just look at my chile, all growed up."

"Dad," she said calmly, "what did Auntie Effie do?"

"She didn't do nothin'," he protested, peering away sheepishly as he held a dripping bag of ice. "They was out, machine went dead here, so I had to go make a run to get some —"

"Daddy . . ." Odelia's hands went to her hips.

"Aw, you know Effie. She just got herself a bad case of the hives . . . you know how high-strung she is. Might be shingles. She had them once or twice, and they say it never really goes away. But, uhm, after the food poisoning passed through her and all her sisters, we was all able to get on the road and travel up in a coupla vans with no problem. You get the dress I sent you, suga'?" Her father flashed her the most dashing smile and his thick bicep wrapped around her in a one-armed bear hug.

"Yes, Daddy," she said calmly, and returned his hug. "It's beautiful."

"I'ma be a proud man to walk down the aisle with ya looking just like yo' momma . . . even if he is *a McCoy*."

She let the dig pass, as well as the sentimental reference to her mother. "You-all don't stop, ain't gonna be no wedding."

"Now, now, don't git yourself all worked up. We all agreed to a truce," he said, patting her arm as he hoisted up the ice higher.

"My maid of honor's hair is green. Black beetles attacked her salad. She threw up in public *in a restaurant*. A crow pooped on her head in the street. The girl is laid out on her sofa, traumatized. Tell Aunt Effie to stop, because whatever she sent toward Jefferson boomeranged, missed me, and hit my best friend."

Her father looped his arm beneath hers and feigned shock as they began to walk. "Do tell. Now, see, that's why I don't fool with them tacky establishments. Your girlfriend oughta be more selective —"

"Dad, I'm serious."

She watched her father swallow away a smile.

"Aw right. Your Nana Robinson made us call a truce, like I said, any ole way. Plus I heard that Rev got up a prayer wall, so it musta accidentally slid onto whoever was near ya."

Odelia stopped walking. "I haven't been able to get in touch with Jefferson all day."

Her father patted her arm and kissed the top of her head. "Oh, he'll be all right. He's covered, I reckon."

"You reckon?"

"Effie and your other aunties was truly offended by Nana Robinson's accusations."

"Where's Nana?"

"Alive. That old bat is fine."

"Daddy!"

Her father sighed. "I don't rightly know. Probably holed up with Reverend Mitchell, and them Jones people. They had the nerve to form an alliance agin' us Hatfields — have you ever heard such? We supposed to be kin, us and the Robinsons!"

"What happened?" Jefferson said in a near whisper as he looked around the hotel room that all his uncles had packed into for a family meeting. Were it not for a lift by another buddy, Jefferson wouldn't have been there at all.

Each one of them had dark red splotches all over their faces and was itching and scratching so badly that it gave Jefferson a nervous tic. His mother stood at his side, arms folded over her big bosom, wig firmly set on her head, her expression a mixture of victory and disgust.

"Serves 'em all right. I done tol' 'em Grandma Jo meant what she said. But they had to tes' my momma and it done boomeranged on all of 'em. They couldn't even eat dinner at Red Lobster, for everybody getting sick."

"Boy, tell your grandma to call off the hoodoo hounds so we can all go to your graduation tomorrow," his uncle Rupert begged, scratching his crotch. "There's conjuring, and then there's just plain ole unfair!"

"Son, I got a suit you can wear; one of us got some shoes," Melville cried, scratched a bald spot in his scalp, and then unbuckled his pants. "Tell that old lady that to make a man itch this bad where the sun don't shine just ain't Christian!"

"Where's Gran?" Jefferson asked his mother, too done for words.

"Over at the church, probably with Rev and the Robinson and Jones clan."

Odelia didn't wait to be told twice. Her mission was to find Nana Robinson — sanctuary. After seeing her thirteen aunts sprawled out on two beds, the floor, and room chairs scratching what looked like quarter-sized mosquito bites, Odelia was out. She lied, telling her fifty cousins who whooped and surrounded her in the hall with glad tidings that she'd be back to eat dinner with them, as soon as she double-checked on her girlfriend. Eat there? Not. She just prayed for all the little kids, too numerous to count, hoping God truly did look after children and fools.

By the time she reached the church grounds, she was close to tears. Obviously, verbal truces aside, an all-out war had started. If Jefferson had been hurt and caught in the cross fire, she vowed to mount her own vendetta — against her own kin. This was absolutely outrageous!

Odelia double-parked, dashed for the church house, rang Pastor Wise's door, and waited, hugging herself. She could hear loud voices and laughter and could smell the fragrance of good home cooking wafting from the windows. Why couldn't her life just be normal, like this? When the burly man with the big smile and warm eyes came to the door wearing a clerical collar, tears streamed down her face in earnest.

"Come on in here, darlin'; you got people waiting on you," he said, enfolding Odelia in his arms. "Reverend Mitchell — the bride's here!"

Odelia buried her face in the pastor's barrel chest and breathed deeply, staving off an all-out crying jag. Another pair of warm, elderly hands petted her back and guided her away from Pastor Wise and across the threshold. Nana Robinson was smiling and standing next to a thin, gaunt woman with a kind face and merry eyes. A roomful of people surrounded the two older matrons, and Reverend Mitchell kept his arm tightly around Odelia's shoulders. But once she saw her nana, it was all over.

Breaking the reverend's hold, Odelia rushed to the thick, safe arms that had always been there for her as a child.

"I know, baby. We all heard about it," her nana cooed, stroking Odelia's hair. "Now you go on upstairs with Pastor Wise's wife, get showered, and put your dress on. We sent your cousin to go git it, and a nice security guard from the building let us in, so we could save your momma's dress from the fire ants that decided to invade your apartment. The door was already open, on account of they had to fumigate."

"Fire ants?" Odelia was slack-jawed.

"Oh, we got the dress and shook 'em out." her nana reassured her. "We's gonna fetch your daddy, and that boy's momma, and bring jus' them here for a little repast. The rest of them fools got contagion." Her nana chuckled and clucked her tongue as she held Odelia back so she could wink at her. "Brought it on dey-selves . . . don't know how that happened?"

"Uhmmm-hmmm," the thin woman beside her nana said. "The Lord do work in mysterious ways."

"Now, Grandma Jo, I thought you old girls agreed to leave this mess in the purview of prayer —"

"We did, Reverend Mitchell," Grandma Jo said, pressing a gnarled hand to her chest in shock. "You know we too ole to be acting like that, and we cooked up some good food that ain't gonna make nobody sick. Got a purty cake for the ceremony . . . lemon butter pound, a real cake, not some sto'-bought mess."

Odelia looked around, confused. "You're Jefferson's Grandma Jo?"

"Yes, baby. Welcome to the family. I'm a Jones. Don't get me confused with being no McCoy."

Healthy shouts of Amens filled the room, as family members from Jefferson's mother's people gathered around Odelia.

Frantic, Odelia's gaze scanned the house. "Is Jefferson all right?"

"That nice young man is fine," Pastor

Wise's wife said. "He's upstairs dressing in the suit his Grandma Jo had presence of mind to buy for him as a graduation present, along with some shoes and whatnot."

"Best to always be prepared," Grandma Jo said, pressing her lips together to stifle a smug smile.

"Well, they do say, the Lord helps those who he'p theyselves," Nana Robinson said, nodding with Grandma Jo.

"What happened to Jefferson's suit he was gonna —"

"There's plenty of time to talk about that later," Pastor Wise's wife said, interrupting Odelia's question. She shot her husband a coy, knowing glance. "I'll take you into my daughter's room so you can get ready for the wedding."

Odelia froze. "The wedding? Tonight?" Her voice had come out in a squeak. "We gettin' a jump on 'em, suga'," Nana Robinson said calmly. "By tomorrow, it'll be all over but the shouting; then maybe you two can graduate in peace. I didn't drive all this way for no nonsense."

"No truer words been said," Grandma Jo concurred. "If you stop crying, hurry up, and get dressed, y'all be married within an hour, then we can finally eat — I done put my big toe in that macaroni and cheese —

and y'all can go on and do what young folks do. Get you a hotel room and get busy, seeing as how neither one of y'all's apartments is fit to live in, right through here. Jus' don't get too love-crazy and fergit to set your clock. Like your nana said, I ain't come all this way to miss my boy's graduation. Hmmph!"

Odelia opened her mouth and closed it.

Both Pastor Wise and Reverend Mitchell discreetly chuckled with the rest of the family as the pastor's wife ushered Odelia through the house toward the stairs, winding a path through widely smiling kinfolk. Her cheeks felt hot, and Mrs. Wise squeezed her arm when Grandma Jo called out to Nana Robinson, "Girl, you ain't fergit to spice them greens with something to bring great-grands quick, did ya?"

"You oughts ta know me better than that, Jolene. We Robinson women don't play, when it comes to the kitchen," Nana Robinson fussed back.

"Good. 'Cause like I said, I put my foot in that macaroni and cheese."

EPILOGUE

Odelia wasn't sure if it was something in the greens, the mac and cheese, the fried chicken, or the lemon butter pound wedding cake. None of the elderly chefs were to be trusted; they all believed in big families. Might've been a sleight of hand by the maker of the tuna mac, potato salad, sweet potatoes, or even something slipped into the snap beans, rice, or ham. Anything was fair game to produce more great-grandbabies. On the other hand, trying to remain logical, it very well could've been the yearlong wait for the right partner, or the peach iced tea could have been spiked, knowing their families. Maybe it was simply love — go figure.

All she was very sure of was, Jefferson Mc-Coy hadn't let her sleep a wink all night and was still sweating like he'd run a marathon this morning. Bottom line, Odelia was married, happy, and it was clear that they were both going to be very late for their graduations.

L. A. BANKS (a.k.a. Leslie Esdaile Banks) is a native of Philadelphia, a graduate of the University of Pennsylvania Wharton under-graduate program, and holds a Masters in Fine Arts from Temple University's School of Film and Media Arts. After a stellar ten-year career as a corporate marketing executive for several Fortune 100 high-tech firms, Banks changed careers in 1991 to pursue a private consulting career — which ultimately led to fiction and film writing. Now, with more than twenty-four novels and ten anthology contributions in an extraordinary breadth of genres, and many awards to her credit, Banks writes full-time, and resides with her husband and children in Philadelphia. Look for her Vampire Huntress Legends series and a full listing of her published works at: www.vampire huntress.com.

SOMETHING BORROWED

JIM BUTCHER

Steel pierced my leg and my body went rigid with pain, but I could not allow myself to move. "Billy," I growled through my teeth. "Kill him."

Billy the Werewolf squinted up at me from his seat and said, "That might be a little extreme."

"This is torture," I said.

"Oh, for crying out loud, Dresden," Billy said, his tone amused. "He's just fitting the tux."

Yanof the tailor, a squat, sturdy little guy who had recently immigrated to Chicago from Outer Sloboviakastan or somewhere, glared up at me, with another dozen pins clutched between his lips and resentment in his eyes. I'm better than six and a half feet tall. It can't be fun to be told that you've got to fit a tux to someone my height only a few hours before the wedding.

"It ought to be Kirby standing here," I said.

"Yeah. But it would be harder to fit the tux around the body cast and all those traction cables."

"I keep telling you guys," I said. "Werewolves or not, you've got to be more careful."

Ordinarily, I would not have mentioned Billy's talent for shape-shifting into a wolf in front of a stranger, but Yanof didn't speak a word of English. Evidently, his skills with needle and thread were such that he had no pressing need to learn. As Chicago's resident wizard, I'd worked with Billy on several occasions, and we were friends.

His bachelor party the night before had gotten interesting on the walk back to Billy's place, when we happened across a ghoul terrorizing an old woman in a parking lot.

It hadn't been a pretty fight. Mostly because we'd all had too many stripper-induced Jell-O shots.

Billy's injuries had all been bruises and all to the body. They wouldn't spoil the wedding. Alex had a nasty set of gashes on his throat from the ghoul's clawlike nails but could probably pass them off as particularly enthusiastic hickeys. Mitchell had broken two teeth when he'd charged the ghoul but hit a wall instead. He was going to be a dedicated disciple of Anbesol unil he got to the dentist.

All I had to remember the evening by was a splitting headache, and not from the fight. Jell-O shots are far more dangerous, if you ask me.

Billy's best man, Kirby, had gotten unlucky. The ghoul slammed him into a brick wall so hard that it broke both his legs and cracked a vertebra.

"We handled him, didn't we?" Billy asked.

"Let's ask Kirby," I said. "Look, there isn't always going to be a broken metal fence post sticking up out of the ground like that, Billy. We got lucky."

Billy's eyes went flat and he abruptly stood up. "All right," he said, voice hard. "I've had just about enough of you telling me what I should and should not do, Harry. You aren't my father."

"No," I said. "But —"

"In fact," he continued, "if I remember correctly, the other Alphas and I have saved your life twice now."

"Yes," I said. "But —"

His face turned red with anger. Billy wasn't tall, but he was built like an armored truck. "But *what?* You don't want to share the spotlight with any of us mere one-trick wonders? Don't you *dare* belittle what Kirby did, what the others have done and sacrificed."

I am a trained investigator. Instincts honed by years of observation warned me that Billy might be angry. "Great hostility I sense in you," I said in a Muppety voice.

Billy's glower continued for a few more steady seconds, and then it broke. He shook his head and looked away. "I'm sorry. For my tone."

Yanof jabbed me again, but I ignored it. "You didn't sleep last night."

He shook his head again. "No excuse. But between the fight and Kirby and . . ." He waved a vague hand. "Today. I mean, *today.*"

"Ah," I said. "Cold feet?"

Billy took a deep breath. "Well. It's a big step, isn't it." He shook his head. "And after next year, most of the Alphas are going to be done with school. Getting jobs." He paused. "Splitting up."

"And that's where you met Georgia," I said.

"Yeah." He shook his head. "What if we don't have anything else in common? I mean, good grief. Have you seen her family's place? And I'm going to be in debt for seven or eight years just paying off the student loans. How do you know if you're

70

ready to get married?"

Yanof stood up, gestured at my pants, and said something that sounded like, "Hahklha ah lafala krepata khem."

"I'm not seeing people right now," I told him, as I took off the pants and passed them over. "Or else you'd have a shot, you charmer."

Yanof sniffed, muttered something else, and toddled back into the shop.

"Billy," I said. "You think Georgia would have fought that thing last night?"

"Yes," he said, without a second's hesitation.

"She going to be upset that you did it?"

"No."

"Even though some folks got hurt?"

He blinked at me. "No."

"How do you know?" I asked.

"Because . . ." He shook his head. "Because she won't. I know her. Upset by the injuries, yes, but not by the fight." He shifted to a tone that he probably didn't realize was an imitation of Georgia's voice. "People get hurt in fights. That's why they're called fights."

"You know her well enough to answer serious questions for her when she isn't even in the room, man," I said quietly. "You're ready. Keep the big picture in mind. You and her."

He looked at me for a second and then said, "I thought you'd say something about love."

I sighed. "Billy. You knob. If you didn't love her, you wouldn't be stressed about losing what you have with her, would you."

"Good point," he said.

"Remember the important thing. You and her."

He took a deep breath and let it out. "Yeah," he said. "Georgia and me. The rest doesn't matter."

I was going to mumble something vaguely supportive when the door to the fitting room opened and an absolutely ravishing raven-haired woman in an expensive lavender silk skirt-suit came into the fitting room. She might have been my age, and had a lot of gold and diamonds, a lot of perfect white teeth, and the kind of curves that only come from surgery. Her shoes and purse together probably cost more than my car.

"Well," she snapped, and put a fist on her hip, glaring first at Billy and then at me. "I see you are already doing your best to disrupt the ceremony."

"Eve," Billy said in a kind of stilted, formally polite voice. "Um. What are you talking about?"

"For one thing, this," she said, and flicked a hand at me. Then gave me a second, more evaluative look.

I tried to look casual and confident, there in my Spider-Man T-shirt and black briefs. I managed to keep myself from diving toward my jeans. I turned aside to put them on, maintaining my dignity.

"Your underwear has a hole," Eve said sweetly.

I jerked my jeans on, blushing. Stupid dignity.

"Bad enough that you insist on this . . . petty criminal taking part in a ceremony before polite society. Yanof is beside himself," Eve continued, speaking to Billy. "He threatened to quit."

"Wow," I said. "You speak Sloboviak-stanese?"

She blinked at me. "What?"

"Because Yanof doesn't speak any English. So how did you know he threatened to quit?" I smiled sweetly at her.

Eve gave me a glare of haughty anger and defended herself by pretending I hadn't said anything. "And now we're going to have to leave out one of the bridesmaids. To say nothing of the fact that with *him* standing up there on one side of you and Georgia on the other, you're going to look like a midget.

The photographer will have to be notified and I have no idea how we'll manage to re-arrange everything at the last moment."

I swore I could hear Billy's teeth grind. "Harry," he said, in that same polite, strained voice. "This is Eve McAlister. My stepmother-in-law."

"I do not care for that term, as I have told you often. I am your mother-in-law," she said. "Or will be, whenever this ongoing disaster you've created from a respectable wedding breathes its last."

"I'm sure we can work something out," Billy assured her, his tone hopeless.

"Georgia is late and is letting the voice mail answer her phone — as though I needed something else to occupy my thoughts." She shook her head. "I assume the lowlifes you introduced her to kept her out too late last night. Just like this one did to you."

"Hey, come on," I said, careful to keep my tone as reasonable and friendly as I could. "Billy's had a rough night. I'm sure he can help you out if you just give him a chance to —"

She made a disgusted sound and inter-rupted me. "Did I say or do something to imply that I cared to hear your opinion, charlatan? Lowlifes. I warned her about folk

74

like you."

"You don't even know me, lady," I said.

"Yes, I do," she informed me. "I know all about you. I saw you on *Larry Fowler.*"

I narrowed my eyes at Eve.

Billy's expression came close to panic, and he held up both hands palm out, giving me a pleading look. But my hangover ached, and life is too short to waste it taking verbal abuse from petty tyrants who watch bad talk shows.

"Okay, Billy's stepmom," I began.

Her eyes flashed. "Do *not* call me that."

"You don't care to be called a step-mother?" I asked.

"Not at all."

"Though you obviously aren't Georgia's mother. Howsabout I call you trophy wife?" I suggested.

She blinked at me once, her eyes widening.

Billy put his face in his hands.

"Bed warmer?" I mused. "Mistress made good? Midlife-crisis by-product?" I shook my head. "When in doubt, go with the classics." I leaned a little closer and gave her a crocodilian smile. *"Gold digger."*

The blood drained out of Eve's face, leaving ugly pinkish blotches high on her cheeks. "Why, you . . . You . . ."

I waved my hand. "No, it's all right; I don't mind finding alternate terms. I understand that you're under pressure. Must be hard trying to look good in front of the old money when they all know that you were really just a receptionist or an actress or a model or something."

Her mouth dropped completely open.

"We're all having a tough day, dear." I flipped my hand at her. "Shoo."

She stared at me for a second, then let out a snarled curse you'd hardly expect from a lady of her station, spun on the heel of one Italian-leather pump, and stalked from the room. I heard a couple of beeps as she crossed to the shop's door, and then she started screeching into a cell phone. I could hear her for about ten seconds after she went outside.

Mission accomplished. Spleen vented. Dragon lady routed. I felt pleased with myself.

Billy heaved a sigh. "You had to talk to her like that?"

"Yeah." I glowered out after the departed Eve. "Once my mouth was open and my lips started moving, it was pretty much inevitable."

"Dammit, Harry," Billy sighed.

"Oh, come on, man. Sticks and stones

76

may break her bones, but one wiseass will never hurt her. It's not a big deal."

"Not for you: You don't have to live with it. I do. So does Georgia."

I chewed on my lower lip for a second. I hadn't thought about it in those terms. I suddenly felt less than mature. "Ah," I said. "Oh. Um. Maybe I should apologize?"

He bent his head and pinched the bridge of his nose between his fingers. "Oh God, no. Things are bad enough already."

I frowned at him. "Is it really that important to you? The ceremony?"

"It's important to Georgia."

I winced. "Oh," I said. "Ah."

"Look, we've got a few hours. I'll stay here and try to sort things out with Eve," Billy said. "Do me a favor?"

"Hey, what's a best man for? Other than tackling a panicked groom if he tries to run."

He gave me a quick grin. "See if you can contact Georgia first? Maybe she's had car trouble or overslept or something. Or maybe she just left her phone on all night and it went dead."

"Sure," I said. "I'll take care of it."

I called Billy and Georgia's apartment and got no answer. Knowing Georgia, I expected her to be at the hospital, visiting Kirby. Billy might have been the combat leader of the merry band of college kids who had learned shape-shifting from an actual wolf, but Georgia was the manager, surrogate mom, and brains when there wasn't any violence on.

Kirby was on painkillers and groggy, but he told me Georgia hadn't been to see him. I talked to the duty nurse and confirmed that though his family was flying in from Texas to see him, he'd had no visitors since Billy and I left.

Odd.

I thought about mentioning it to Billy, but I didn't really know anything yet, and it wasn't like he needed *more* pressure.

"Don't get paranoid, Harry," I told myself. "Maybe she's got a hangover, too. Maybe she ran off with a male stripper." I waited to see if I was buying it, then shook my head. "And maybe Elvis and JFK are shacked up in a retirement home somewhere."

I went to Billy and Georgia's apartment.

They live in a place near the University of Chicago's campus, in a neighborhood that missed being an ugly one by maybe a hundred yards. It still wasn't the kind of place you'd want to hang around outside after dark. I didn't have a key to get in the building, so I pressed buttons one at a time until someone buzzed me in, and took the stairs up.

As I neared the apartment door, I knew that something was wrong. It wasn't like I saw or heard anything, magical or otherwise, but when I stopped before the door I had a nebulous but strong conviction that something bad had gone down.

I knocked. The door rattled and fell off the lower hinge. It swung open a few inches, drunkenly, upper hinges squealing. Splits and cracks that had been invisible until the door moved appeared in the wood, and the dead bolt rattled dully against the inside of the door, loose in its setting.

I stopped there for a long second, waiting and listening. Other than the whirring of a window fan at the end of the hall and someone playing an easy-listening station on the floor above me, there was nothing. I closed my eyes for a moment and extended my wizard's senses, testing the air nearby for any touch of magic upon it.

I felt nothing but the subtle energy that surrounded any home, a form of naturally occurring protective magic called the threshold. Billy and Georgia's apartment was the nominal headquarters of the Were-wolves, and members came and went at all hours. It was never intended to be a permanent home — but there had been a lot of living in the little apartment, and its threshold was stronger than most. I slowly pushed the door open with my right hand.

The apartment had been torn to pieces.

A futon lay on its side, its metal frame twisted like a pretzel. The entertainment center had been pulled down from the wall, shattering equipment, scattering CDs and DVDs and vintage *Star Wars* action figures everywhere. The wooden table had been broken in two precisely in its center. One of the half-dozen chairs survived. The others were kindling. The microwave protruded from the drywall of an interior wall. The door of the fridge had taken out the bookcase across the room. Everything in the kitchen had been pulled down and scattered.

I moved in as quietly as I could — which is pretty damned quiet. I've done a lot of sneaking around. The bathroom looked like someone had taken a chain saw to it and followed up with explosives. The bedroom used to house computers and electronic stuff looked like the site of an airplane crash.

Billy and Georgia's bedroom was the worst of all of them.

Because there was blood on the floor and

one wall.

Whatever had happened, I had missed it. Dammit. I wanted to kill something and I wanted to scream in frustration and I wanted to throw up in fear for Georgia.

But in my business, that kind of thing doesn't help much.

I went back into the living room. The phone near the door had survived. I dialed.

"Lieutenant Murphy, Special Investigations," answered a professional, bland voice.

"It's me, Murph," I told her.

Murphy knows me. Her tone changed at once. "My God, Harry, what's wrong?"

"I'm at Billy and Georgia's apartment," I said. "The place has been torn apart. There's blood."

"Are you all right?"

"I'm fine," I said. "Georgia's missing." I paused and said, "It's her wedding day, Murph."

"Five minutes," she said at once.

"I need you to pick something up for me on the way."

Murphy came through the door eight minutes later. She was the head of Chicago P.D.'s Special Investigations Department. They were the cops who got to handle all the crimes that didn't fall into anyone else's purview — stuff like vampire attacks and mystical assaults, as well as more mundane crimes like grave robbing. Plus all the really messy cases the other cops didn't want to bother with. SI is supposed to make everything fit neatly into the official reports, explaining away anything weird with logical, rational investigation.

SI spends a lot of time struggling with that last one. Murphy writes more fiction than most novelists.

Murphy doesn't look like a cop, much less a monster cop. She's five nothing. She's got blond hair, blue eyes, and a cute nose. She's also got about a zillion gunnery awards and a shelf full of open-tournament martial arts trophies, and I once saw her kill a giant plant monster with a chain saw. She wore jeans, a white tee, sneakers, a baseball cap, and her hair was pulled back into a tail. She wore her gun in a shoulder rig, her badge around her neck, and had a backpack slung over one shoulder.

She came through the door and stopped in her tracks. She surveyed the room for a minute and then said, "What did this?"

I nodded at the twisted futon frame. "Something strong."

"I wish I was a big-time private investigator like you. Then I could figure these things out for myself."

"You bring it?" I asked.

She tossed me the backpack. "The rest is in the car. What's it for?"

I opened the pack, took out a bleached-white human skull, and put it down on the kitchen counter. "Bob, wake up."

Orange lights appeared in the skull's shadowed eye sockets, and then slowly grew brighter. The skull's jaws twitched and then opened into a pantomime of a wide yawn. A voice issued out, acoustics odd, like when you talk in a racquetball court. "What's up, boss?"

"Jesus, Mary, and Joseph," Murphy swore. She took a step back and almost fell over the remains of the entertainment center.

Bob the Skull's eyelights brightened. "Hey, the cute blonde! Did you do her, Harry?" The skull spun in place on the counter and surveyed the damage. "Wow. You *did!* Way to go, stud!"

My face felt hot. "No, Bob," I growled.

"Oh," the skull said, crestfallen.

Murphy closed her mouth, blinking at the skull. "Uh. Harry?"

"This is Bob the Skull," I told her.

"It's a skull," she said. "That talks."

"Bob is actually the spirit inside. The skull is just the container it's in."

She looked blankly at me and then said, "It's a *skull.* That *talks.*"

"Hey!" Bob protested. "I am not an it! I am definitely a he!"

"Bob is my lab assistant," I explained.

Murphy looked back at Bob and shook her head. "Just when I start thinking this magic stuff couldn't get weirder."

"Bob," I said. "Take a look around. Tell me what did this."

The skull spun obediently and promptly said, "Something strong."

Murphy gave me an oblique look.

"Oh, bite me," I told her. "Bob, I need to know if you can sense any residual magic."

"Ungawa, bwana," Bob said. He did another turnaround, slower, and the orange eyelights narrowed.

"Residual magic?" Murphy asked.

"Any time you use magic, it can leave a kind of mark on the area around you. Mostly it's so faint that sunrise wipes it away every morning. I can't always sense it."

"But *he* can?" Murphy asked.

"But he *can!*" Bob agreed. "Though not with all this chatter. I'm working over here."

I shook my head and picked up the phone again.

"Yes," said Billy. He sounded harried, and

there was an enormous amount of background noise.

"I'm at your apartment," I said. "I came here looking for Georgia."

"What?" he said.

"Your apartment," I said louder.

"Oh, Harry," Billy said. "Sorry, this phone is giving me fits. Eve just talked to Georgia. She's here at the resort."

I frowned. "What? Is she all right?"

"Why wouldn't she be?" Billy said. Someone started shrieking in the background. "Crap, this battery's dying. Problem solved, come on up. I brought your tux."

"Billy, wait."

He hung up.

I called him back, and got nothing but voice mail.

"Aha!" Bob said. "Someone used that wolf spell the naked chick taught to Billy and the Werewolves, back over there by the bedroom," he reported. "And there were faeries here."

I frowned. "Faeries. You sure?"

"One hundred percent, boss. They tried to cover their tracks, but the threshold must have taken the zing out of their illusion."

I nodded and exhaled. "Dammit." Then I strode into the bathroom and hunkered down, pawing through the rubble.

"What are you doing?" Murphy asked.

"Looking for Georgia," I said. I found a plastic brush full of long strands the color of Georgia's hair and took several of them in hand.

I've gotten a lot of mileage out of my tracking spell, refining it over the years. I stepped out into the hall and drew a circle on the floor around me with a piece of chalk. Then I took Georgia's hairs and pressed them against my forehead, summoning up my focus and will. I shaped the magic I wanted to create, focused on the hairs, and released my will with a murmur of, "Interessari, interressarium."

Magic surged out of me, into the hairs and back. I broke the circle with my foot, and the spell flowed into action, creating a faint sense of pressure against the back of my head. I turned, and the sensation flowed over my skull in response, over my ear, then my cheekbone, and finally coming to rest directly between my eyes.

"She's this way," I said. "Uh-oh."

"Uh-oh?"

"I'm facing south," I said.

"Which is a problem?"

"Billy says she's at the wedding. Twenty miles north of here."

Murphy's eyes widened in comprehension. "A faerie has taken her place."

"Yeah."

"Why? Are they trying to place a spy?"

"No," I said quietly. "This is malicious. Probably because Billy and company backed me up during the battle when the last Summer Knight was murdered."

"That was years ago."

"Faeries are patient," I said. "And they don't forget. Billy's in danger."

"I'd say Georgia was the one in danger," Murphy said.

"I mean that Billy's in danger, too," I said.

"How so?"

"This isn't happening on their wedding day by chance. The faeries want to use it against them."

Murphy frowned. "What?"

"A wedding isn't just a ceremony," I said. "There's power in it. A pledging of one to another, a blending of energies. There's magic all through it."

"If you say so," she said, her tone wry. "What happens to him if he marries a faerie?"

"Conservatives get real upset," I said absently. "But I'm not sure, magically speaking. Bob?"

"Oh," Bob said. "Um. Well, if we assume this is one of the Winter Sidhe, then he's going to be lucky to survive the honeymoon. If he does, well. She'll be able to influence him, long-term. He'll be bound to her, the way the Winter Knights are bound to the Winter Queens. She'll be able to impose her will over his. Change the way he thinks and feels about things."

I ground my teeth. "And if she changes him enough, it will drive him insane."

"Usually, yup," Bob said. His voice brightened. "But don't worry, boss. Odds are he'll be dead before sunrise tomorrow. He might even die happy."

"That isn't going to happen," I said. I checked my watch. "The wedding is in three hours. Georgia might need help now." I looked back at Murphy. "You carrying?"

"Two on me. More in the car."

"Now there's a girl who knows how to party!" Bob said.

I popped the skull back into my backpack harder than I strictly had to, and zipped it shut. "Feel like saving the day?"

Her eyes sparkled, but she kept her tone bored. "On the weekend? Sounds too much like work."

We started from the apartment together. "I'll pay you in donuts."

"Dresden, you pig. That cop-donut thing is a vicious stereotype."

"Donuts with little pink sprinkles," I said.

"Professional profiling is just as bad as racial profiling."

I nodded. "Yeah. But I know you want the little pink sprinkles."

"That isn't the point," she said loftily, and we got into her car.

We buckled in, and I said, more quietly, "You don't have to come with me, Karrin."

"Yes," she said. "I do."

I nodded and focused on the tracking spell, turning my head south. "Thataway."

The worst thing about being a wizard is all the presumption, people's expectations. Pretty much everyone expects me to be some kind of con artist, since it is a well-known fact that there is no such thing as magic. Of those who know better, most of them think that I can just snap my fingers, poof, and have whatever I want. Dirty dishes? Snap my fingers and they wash themselves, like in *The Sorcerer's Apprentice.* Need to talk to a friend? Poof, teleport them in from wherever they are, because the magic knows where to find them, all by itself.

Magic ain't like that. Or I sure as hell wouldn't drive a beat-up old Volkswagen.

It's powerful, true, and useful, and enormously advantageous, but ultimately it is an art, a science, a craft, a tool. It doesn't go out and do things by itself. It doesn't create something from nothing. Using it takes talent and discipline and practice and a lot of work, and none of it comes free.

Which is why my spell led us to downtown Chicago and suddenly became less useful.

"We've circled this block three times," Murphy told me. "Can't you get a more precise fix on it?"

"Do I look like one of those GPS thingies?" I sighed.

"Define 'thingie,' " Murphy said.

"It's my spell," I said. "It's oriented to the points of the compass. I didn't really have the z-axis in mind when I designed it and it only works for that when I'm right on top of the target. I keep meaning to go back and fix that, but there's never time."

"I had a marriage like that," Murphy said. She stopped at a light and stared up. The block held six buildings — three apartments, two office buildings, and an old church. "In there. Somewhere. It could take a lot of time to search that."

"So call in all the king's horses and all the king's men," I said.

She shook her head. "I might be able to get a couple, but since Rudolph moved to

Internal Affairs, I've been flagged. If I start calling in people left and right without a damned good logical, rational, wholly normal reason . . ."

I grunted. "I get it. We need to get closer. The closer I get to Georgia, the more precise the tracking spell will be."

Murphy nodded once and pulled over in front of a fire hydrant, parking the car. "Let's be smart about this. Six buildings. Where would a faerie take her?"

"Not the church. Holy ground is uncomfortable for them." I shook my head. "Not the apartments. Too many people there. Too easy for someone to hear or see something."

"Office buildings on a weekend," Murphy said. "Empty as you can find in Chicago. Which one?"

"Let's take a look. Maybe the spell can give me an idea."

It took ten minutes to walk around the outside of both buildings. The spell remained wonderfully nonspecific, though I knew Georgia was within a hundred yards or so. I sat down at the curb in disgust. "Dammit," I said, pushing at my hair. "There has to be something."

"Would a faerie be able to magick herself in and out of there?"

"Yes and no," I said. "She couldn't just

wander in through the wall, or poof herself inside. But she could walk in under a veil, so that no one saw her — or else saw an illusion of what she wanted them to see."

"Can't you look for residual whatsis again?"

It was a good idea. I got Bob and tried it, while Murphy found a phone and tried to reach Billy or anyone who could reach Billy. After an hour's effort, we had accomplished enormous amounts of nothing.

"In case I haven't mentioned it before," I said, "dealing with faeries is an enormous pain in the ass." Someone in a passing car flicked a still-smoldering cigarette butt onto the concrete near me. I kicked it through a sewer grate in disgust.

"She covered her tracks again?"

"Yeah."

"How?"

I shrugged. "Lot of ways. Scatter little glamours around to misdirect us. Only used her magic very lightly, to keep from leaving a big footprint. If she did her thing in a crowded area, enough people's life force passing by would cover it. Or she could have used running water to —"

I stopped talking and my gaze snapped back to the sewer grate.

I could hear water running through it in a

low, steady stream.

"Down there," I said. "She's taken Georgia to Undertown."

Murphy stared at the stairs leading down to a tunnel with brick walls and shook her head. "I wouldn't have believed this was here."

We stood at the end of an uncompleted wing of Chicago's underground commuter tunnels, at a broken section of wall hidden behind a few old tarps that led down into the darkness of Undertown.

Murphy had thrown on an old Cubs jacket over her shirt. She switched guns, putting her favorite Sig away in exchange for the Glock she wore holstered on one hip. The gun had a little flashlight built onto the underside of its barrel, and she flicked it on. "I mean, I knew there were some old tunnels," Murphy said. "But not this."

I grunted and took off the silver pentacle amulet I wore around my neck. I held it in my right hand, my fingers clutching the chain against the solid, round length of oak in my right hand, about two feet long and covered with carved runes and sigils — my blasting rod. I sent an effort of will into the amulet, and the silver pentacle began to glow with a gentle, blue-white light. "Yeah.

The Manhattan Project was run out of the tunnels here until they moved it to the Southwest. Plus the town kept sinking into the swamp for a hundred and fifty years. There are whole buildings sunk right into the ground. The Mob dug places during Prohibition. People built bomb shelters during the fifties and sixties. And other things have added more, plus gateways back and forth to the spirit world."

"Other things?" Murphy asked, gun steady on the darkness below. "Like what?"

"Things," I said, staring down at the patient, lightless murk of Undertown. "Anything that doesn't like sunlight or company. Vampires, ghouls, some of the nastier faeries, obviously. Once I fought this wacko who kept summoning up fungus demons."

"Are you stalling?" Murphy asked.

"Maybe I am," I sighed. "I've been down there a few times. Never been good."

"How you wanna do this?"

"Like we did the vampire lair. Let me go first with the shield. Something jumps out at us, I'll drop and hold it off until you kill it."

Murphy nodded soberly. I swallowed a lump of fear out of my throat. It settled into my stomach like a nugget of ice. I prepared my shield, and the same color light as emanated from my pentacle surrounded it, drizzling heatless blue-white sparks in an irregular stream. I prepared myself to use my blasting rod if I had to, and started down the stairs, following the tracking spell toward Georgia.

The old brick stairs ended at a rough stone slope into the earth. Water ran down the walls and in rivulets down the sides of the tunnel. We went forward, through an old building that might have been a schoolhouse, judging by the rotted piles of wood and a single old slate chalkboard fallen from one wall. The floor was tilted to one side. The next section of tunnel was full of freezing, dirty, knee-deep water until it sloped up out of the water, went round a corner where the walls had been cut by rough tools, then opened into a wider chamber.

It was a low-ceilinged cave — low for me, anyway. Most folks wouldn't have been troubled. Three feet from the doorway, the floor dropped away into silent, black water that stretched out beyond the reach of my blue wizard light. Murphy stepped up next to me, and the light on her gun sent a silver spear of white light out over the water.

There, on a slab of stone that rose up no more than an inch or two from the water's surface, lay Georgia.

Murphy's light played over her. Georgia was a tall woman — in high-enough heels, she could have looked me in the eye. She'd been stork-skinny and frizzy-haired when I met her. The years in between had softened the lines of her and brought out a natural confidence and intelligence that made her an extraordinarily attractive, if not precisely beautiful, woman. She was naked, laid on her back with her arms crossed over her chest in repose, funeral-style. She took slow breaths. Her skin was discolored from the cold, her lips tinged blue.

"Georgia?" I called, feeling like a dummy. But I didn't know of any other way to see if she was awake. She didn't stir.

"What now?" Murphy asked. "You go get her while I cover you?"

I shook my head. "Can't be as easy as it looks."

"Why not?"

"Because it never is." I bowed my head for a moment, pressed my fingertips lightly to my forehead, between my eyebrows, and concentrated on bringing up my Sight.

One of the things common to all wizards is the Sight. Call it a sixth sense, a third eye, whatever you please, around the world everyone with enough magic has the Sight.

It lets you actually see the forces of energy at work in the world around you — life, death, magic, what have you. It isn't always easy to understand what I see, and sometimes it isn't pretty — and anything a wizard views with his Sight is there, in Technicolor, never fading. Forever.

That's why you have to be careful what you choose to Look at. I don't like doing it, ever. You never know what it is you'll See.

But when it came to finding out what kinds of magic might be between me and Georgia, I didn't have many options. I opened my Sight and Looked out over the water to Georgia.

The water was shot through with slithery tendrils of greenish light — a spell of some kind, just under its placid surface. If the water moved, the spell would react. I couldn't tell how. The stone Georgia lay upon held a dull, pulsing energy, a sullen violet radiance that wound in slow, hypnotic spirals through the rock. A binding, I was sure, something to keep her from moving. Another spell played over and through Georgia herself — a cloud of deep blue sparkles that lay against her skin, especially around her head. A sleeping spell? I couldn't make out any details from here.

"Well?" Murphy said.

97

I closed my eyes and released my Sight, always a mildly disorienting experience. The remnants of my hangover made it worse than usual. I reported my findings to Murphy.

"Well," she said. "I sure am glad we have a wizard on the case. Otherwise we might be standing here without any idea what to do next."

I grimaced and stepped to the water's edge. "This is water magic. It's tricky stuff. I'll try to take down the alarm spell on the surface of the pool, then swim out and get Geo —"

Without warning, the water erupted into a boiling froth at my feet, and a claw, a freaking pincer as big as a couple of basketballs, shot out of the water and clamped down on my ankle.

I let out a battle cry. Sure, a lot of people might have mistaken it for a sudden yelp of unmanly fear, but trust me. It was a battle cry.

The thing, whatever it was, pulled my leg out from under me, trying to drag me in. I could see slick, wet black shell. I whipped my blasting rod around to point at the thing and snarled, "Fuego!"

A lance of fire as thick as my thumb lashed from the tip of my blasting rod, which was pointed at the thing's main body. It hit the water and it boiled into steam. It smashed into the shell of the creature with such force that it simply ripped the thing's body from its clawed limb. I brought my shield up, a pale, fragile-looking quarter dome of blue light that coalesced into place before the steam boiled back into my eyes.

I squirmed away from the water on my butt, shaking wildly at the severed limb that still clutched me.

The waters surged again, and another slick-shelled *thing* grabbed at me. And another. And another. Dozens of the creatures were rushing toward our side of the pool, and the pressure wave rushing before them rose a foot off the pool's surface.

"Shellycobbs!" I shouted, and flicked another burst of flame at the nearest, driving it back. "They're shellycobbs!"

"Whatever," Murphy said, stepped up beside me, and started shooting. The third shellycobb took three hits in the same center area of its shell and cracked like a restaurant lobster.

It bought me a second to act, and I raised the blasting rod and tried something new on the fly, a blending of a blast of fire with my shield magic. I pointed the rod at one side of the shore, gathered my will, and thundered, "Ignus defendarius!"

A bar of flame, bright enough to hurt my eyes, shot out to one side of the room. I drew a line across the stone with the tip of the blasting rod, and as the flame touched the stone it adhered, spooling out from my blasting rod until it had formed a solid line between us and the water, and an opaque curtain of flame three feet high separated us from the shellycobbs. Angry rattles and splashes came from the far side of the curtain.

If the fire dropped, the faerie water monsters would swarm us.

The fire took a lot of energy to keep up, and if I tried to hold it too long I'd probably black out. Worse, it was still fire — it needed oxygen to keep burning, and in those cramped tunnels there wasn't going to be much of it around for breathing if the fire stayed lit too long. All of which meant that we only had seconds and had to do something. Fast.

"Murph!" I snapped. "Could you carry her?"

She turned wide blue eyes to me, her gun still held ready and pointing at the shellycobbs. "What?"

"Can you carry her?"

She gritted her teeth and nodded once.

I met her eyes for a dangerous second and asked, "Do you trust me?"

Fire crackled. Water boiled. Steam hissed.

"Yes, Harry," she whispered.

I flashed her a grin. "Jump the fire. Run to her."

"Run to her?"

"And hurry," I said, lifting my left arm, focusing as my shield bracelet began to glow, blue-white energy swiftly becoming incandescent. "Now!"

Murphy broke into a run and hurtled over the wall of fire.

"Forzare!" I shouted, and extended my left arm and my will.

I reshaped the shield, this time forming it in a straight, flat plane about three feet wide. It shot through the wall of flame, over the water, to the stone upon which Georgia lay. Murphy landed on the bridge of pure force, kept her balance, and poured on the speed, sprinting over the water to the unconscious young woman.

Murphy slapped her gun back into its holster, grabbed Georgia, and with a shout and a grunt of effort managed to get the tall girl into a fireman's carry. She started back, much more slowly than she'd gone forward.

The shellycobbs thrashed even more furiously, and the strain of holding both spells started to become a physical sensation, a spidery, trembling weakness in my arms and legs. I clenched my teeth and my will, focusing on holding the wall and the bridge until Murphy could return. My vision distorted, shrinking down to a tunnel.

And then Murphy shouted again and plunged through the fire, this time more slowly. She let out a gasp of pain as she got singed, then stumbled past me.

I released the bridge with a gasp of relief. "Go!" I said. "Come on, let's go!"

Together, we were barely able to get Georgia lifted. I was only able to hold the wall of flame against the shellycobbs for about fifty feet when I had to release the spell or risk passing out. I guess the shellycobbs weren't sprinters, because Murphy and I outran them, dragging the naked girl out of her Undertown prison and back to Murphy's car.

In all that time, Georgia never stirred.

Murphy had a blanket in her trunk. I wrapped Georgia in it and got in the backseat with her. Murphy gunned the car and headed for the Lincolnshire Marriott Resort Hotel, twenty miles north of town and one of the most ostentatious places in the area to hold a wedding. Traffic wasn't good, and according to the clock in Murphy's car, we had less than ten minutes before the wedding was supposed to begin.

I struggled in the backseat, fumbling to keep Georgia from bouncing off the ceiling, to get my backpack open, and to ignore the cuts the shellycobb's pincer left on my leg.

"Is that blood on her face?" Murphy asked.

"Yeah," I said. "Dried. But I figure it wasn't hers. Bob said she wolfed out in the apartment. I think Georgia got her fangs into Jenny Greenteeth before she got grabbed."

"Jenny who?"

"Jenny Greenteeth," I said. "She's one of the sidhe. Faerie nobility, sidekick to the Winter Lady."

"Are her teeth green?"

"Like steamed spinach. I saw her leading a big old bunch of shellycobbs just like those guys, back at the faerie war. If Maeve wanted to lay out some payback for Billy and company, Jenny's the one she'd send."

"She's dangerous?"

"You know the stories about things that tempt you down to the water's edge and then drown you? Sirens that lure sailors to their deaths? Mermaids who carry men off to their homes under the sea?"

"Yeah?"

"That's Jenny. Only she's not so cuddly."

I dug Bob out of my backpack. The skull took one look at the sleeping, naked Georgia and leered. "First you get demolition-level sex with the cop chick, and now a threesome, all in the same day!" he cried. "Harry, you have to write *Penthouse* about this!"

"Not now, Bob. I need you to identify the spell that's been laid on Georgia."

The skull made a disgusted sound but focused on the girl. "Oh," he said after a second. "Wow. That's a good one. Definitely sidhe work."

"I figure it's Jenny Greenteeth. Give me details."

"Jenny got game. It's a sleep spell," he said. "A seriously good one, too. Malicious as hell."

"How do I lift it?"

"You can't," Bob said.

"Fine. How do I break it?"

"You don't understand. It's been tied into the victim. It's being fueled by the victim's life force. If you shatter the spell . . ."

I nodded, getting it. "I'll do the same to her. Is it impossible to get rid of it?"

"No, not at all. I'm saying that *you* couldn't lift it. Whoever threw it could do that, of course. But there's another key."

I grew wroth and scowled. "What key, Bob?"

"Uh," he said, somehow giving the impression that he'd shrugged. "A kiss ought to do it. You know. True love, Prince Charming, that kind of thing."

"That won't be hard," I said, relaxing a little. "We'll definitely get to the wedding before he goes off alone with Jenny and gets drowned."

"Oh, good," Bob said. "Of course, the girl still kicks off, but you can't save all the people, all the time."

"What?" I demanded. "Why does Georgia die?"

"Oh, if the Werewolf kid goes through the ceremony with Jenny and plights his troth and so on, it's going to contaminate him. I mean, if he's married to another, it can't really be pure love. Jenny's claim on him would prevent the kiss from lifting the spell."

"Which means Georgia won't wake up," I said, chewing on my lip. "At what point in the wedding does it happen, exactly?"

"You mean, when will it be too late?" Bob asked.

"Yeah. I mean, when they say, 'I do,' when they swap rings, or what?"

"Rings and vows," Bob said, mild scorn in his voice. "Way overrated."

Murphy glanced up at me in the rearview mirror and said, "It's the kiss, Harry. It's the kiss."

"Buffy's right!" Bob agreed cheerily.

I met Murphy's eyes in the mirror for just a second and then said, "Yeah. I guess I should have figured."

Murphy smiled a little.

"The kiss seals the deal," Bob prattled. "If Billy kisses Jenny Greenteeth, the girl with the long legs ain't waking up, and he ain't long for the world, either."

"Murph," I said, tense.

She rolled down the car's window, slapped a magnetic cop light on the roof, and started up the siren. Then she stomped on the gas and all but gave me whiplash.

Under normal circumstances, the trip to the resort would have taken half an hour. I'm not saying that Murphy's driving was suicidal. Not quite. But after the third near collision, I closed my eyes and fought off the urge to chant "there's no place like home."

Murphy got us there in twenty minutes.

Tires screeched as she swung into the resort's parking lot. "Drop me there," I said, pointing. "Park behind the reception tent so folks won't see Georgia. I'll go get Billy."

I bailed out of the car, which never actually came to a full stop, clutching my blasting rod, and ran into the hotel. The concierge blinked at me from behind her desk.

"Wedding!" I barked at her. "Where?"

She blinked and pointed a finger down the hall. "Um. The ballroom."

"Right!" I said, and sprinted that way. I could see the open double doors and heard a man's voice over a loudspeaker: ". . . until death do you part?"

Eve McAlister stood at the doorway in her lavender silk outfit, and when she saw me her eyes narrowed into sharp little chips of ice. "There, that's him. That's the man."

Two big, beefy guys in matching badly fitted maroon dress coats appeared — hotel security goons. They stepped directly into my path, and the larger one said, "Sir, I'm sorry, but this is a private function. I'll have to ask you to leave."

I ground my teeth. "You have got to be kidding me! Private? I'm the best fucking man!"

The loudspeaker voice in the ballroom said, "Then by the power vested in me . . ."

"I will not allow you to further disrupt this wedding, or tarnish my good name,"

Eve said in a triumphant tone. "Gentlemen, please escort him from the premises before he causes a scene."

"Yes, ma'am," the bigger goon said. He stepped toward me, glancing down at the blasting rod. "Sir, let's walk to the doors now."

Instead, I darted forward, toward the doors, taking the goons by surprise with the abrupt action. "Billy!" I shouted.

The goons recovered in an eyeblink and tackled me. They were professional goons. I went down under them, and it drove the breath out of me.

The loudspeaker voice said, ". . . man and wife. You may now kiss the bride."

I lay there on my back under maybe five hundred pounds of security goon, struggling to breathe, staring at nothing but ceiling.

A ceiling lined with a whole bunch of automated fire extinguishers.

I slammed my head into the Boss Goon's nose and bit Backup Goon on the arm until he screamed and jerked it away, freeing my right arm.

I pointed the blasting rod up, reached for my power, and wheezed, ". . . fuego . . ."

Flame billowed up to the ceiling.

A fire alarm howled. The sprinklers flicked on and turned the inside of the hotel into a miniature monsoon.

Chaos erupted. The ballroom was filled with screams. The floor shook a little as hundreds of guests leaped to their feet and started looking for an exit. The security goons were smart enough to realize that they suddenly had an enormous problem on their hands, and then scrambled away from the doorway before they could be trampled.

I got to my feet in time to see a minister fleeing a raised platform, where a figure in Georgia's wedding dress had hunched over, while Billy, spiffy in his tux, stared at her in pure shock. That much running water grounded out whatever glamour the bride might have been using, and her features melted back into those I'd seen before — she lost an inch or two of height and her proportions changed. Georgia's rather sharp features flowed into a visage of haunting, unearthly beauty. Georgia's brown hair became the same green as emeralds and seaweed.

Jenny Greenteeth turned toward Billy, her trademark choppers bared in a viridian snarl, and her hand swept at his throat, inhuman nails gleaming.

Billy may have been shocked, but not so much that he didn't recognize the threat.

His arm intercepted Jenny's and he drove into her, pushing both hands forward with the power of his arms, shoulders, and legs. Billy's got a low center of gravity, and he's no skinny weakling. The push sent Jenny back several steps and off the edge of the platform. She fell in a tangle of white fabric and lace.

"Billy!" I shouted again, almost managing to make it loud. My voice was lost in the sounds of panic and the wailing fire alarms, so I gritted my teeth, brought my shield bracelet up to its flashiest, sparkliest, shiniest charge, and thrust into the press of the crowd. To them, it must have looked like someone waving a road flare around, and there was a steady stream of interjections that averaged out to, "Eek!" I forged ahead through them.

By the time I was past the crowd, Jenny Greenteeth had risen to her feet, tearing the bridal gown off like it was made of tissue paper. She stretched one hand into a grasping claw and clenched at the air. Ripples of angry power fluttered between her fingers, and an ugly green sphere of light appeared in her hand.

She leaped nimbly back up to the platform, unencumbered by the dress, and flung the green sphere at Billy. He ducked. It flew over his head, leaving a hole with blackened, crumbling edges in the wall behind him.

Jenny howled and summoned another sphere, but by that time I was within reach. Standing on the floor by the platform gave me a perfect shot at her knees, and I swing my blasting rod with both hands. The blow elicited a shriek of pain from the sidhe woman, and she flung the second sphere at me. I caught it on my shield bracelet and it rebounded upon her, searing a black line across the outside of one thigh.

The sidhe screamed and threw herself back, her weight mostly on one leg, and snarled to me, "Thou wouldst have saved this one, wizard. But I will yet exact my Lady's vengeance twofold."

And with a graceful leap, she flew over our heads, forty feet to the door, and vanished from sight as swiftly and nimbly as a deer.

"Harry!" Billy said, staring in shock at the soaking-wet room. "What the hell is happening here? What the hell was that thing?"

I grabbed his tux. "No time. Come with me."

He did but asked, "Why?"

"I need you to kiss Georgia."

"Uh," he said. "What?"

"I found Georgia. She's outside. The

111

watery tart knows it. She's going to kill her. You gotta kiss her, *now*."

"Oh," he said.

We both ran, and suddenly the bottom fell out of my stomach.

Vengeance twofold.

Oh God.

Jenny Greenteeth would kill Murphy, too.

Outside the hotel was a mess. People were wandering around in herds. Emergency sirens were already on the way. A couple of cars had smashed into one another in the parking lot, probably as they both gunned it for the road. Everyone out there seemed to be determined to get in our way, slowing our pursuit.

We ran to where Murphy had parked her car.

It was lying on its side. Windows were broken. One of the doors had been torn off. I didn't see anyone around. But Billy suddenly cocked his head to one side and then pointed at the reception tent. We ran for it as quietly as we could, and Billy threw himself inside. I heard him let out a short cry.

I followed.

Georgia lay on the ground, hardly covered by the blanket at all, limbs sprawled bonelessly. Billy rushed over to her.

Just past them I saw Murphy.

Jenny Greenteeth stood over her at the refreshments table, hands locked in Murphy's hair, pushing her face down into a full punch bowl. The wicked faerie's eyes were alight with rage and madness and an almost sexual arousal. Murphy's arms twitched a little, and Jenny gasped, lips parting, and pushed down harder.

Murphy's hand fluttered one more time and went still.

The next thing I knew, I was smashing my blasting rod down onto Jenny Greenteeth, screaming incoherently, pounding as hard as I possibly could. I drove the faerie back from Murphy, who slid limply to the ground. Then Jenny recovered her balance, struck out at me with one arm, and I found out a fact I hadn't known before.

Jenny Greenteeth was something strong.

I landed several feet away, not far from Billy and Georgia, watching birdies and little lights fly around. On another table, next to me, was another punch bowl.

Jenny Greenteeth flew at me, lust in her inhumanly lovely features, her feline eyes smoldering.

"Billy!" I slurred. "Dammit, kiss her! Now!"

Billy blinked at me.

Then he turned to Georgia, lifting the upper half of her body in his arms, and kissed her with a desperation and passion that no one can fake.

I didn't get to see what happened, because faster than you could say "oxygen deprivation," Jenny Greenteeth had ahold of my hair and my face smashed against the bottom of the punch bowl.

I fought her, but she was stronger than anything human and she had all kinds of leverage. I could feel her pressed against me, body tensing and shifting, rubbing against me. Getting off as she murdered me. The lights started to go out. This was what she did. She knew what she was doing.

Lucky for me, she wasn't the only one.

I suddenly fell, getting the whole huge punch bowl to turn over on me as I did, drenching me in bright red punch. I gasped and wiped stinging liquid from my eyes and looked up in time to see a pair of wolves, one tall and lean, one smaller and heavier, leap at Jenny Greenteeth and bring her to the ground. Screams and snarls blended, and none of them sounded human.

Jenny tried to run, but the lean wolf ripped across the back of her unwounded leg with its fangs, severing the hamstring.

The faerie went down. The wolves were on her before she could scream again. The wheel turns, and Jenny Greenteeth never had a chance. The wolves knew what they were doing.

This was what *they* did.

I crawled over to Murphy. Her eyes were open and staring, her body and features slack. Some part of my brain remembered the steps for CPR. I started doing it. I adjusted her position, sealed my lips to Murphy's, and breathed for her. Then compressions. Breathe. Compressions.

"Come on, Murph," I whispered. "Come on."

I covered her mouth with mine and breathed again.

For one second, for one teeny, tiny instant, I felt her mouth move. I felt her head tilt, her lips soften, and my oh-so-professional CPR — just for a second, mind you — felt almost, *almost* like a kiss.

Then she started coughing and sputtering, and I sank back from her in relief. She turned on her side, breathing hard for a moment, and then looked up at me with dazed blue eyes. "Harry?"

I leaned down, causing runnels of punch to slide into one of my eyes, and asked quietly, "Yeah?"

"You have fruit punch mouth," she whispered.

Her hand found mine, weak but warm. I held it. We sat together.

Billy and Georgia got married that night in Father Forthill's study, at Saint Mary of the Angels, an enormous old church. No one was there but them, the padre, Murphy, and me. After all, as far as most anyone else knew, they'd been married at that disastrous travesty of a farce in Lincolnshire.

The ceremony was simple and heartfelt. I stood with Billy. Murphy stood with Georgia. They both looked radiantly happy. They held hands the whole time, except when they were exchanging rings.

Murphy and I stepped back when they got to the vows.

"Not exactly a fairy-tale wedding," she whispered.

"Sure it was," I said. "Had a kiss and an evil stepmother and everything."

Murphy smiled at me.

"Then by the power vested in me," the padre said, beaming at the pair of them from behind his spectacles, "I now pronounce you man and wife. You may kiss th—"

They beat him to it.

■ ■ ■ ■

JIM BUTCHER'S bestselling *Dresden Files* from ROC chronicles the life of modern-day Chicago's only professional wizard, Harry Dresden. (*Lost Items Found. Paranormal Investigations. Consulting. Advice. Reasonable Rates. No Love Potions, Endless Purses, Parties or Other Entertainment.*) You may learn more at www.jim-butcher.com.

Jim Butcher is a martial arts enthusiast with fifteen years of experience in various styles including Ryukyu Kempo, Tae Kwan Do, Gojo Shorei Ryu, and a sprinkling of Kung Fu. He is a skilled rider and has worked as a summer camp horse wrangler and performed in front of large audiences in both drill riding and stunt riding exhibitions.

Jim enjoys fencing, singing, bad science fiction movies, and live-action gaming. He lives in Missouri with his wife, son, and a vicious guard dog.

DEAD MAN'S CHEST

RACHEL CAINE

"Now this," Ian Taylor said with satisfaction, surveying the ship bobbing just outside of the harbor, "is what I call an *adventure!*" He turned a blinding grin on his wife-to-be as he patted her hand. He had to hunt for it; it only wrapped partly around his well-muscled forearm. "It's going to be amazing. Better than any church wedding, eh?"

She looked up at him, speechless. He stood six feet, five inches to her dumpy five-foot-four and had the kind of rippling, tanned body usually only seen onstage in gay strip clubs. Silky blond hair. Impossibly white, even teeth. Big blue eyes.

And he was — unbelievably — a *romance-novel cover model.*

For a woman whose self-image most often involved the words "mousy" and "short," meeting Ian had been like being run down by the speeding Love Train. Ian had knocked her off her feet (literally, with a shopping cart to her midsection), and upon reviving her in the parking lot of the local Wal-Mart, he'd set about seducing her by wearing ruffled poet shirts and declaiming flowery compliments.

Their romance — two months along, yesterday — had been one big, rose-colored dream, and she kept waiting to wake up. But the dream was starting to take on a surreal edge of panic, and all Cecilia could finally sum up in response to Ian's enthusiasm was a wan smile and a quiet, "It looks great."

She supposed it did, if you were a romance-cover heroine. When Ian had mentioned the surprise, she'd been thinking with desperate optimism of a cruise ship. Something like a floating city, with beauty shops and bowling alleys and seven ballroom-sized dining rooms. (She'd done considerable last-minute research.)

The huge ship bobbing like a cork was, in true Ian fashion, *not* a boring old honeymoon cruise ship. No, this was straight out of some sweeping pirate tale, with towering masts and yo-ho-ho on a dead man's chest. It was even flying a pirate flag. Cute.

"When —" She tried to banish the squeak from her voice. "When do we —" Drown. Yes, sink and drown, arrrrrr, matey. "Sail?"

"Sail?" Ian echoed, and picked her up to whirl her around in a nauseating spiral. "Within the hour, Cess! Isn't that wonderful?"

It was a measure of how overwhelmed she was that she hadn't complained about that damn nickname. *Cess.* Ugh. *Cecilia, if you please,* she imagined herself saying coolly, like those heroines in the novels, as she pulled her shoulders straight and cowed him with an imperious gaze.

Of course, none of those women would have gotten themselves into a fix like this in the first place.

Cecilia squeezed her eyes shut and clung for dear life until Ian, and the world in general, stopped whirling. Well, at least she had manly thews to which she could cling. Hadn't had those, a couple of months ago. Hadn't had anything at all but herself.

Ah, some traitorous part of her heart sighed, *hadn't that just been the life?*

With shock, she realized what he'd just said. *SAIL? Within the hour?!*

She must have made some squeak of protest. Ian, hair blowing in cornsilk waves on the wind, shirt billowing romantically, looked down at her. "Trust me," he said. "You're going to *love* this."

■ ■ ■ ■

Somehow, he managed to get her down the boardwalk, mostly by bum's-rushing her with an arm around her shoulders. Terror rendered her effectively mute and manageable.

"There she is, Cess. Isn't she beautiful?"

She supposed, in a scary piratical way. The ship was anchored out in the harbor, riding the waves, its skeletal spires draped with ropes like cobwebs in the mist. The day was clouding over and fog boiling in from the ocean. Perfect. Well, maybe she could use it to slip away.

She'd just taken the first sidle in that direction when Ian pulled her into a smothering embrace. She tried for that square-shouldered dignity she'd been imagining earlier. "Ian, we can't do this. It's impossible."

"Can't? What do you mean? You said you'd marry me, didn't you?"

Well . . . yes. She had. But it had been one of those *yes, of course, someday* things, not a *yes, God, drag me to the docks and throw me on a pirate ship* thing.

"Ian, listen to me," she said. "I really can't —"

She paused, because Ian had been walking her toward the edge of the wooden pier, and suddenly there was nothing between her and the greasy, slippery water except his arm and about an inch of foothold. Her voice locked tight in her throat.

Out in the growing mist, she heard the rhythmic splash of oars.

Tell him. Tell him you can't marry him. TELL HIM!

She opened her mouth to do it, and a boat glided out of the gray fog. A black, glossy boat with six men at the oars and another standing straight as a pike with his arms folded. Clearly the man in charge. Pirate in charge. Whatever.

Well, Cecilia thought numbly, you couldn't say Ian didn't go in for authenticity. She'd never in her life seen a more likely brigand. Sun-browned skin. A mass of coiling dark hair shot with gray, the lot barely contained by some braids to either side and a battered tricorn hat. He wasn't tall — not as tall as Ian, certainly — and wore a heavy, antique-style coat with corroded brass buttons and fraying bullion on the sleeves. Faded and sea stained.

His eyes were fierce and dark, and under a bristle of mustache and goatee she couldn't see any expression at all. For all she could tell, he was about to draw that frightening-looking cutlass at his belt and demand that she stand and deliver.

"Ah," Ian said. "Captain Lockhart. May I present my wife-to-be, Cecilia Welles?"

Captain Lockhart flicked that impenetrable glance from her to Ian and then back. "If you must," he said, in the most dismissive tone she'd ever heard.

She'd been about to turn around and bolt, but that did it. It came to her in a blinding, angry rush, exactly why she was doing this. She'd found the perfect man, and there was no reason, no reason at all, not to see this for the incredible lucky break it was. She'd be stupid to turn away. Some other woman would be all over Ian like spray-on tan the second she did.

Cecilia squared her shoulders and fixed the ragged pirate with the glare she wasn't capable of aiming at Ian. "Yes," she said. "He must. Is this our ride?"

Captain Lockhart clasped his hands behind his back and easily rocked with the waves that battered the small boat. His face remained bland. "No horses," he said.

"What?"

"Not a ride, love. No horses."

She felt an obscure sense of satisfaction at having provoked even that much reaction.

"Our . . . conveyance." That was a good romance-novel word. "Conveyance." She saw a sudden, startling flash of teeth.

"Aye," he said. "It's a conveyance, if you're not too particular about your terms. Get in, if you're getting. Tide's about to turn."

Ian jumped into the boat with a solid thump and swung Cecilia in before she could suck in breath to protest.

Too late. She sat and clung to the side convulsively as it lurched in the waves. The left-side oarsmen pushed off from the pier, and the boat began a hideous rocking motion. "Ian, wait! Isn't — isn't anybody else coming? Your family? My friends? We should have witnesses. . . ."

Ian patted her shoulder. "Captain Lockhart and his men will sign all of the necessary papers, Cess." She shivered, damp and miserable in her thin T-shirt and blue jeans. "See? I told you it'd be a surprise."

Captain Lockhart cast her a look, raised an expressive eyebrow, and turned to watch the unseen horizon as they rowed into the mist.

The ship was called *Sweet Mourning.* Cecilia knew that, because she saw the name on the stern as they rowed toward it. If she'd thought the ship was big before, well, it was *enormous*. And she had to admit, she felt a thrill when the black glossy mountain of a hull appeared out of the fog. The sails were down, neatly tied to the crosspieces — yardarms? — and men up in the webs of rigging swarmed like spiders.

Captain Lockhart's oarsmen maneuvered the boat next to the gigantic bouncing hull of the ship, and a contraption that looked like a worn wooden swing came over the railing to hang at the level of the boat. "Right," Ian said cheerfully. "In you go, Cess."

Before she could, once and for all, tell him to *stop calling her that,* he grabbed her around the waist and settled her in the swing.

"Heave!" Lockhart bellowed, which was offensive, really — and then she was rising into the air. She grabbed for the ropes. Within five feet, the mist closed in, and she could barely see the boat below; in ten, she might as well have been alone in the fog, suspended like a puppet from a giant's finger.

And then she heard the squeal of pulleys and the creak of rope, and a shadow leaned over the rail and hauled the swing over the side. Her feet hit the deck with a thump.

125

She promptly lost her balance in the dip of a wave and grabbed for the first available hold.

It was the fraying collar of Captain Lockhart's coat. She stared at him in numbed surprise as he distastefully pried her fingers loose and settled her back on balance.

"How did you get here first?" she demanded.

"Climbed," he said, and nodded toward a knotted rope thrown over the rail. It was creaking with strain. Sure enough, the top of Ian's head appeared, and then his reddened face. Captain Lockhart hadn't even broken a sweat. "Now, there's work to be done on deck. You and your" — his eyes flicked toward Ian, who was clambering over the railing — "your intended can wait up on the quarterdeck."

"I have no idea what that means."

Lockhart grabbed her by the arm, spun her around, and pointed over her shoulder through the thick forest of masts and ropes, up a ladder to a second level. A huge black wheel was revealed by an eddy in the mist. "Quarterdeck," he said, and gave her a push. She glared after him, furious, but he dismissed her and moved on. Ian was there to grab her when she stumbled again. The whole ship seemed to be lurching violently from one wave to the next.

"Isn't this *grand?*" Ian enthused, panting. "She's an East Indiaman. You'll never see a bigger sailing ship, Cess. Nothing like her has sailed the seas for a hundred years, at least."

"Lovely," she said. "Look, he said —"

"Normally there'd be about three hundred men on board, but I was told they run with fewer, since they're not really taking on cargo." Ian, on a roll, ignored her. "Funny story, how I found —"

"Ian, the captain said —"

"Funny story, how I found the ship, but I was at this pub, and —"

"I told you to get to the quarterdeck!" Captain Lockhart's bellow. The deck was suddenly awash with sailors boiling out of hatchways — a blur of sun-blackened faces, scars, disfigurements. She doubted any of them had bathed in months, and from what she could see of their bare, calloused feet, they'd spent more than half their lives shoeless. She fought her way out of the mob and reached the ladder and scrambled up to the relative sanity of the quarterdeck. Ian was right behind her, broad as a wall. She was grateful for that, because for the third impossible time Captain Lockhart was ahead of them, standing at a military parade

127

rest in his shabby, water-stained coat. He rode the waves with feline grace.

"How did you —," she blurted.

He gave her a sad shake of his head, and watched as another wave sent her reeling. "Mr. Argyle, weigh anchor and take us out."

"Aye, Cap'n," said a small man standing behind him, resplendent in a blaring red coat marred by at least three blackened holes in the breast. He had a Napoleonic haircut, fussy little spectacles, and he looked rather sweet until he began bellowing like a foghorn. "Richards! Weigh the anchor! Topsails, Mr. Simonds, *today,* or I'll see you kissing the mast tomorrow!"

A heavy, vibrating clank echoed through the fog, and the ship groaned like a living thing. Repeated commands echoed from one end of the ship to the other, growing distant in the mist. Cecilia clung to the railing and listened to the creak of ropes and the sudden snap of canvas.

She was suddenly sickly aware that her life was totally out of control.

Captain Lockhart had his hands on the massive oversized wheel, moving it by small increments. Steering by feel, she supposed; she couldn't see a damn thing, but his dark eyes never wavered from some distant spot in the mist. Maybe he had an earpiece under that wig. Maybe someone was hiding belowdecks with radar to guide him out. Yes, that must be it. Otherwise . . . No. She wasn't going to think about some *actor* sailing them blind out of a harbor.

Canvas creaked, and she felt a sudden surge of acceleration. Lockhart's face relaxed into something that almost looked like a grin. His fingers caressed the wheel gently, and he shot a glance to the small man standing next to him.

"East-sou'east, Mr. Argyle. I leave her in your hands." He let go of the wheel, and Argyle stepped quickly up to grab it. "I'll see our . . . guests . . . to their quarters."

"Aye, sir," Argyle said, stone-faced.

Lockhart descended, agile as a monkey, to the main deck and threw open a door between the two ladders. Cecilia, following, slipped on the wet decking despite her sneakers. "Get rid of the fancy slippers," Lockhart said. "Bare feet's best. Wouldn't want you going overboard, now, would we?"

The words were bland, but the men working nearby laughed. Cecilia swallowed hard and remembered her resolve. She drew herself up straight and looked Lockhart in the eye.

"I'm sure you wouldn't, Captain," she said, which wasn't exactly the comeback of the year, but it was, after all, her first attempt. "That wouldn't be a great advertisement for your cruise line, would it?"

"Cruise line?" Lockhart echoed, and slowly smiled. "Ah. Yes. Of course."

The cabin was a closet. Well . . . not *quite* a closet, maybe. It had two chancy-looking hammocks, a nice porcelain sink and pitcher, an oil lamp hanging from a safety hook, and a closed pot in the corner on the floor. There were also two outfits laid out on the bed — something true to the period, so far as her inexperienced eye could tell. Ian's was composed of a nice blue coat, a frilled white shirt, and some gray trousers. Knee boots.

Well, at least Ian's looked like some approximation of Lord of the Manor. Hers came from Central Tavern Wench Casting.

"Oh, hell, no," she muttered, holding up the low-cut shirt and bodice. "Ian, no way am I wearing this! — Ian?"

There was a thumping out in the corridor, and then Ian squeezed through the door, long hair straggling around his face. She'd never actually seen him look messy before. He tried to straighten up, bumped his head on the wooden ceiling, and cursed, glaring at the rafters.

Lockhart's lips twitched. "Argyle will fetch

you later," he said. "Be dressed."

He slammed the door, and metal rattled. Cecilia, curious, went to it and tried the handle.

It didn't turn. She tried harder. "Ian! Ian, he's locked us in!"

"Probably stuck," Ian said grumpily. "Sea air."

"No, seriously. It's locked." She braced one foot on the wall and yanked until it felt like her shoulder muscles might snap, then subsided, panting.

Ian was holding the pot that had been in the corner. It was a nice one, white enamel, with painted flowers. "Why is there a pot under the bed? What are we supposed to cook?"

She had to laugh when she explained the uses of a chamber pot. Authenticity. She suspected he hadn't wanted quite that much.

And then . . . nothing happened. For what seemed like hours. Nothing to do, no television, no books, nobody but Ian to talk to, and she was afraid to admit it, but that was losing its charms. She tried out the hammock. It was surprisingly comfortable, and in fact, the swaying motion combined with Ian's monotonous pacing sent her right off into a doze.

She woke up with a start when the door rattled again and banged open. Mr. Argyle, still in his fire-engine red coat with its burnt holes over the breast, looked in.

"Bother. You were told to get dressed," he said. "Captain expects you looking proper. Hop to it, then."

He slammed the door again. She sat up, realized that there was no graceful way to get out of a hammock, and nearly ended up on her butt on the floor. Ian grabbed her arm to hold her upright, and she blinked at him in surprise.

Ian was all togged out, and on him, it looked . . . breathtaking. Most things did, though. He flashed a blindingly confident grin. "Better get ready, Cess. I think they mean it."

She looked at the tangle of clothing at the end of the bunk. The long pink-and-white striped skirt wasn't too horrible, but the tight-lacing black bodice was downright terrifying. She was staring at it miserably when the door banged open again. This time it was Lockhart, flanked by Argyle.

Lockhart sighed and turned to Argyle. "I told you to get her dressed."

"Aye, sir, well —"

"Next time I see her in men's trousers,

Argyle, you'll be the one wearing the dress."

"Aye, sir," Argyle said, and touched his forehead. "Sorry, sir."

Lockhart dismissed it and focused on her. "Well then, Miss Welles. Do you intend to be wed in breeches?"

"Will I — what?" She clutched the bodice tight in both hands. "Um . . . ?"

"Be wed," he said, very clearly enunciating the words. "Married. Joined in sacred union. Tie the knot. Become one flesh, so help ye God."

"I don't — what, you mean *now?* Right now?"

Ian, who was cautiously settled on the edge of one of the hammocks, frowned. "What's wrong with now?"

"Well —" Nothing, she supposed, except that she felt ice-cold at the prospect, barely able to control her shaking knees. "All right." She tried raising her head. It made her feel seasick again, and she hastily tucked her chin back in a less exposed position. "Um . . . I think I'd like to change, in that case. Please leave me, gentlemen."

"Leave?" Lockhart raised an eyebrow. "Aye. Five minutes, and then you're coming out; dressed or naked is all the same to me."

He banged the door back shut. Cecilia,

133

openmouthed, stared after him.

"Maybe you'd better get dressed, Cess," Ian said. "Sounds like he means what he says."

"You, too," she said. "Please. Out?" She wasn't used to giving him orders, and it sounded more like a plea. Or maybe a question.

But after a few seconds, he sighed. "Women," he said, and went to the door. To her surprise, it opened right up, and he ducked out. She heard the sound of male chuckles. Great. So much for chivalry, or gallantry, or whatever it was.

In five minutes, she was struggling with the ties. She overflowed the low-cut, tightly laced black bodice by a considerable margin — a lot more than most wedding consultants would have considered suitable, she was sure. The striped pink and white skirts were heavier than she'd thought, but they felt . . . nice. Almost formal. At least with the bodice laced tightly, she had an excuse for feeling faint and being short of breath.

This time, it didn't surprise her when the door banged open again. Lockhart, who'd been meaning to deliver some cutting remark, paused and actually blinked. Even the dry Mr. Argyle cast a significantly surprised look at her.

Lockhart cleared his throat. "Good enough, I suppose. Out with you, and let's be quick about it."

He stepped away, and she sailed through the open door, attempting regal and missing it by tripping on the fabric of her heavy skirts. Ian and Argyle were already halfway down the corridor. She felt a hot blush of shame and knew Lockhart would be sneering at her. She kept her chin up, somehow. That was a major victory.

Outside on the deck, a dizzying breath of sea air swept over her. It ruffled her hair and made her weak at the knees. Fresh, cool, misty air. She hadn't realized how starved she was for it until it slid over her skin. Spending a few hours in that cabin had been worse than a week penned up in her cubicle at work.

Lockhart jostled her elbow impatiently, and as she moved farther onto the open deck, she looked up . . . and fell in love. *Magic,* she thought numbly. *This is what magic looks like.* It wasn't the ship, or the quaintly costumed pirates. It was the sky. Stars spilled thick and diamond-hard overhead, veiled here and there by a silver net of mist — more stars than she'd ever seen in her life. The moon was a breathtaking, pure crescent of silver-white, so bright it burned.

And the *sea* — a vast, mesmerizing net of glints and sparks and liquid silver. Cold and beautiful.

"You locked us in," she said. She meant it to be accusatory, but there was something so beautiful about the night that she couldn't even begin to be angry.

"Ah, well, I'd prefer to define it as 'kept you out of my way,' " Lockhart said. She couldn't tell if he was mocking her or not. "The sea's a treacherous bitch, but she's a looker when she's in the mood." His low, dark-honey voice turned unexpectedly rough. "Like most women, I'd suppose. Best move on now. Don't keep your true love waiting."

A whole audience had assembled — the whole crew, maybe, or as many as could be spared — and she edged past the men nervously and considered the issue of the ladder leading up to the quarterdeck. Not a problem in pants. Big problem in skirts.

Ian, resplendent as a lost prince in his finery, struck a bold pose at the top of the ladder. Wind billowed his frock coat and feathered the lace at his throat, and his hair spilled out like a silk flag. Very romantic.

He didn't offer to help her up.

She climbed fast, trying to keep her skirts as tight around her legs as possible. She settled herself breathlessly, and Ian moved away after a perfunctory peck on the cheek.

A hand closed over hers as she lurched for balance. Not Ian's big, strong hand — this one was darker, sinewy, rougher, and had never seen a manicure in its entire existence. She looked up into Captain Lockhart's face, and for a second she saw something odd there. A kind of searching regret, something that brought him into real focus for the first time not as a parody or an archetype in tattered clothing but a man. He placed her hand over his arm, in an old-world gentlemanly way, and walked her to her husband-to-be.

The comparison was inevitable. Ian had a carefully sculpted body, courtesy of personal trainers. A tan delivered weekly at the best salon in the city. Fine, gorgeous hair that required more maintenance than Cecilia's entire (mostly nonexistent) beauty regimen. He was polished and buffed and engineered into every woman's fantasy, and as he smiled at Cecilia she felt the doubts that had been growing in her mind spread like an oil slick to her heart.

Lockhart placed her chilled fingers in Ian's and then held out his right hand. Argyle hastily stepped forward and put his small book into it. Lockhart opened it, squinted at the pages, turned it around, and made a show of flipping until he found the appropriate passage.

"Right," he said, and cleared his throat. "Ian Taylor, do you take this woman as your lawfully wedded wife, et cetera?"

" 'Et cetera'?" Ian repeated blankly, and then, "Er, yes. Sure. I do."

Lockhart was already moving on before the last syllable was out of Ian's mouth. "Right. Cecilia Welles, think you carefully: Do you take this man, Ian Taylor, as your lawfully wedded husband, giving him power and authority over your worldly goods as well as your earthly body, until death do you part?"

She was no expert, but she was pretty sure that most marriage ceremonies weren't that sinister. Lockhart's dark eyes seemed to see everything — all the doubt, the fear, the horrible lack of self-confidence that had led her to this terrible, unhappy moment.

I hate oceans. I hate boats. I hate pirates.
I hate Ian.
I hate myself. That's the real problem.

"I do," she heard herself whisper.

Lockhart's eyes widened just a fraction, but then his face went entirely still. "Ah. Then ye be a wedded woman, Mistress Taylor," he said, and tossed the book over his shoulder at Mr. Argyle. "God preserve you."

Argyle fumbled the book out of the air, tsked over a bent page, and carefully stowed the book in a pocket of his coat. Lockhart threw his arms wide for a metaphorical embrace of his crew watching below. "That's it! Finished! Back to work, you scurvy dogs!"

The sailors muttered. She found herself clinging to Ian's warm hand for more than just moral support. The sails creaked, banners cracked in the fresh, cool wind, and the moon seemed eerie now, not beautiful. The constant hissing rush of the sea made her feel faint.

"He didn't say, 'You may kiss the bride,' but I'll take the liberty anyway," Ian said, and grabbed her in a bruising embrace and kissed her, all wet lips and slick teeth, and she tried to struggle away, but he seemed to think that was funny, somehow. Even when he pulled back, he held on to her with her feet flailing uselessly for the deck. "Captain Lockhart!"

Lockhart turned, hands clasped behind his back. The momentary humanity Cecilia had seen was gone like a pebble dropped in the ocean. "Your servant."

"I'll need the paperwork you promised. With witness signatures."

"Yes, of course." His lips parted in that surprisingly white smile. "Witnesses. Aye, Mr. Argyle, you'd swear these two were wed, wouldn't you?"

"Completely legal," Argyle said.

"Completely," Lockhart agreed. "All that remains is for you to consummate your sacred union as you see fit."

"Absolutely," Ian said. He moved to the railing and sat Cecilia roughly on the thin wooden support. She grabbed for his broad shoulders, then his lapels, as the ship heaved again. He gave her a slow, entirely unpleasant smile. "You never got it, did you?"

"What?"

He pulled a letter out of his pocket. "One thing about working at the post office, you come across all kinds of great stuff. For instance, this one — from Mr. Tom Carruthers, Attorney-at-Law." He unfolded it. " 'To Miss Cecilia Welles, I regret to inform you of the recent passing of your aunt Nancy Welles Paulson, who died after a short illness . . .' yadda yadda . . . ah! Here's the good part. *Please call me to discuss the details of your estate.*' Estate, Cess. Two-point-four million, and as your widower, I'm entitled to the whole thing. Tragic honeymoon accident. I'll bet I end up get-

ting so much sympathy tail after the funeral."

And he pitched her over the railing.

She screamed on the way down — all the
way — and hit the water with a breath-
stealing smack. Cold. She flailed, was
slapped in the face by a wave, and then
another, before she could suck in a gasp.
Salt water burned in her throat and eyes.
She choked, coughed, and got a cold
mouthful of sea spray. It felt like there were
hands on her ankles, hands dragging her
down, and she couldn't feel anything below
her neck but pressure and cold. . . .

Her head slid under the next wave. When
she fought back to the surface, there was
someone standing up on the top deck of the
passing ship, looking down at her. Tricorn
hat. A mass of dark hair. A tattered antique
coat.

She didn't even know why she did it, but
she lifted a hand to him.

Please.

The next wave buried her. The pressure of
air in her lungs turned stale and useless,
and she let it dribble out in pretty silver
bubbles, a part of her escaping even though
the rest was sinking into the dark. . . .

And then there was a viselike grip on her
arm, and she was hauled to the surface.

Moonlight exploded pale in her eyes. Captain Lockhart, seal-sleek, hatless and coatless, turned her on her back. "Stay still," he ordered her. "Don't fight me!"

He clapped an arm as unyielding as an iron bar under her breasts and swam like a dolphin — but it wasn't going to be enough. The ship was pulling away, leaving them in its wide, silvery wake.

He couldn't swim forever, could he?

He didn't need to. The sails suddenly luffed, flapped, and slumped into pools of canvas on the yardarms. Shouts echoed over the water, and a rope ladder hit the water with a smack nearby and clattered against the black-painted hull.

Ian was now at the tall railing, leaning over. She couldn't really make out his face, only the broad details, but he didn't look happy. "You were supposed to let her drown!" he yelled down at Lockhart. "I paid you, you bastard! I paid you good hard cash —"

Lockhart waved a hand and shouted. "Mr. Argyle!"

"Aye, sir!" floated back the reply.

"Belay that noise!"

"Aye-aye, sir!"

Argyle bashed Ian smartly over the head and hauled him away. Cecilia screamed, not so much in fright as in surprise at the efficient way it was done.

"Best thing for it, really," Lockhart said, and bared his teeth in a broad white grin. "No refunds. Now climb, lass. It's too dark for me to look up your skirts."

Screaming wasn't doing her any good.

Cecilia shouted and battered at the bolted door, to absolutely no avail. If she'd thought being rescued meant that she had some kind of status, she'd been dead wrong. As soon as Lockhart had set foot on deck, he'd had her tossed into a lightless black hold. It smelled of rotten fish and moldy bread, and didn't even have the meager creature comfort of a hammock like her guest quarters. And to add insult to injury, a few minutes later another limp body was tossed inside, groaning. Ian. Oh, joy. They might not let her drown, but they probably wouldn't care if Ian finished the job for them.

The ocean's bounce seemed to be getting worse. She clutched her head as the ship leaped weightless, then crashed down into a trough . . . then rose . . . and fell. . . .

Ian groaned feebly, and she heard him scrabbling around as the door was bolted shut again behind him. No light, so she couldn't see him, but she could imagine how miserable he looked. "Oh God," he moaned. "I think I have a skull fracture."

"Then die already," she said. "I wish they'd shot you. With . . . with great big musket balls."

"Cess —"

"Don't call me Cess!" she yelled furiously. It was easier when she couldn't see him. "This is all your fault! I can't believe you tried to kill me!"

"Now, um, Cecilia —" More fumbling noises. Oh God, he was coming her way. "It was a mistake, that's all. You're just . . . confused, and —"

"I'm not the one with a skull fracture, Fabio. Now, let me see if I got this straight: You found the letter while you were working at the post office, and you intercepted it and decided to what? Seduce me? Marry me and then do away with me?"

"Um —"

"On a *pirate ship?* What are you, crazy? What kind of plan is that?"

"It's not a real pirate ship! It's . . . just an act."

"Who told you that?" she demanded furiously.

"Well . . . a guy at the docks —"

"Let me guess: some shifty-looking guy at the docks? Were you looking for a honeymoon cruise or body disposal?" She was screaming at him now, and she didn't care. She felt around and found something rolling on the floor. A filthy, ancient potato, it felt like. She hefted it in her right hand.

"It's not like that; it's just — um — look, I can explain."

She pelted the potato at the sound of his voice and sidestepped his lunge. She tripped over a box, went sprawling in a tangle of wet skirts, and his weight landed awkwardly on top of her.

Oh, damn.

"Oh, Cess . . . ilia, I just don't know what I — it was just temporary insanity, I swear; I don't know what happened. . . . I lost my grip on you. . . . It was an accident!"

She slapped him. He pinned her hands to the deck. "I want a divorce!" she shouted.

"Fine! We split the money fifty-fifty!"

"I don't have any money, you idiot!" she shouted, right in his face. *"And I don't have an aunt Nancy!"*

There was a long, ringing silence.

"You don't have an Aunt Nancy?"

"No."

"Then you didn't inherit two million dollars?"

"Not a chance."

"But it was addressed to —"

"The wrong Cecilia."

A long pause. "Oh."

"I can't believe I ever thought that somebody like you would — could — did you ever like me at all?"

"Well," he said judiciously, "I'd have probably taken you to bed at least once, you know. Things just got . . . out of hand."

She was hunting around for something hard enough to give him a *real* skull fracture but froze at the metallic clatter of latches. The door — hatch? — swung open and she was blinded with a lantern's glare.

"You," said a male voice. "Lass. Out with you."

She swallowed hard and started to get up, but suddenly Ian was there between her and the light. "Wait! You can't leave me here!"

Her eyes were adjusting to the dazzle, and she picked out the gleam of fussy spectacles perched on a narrow nose, short graying hair, and a deadly-looking pistol being pressed to Ian's temple. Mr. Argyle, her hero.

"Can and will. Come on, me laddie, you're too pretty to die. Fetch a good price at some of our less savory ports of call, I expect." He nodded toward Cecilia. "Let's go, then."

Cecilia edged around Ian to step out into

the larger darkened cabin. Even short as she was, she had to duck to pass under the low beams. The main crew quarters were partly filled with men sitting at trestle tables, knotting ropes, mending shirts, drinking. They eyed her as she passed, with varying degrees of sinister leering.

"Up," Argyle said, and prodded her with his pistol. She climbed.

Outside, it was dark and breathtakingly clear. Argyle hustled her through the now-familiar black door and down the corridor. Instead of taking the left-hand door, he opened the right, and ushered her through.

She blinked and paused a couple of steps in, because it looked as if she'd stepped off of the ship and into an elaborate manor house. Fine tables, linens, candles, hung from clever brackets that tilted with the motion of the ship. Thick carpet underfoot.

There were seven men seated at the table. Dinner, it seemed, had just ended. Plates were empty, serving dishes ravaged, and the only things filled were crystal glasses. Filled, emptied, and filled again before she'd managed to cross the long room with Mr. Argyle at her side.

"The wee lass," Argyle said, unnecessarily. They'd already looked up, and she was the focus of seven sets of assessing male eyes.

The most disconcerting were Captain Lock-hart's, because he seemed to see nothing in particular that appealed. "Or shall we say, the soon-to-be widow?"

"Sit," the captain said, and kicked out a chair. Or tried. His boot missed it by an inch. He aimed with great concentration and succeeded in thumping it ass-over-cushion to the carpet. "Damn."

"I've seen this movie," Cecilia blurted. "This is where you leer at me and tell me that food doesn't satisfy you, and you turn into zombies in the moonlight. Right?"

There was a long, surprised silence, and then they roared drunkenly with laughter. Argyle — sober, monkish Mr. Argyle — laughed so hard he reeled into the paneled wall. "Now, lassie," Argyle gasped, "does it *look* to you as if food doesn't satisfy this lot? They've done their level best to lick the shine from the plates! The best part of our cargo's food and drink!"

"Zombies in the moonlight!" roared a lop-eared fellow near Lockhart's left elbow. "Zounds, that's rich. . . . What the devil is a zombie?"

"From the Caribbean," Lockhart said contemplatively. He was decidedly not laughing. "Means the walking dead."

The laughter cut off abruptly. In the odd

silence, Cecilia clumsily bent down and set the chair upright again and let herself sink into it, because she wasn't sure her trembling knees would hold her. It had been a long, long day.

"Zombies," Argyle repeated blankly. "Well. I do stand corrected."

After a cutting glance around the table, Lockhart reached for the bottle and poured the crystal glass in front of Cecilia's empty plate to the brim.

"Drink up," he said.

"No, thank you."

"You need it. Not every day you get married and murdered," he said, and leaned his chair back precariously on two legs. She waited for him to tip straight over backward. It wasn't possible to keep a chair balanced with the constant gyrations of the damn ship, especially as drunk as he was. "Excuse me. Nearly murdered."

She waited, breathless. He stared back, the chair gently moving back and forth, never quite off center, never quite still.

She slowly reached for the glass and sipped, then coughed. Good British rum, burning a wide path down her throat. Argyle rapped the table and nodded his appreciation. "Braw lass," he said. "Fill her glass, Jacks."

Lockhart's neighbor cheerfully obliged, his face mottled red as he chuckled. Someone started up a drinking song, and Argyle took it up with a startlingly clear tenor voice; at the chorus, everyone lifted a glass, even Lockhart. She hastily followed suit.

There were several refrains and quite a lot of choruses. Lockhart, she noticed, only raised his glass and touched it to his lips. She tried, but the ship kept deceiving her with its dips and swirls, and the liquor spilled either over her or into her mouth, and one way or another, she was getting mightily drunk. Not to mention sticky.

"A bit of business," Argyle said once the song was over and glasses were being refilled. "What about the lad, Cap'n?"

Lockhart shrugged. "Over the side, I suppose. No great loss to anyone."

Argyle looked sad. "Could've fetched a pretty penny for him, back in the good times. Sold him in Tortuga —"

"Tortuga's gone soft," Lockhart said. "So's every damn port in the world, even Singapore. We'll never get a profit out of his pretty hide. Might as well save ourselves the bread and aggravation."

"Wait!" Cecilia blurted, alarmed. "You're . . . you're talking about —"

"Pitching your would-be killer over the

side," Argyle said. "You don't have to thank us."

"No!"

"No?" He looked momentarily non-plussed, and then downed his rum and slapped the table in comprehension. "Ah! You want to put a musket ball through his black heart first! Done, lassie! A fine piece of vengeance!"

"No! No, of course I don't! I want —"

Lockhart raised one ironic eyebrow. "Drink first," he said. "I never negotiate with a dry throat."

She got most of it down in long gulps, choked, and swayed. She was getting used to the up-and-down lurch of the ship, she decided. Like riding a horse. Or a cowboy. Oh, dear. The pirates howled their approval and downed their own rum. "Another round!" Argyle shouted.

Lockhart, who hadn't taken a single drink, suddenly crashed all four legs of his chair to the deck, causing an instant and precari-ously sober silence. "Everybody out," he said. He didn't raise his voice, but all of the other men shoved their chairs back and took their leave. Cecilia tried, but Lockhart reached out to place two long fingers on her wrist to press it to the table. She froze. "Not you." He exerted no pressure, but she couldn't find the strength to get up.

In seconds, the cabin was empty except for the two of them. Lockhart let go of her wrist and rested his elbow on the table.

"Well," he said. "You're set on mercy for your would-be killer?"

"Yes," she said. The room lurched, and she swayed with it. Well, this wasn't so difficult after all, now, was it? She was on a pirate ship, aye, avast, and all that crap. "Yes, I'd like you to . . . to . . . let him go."

"That's what we're going to do, Mistress Taylor. Let him go. If he sinks, well, that's purely a flaw of character."

"Hey! *I'm not married!*" She got her thoughts back on track with an effort. "And no fair dumping him in the middle of the osh . . . osh —"

"Ocean."

" 'Zackly."

"An island, perhaps? Something . . . harsh. With hostile natives. Possibly cannibals."

She considered it. It did have an appeal. "No cannibals. But everything else is okay."

He cocked his head slowly to one side. "Then my felicitations, Miss Welles. Consider yourself divorced. Of course, you'd be far more unattached if you'd let us put a musket ball in his back."

The room spun. Were they caught in a

whirlpool? She pressed her hands flat against the table and tried to hold steady, but the damned boat turned over and her legs went to warm jelly and all of a sudden she toppled.

And when she caught her breath, she was sitting in Captain Lockhart's lap.

Apart from a very slight widening of his eyes, he didn't move. She sucked in a deep breath, and the smell of him washed through her — sharp male sweat, old rum, clothes worn too long without more than an opportune rainstorm. The coat puffed out an aroma of patchouli. Her left hand was braced on Lockhart's chest, and she felt his muscles tensing pleasantly under the thin cloth of his shirt.

He slowly tilted his head, keeping his gaze steady and level on hers. "Yon Ian's a pretty, empty-headed fool, and no match for a woman of your . . . potential. You should have known that."

She let loose of the table to make a grand sweeping gesture with her right hand, which made her sway alarmingly on the captain's lap. "Potential," she said. "Right. I have loads of that. A dead-end job, no money, no friends . . . and Ian, he was just so —"

"Pretty?" Lockhart supplied dryly.

"Considerate!"

Lockhart smiled slowly. "Oh, aye," he said. "We offered to make sure you were dead before he tossed you overboard, for a bit extra, but he'd have none of that. Very considerate of his pocketbook, your husband-to-be. It was a considerable savings to let you drown."

Heat rushed over her — physical, sticky, painful — and she thought for a miserable second that she would simply pass out. *Oh, Ian . . .*

"Cecilia," Lockhart said quietly. It was the first time he'd called her by her name. "He meant to have you dead, one way or another. Be sure of that."

She pulled her hand back from his chest, and sure enough, the ship's next lurch sent her head and balance spinning. The world spiraled away in a hiss of gray sparkles, and she slid sideways toward the lurching deck.

He caught her, both arms around her, and she was in a very indecent position for a woman who just, well, *tonight* had been saying yes to a different man altogether, but in the candle's glow his eyes were unguarded and dark and lovely, and she buried her fingers in the still-damp curl of his hair and kissed him.

After a second of surprise, his lips moved, molding into hers, still cool from the water, and she put her arms around his neck and moaned into his mouth and, *My God, you're drunk,* she told herself, but it wasn't really the rum; the rum just let her forget about all the reasons why this was a very, very bad idea.

It was a long, silent, slow kiss. Not full of energy, like Ian's kisses . . . full of promises. Full of restraint and the tantalizing taste of some vibrating mad energy she could feel inside of Lockhart, tingling under the skin.

And then she felt him lurch, as if he'd been stabbed in the guts, and tremors went through every muscle of his body. Nearly a seizure. He dumped her off his lap and stood up himself so suddenly that his chair toppled to the deck with a crash. She swayed, disoriented.

"What . . . ?"

Lockhart grabbed her by the elbow and rushed her across the room. Mr. Argyle, rubbing his chest and looking shaken, snapped to attention as Lockhart threw the compartment's door open.

"Take her," Lockhart said roughly.

Argyle blinked, as if this was not at all what he'd been expecting. "Captain —"

"Take her!" Lockhart roared. He was white-faced, shaking, and there was a bitter fire in

his eyes she couldn't even begin to understand.

He thrust her into Argyle's arms, crowded past, and was gone.

"Well," Argyle said slowly. "You do make an impression, don't you? In you go." He opened her cabin door.

"Wait," she said, and put one hand flat on his coat, right over the three black-edged holes.

His eyes went wider. "You're a forward sort of lass, aren't you?"

She barely noticed the words, because something was slowly penetrating her rum-pickled brain.

She slid her hand down to Argyle's wrist. He watched curiously, eyes brilliant behind those Benjamin Franklin spectacles, as she turned his hand over and put two fingers on the pallid skin there, over the blue trace of veins.

"No pulse," she said. "He didn't have one, either."

Argyle silently moved the fabric of his coat aside. In the shirt beneath, there were three matching black-edged holes. And beneath that, she could see the scars over his heart — closed, but not healed. Still fresh, but not bloodied.

"Sit down," Argyle said. "I suppose you'd

best know everything."

She sat. He paced awhile, then perched nervously on the bed beside her. When he finally started talking, it came in a low-voiced rush.

"Being a privateer was an honorable profession when it began, lass. We had a marque from the Crown to batten on the Frenchies and the Spanish. But things changed; royal favor moved on. Some claimed we'd put loyal English merchant-men on the bottom, and soon enough, we'd gone from privateers to pirates, with no chance to tell our side of it. We sailed out heroes, and sailed back condemned men."

He paused, cleared his throat, and fixed his gaze on the deck between his feet. "We put in to Jamaica, always a friend to us. Found the local governor had raided our homes, took all we owned. And for the officers — he hanged our families as thieves. Harsh times, lass. Very harsh."

She turned her head, shocked. He wasn't looking at her, and his face was set and grim.

"Captain Lockhart had a new wife," he said. "Much in love, he was. Came home in triumph to find her dangling, three days ripe. I lost my own two sons."

"Oh God," she whispered.

Argyle shook his head. "God was in no part of this. The governor's wife was the one spreading the tales, pouring her evil poison into willing ears. She was the cap'n's lover once, but he turned from her, and she never forgot it. This was purely a petty woman's revenge, and innocents died for it."

Cecilia couldn't seem to breathe. Argyle's tone was stripped bare of emotion, but she caught a ghost of the pain in it even so.

He was shaking his head slowly, lost in memory. "I tell you frankly, lass, we were like madmen, and we were out for blood. We fought our way to the governor's house, carried him and his wife away, and sailed out under fierce pursuit. Soon as we found a good deep spot and some decent-sized sharks, we chummed the waters and put out the plank." He let his shoulders rise and fall. "It wasna right, and we all knew it, but grief and anger can make men do vile things. Still, I'll never forget seeing that water bloom red, or stop hearing the screams. Even hers, for all she deserved no better."

Cecilia couldn't begin to speak. Argyle's voice continued dry and bleak, full of despair. "As she was on the plank, the witch called out a curse on us. A storm took us hard at midnight, and in the midst of it came an English ship, captained by the devil himself, I say. We had no chance. No chance at all. He took the ship straight down to hell."

"But . . ." She licked her lips. "But you're not —"

"Oh, we're dead all right, lassie. Every man jack among us. But we don't rest. Cursed to sail for eternity without rest, without the comfort of land or family. We'll never set foot at a port again. She made sure of that, when she put her curse on us."

Cecilia decided it must be the rum making her simultaneously dizzy and credulous. Sane people didn't believe things like this, did they? Sober people certainly wouldn't. "How long have you been . . . well . . ."

"Cursed?" he asked. "Far too long. Captain keeps us sailing, but there's not much heart left in us. We all ache for an end to it, if we were to put an honest face on things."

"Haven't you tried to break the . . ." She felt stupid even saying it. ". . . curse?"

"Oh, aye." Argyle turned his head and looked at her, then patted her hand with his cool, pale fingers. "We've tried everything, but when that dying witch called on the devil, she put the doom on us, no doubt about it." He considered Cecilia for a moment, then said, "Do you want to hear it? The words?"

Cecilia nodded. Argyle shut his eyes, and eerily, the voice that came out of his mouth wasn't his own at all — it was a woman's, high and thin and strange, quavering with fear and fury. "I curse you, Liam Lockhart, and through you, this ship and its crew. Your blood will lie cold in your veins before this night is done, and your heart will lie cold and silent in your chest. No home, no shelter, no comfort, no port, no rest, for as long as love forsakes you as it has forsaken me. I lay my doom on you, and curse you all to hell."

He relaxed, let his breath out, and shivered. When his voice came again, it was his own — a little breathless, maybe. "Love," he said. "As if she knew anything of it. No, there's no breaking that kind of curse. But it's kind of you to think on it, lassie."

"But if you're not trying to break the curse, why . . . why take on me and Ian?"

"We stop to take on supplies, here and there. Must do. She cursed us to sail; she didn't say we had to starve." A smile lit up his face for a moment, and Cecilia thought that she'd like to see him smile more. Under better circumstances, and when she wasn't so drunk and vulnerable. "It's terrible expensive even boarding rum and water, and precious little prizes to be taken. We board ships, and find 'em filled with black sludge, or foolish toys instead of real solid goods. No gold on these seas anymore, and precious few cargoes of any real worth. That's why we put out the word among other crews, like. That we'd take on passengers for money. We planned on robbing you and dumping you penniless in another port, but young Ian's proposal was sommat different."

"And you were just going to let him kill me."

"Cap'n considered anything that happened after he said the words were what you might call a domestic affair. I'm sorry, pet. But after all, we are pirates."

She sat, numbed and disoriented and drunk and cold, and for no reason she could put her finger on burst into tears.

Argyle *tsked* under his breath, shut the door, and locked her in.

"Lassie?"

Cecilia cracked hot, thick eyelids and wet her lips. She was still dressed, and wrapped in the rough woolen blanket as well. A chill had come on hard, in the middle of the night, and then she'd started sweating. Her head felt lighter than air.

She coughed rackingly when she tried to swallow.

"Holy Jesus!" Argyle said, and his cool hand felt her forehead. "You're ill, lass. Why did you not call out . . . ?"

She murmured something, but it must not have made any sense. Argyle's hand withdrew, and cool water bathed her face, then dribbled into her parched mouth. "Easy, now. You've got an ague, no doubt about it. Most like from that ducking you took. Easy, lass. We'll see you through."

She dozed. When she woke, lantern light dazzled her eyes, and there was a hissed argument being conducted somewhere a few feet away. The sense of it escaped her, but it had something to do with pills, and she thought she recognized Ian's voice.

Someone forced her mouth open. It hurt. Water splashed in, and a pill that felt chokingly huge on her swollen tongue. "Swallow," she was ordered, and it was a voice she felt she should obey. Not Ian's. Never obey Ian again. Ian had . . . done something terrible —

She dreamed of someone whispering her name like a secret in a low, dark-honey voice.

■ ■ ■ ■

The next time she woke, she felt weak but clear. Captain Lockhart was sitting in a chair beside her, balanced on two legs. He was reading a tattered, water-stained magazine that looked strangely familiar to her. Where in the hell had he gotten hold of a copy of *Oprah's* magazine? Granted, it looked a couple of years old. . . .

For a moment she didn't think he'd realized her eyes were open, and then he said, "Argyle collects such things. Books and papers and the like. Takes them from the ships we . . . visit. Most of the crew don't like to look at them. Think such things must be witchcraft. I've only just gotten them used to the flying metal monsters."

He handed her a cup, and she drank convulsively. The water slid down, smooth as glass, and pooled like silver in her stomach. She managed a croak. "How long . . . ?"

"Three days since you last woke," Lockhart said. He reached into a bowl, wet a cloth, and wiped her forehead. "Can't say that your dearly beloved has been too distressed."

"Ian was here."

"Needed his opinion about some supplies we'd taken off a freighter a few years back. Anti-somethings."

"Antibiotics." The long word just about sapped her strength. Lockhart nodded and squeezed cool water from the cloth to dribble over her neck. "He helped?"

"Well, we did make it clear that if you failed to thrive, he'd be investigating the bottom in short order. So he seemed motivated."

"Thank you."

Lockhart tossed the cloth back in the bowl. "Argyle's tended you. I'm only here while he takes his watch. I'm no kind of nursemaid."

"Doing it pretty well, though."

His eyes strayed, lightning fast, and came back to lock on hers. "Best pull up the blankets, Miss Welles. We've been at sea for some time without . . . outlets."

She looked down and realized that at some point someone — most likely Argyle — had stripped off her skirt and bodice and left her in the white chemise, with the drawstring neck gaping low. Dribbles of water had turned the fabric transparent. It clung to her breasts, clearly outlining the dark rings at their tips and tightening nipples.

"Oh," she whispered, and felt heat climb into her cheeks. Nothing like being sick to make you feel violated, and now this. . . . She fumbled ineffectively at the covers. After a hesitation, he reached over and pulled them to her shoulders. His fingers brushed her damp skin, and lingered.

She saw him wince suddenly, and hunch over, as if he'd taken a terrible blow to the guts.

"Captain?" she croaked, alarmed.

He held up a shaking hand and breathed, in and out, labored, agonized breaths. He leaned back in the chair and avoided her eyes for a few long moments, then stood. "We'll be near a port soon. I'll have Argyle row you out. No doubt you can make your own way from there. Women do have their clever ways."

"What?"

His voice turned rough. "If you're imagining anything's between us, put an end to girlish fancies. What happened before — well, rum was involved, and when rum goes in, sense goes out. I have no desire to burden myself with a doxy. You'll go ashore, or over the side."

She watched him leave, too stunned to protest. Every time she saw a flicker of something kind, he went out of his way to be insulting. Even for a pirate, he was rude.

He stopped in the doorway, facing away. As she watched, he clapped his battered tricorn hat back over his hair and turned so that a bare inch of his profile was exposed to her.

She didn't mean to apologize — didn't have any reason to, either! — but it just came out, unguarded. "I'm sorry," she said. "I keep offending you."

He flinched. "You mistake me. I offend myself."

It took another day to recover her voice fully and two more for her strength, but by nightfall she was on deck, strolling arm in arm with Argyle. From him she learned that Ian was back in the hold, for crimes that Mr. Argyle vaguely defined as "insubordination." Not too surprising.

Lockhart was a dark, silent presence on the quarterdeck, pacing in the moonlight. If he noticed her, he gave no sign; he hadn't been back to speak to her again. She had the feeling that if he had his own way, he'd put her ashore without another word of any kind. That made her furious, in a way that Ian's outright assault hadn't.

"I've been thinking," Argyle said. "About what you said. About the curse."

"What I said? Um . . . what did I say?"

"About breaking it. There's a possibility —" Argyle sucked in a deep breath and let it out in deliberately slow increments before finishing the thought. "— a possibility that it could be done. The curse broken."

"How?"

Argyle cast her a sideways, cutting glance. "Love, obviously. *For as long as love forsakes you,* she said. But what if it doesn't?"

"I don't — oh, you've got to be kidding me."

"He's not cared about anyone or anything for a long, long time, lass. But he threw himself over the stern of the ship when you did no more than hold up a hand."

"You're crazy."

"Twice I've felt something coming over me — something like the shadow of death. I think it started with the cap'n, and you, there after dinner."

When she'd been so drunk. When she'd kissed him. She felt a warm bloom inside that should have been shame, and wasn't, quite. "I — ," she began.

"I don't need to know," he said, which was kind. "Doesn't matter what happened. Point is, we feel the ache of it every time he's near you. Makes the wounds twinge something awful." He unconsciously rubbed his chest, where the musket balls had pierced. She wondered if they were still in there, black pearls at the heart of a bony oyster.

"You all feel it? Everybody?"

"Every lad I've asked. Well, two of them lied, but I saw it in their eyes. The curse holds us all, and if it breaks, it breaks for all. She cursed him, and through him, us. The cap'n's the key."

"No wonder he's afraid, if he's hurting you all."

"Afraid?" Argyle laughed softly, sourly. "Nay, lassie. Not Liam Lockhart, not over causing his crew a wee bit of pain. He's a ship's master. Men suffer and die, and that's the way of the sea, and well he knows it. The point is, the pain means you're making him feel, warming his blood, and his heart."

"Breaking the curse."

"Aye." Argyle sighed. "Not that he'll ever let himself truly love you."

"What? Why not?"

"The harpy that doomed us dinna have a happy end in mind, in this world or the next. If he lets himself love, he might well break the curse — and likely the moment he does, we fall dead in our tracks, or turn to dust, or some such nasty bit of business. Captain Lockhart has two hundred crew on this ship, and he puts considerable store by that responsibility. Better half a life than none, he'd say."

"But if there's a chance it could save you, maybe I should talk to him —"

Argyle took her firmly by both arms, looking her straight in the eyes. "It's not for you to save us, lassie. Everyone saves themselves. Everyone. Look to your own skin, and don't you worry about —"

He winced suddenly, and looked around toward Captain Lockhart.

So did every sailor visible on the deck of the *Sweet Mourning,* an eerily orchestrated turning of heads.

Captain Lockhart was watching them, leaning on the rail. If he was in pain, there was no way to tell from this distance.

A sigh rattled uneasily out of Argyle's narrow chest, and he rubbed the area over his heart.

"He's jealous." That made her feel annoyed and flattered at once.

"Aye. Knew that already."

"Then why parade me around like this?"

"Had to be sure, didn't I? I've been doing a bit of thinking, too, lass, on behalf of the crew. Most don't find half a life to be worth living. Not if there's a chance of ending it. So I've a mind to . . . provoke a reaction."

"Does the captain know what you're doing?"

He let out a soft bark of laughter. "Conspiracies on a sailing vessel get you flogged, or worse. We're having a theoretical discussion, like two people of reason. Do you trust me?"

"Of course." She did, she found, crazy as that was.

"Then stand fast, for I'm about to betray a man I've served for close on three hundred years. For his own good, mind."

She was about to ask what the hell he was talking about when Argyle yanked her forward and, quite firmly, kissed her.

He was clumsy, and she could tell his heart wasn't in it, but he made it quite a show. She stood shocked, wondering whether she ought to push him away, but it didn't matter. In the next heartbeat he was lurching away with both hands clutching his chest. He hit the rail and slid down to an awkward sitting position, panting. Cecilia lunged toward him and then hesitated. What was she supposed to do? Feel for a pulse? Take his temperature? How did you diagnose a dead man, anyway?

Under the red coat, she saw the grubby white shirt flower with fresh blood. Gouts of it. Argyle gasped in shallow breaths, color gone a pale, unsettling green. All around them, sailors groaned and slumped and fought back cries of pain.

"What did you do?" she cried, and grabbed Argyle's lapels to shake him. "Oh my God, what is this? What's happening?"

"Proof," he said, white to the lips. "Proof he loves you. You have to find a way, lass. Don't let him put you off the ship before you do. Break the curse. It's all on you now."

Lockhart was on the quarterdeck, clutching the rail. She saw his knees bend and then straighten with what must surely be a superhuman effort. When his voice came, it sounded angry and ragged. "If you want the woman, Argyle, take her below and ride her proper. Get out of my sight, the both of you!"

Cecilia bolted up, furious and wild. "You're an unbelievable bastard!" she screamed. "He's your *friend!*"

Lockhart jumped down from the quarterdeck and stalked toward her, sinuous as a cat. If he was hurting — and he had to be, because Argyle was still white to the lips and panting with pain — he was hiding it under a mask of pure fury. "Woman, if you fancy rough trade with my crew, there should be a lottery. Wouldn't want anybody saying it wasn't fair."

Well, if Argyle had wanted to provoke a reaction, he'd certainly succeeded. She cast a tormented look down at Argyle, who was trying to say something. She read his lips in the moonlight. *Finish it.*

Lockhart was coming. She dodged around him, charged through the black door and down the narrow passage. She burst into her tiny cabin and slammed the door. Then slammed it again, just for the catharsis of it. "He's trying to save you!" she shouted. *Slam.* "You don't deserve him, you black-hearted, cold-blooded —"

"Bastard," Lockhart finished, cool and low, and caught the door on its last slam. "I did hear you the first time." She gasped and pulled back. "Mistress Taylor —"

"I'M NOT MARRIED!" she shouted, at the end of her patience. "You know, curse or no curse, I'll bet you've always been like this. A cold-blooded, vile little leech, feeding off of others. That's what a pirate is, a parasite —"

"You seem drawn to parasites," Lockhart observed, and set his shoulder against the doorway. "Young Master Taylor, for instance. But then, he must have other talents you enjoy."

She felt a blush burn across her face and down her throat. "I haven't. Not that it's any of your business!"

"Indeed not. Nor would I care."

"Yeah, well, you cared just now, didn't you? When Argyle had his tongue in my mouth?"

She wanted to take that back, but it was too late. Lockhart was raising that famously satirical eyebrow at her, intending to lock all of his anger and jealousy and emotion inside. She lunged up off the bed and came very close to touching him. "You cared. You damn well care right now, too."

Very close. He didn't move back. Each deep breath she took strained the seams of the bodice and crossed the narrow fraction of an inch between them. A bare whisper of a touch. Oh yeah, he was in pain. She could see it flickering in his eyes. There was fresh blood staining his shirt, and smeared dark across his faded blue coat. She heard the slow patter of drops as they splashed on the leather of his boots.

"You're killing us," he said. "You're as much a witch as that sea hag we put over the side."

"I certainly hope I am, because I curse you, too! I curse you to have what you want. Go on, condemn yourself to feel nothing, *nothing,* forever —"

He captured her face between his hands

and stared into her eyes. "Too late to feel nothing. Whether you're a witch or a saint, I don't know, but you're . . . inside me —"

His knees gave way, and he hit the deck, gasping. Cecilia followed him down and caught him as he swayed. "I'm not a witch," she said. "I'm definitely not a saint. I'm just . . . just a dreamer. That's why I said yes to Ian. Because . . . it was a dream come true."

"Argyle's a dreamer," Lockhart said. "He thinks . . . it will all end well . . . but —" His breath caught hard. There was blood pouring out of the wound under his shirt, not just a trickle but a flood. He was dying, and it was because of her. "I'm not a dreamer, Cecilia."

She braced him on her lap, stroking his hair. This was too hard. Too much. Maybe half a life was better, maybe never having passion or love or life again would be all right, if only you didn't have to go through this. She never wanted to feel her heart come apart like this again.

He was bleeding, great gouts of it flooding hot across her lap. Time was running out. His dark eyes opened, wild and beautiful and full of warmth. Full of life. "Argyle tried to stop me, you know. She begged for mercy, but I wouldn't hear her, I made myself cold, so cold, and I watched the sharks —"

"Liam, stop it; just — look, I know what to do. I'll go. I'll take a boat and I'll leave —"

"You should have gone before you smiled."

"Liam —"

His eyes stayed open, but the pupils slowly relaxed, eclipsing the brown with black. A sky without moon or stars. She felt unnaturally calm, and everything seemed so bright, so sharp, so still. His long hair curled around her fingers, warm and intimate.

"You have to live," she told him. "It doesn't end this way. You have to live."

She let Ian out of the hold at dawn, because she needed him. It took more than two to sail a ship of this size, but at least the sails were still set, and after some trial and error, she found she could steer the ship into the wind. Her arms ached with the effort, but it kept her from thinking.

She'd waited all night for the fairy godmother to drop in, pronounce it all a terrible mistake, and wave her magic wand. But it wasn't a Disney movie after all. It was a story about a curse, and blood, and pain, and it wasn't going to end well.

Cecilia put Ian to work gathering up bodies.

"We should dump them overboard," he called up, panting, as he dragged another body to the port rail. He no longer looked elegant and princely. He looked fey and dirty and savage, and she didn't imagine she looked any better.

"No," she said. She wasn't giving them to the sharks. As Ian reached for Argyle, she snapped, "Don't touch him!"

"What, is he some personal friend, Cess?"

She pulled one of Lockhart's deadly-looking pistols from the makeshift leather belt wrapped around her waist. "I swear, if you call me Cess again . . ."

He held up filthy, bloody hands. "Right. Whatever, *Captain*." He put a lot of contempt into it, but she was the one with the pistols. She'd spent the night clearing away all of the weapons she could find and locking them away in Lockhart's cabin. She was wearing his tricorn hat. It did a good job of keeping the sun off of her nose, and besides, it smelled like him, and she found that an odd comfort.

"Crazy bitch," Ian muttered. She fired the pistol, bracing it with both hands. The mule kick of it stung. She was aiming for him, but she missed, and it gouged an impressive chunk out of the railing next to him. "Hey!"

"Hey, what?" she challenged, and pulled the other gun. "Warning shot. Next time I see daylight through your chest. Be nice."

The sails flapped. She'd lost the wind. She put the pistol away and turned the wheel to find it again.

"Where are we going?"

"That way," she said, and nodded at the horizon. "Funny thing about the planet, it's round. Sooner or later, we'll hit land."

"Oh, great. Brilliant navigation. Here there be monsters." Ian swore and wiped his grimy forehead on an equally grimy sleeve.

"Just keep in mind that out of everybody on this ship, I like you the least."

They ate tough bread and salted beef in midafternoon, and drank enough water to fight off the sun's relentless glare. Nothing to talk about, except for Ian's periodic attempts to bait her into doing something stupid. She was too numb to respond. She wanted to curl up somewhere and cry, but she couldn't. Lockhart wouldn't have approved. Besides, she had to survive this. It had to mean something, in the end. It had to be . . . worth it. *Worth that many dead men? You've got one hell of a price tag, honey.*

As the sun moved toward the western

edge of the sea, Ian ambled off toward the poop deck — aptly named — and came down the ladder fast. "Cecilia!" he yelled. "There's a ship!"

"What? Where?" She turned, startled, and saw a small, iron gray freighter steaming toward them on the port side. "Oh my God!" Salvation. Civilization. Home. She felt tears burn, and then blinked them resolutely away. "Well, don't just stand there! Signal them!" Ian tore his shirt off and waved it energetically over his head, whooping.

This was it. This was how the story ended. Yo-ho-ho, and a floating ship of the damned. It didn't seem right. She'd left Lockhart below in her cabin, silent and pale, and she wanted to see him again. She wanted to hear him say her name in that low, caressing tone, the way she'd heard it when she was sick and lost. She wanted . . . wanted . . .

It came to her, finally, with the force of a sun bursting inside, that she wanted Liam Lockhart, in a way she'd never in her life wanted anyone else.

"I love you," she whispered, and the tears spilled over. "You evil pirate bastard. You can't leave me like this. I love you, do you hear me? I *love you.* And I know you can hear me. Being dead is not an excuse. Now *wake up!*"

She held her breath. *Come on, fairy godmother, you dithering old biddy. . . .*

The moment came, and went. A gust of wind whipped tears from Cecilia's eyes.

It was over. There was no magic, there was no happy ending, and she was going to get off this ship and go home and never, ever dream again.

"They're coming!" Ian yelled, and swarmed down the ladder. "Slow down or something! Hit the brakes!"

She turned the wheel and dumped the wind out of the sails, and the *Sweet Mourning* slowed to a hissing amble as the sun began to slip beneath the waves.

"Um, Cecilia?" Ian was backing away from the starboard rail. "Remember when you said there were still pirates out here?"

"Yeah?"

"You might have been right about that."

She rushed over to take a look. Yep, pirates. Not the quaintly costumed kind. These were modern killers, at least twenty or thirty men armed to the teeth with modern weaponry. And worse, they looked like they knew exactly what they were doing as they lined up at the rail, grinning and gesturing.

"Maybe we should run," Ian said. "We're fast, right?"

"With a *crew!* The two of us are not a crew!"

A hail of gunfire erupted from the other ship. She ducked. Ian hit the deck. Bullets gouged chunks from wood, and she felt flying splinters cut her arm.

She lunged up, grabbed the wheel, and steered for the wind. Ian screamed as the deck heeled sharply and bodies rolled into him. Mr. Argyle slid sideways along the rail, and out of the corner of her eye Cecilia saw Argyle's hand grab the rail. *That's it. I've gone totally around the bend.* As she was debating it, Argyle raised his head and prodded at his chest with trembling fingers.

"Christ," he said faintly. "That was fucking unpleasant. Remind me not to kiss you again."

"Argyle!" She fairly shrieked it, and waved both arms over her head. "*Yesssssss!* Thank you!"

He waved shakily and stood up. "Don't thank me, lass; I've only —" He threw himself flat as another volley of gunfire raked the ship. "What the hell have you got us into?"

"Pirates!" she yelled.

The pile of bodies Ian had made was

180

squirming, men cursing one another in round, ripe accents as they fought to sit up. Argyle grabbed the nearest man and shook him by the shoulder. "Get in the rigging!" Argyle shouted, and favored a few more with kicks and foghorn-volume curses. "Come on, you sons of whores; we have fighting to do! — Fuck me, where's my pistols?"

Oh God, she'd locked them all away. "Take the wheel!" she shouted, and let go. More bullets whizzed past her as she ducked down the left-hand ladder. Argyle swarmed up the right. She pounded down the corridor to her cabin, fumbling with the massive iron ring of keys from Argyle's coat pocket.

Hands slid around her waist, picked her up, and set her aside. Brown, scarred fingers plucked the ring from her grasp, expertly parsed the choices, and unlocked the door.

Captain Lockhart looked her up and down, and his sun-browned face split into a wide, piratical grin. "That's my hat," he said, and reclaimed it. "Not to mention a few more things I want."

He put an arm around her waist and pulled her close. She gasped. "Um, Captain . . . I don't think we have time for —"

Lockhart's grin turned sharply seductive,

and he liberated the pistols from her belt. Took his time about it, too. She remembered to breathe when her ribs started to ache.

"You'll need to reload," she said. "I shot at Ian."

"Ah. Hit him?"

"Missed."

"Pity." Lockhart unbuckled the leather belt from around her waist. "You make a fierce little wench, Cecilia, but then, I did tell you, you had potential." He buckled on the sword, added the pistols, and kissed her. Brisk and efficient and warm, so warm.

"Wait," she said, and caught his arm when he moved to duck back down the corridor. "You're alive, right?"

"Aye," he said. "Mortal. And that means I can die, lass. Good timing, eh? Bring more guns."

"Well," Argyle sighed regretfully, "we *were* a bit out of practice. Haven't had a decent fight in decades, really. It was over too soon."

He poured a tot of rum into a crystal glass and handed it across the table. Cecilia accepted it and knocked it back.

"All together and drown the devil!" Argyle grinned and slopped more liquor into the glasses. "We'll make a pirate of you yet, lass."

"I wish you'd warned me about the cannons," she sighed.

"Don't be daft," Mr. Jacks said, his portly face red with drink. "Only managed one decent barrage. Didn't even get in a good broadside. Only the larboard guns. We carry fifty-four, you know. Haven't had to use more than a dozen in years."

Cecilia shuddered, remembering that metal freighter — with no battleship armor — taking the full force of the cannonballs. "They didn't have a chance," she said.

"Regrets, lass? You saw the holds of that ship," Argyle reminded her, and cut himself a slice of pineapple with his dirk. "They barely made an effort to rinse out the blood from their last massacre. Mind you, you should never let blood sit like that for long; it raises a terrible stink. Always clean up after yourself."

"I'll remember," she said faintly.

"Unsanitary bastards," he said, and bit into the pineapple. "Damn fine produce, though."

Another dirk speared the unfortunate pineapple and moved it to an empty place. Cecilia looked over her shoulder just as Lockhart dropped into his chair beside her.

"It's done," he said. "We're on course for Boston Harbor. Though what you mean to do when we get there —"

"Go ashore," she said. "Use my ATM card. Buy some cute shoes. Get married."

Argyle froze in midmotion. So, across the table from him, did Ian, who choked on a mouthful of rum. Mr. Simonds cheerfully slapped him on the back, hard enough to leave hand-sized bruises, while her former fiancé coughed. "Easy, lad; she don't mean you," he said. "Ain't you relieved?"

Lockhart rocked his chair back on two legs and balanced. "Got a plan, do you, Miss Welles?"

"A pretty good one, as a matter of fact. And Ian, you're going to love this — it's even profitable."

He stopped coughing. "Yeah?"

"See, when we sail this ship into Boston Harbor and these men walk off this ship, it's going to raise some questions, right? Serious questions."

"Absolutely," he said. "Like, who are they and where did they come from."

"Two hundred men out of the past," Cecilia said. "Everybody will want to know their story."

"Yes," Ian said slowly, and then leaned forward to stare at her. "Yes! *Everybody!* My

184

God, think of the possibilities: book deals, movie deals, pricey talk show appearances, merchandising —" The light went out in his face, and he slumped back into his chair. "Damn. No way is anybody going to buy this stupid curse story, though. We're all going to end up in the loony bin."

The pirates growled. *Growled.* "They'll take me to one of those hellpits when they pry my pistol out of my cold, dead hand," Argyle said. "I've seen what happens in madhouses."

"Well, it's better now," Cecilia said quickly. "Not that I've got personal knowledge of, you know, the mental health industry, but —"

"I'm not getting shut in any Bedlam!" Jacks said, and drank more rum. There was a chorus of "Ayes!" and glasses lifted around the table.

Lockhart sighed and sent her a private look. "Sorry, lass. No church weddings in your future, it seems."

"Well . . . not if we tell the whole truth . . . but . . ."

"But?"

She took a deep breath. "Nobody believes in curses anymore. Ian's right about that. But there's something they do believe in — or want to, anyway. They may think we're crazy, but they won't be measuring us for straitjackets, just laughing."

Argyle leaned elbows on the linen tablecloth, eyes bright. "Tell us, lass."

"There's only three things you need to remember. One: The last thing you remember, you were sailing out from Bermuda."

"Simple enough."

"Two, and this is important, there was a bright white light —"

"Oh! I get it!" Ian yelled. "Bermuda Triangle! Right! And what the hell, throw in some little gray alien guys, too. Give it some local color. Oh, I'm going to get *so* rich with this story —" Another growl from the pirates. He gulped. "I mean, straight fifteen percent. Standard commission."

"Ten," Lockhart growled.

"Ten's good. Ten's fabulous." Ian gulped rum. The pirate sitting next to him filled his glass to the brim.

"Three," Lockhart said.

"*Three percent?* Mercenary bastard," Ian muttered.

Lockhart quelled him with a look, then turned a seditious smile toward Cecilia. "You said three things, love. One, Bermuda. Two, bright white light. Three . . . ?"

"Three . . ." She reached out, grabbed the arm of his chair, and thumped all four feet back to the deck. He slid forward, off balance, and she kissed him, to the appreciative table slaps of the other men.

"Now, you see, I *like* three," he said, pulling back just enough to get the words out. "I think I like three a great deal. Though I could do with more research."

"Well then, four things," she amended, and settled her arms around his neck. "We get married before you go on *Oprah,* because after that, you won't be able to fight the girls off with a cutlass."

There was a short, considering silence around the table.

"Oprah," Argyle said, and toasted her. "I like the sound of that."

RACHEL CAINE is the author of the *Weather Warden* series, the latest of which is *Firestorm* (book 5). She also writes romance for the Silhouette Bombshell line (most recently *Devil's Bargain* and *Devil's Due*), as well as short fiction and nonfiction when time and sanity permit. She prefers her personal details to remain alluringly mysterious, but her Web site is www.rachelcaine.com, and we have it on good authority that she can be bribed with chocolate.

"ALL SHOOK UP"

P. N. ELROD

"Hey there, little sister, pull my pants down, would ya please?"

Frankie halted cold in her tracks at the sound of the man's velvety, uncannily familiar voice, which originated somewhere above her, frozen in a "what the . . . ?" reaction. Normally she'd have blown off any guy daring such a line with her, but that *voice.*

She'd been raised on that voice.

Frankie looked up and, oh yeah, it was *him* — standing tall on the backstage platform getting ready for his opening set.

It couldn't have been, but it was; *Elvis* had just asked her to pull his pants down.

What the hell . . . ?

"The legs, darlin'." He pointed, a half smile curling the famous lips and a glint of mischief in his blue, blue eyes.

His knees were just at her eye level, and his pant hems were hung on the tops of his shiny black half boots. She stared, blinking, then gaped up at him again. He sure *looked* like the real deal, but it belatedly registered in her harried brain that this was the special wedding singer the bride had insisted on. Dang. She had good taste.

"Uh, sure," Frankie said, abruptly aware she was holding a wide platter heavy with stuffed mushrooms. She owned the catering service hired for the wedding but pitched in with the rest of the staff when the heat was on. Things were in swelter mode tonight. She'd been forced to find an alternate way around to the buffet tables because of a drinks spill. Her idea to take a backstage route hadn't been well considered; the cramped area was littered with sound equipment, cases for musical instruments, and lots and lots of trip-worthy electrical cables and little to no lighting. A bad choice on her part until now. She quickly edged the tray onto the platform and, hands free, yanked at the man's cuffs. Leather pant cuffs. He was Comeback Elvis from 1968, head to toe in black leather and at his absolute sexiest.

"Just a little harder, darlin'," he said, apparently in full character. Only Elvis could get away with it. But he wasn't *really* Elvis, just a damned excellent hunky substitute, built exactly the same, with a tight butt and wide shoulders stretching the limits of the leather jacket. Nothing fake there. Wow, they still made guys like that?

She pulled and the black leather rutched up the length of one of his long legs suddenly smoothed into a lean second skin. She did the same again for the other leg. Not exactly listed on her job description, but . . . wow, no trouble, nope, none at all.

"How's that?" she asked.

He shot her the *look* — the one that had once caused her then twenty-year-old grandmother to scream and fall into a dead faint at one of his concerts in 1956. Gramma had been proud of that incident, if ticked off for missing things while being revived by her friends.

Frankie suddenly understood what Gramma had felt. Knees going, heart leaping, eyes bugging out a little with the shock of impact, but Frankie held her ground and looked right back. The view was great even if it resulted in the temporary loss of her higher brain and motor functions.

And that was from just a look. Wow. Again.

Then Frankie pulled herself together. Elvis was the hottest of the hot, but hey, he was hired help, too, just in a different ranking on the wedding industry food chain. No need to go all groupie-girl. He was the result of costume, makeup, and assumed attitude. He probably had a dorky real name.

"What's your name, honey?" he asked, as though reading her mind. His smile wattage increased. The son of a gun was obviously aware of his effect on her and enjoying the moment.

"Yummy Catering," she blurted. It was the name of her tiny company, the name she proudly announced into the receiver each time the phone rang, and for the life of her she couldn't think why she'd said that.

On the other hand, it made him blink, a little startled. Then the eye-glint thing happened again, and he flashed very white teeth. "Well, now, your momma 'n' poppa sure got that right. May I call you Yummy Cat for short?"

She felt a completely idiotic giggle trying to flutter out and firmly slammed it down. Frankie was a lot of things, but a brainless, giggling ditz was not one of them. "I mean, my name is Frankie Foster. I'm the caterer for this job."

"Pleased to meet you, then. Those sure smell good." He gave a nod at the mushrooms.

"Have one?"

"Not before a show, how about after? Save some for me and my crew?"

"Sure!" she chirped. Again without thinking. The food had been paid for by someone else; it belonged to them, but she'd yet to get through a wedding where they bothered about the leftovers.

And this was *Elvis* for crying out loud. Okay, Tribute-Artist Elvis. She heard they preferred that over "impersonator." But still . . .

He winked. "Well, that's all right. See you then, Miss Foster." He swept away, tossing her a last look — oh, that was another glint all right, but who was counting? — then went to consult with one of the technicians in his group.

Frankie sagged, suddenly drained. It felt like every muscle in her body had gone through a major workout. This was no surprise — she'd always had a weakness for performers. Their energy was unique, addictive, and not always good for her. Better to enjoy it from the safe distance of audience seating than up close and-and-and . . . up close. She grabbed the platter of mushrooms and continued on, picking her way forward over the junk on the floor. Breaking through to the other side of the platform, she made it to the buffet tables.

"I gotta stay away from the showbiz types," she muttered. They were exciting but more often than not came with baggage, or expected her to know all the unwritten rules of their trade. Oh, and egos; don't forget egos. It was a very different world from hers, and the culture shock tended to mess with her head and heart too much.

She'd once wasted six weeks dating a gorgeous but terminally insecure mama's boy. He'd finally picked one fight too many when she hadn't applauded hard enough for his performance as the second murderer in a community theater production of *Macbeth*.

The Elvis guy . . . devastatingly hot, but off her menu. She would appreciate his talent from a distance.

Catering was her speed and her life, and she was good at it. She could cook like a demon and calculate the cost (gross and net) for a sit-down feast for a hundred in her head and was able to guide the most nervous of brides through the complex process of planning a wedding supper. Yes, better to stick to what she knew best and not mix worlds.

Of course, it never hurt to peek over the fence at the guest talent now and then.

Frankie took an empty platter from the appetizers table, slipping her full one into place so quickly that the guests filing past hardly noticed. She checked the food levels at the various tables and was pleased (and relieved) to see she'd figured things right yet again. The salad bar was popular. The bridesmaids, all of them rail-thin magazine models like the bride, were chewing through the lettuce, veggies, and tofu like starved rabbits. That had been a clever call, to find out how many guests were vegetarians and allow for it. Raw green edibles were cheap, allowing one to get fancy with the meat dishes and still stay within the budget.

The prime rib (a costly but popular classic) was steadily shrinking along with the chicken and fish as lines of guests inched by filling their plates. Her second-in-command, Omar, had everything in hand. As the last of the rib vanished, he produced another, expertly carving it up with one of his big knives.

Except for the spill (sticky fruit juice, not pricey wine), this job was going exceptionally well. It was the bride's third time at marriage, so she'd known exactly what she wanted. Planning had been easy, though the numbers had staggered Frankie at first. She'd never done a wedding of this size before and was grateful the bride had opted for a buffet. Frankie didn't have the staff to deal with serving so many tables. Not with food, anyway. There were a number of fleet-footed temps rushing around making sure everyone had their drink of choice. If the staff had to serve food as well it would have been too big a job and Frankie would have had to turn it down altogether.

Which meant she'd have missed meeting the Elvis guy.

"What's he like?"

She tried not to give a start. The question had come from Gramma, who was in charge of the dinner rolls. A nicely preserved seventy, she liked to keep busy and loved helping out on weddings.

"He, who?" Frankie asked.

"The groom. You know — Santiago."

Because she had lots of practice, Frankie kept from making a face at the name she presumed the man had chosen for himself. He was a flashy TV wrestler, big and muscled through and through. Somehow the magic of a tuxedo (a custom extra-extra-large fit) had given sophisticated class to his shaved head and the tattoos all over his scalp. "Not my type," she answered.

Gramma made a frustrated noise involving both nose and throat. "Wake up and smell the sweat, girl; he's awesome!" She quivered a bit, not from infirmity but adrenaline. The buckets of testosterone floating around the wedding party — as represented by the groom's many beefcake pals from the wrestling world — had its effect on her. She was fond of saying, "I'm old, not dead!"

"Still not my type." Frankie shrugged. Santiago put her off, and it wasn't anything to do with his fearsome outward looks. There was something inside him she'd picked up on but hadn't bothered to identify.

Regardless of what was hidden within, the man had netted himself a beauty, a cover model for the slicks who was fast gaining international recognition.

The bride had been on a photo shoot requiring she be in evening clothes surrounded by wrestlers, the tougher looking the better, and he was the toughest of the lot. Somehow they'd hit it off. Perhaps they'd found common ground — so to speak — with their geographically inspired names. Hers happened to be Trinidad. Frankie wondered if they would continue the tradition of place names for their kids. She had a mercifully brief mental picture of them posing for a Christmas card photo before the fireplace, Santiago with his beefy arm around Trinidad and on their laps little

Tierra del Fuego and his sister, Peru.

But somehow Frankie knew that would never happen. Santiago . . . what was it about him?

Frankie had a clear view of him across the crowded room. She didn't do it often since it was sort of like invading another's privacy, but now she was curious. She focused and let it come to her. The smallest nuances of expression and body language took on predictable meaning. Just a bare hint was all she got at this distance, but she had it. Oh, dear. This was bad. He would want Trinidad to stay home, wait on him hand and foot, have babies, and cheer nonstop at his wrestling bouts, her modeling days over.

That wouldn't work with her; she loved her career and had left two ex-husbands (a minor rock star and an accountant) in her wake to pursue it.

Well, darn. Frankie grimaced. The split, and there would be one, would start within months of the couple's return from the honeymoon. Any warning Frankie gave wouldn't be believed. They were both past the age of consent, hitched, and happy for now. Matters would take their course.

No one liked a Cassandra, as Frankie had figured out during puberty when her talent for reading people first manifested itself.

She didn't always get a handle on a person's future, but she could tell friend from foe. It came in very handy for her business. She could accurately determine who would bounce her check and who would not, thus booting a number of mystified deadbeats out the door long before they ordered anything.

But sadly, she wasn't all-knowing. There was the hormone factor. If a man hit all her buttons at the same time, then her talent seized up and stopped working. Like what happened with the actor.

Like what had just happened with the Elvis guy.

No regrets there, and no big problem, since Frankie wouldn't be dating him even if he asked. A nice meal on the leftovers and maybe some shop talk would be the limit. Gramma would get a big kick out of it, though. She adored Elvis and had volunteered to help at this reception as soon as she heard an impersonator — er — tribute artist had been hired as the wedding singer. This man's resemblance to the original was uncanny — at least when seen backstage in low lighting. Maybe a picture or two of Gramma with him could be arranged. He had seemed a friendly sort . . . unless that was just part of his act. Until she could mentally settle down, Frankie wouldn't be reading him.

Hoping to catch a glimpse of him again, Frankie looked across the wide reception hall toward the platform stage. It glittered with gold tinsel and Mylar balloons. A girl in a maroon coat with wide padded shoulders that marked her as one of the musicians was messing around with the drums, while two guys in matching maroon T-shirts checked the microphones and soundboard. A second musician had both acoustic and electric guitars in place onstage and was making sure the latter were hooked up to power. This promised to be more like a concert than wedding entertainment. She caught the group's name from the front of the bass drum: "Coop's Cool-Cats." The three Cs were linked to one another in a fiftie's-style font. Very retro. No sign of the star, though.

"How's it going?" asked a girl who eased up next to her.

"Pretty good, but I don't want to jinx things," said Frankie. The question had come from Aleen, one of the bridesmaids. She actually looked good in her special dress, though tradition held that such things had to be walking eyesores. On Aleen it worked. She went in for piercings, lots of piercings: ears, tongue, and other places that didn't bear thinking about, soot black hair, and tattoos. So what was a little purple satin with flounces against all that? Like Trinidad, Aleen was a professional model. She was very popular for the more edgy fashion layouts. She and Frankie had been best friends since grade school, and she'd suggested Yummy Catering to the bride, for which Frankie was still thanking her. Trinidad had taken quite a chance bestowing her trade on an unknown.

"Trini was so nervous before the ceremony," said Aleen. "Didn't show one flicker of it when she went down the aisle. What a pro."

"Nervous? Five hundred guests, bodyguards, and the tabloid press to juggle, why should she be nervous?" Frankie shook her head.

"The usual. Third time's supposed to be the charm. She really wants this one to work."

"Then she picked the wrong guy," said Gramma, who had leaned sideways from the bread tray to listen.

"Oh, don't tell me your vibe twanged again." Aleen looked distressed. Of course, it was hard to tell, as her trademark chalk-white-and-gray-toned makeup made her look distressed all the time.

"Like a guitar with a bad string." Gramma pronounced.

"Frankie?"

She nodded agreement. Gramma *had* picked up on Santiago's inner man, just chosen not to mention it. " 'Fraid so."

"You guys are just spooky with that."

"A blessing and a curse," said Gramma, raising her gaze briefly to the ceiling as though to apportion blame; then she resumed dishing out rolls with a smile.

"What's going to happen?"

Frankie haltingly gave what few deductions she'd drawn concerning Santiago.

Gramma backed her up on it, then added: "It won't necessarily turn out that way. Things can change."

"How?" Aleen demanded.

Gramma shrugged. "That's up to the happy couple. Maybe Trinidad will suddenly go all domestic; maybe Santiago will join the twenty-first century and back off from pushing her into being something she's not. The key to any solid relationship is seeing your partner for what he or she is, not for what you've projected onto them. Projections always disappoint."

"But poor Trini," said Aleen. "I feel I should warn her or something."

"Never works. Trust me, it's been tried."

"Is your vibe *ever* wrong?"

"Never. But it's handy. Helped me pick the right man. Helped Frankie's mom do the same. Hopefully she'll have the same good luck if and when she takes a crack at it."

Frankie rolled her eyes. "Just not tonight. I'm too busy." So saying, she hurried to another part of the serving line that was about to run out of potatoes. Aleen remained with Gramma, probably hoping to find a way to save Trinidad's marriage.

"Vibe" had always been Aleen's word for whatever-it-was that ran in the distaff side of Frankie's family. Way back when, the women might have called it the Sight or the Eye, if they called it anything. Gramma never made a big to-do about it, no more than one would for a birthmark, and just as well. Frankie had grown up with a minimum of trauma attached.

The initial assault of hungry guests was over, with everyone but a few table hoppers seated. The big hall echoed loud with simultaneous conversations, the clink and clank of utensils on plates, the noise visually punctuated by the official photographer's flash unit. Weddings ran more or less on a schedule, even one this large. Next would come the second-helping crowd, and sure enough, some of the wrestler types were already in line again.

Those were pretty big guys. Frankie hoped she'd allowed enough food for them. Coop's Cool-Cats might be out of luck for a post-show meal otherwise.

Everything was under control, though, and running smoothly. The bride would be pleased, and might recommend Yummy Catering to her friends. It wouldn't hurt to have a picture of Trinidad's wedding up in the front office, either. Status-wise, this wedding was a hell of a good windfall for the business.

Frankie was in the kitchen supervising an early start on the cleanup when the loud twang of a very much in tune electric guitar thrummed through the walls, announcing the show. She wiped her wet hands and rushed out for a look. The catering line for the main meal was shut down and cleared. Nothing to do but clean until the cake cutting began. She was allowed a break.

Twa-a-a-ng again; then the drummer began thumping a vigorous beat, building for the star's big entrance. Frankie could guess that Gramma would find the best view for the show, spotted her, and stood next to her. They had a clear field to the stage.

"This is sooooo cool," said Gramma, who was able to get away with teen-talk simply because on her it was cute, not forced. The glow on her face and spark in her eyes showed that she'd not changed much from that swooning twenty-year-old of fifty years past.

"Totally cool," Frankie agreed, having to raise her voice to be heard above the rising fanfare. The group had saxophone and trombone players, both instruments adding to the tapestry of sound, enriching it. She loved live music, done well; tonight would be a treat. She craned her neck, looking for the first sign of the Elvis guy coming on-stage.

" 'Scuse me, pretty ladies."

The *voice.*

Frankie gave a jellied-knees start, for the man was behind her and had bent to speak almost in her ear.

Gramma also jumped, gaping, then mouthing a silent *oh, my goodness* at the sight of him. What big eyes she had.

Elvis smiled down at both in turn and winked. " 'Scuse me. Gotta take care of business." Clearly he was intent on a grander entrance than simply stepping out from behind a partition onstage.

He passed between them. Frankie caught

a whiff of a clean, sharp aftershave mixed with the black leather; then he was gone and on the move. The drums and guitar cut loose in frenzied earnest, and a spotlight flashed bright in her eyes before it centered on Elvis.

The guests gave a collective gasp. Many must have known the specifics of the entertainment but were clearly unprepared for the quality. Spotlights were merciless and could pick out every flaw, only in this case none were to be found. He was perfect from every angle. He moved easily through the crowd, pausing at tables, throwing the *look,* and collecting squeals of reaction from dozens of stirred-up girls. Hands reached for him; he brushed at a few, grinned as though sharing a secret joke, and steadily made his way to the stage. The audience began to spontaneously applaud as though for the real deal. Frankie was surprised to find she'd joined in, caught up by the phenomenon.

He took the two steps up to the stage, plucked a cordless mic from a stand, and paused, his back to the house, feet apart, legs braced. His shoulders shifted, settled, and the ovation increased. Then he held up his free hand, fingers spread, and pointed to the ceiling. The music cut off, and as though by magic so did the applause. The whole place went utterly silent.

He slowly turned, head tilted and shoulders slightly hunched, arm still high. Everyone seemed to be holding their breath.

He brought the mic to his lips. The deep "huh-huh-huh" that came forth boomed through the room, and everyone, Frankie included, roared in response. The show could have ended right then and been considered a success, but the drummer resumed her driving beat, the guitar player joined in, and Elvis launched into "Hound Dog."

The voice was the same one Frankie had heard on Gramma's records, then her CD collections. The timbre, tone, and range were identical, but this was no lip-sync performance; the man onstage was belting it out himself and throwing everything into it. He had the moves and mannerisms nailed so accurately it was as though he'd invented them himself. The blast of raw energy rolled from him to the audience, and though it was not the time for it, several stood up and danced in place, unable to hold still.

"What do you think, Gramma?" Frankie asked. The noise levels were such that she had to bellow to be heard. "We're feeding them afterward. Does that work for you?"

Gramma stared, still wide-eyed, at the man onstage and made no reply. Something was off. Maybe she didn't like impersonators, after all, but she'd never once said anything against them.

"Gramma?"

She only shook her head. *Not now,* she mouthed, and flapped her hand at the show.

Okay, fine, Frankie wanted to enjoy it. If Gramma had a problem, they could tackle things later.

The opening number over, Elvis took a bow. Frankie scanned the crowd, noting amazement on some faces and blatant hero worship on others. The older folks who had memories of the real man seemed the most stunned. The rest, born years after his passing, were apparently realizing what their parents and grandparents had seen in him. She was willing to lay down money that they'd be at a music store the next day looking to add to their CD collections.

He was timeless, and she was suddenly glad Gramma had instilled an appreciation for him in her from an early age.

The man onstage thanked everyone — yes, his speaking voice was the same, too, right down to the melting accent — and launched into the master-of-ceremonies part of his job. He introduced the bride and groom, poked gentle fun at their unique names, and made it seem as though he were close personal friends with them and their respective families.

"Now bachelorhood isn't everything it's cracked up to be, isn't that right, Santiago?" he asked. "That's right; some of your pals have been tellin' tales, tellin' me what it was like for you before you met that pretty lady you're sittin' next to. . . ."

The music swelled and he began singing "Are You Lonesome Tonight?"

The groomsmen hooted — at the groom, who was grinning and nodding agreement to the words. Then he cocked his shaved, tattooed head, listening as though he'd never heard them before. He almost looked somber as the song ended.

"Of course," Elvis continued, "you've had plenty of dates, you're a popular guy, but when you don't find that special gal, there's only one place you can go . . ."

He sang "Heartbreak Hotel."

The small band was inspired; it was as though he had a full orchestra backing him instead of just a few players and a lot of amps. Frankie had seen her share of wedding singers, but nothing came close to this.

When the applause settled, he continued,

"And then one day, if you're real lucky, out of the blue she's *there,* right next to you as though you've known her your whole life — that one woman you can love forever. And she's precious, man, precious."

Santiago, nodded, looking at his bride as Elvis sang "I Can't Help Falling in Love." Before he'd gotten halfway through, the bride's mother broke down into tears. Her husband put his arm around her. There was a general shifting of several couples as they also reacted to the music and the voice. Frankie felt her own throat getting a lump and glanced around for a glass of water she'd put on the serving table earlier.

"Gramma? You okay?"

Her grandmother was openly crying, a wad of paper napkins in one hand for her tears. She shook her head and waved Frankie off, clearly having a wonderful time.

Said Elvis: "But it's one thing to love a woman, and another to appreciate her. You think about it, Santiago: Out of all the handsome men in this whole wide world" — he gave a sly smile — "and I'm sure one of 'em . . ."

The cheering and whistling took up a few moments.

". . . Out of all of those guys this beautiful, wonderful lady picked *you.* Now why do you think she did that?"

Santiago shook his head. His expression had gone serious, as though he truly needed to have the answer.

" 'Cause she loves you, man. You don't ever want to take that for granted. You respect her, you love her, you *be* there for her, and . . ."

"Love Me Tender" came next, and it was the softest, sweetest rendition of the ballad Frankie had ever heard. Elvis came down from the stage so he could sing directly to the couple at their table.

Frankie's lump in the throat came back, and Gramma tore through another stack of paper napkins. Everyone in the place, from the guests, to the servers, to the hard-faced bodyguards keeping out the uninvited, seemed deeply moved by it.

"This guy is beyond amazing," Frankie whispered to Gramma.

"Sweetheart, you don't know the half if it," Gramma whispered back.

When he finished, the couple kissed. It wasn't a planned thing, it just happened, and they weren't the only ones. Frankie abruptly wanted someone to kiss and this Elvis counted for at least twelve slots on her top-ten list for that experience. Yes, he was an illusion, but damn — he was a *good* illusion, a *hot* illusion.

He'd returned to the stage, accompanied by the sounds of sniffles and the occasional goose honk as someone blew their nose. Unbelievable. The big, tough groomsmen were doing most of it.

"You've found her and she's picked you — now what happens?" Elvis asked, and in reply he sang "One Night" so plaintively, his whole heart so clearly into it, that Frankie had to quell the urge to shout, *Yes!* and charge the stage to jump on him.

The song proved a showstopper. The guests were wild now, and needed settling. Frankie couldn't make out what he said through it, but the next number was "Hawaiian Wedding Song."

Perfect. The man, whoever he was under the hairstyle and makeup, was a genius. There wasn't a dry eye in the house. They'd remember this wedding for years to come.

"Now I want the new mister 'n' missus to come out on the floor. Don't be shy; we're all friends here."

The couple's first dance was to a reprise of "Can't Help Falling in Love," and Elvis encouraged the audience to sing the chorus with him. Other couples got out on the floor. Frankie was sorry she wasn't a guest as well.

211

Someone tapped her shoulder. She expected a kitchen crisis, but it was Omar, his arms wide in invitation. In his late fifties and wholly devoted to his large family, he was just playing the polite gentleman with an offer to dance, but apparently the music had touched him as well. She laughed, accepted, and they did a couple of dignified turns in a clear area behind the tables.

Another shoulder tap — this time from Gramma, who wanted some of the action.

"C'mon, kid," she said. "Share."

Omar bowed gravely and took her hand. She liked younger men; she claimed they were the only ones who could keep up with her.

Frankie was delighted. She was drawn back to her catbird view of the dance, getting there in time to see the newlyweds finish out with another kiss. The whole room cheered.

It was wonderful. A bona fide Moment, with a capital *M.*

And . . . there was something odd about them . . . no . . . *changed.* What the hell . . . ?

She stared, but there was no mistaking that they were different now. Yes, it was still Santiago and Trinidad, ridiculous names for anyone, but the two people who bore them were giving off a wholly different vibe. They were together, *really* together, two adults on the same page with common goals and a rock-solid love that would last, truly last. That hadn't been there half an hour ago. Frankie had known that for a fact. Gramma had seen it, too.

Frankie looked at the Elvis guy, her jaw dropping.

Oh no . . . *no* way. That kind of thing only happened in the movies. Someone sings a song and makes everything all better? Sweet, but never in the real world. No way. *No* freakin' way. . . .

Elvis looked at Frankie across the space, seemed to fix on her despite the fact that she was in the dim background of a huge hall. She opened up a little, thinking to catch his vibe and be able read him this time, but it wasn't working the way she expected. She felt his gaze locking on to hers like a searchlight.

Make that a cruise missile.

Her breath caught, her heart leaped again, and every light in the room suddenly flared up too bright to bear.

All the strength left her knees, and her brain spun. She grabbed a chair for balance, but it wasn't enough and down she dropped, taking the chair with her. They made quite a crashing clatter.

Startled cries and an instant later she was surrounded by concerned voices and helping hands. By some miracle she'd not cracked her head, nor had she fully lost consciousness, but she'd swooned away like a schoolgirl.

Gramma was there, dribbling water on her face from a dishcloth. Ugh. "It's all right, honey."

When she tried to get up it didn't work. Omar held her shoulders, and someone she couldn't see had her feet raised comically high. She was damn-for-sure glad she'd opted for pants instead of a skirt tonight.

"I'm *fine,*" she rasped, struggling. "Lemme up."

"No," said Omar. Firmly. It was his don't-even-think-it tone, usually reserved for inept kitchen help about to be fired.

Okay, she could lie here for a bit longer if it made him not-mad. She would work on making the dizziness go away.

Can I be any more mortified? Frankie thought.

The answer wasn't just *yes* but *hell-yes.* Elvis was now one of the people leaning into her view.

Arrgghh. She couldn't think how he'd gotten over here so fast through the crowd, and

214

wished he'd stayed away. Lying sprawled with her legs in the air . . . oh yeah, that would make an impression.

"Lemme through," he said. "I had a little first aid in the army."

No one argued with that soft voice. People parted and he checked her over. She squeezed her eyes firmly shut, hoping that when she opened them this would all be done. Embarrassing as it was, she couldn't help noticing his aftershave again (*oh yeah, and the leather*), and how gentle he was, murmuring questions on whether this or that hurt. This would have been a fine time for him to cop a feel, but he remained a perfect gentleman.

He ascertained her skull was intact and nothing broken. That pronounced, she was ready to get up again, her dizziness gone now that she'd caught her breath.

More embarrassment. As soon as she was helped to her feet a cheer went around the hall. She hung on to Elvis's arm for dear life and wanted to throw a grenade at the genius who had swung the spot square on them.

"You've got that deer in the headlights look, Frankie," Gramma urgently whispered. "Smile and wave like an astronaut."

Those instructions were her solution to a

wide number of life's disasters, major and minor. Frankie did as she was told. It worked. Another round of cheers. The best man had shouldered his way over along with the father of the bride, who looked justifiably nervous, probably worried about lawsuits. She smiled, gave them a thumbs-up, still holding on to Elvis with her other hand. He was pretty dang solid under that leather.

Gramma ran interference for her, God bless the woman, saying that the kitchen had been too warm and Frankie had been working too hard. While she held their attention Frankie glared up at Elvis.

"Just what the hell did you do to me, buster?" she snarled.

He returned her gaze, steady, with no excuses, no denials, no what-are-you-talking-abouts. "I'm sorry about that, truly sorry. I'm as surprised as you. I didn't know that could happen."

"*What* could happen?" She was furious.

"Well — uh — maybe we could talk later? I am truly, truly sorry." He started to pull away.

She held fast. "Who *are* you?"

An odd expression whipped over his face and was gone, a touch of sadness, a hint of sly charm, then the smile, the shy, sweet smile exactly as she'd seen in the movies.

"Why, Yummy Cat, I think you know already. No need for me to say."

Frankie's grip went slack as her fingers lost feeling, and he went away to finish his set.

She'd have been happier if the rest of the evening had passed in a nice, foggy haze, but everything was crystalline sharp and seemed to take far too long.

Speeches were made, the cake cut, photographs taken, video shot. The bride tossed the bouquet; the groom tossed her garter, inspiring a violent shouting match and scuffle among four of the groomsmen. It looked ugly for a moment, then turned out to be a wrestling gag they'd cooked up. They all shook hands and did the macho slap-on-the-back/shoulder thumping thing, laughing.

And Elvis sang. They couldn't get enough of him.

The unexpected pause in the proceedings had no effect on the show. Coop's Cool-Cats kept the energy high and moving. Every song was a hit you could dance to and so well done that Frankie felt her anger vanish after just a few bars. That annoyed her. She'd wanted to hang on to her mad so as to have it in reserve for the talk he'd promised. The music wouldn't let her keep that particular kind of momentum.

He *had* been genuinely contrite. Her vibe still wasn't up to full speed and now cut out entirely when she turned it on him, but she was sure he'd been sincere on the apology.

Elvis got the bridesmaids lined up before the stage, requesting their help with the next number, "Rock-a-Hula Baby." Considering that none of them really had much in the way of hips for the hula, they made a game effort. He had better luck with one of the wrestlers who turned out to be Hawaiian and had remarkable muscle control, much to the delight of the ladies, especially when he took off his coat and shirt, leaving only the bow tie in place, like a Chippendales dancer.

But no one came close to matching the star's moves and sheer raw sexiness.

Frankie marveled that the leather stood up to what he put it through. Damn, but he looked *fine.* Hips, shoulders, long legs, all working perfectly, thank you very much. No hint of exaggeration or parody here. The man had talent.

It was kind of sad.

For the sake of her own sanity Frankie chose to conclude that the Elvis guy was one of those who had let the persona take over. That was it. That *had* to be it. She'd seen it when dating the actor. One of his friends couldn't drop character after the curtain rang down. Long after a play had closed he was still playing his part, improvising until called out on a new audition for a new play. Even the other actors gave him space and suggested therapy. She'd fervently hoped he never got cast as Jack the Ripper.

Clearly the man onstage had the same problem.

She felt bad for him, but it was his life, and he seemed to be enjoying it. Heck, there were worse people to be than Elvis.

The cake serving marked the beginning of the end for her catering job. Frankie saw to it that the gigantic confection's top part was boxed and saved, sent the temps around the tables to gather dishes and cutlery, and made sure the cleaning and packing up was thorough. They had access to the hall until 3:00 a.m. but she had no intention of hanging around that late. It had been a horrendously busy night, with or without the fainting incident, and weariness was creeping up on her.

Sticking to her promise, she reserved more than enough leftovers for Coop's Cool-Cats. Usually those were divided among her own crew, but no one minded when they found

219

out the band would be coming back for a meal. Her crew was apparently starstruck. Omar, who wasn't one for much talk, nodded and took over organizing the pending feast, keeping the dishes warm. There was an anticipatory smile lurking under his bush of a mustache. Gramma helped him, relating the story of the concert where she'd fainted. Omar good-naturedly pretended that he'd never heard it before.

The bride disappeared to put on her traveling clothes and pack her wedding gown. Aleen had let slip that the simple white sheath had cost more than the whole reception. Good grief. All that on a dress? A one-time-only dress? That would be — in the fashion world — out of style in two days or less? Yikes.

Elvis kept the party going until it was time for the big departure. He got a signal from the best man, then launched into the finale, "Viva Las Vegas," the couple's honeymoon destination. On what they leaked to the tabloids. Aleen had the real skinny: They were going to Niagara Falls, then taking a road trip through Canada. Who'd have thought it?

Gramma was tired but refused Frankie's suggestion to catch a ride home with one of the temps. "I want another gander at that stud," she said, and found a chair at a folding table they'd set up in the kitchen. No need to ask which stud.

The band had their own routine to follow as they broke things down and packed them into a van parked at the loading dock. Everyone had their area of expertise, and there was little conversation. They rolled up wires, shut instruments into shockproof carriers, and took it away. Soon all that was left was drooping tinsel and a few Mylar balloons not snagged by guests as souvenirs. The hall's resident staff would clear things for the next event, a class reunion or political rally, whatever. Frankie might even see the place again for another big wedding.

Aleen came from somewhere or other, the purple dress on a hanger and cocooned in plastic, a big purse hanging from one slim shoulder. She'd pulled on black jeans and a tight red tank top. As always, she looked like she'd not eaten since grade school, which was the result of genetics and a dedicated fitness routine.

"Where's the dead-hound-dog party?" she asked brightly.

Gramma must have passed the word to her. It was a miracle more people hadn't heard and lingered.

"Kitchen." Frankie felt a reluctance to go

back there and had been hanging around the main hall, putting things off. When still mad she'd wanted to get in the guy's face for that explanation; now it was no longer important. She'd figured things out on her own and further contact with him would only be uncomfortable for them both. He was welcome to his method-acting musical fantasy, and she would stick to the weirdness-free zone that was catering.

With a slightly bruised vibe.

Have to be more careful with that, she thought. The fainting incident . . . maybe that's what hit Gramma fifty years back. The real Elvis had that raw power, and like many girls of the time, Gramma had a mad crush on him. She might have had her vibe tuned to him at the concert, he hit her with a flash of his energy, then *boom,* another fan fainting in the aisles.

In Frankie's case it was an Elvis impers— tribute artist but no less real for the energy. He'd been pouring that out on the stage, flinging it at the audience, revving them to the max; you couldn't fake it.

But he'd *known* something.

"Yo. Zombie-girl." Aleen nudged her. "Kitchen? Par-tay?"

"Yeah, okay-fine."

"That was massively well done. Your first

really big job. You impressed the hell out of Trini."

"I just underbid the competition."

"Actually, they overbid you. Soon as they knew it was Trinidad they doubled their prices. You charged her the same as you would a nonfamous person and that got you on her good side."

"I'll keep it as company policy then." Frankie hadn't known about the other catering services and their price gouging. Well, good for her; playing fair had paid off.

Her absence from the kitchen hadn't impeded the feeding of the band. They'd apparently eaten their fill and were kicked back and relaxing with the Yummy crew. The plates were cleared, and only soda cans remained on the table. Everyone looked content.

The Elvis guy was saying, still in his Elvis voice, "Omar, that was the best I've had in a long time. I'd be pleased to kiss the cook, but your mustache is mighty in the way."

Laughter, everyone in a great mood. He was the star back here as much as he had been out front. Gramma had a chair right next to him and looked impossibly pleased with herself.

Omar nodded once with much dignity. "I and the mustache are very relieved to hear that, Mr. Presley." He was utterly serious, as though speaking to the real deal. Maybe they were all just being polite by playing into the man's fantasy . . . out of respect for his talent. That was nice of them.

Elvis spotted Frankie and Aleen and stood up. Still the gentleman. "Ladies. It sure is pleasing to have you join us. Miss Foster, on behalf of my poor starvin' group I want to thank you for a doggone good meal."

For a second Frankie didn't know what to say. Smiling and waving like an astronaut didn't suit this one, so she cut the waving part and kept the smile. "You're welcome. Anytime." *Arrgh.* Why had she added that? "Everything okay, then?" she asked the others, and got approval all around. No one seemed inclined to go home just yet, which was strange. "Anybody ready to leave?"

"They're still coming down from the show, dear," said Gramma. She looked about to say something more, then shut her mouth and smiled.

Okay, Gramma, what's the subtext here? There was something on her mind, the whatever-it-was that had bothered her when the show first started.

But Gramma only picked up a canned lemonade and sipped from it.

Elvis guy hadn't resumed his seat and

stepped sideways to get out from the middle of the crowd. He came up to Frankie, who was subjected to another nudge from a grinning Aleen.

"Oh — this is my best friend, Aleen Nuutzenbaum."

"Pleased to meet you," he said, shaking her hand. "German name?"

"Dutch. No cracks about nuts, okay?"

"I wouldn't dream of it."

Frankie bit her tongue, so as not to say anything about nut cracking. She didn't know him well enough to make that kind of joke, and — damn it! — his gentlemanly manner made her want to behave.

"Did you get teased about your name at school?" Aleen asked.

He flashed her that half grin and shook his head. "Not much. It was about me carrying a guitar all the time. I was kinda shy. But I don't think about that stuff anymore."

Frankie went cold inside. *Aleen had fallen for it, too?*

Okay, enough. Everyone out of the pool; it was reality check time. He was just an actor, singer, what have you, scratching a living by cashing in on another man's fame. Running around after the show was over and pretending to *be* that man was just an insult to his memory.

She drew a deep breath to speak, feeling the anger building up fast and furious . . . then looked up into his eyes.

Something there stopped her. Stopped her hard. That something asked her not to shatter the moment, not to spoil the good time everyone was having.

They were enjoying the illusion, loving every minute of it.

She couldn't strip that from them with harsh words, especially not from Gramma. For their sakes Frankie made herself slowly deflate and pull back. She'd been damn close to the edge. Common sense and common courtesy had saved her from putting her foot into things.

He smiled at her as though he'd been inside her head just then, as though he'd known every thought that had whipped through her brain in the last few seconds.

She went beet red, and knowing that she had a blush on only made it worse.

Okay, then ignore it, girl. She went to an ice chest, got a cold soda, and held it to her forehead to cool down.

"You feeling all right, Frankie?" Gramma asked.

"I'm gonna get some air. I've been smelling this food all day and need a break."

They all understood that. She pushed out

the back door. Her catering van was backed into the loading dock area right next to the band's vehicle. The latter bore the same retro logo as the bass drum: "Coop's Cool-Cats."

Her car was parked farther out, as were those of her crew — and one other. She'd not expected it, but yeah, it was definitely there, a pink 1955 Cadillac Fleetwood — her eyes bugged — in *cherry* condition. White sidewalls, white roof, chrome gleaming like new under the parking lot lights . . . good God, but the man was thorough.

She popped the soda open and chugged, not tasting it, just relishing the icy, tickling fizz clearing her throat.

"Take you for a spin, Yummy Cat?"

She sputtered and choked. Recovered. No one else was here, so she rounded on him. "Stop that!"

Again, no denial, no asking what she was talking about. He did look troubled and kept a respectful distance from her body space. "I am sorry, Miss Foster. I don't blame you for being creeped out. Is that what they call it? That's the last thing I want."

She chugged more soda to give herself time to think, only she couldn't think of anything, which was annoying. She was usually faster than this, but as she had never been in such a situation before, it was hard to be brilliant. "Look, it's fun to pretend, but sometime you have to drop character."

"I hear ya. It's just that I get wound up for a show and it takes a while to let go."

Frankie nodded. "Okay. Just so you know, I did enjoy it; you're fabulous. It was an incredible show. At least until I hit the floor. You wanted to talk about that?"

"And apologize again. I was all opened up, and then I looked at you and you were lookin' back an' . . . well, it was like my whole world stopped."

World stopped? What the hey? "Opened up?"

"Gotta do a little of that for every show, just part of the gig. It's what I do to get everyone goin'. But this one . . . I could tell that couple was heading for trouble. They needed a push in the right direction or there'd have been all kinds of misery down the road."

It took her a moment to digest. "You've got the vibe, too?" And he could actually *influence* people? Ye gods.

"That what you call it? Never did have a name before. Never could talk to anyone about it, not 'til you came trottin' along backstage. Soon as I laid eyes on you I saw you were different, that you had something more than those good looks you're carryin' around."

"Whoa, you laying a line on me?"

"No'm. Just fact. You're one cute head turner."

Her face worked hard to project and maintain a calm façade. Now was not the time to go all girlie and break out in a big smile. "Well . . . thank you . . . but the other thing. The vibe?"

"If that's your name for it, then that's what I got. I can tell a lot about people without ever askin'. The stuff just comes to me. Sometimes too much."

She'd never heard of a guy having the talent, but why not? It wasn't anything she or Gramma talked about much with others, so why should anyone else?

"You know of a way of shutting it off?" he asked.

Shutting it off? "Uh, not really. What, you get stuff twenty-four/seven?"

"Sometimes, when I'm around too many people. I use the music. It's a buffer between me and the world. And I use the getup."

She presumed he referred to the Elvis gear. "How?"

The shy grin flashed. It was a nice grin. "Well, everyone loves Elvis. I get mostly positive stuff coming at me then. If I went around too much as Rick Cooper I'd be crazy. I'd be picking up all kinds of misery otherwise, and a body can only take so much."

"So . . . you impersonate Elvis to *keep* from going crazy. That's . . . crazy."

"I guess so, but it sure works."

"Your real name's Rick Cooper?"

"That's what's on the drivin' license." He gestured at the van. "Originator of Coop's Cool-Cats."

"Do they know about your vibe?"

"They're like my family; they know everything. No one seems to mind. We do good, too. Like tonight. We kept something fine from breakin'."

"I saw that. I never knew things could be changed."

"It takes some work, an' I don't do the changing. It's the music going out of me that does it. If I sat down in front of those two an' gave 'em a talkin' to it wouldn't have done a lick a good. But music can come out of one soul and touch another in amazin' ways. I see it all the time and it still gets to me. Pretty humblin'."

"Look, uh, Coop?"

"Coop's fine. Rick if you ever get the notion for it."

"Okay, Coop, maybe you and my gramma should talk. She knows more about this stuff than I do. She's got the vibe, too."

"Oh, I could tell that. She is one sweet little lady. I'd be pleased to call on her and you both, any day you name."

"In what persona? I don't mean to be rude, but —"

"I know. If it's just the two of you I can shed the getup. I can't change the face or hair, though. This is what the Good Lord gave me, so I have to live with it."

Wow. "It's amazing."

"Uncanny?"

She nodded.

"Yeah, I've heard all that. Seemed only right to just take it and run. It's worked out. I got a good life."

"How did it start?"

"You won't believe it."

"Try me."

"Well, when I was beginnin' my teens my folks took me on a tour of Graceland."

"Me, too! Gramma took me."

"Then you know how that place is; everything's so well cared for and clean and just plain *loved.* When we were going through the rooms I couldn't shake the feeling that Elvis would walk in at any moment. It *is* like he's still there. That's about when I first

231

started perceivin' things. And what I perceived first was *him*."

"You saw his ghost?"

"No, nothin' like that. It was . . . like a presence . . . only it wasn't him so much as the love everyone who'd ever crossed that threshold had for him. It was love for him, for his gifts, for all that he gave the world. That's a mighty powerful lot of energy, and it's permeated into every square inch of the whole place. That's how he's there. I don't hold nothing about ghosts, but I do believe a place can pick up . . ."

"A vibe?"

"Surely. What I think is maybe some of it got into me and found a home. And if any of that has even a single atom of himself inside me, then I'm pleased and honored to carry it."

She liked his attitude. "And you spotted the vibe in me?"

"Right away."

"But I didn't see it in you. I shut down."

"You saw the getup, is all. Give it a while. Maybe you'll get past it."

No time like the present. She decided to risk another faint; she had to know.

Frankie opened up . . . and . . . wow, again. Now she was able to see the guy who was Rick Cooper, and something more. The Elvis energy. Dampened down quite a lot, but it was as much a part of him as his skin and went far deeper. Very reassuringly, it wasn't the least bit scary but rather comforting, like a piece of Elvis truly did live on. This must have been what Gramma had seen, and it had thrown her, virtually two guys sharing the same space.

She would have also figured that it was all right, though. Had it been bad, Gramma would have had nothing to do with him.

Damn, but the universe was a strange place to hang out. Strange, but never boring.

"You got it, didn't you?" he asked.

"I did." She really liked what she'd seen, too. Of Rick Cooper, that is. Elvis was mighty fine, but so was Rick. He looked just as interesting; for one thing, he'd also made it to adulthood with an oddball gift and not gone raving nuts. He'd opted for a unique way of dealing with it, but hey, whatever worked. Frankie wanted to see more of him, on a lot of levels.

"Uh, about me talkin' to your gramma?" he began.

"Yeah?"

"I shouldn't like to impose unless I could . . . well, I know of this diner where they do the old-fashioned burgers an' milk shakes an' have a real jukebox with forty-fives. If you think she —"

"She'd love it. Tomorrow for lunch?"

"I'd be mighty pleased with your company, Yummy — oh, sorry."

"You can call me Yummy Cat. If anyone else does, I'll bust 'em."

"Well, that's all right, then. There's just one more thing, an' it's been on my mind all evenin', but . . ."

She didn't have to read his vibe to have seen that in his blue, blue eyes. She tossed her soda can away, grabbed the black leather lapels of his jacket, and pulled him toward her.

Oh. My. God.

Rick Cooper or Elvis, it didn't matter; he, they, whoever, was a world-class kisser. He knew exactly what to do and how much to do it and the breath went right out of her for a third time that night, and it felt *great.*

Better than great.

Oh yeah, baby . . . he had her *all* shook up.

P. N. ELROD is best known for *The Vampire Files,* featuring her wisecracking undead gunshoe, Jack Fleming. She's written over twenty novels and twenty short stories in the paranormal genre, edited several collections, and branched into fantasy and mystery. You can check out all her projects at www.vampwriter .com. Yes, she really does love Elvis, huh-huh-huh!

THE WEDDING OF WYLDA SERENE

ESTHER M. FRIESNER

It has been said that God makes marriages, but the Devil plans weddings. I know this has been said, because I said it.

I coined the aforementioned *bon mot* upon the occasion of my elder sister's third wedding of a career-best total of six. The nuptial rut that dear Katherine wore into the aisle of St. George's Anglican is one reason for my own continued bachelorhood. If one cannot learn from the mistakes of others, one might as well become a Democrat.

One would presume that when a woman has gone through the same ceremony so many times (not counting an ill-considered elopement with one of the pool boys during her fourth honeymoon on Maui), the mechanics of a wedding, if not the subsequent marriage, would go more smoothly as experience was garnered along the way.

Ah, but when has logic ever refused to defer to human stupidity? Our dear Katherine somehow managed to turn each wedding into an even greater display of obsessive perfectionism, spectacular tantrums, and alienated bridesmaids. By the time she embarked upon Marriage VI she hadn't a female friend left with whom she was on speaking terms, let alone one who would be willing to stand up for her in a cloud of mint green tulle at the altar of St. George's.

Thus my sister made a virtue of Necessity and struck up an instantaneous friendship with one Nora Scruggs. La Scruggs was a part-time employee at the florist's shop that had provided Katherine with so many wedding bouquets, boutonnieres, pew decorations, altar flowers, and table centerpieces that the proprietor had to be forcibly restrained from falling to his knees and covering my sister's hands with kisses every time they met.

Miss Scruggs was an attractive, well-meaning young woman of gentle mien and biddable disposition. She seemed to have about as much self-determination as a tablespoon of tomato aspic. When, within the space of twenty minutes, my sister took their conversation from, "I'm getting married in May," to, "Your bridesmaid dress fitting will be this Saturday at ten a.m. I'll pay for it, of course," the poor girl was thrilled.

Katherine's sixth wedding proved to be an historic occasion for many reasons, not the least of which being that it was her last. Apparently her latest husband, Bryce Calhoun III, took exception to a torrid Internet romance that Katherine initiated in a cybercafe on St. Bart's during their first Christmas together. As they flew home together in one of Bryce's smaller private planes, they had a dreadful falling-out about it. For my sister, the falling-out was quite literal, helped along by a hearty push from her exasperated spouse. By a remarkable stroke of luck, Bryce was both defended (well) and prosecuted (weakly) by two of Katherine's former husbands, although I hope for our family's sake that there is little or no truth to the rumor that my late sister also had dated nine out of the twelve jurors.

Katherine's hymeneal excesses aside, her final wedding was also significant in that it provided her makeshift bridesmaid, the bewitchingly blue-collar Miss Scruggs, with unexpected entrée to the higher strata of Society. It happened at the reception, which of course took place at The Club. It was there, in an earthly paradise of scrupulously groomed lawns, tastefully decorated function rooms, and perfectly chilled champagne, that the winsome florist's assistant made the acquaintance of young Frederick Austin-Cowles. The rest was history, as written by Cinderella.

Frederick came from an American lineage so old, rich, and respectable that defending its age, wealth, and honor was his parents' sole preoccupation. The burden of nigh four hundred years of ancestral obligation had made them into blue-blooded martinets of the first order, intent on raising their only child to be nothing more than top-grade mulch for the family tree. The lad spent the first twenty-five years of his life firmly compressed beneath their totalitarian thumbs. Each aspect of his existence — eating, sleeping, clothing, schooling, playing, and more — was regimented with a strictness to make the ancient Spartans look like fifth-string yoga instructors.

No one but a confirmed masochist or a member of Yale's Skull and Bones club would doubt for an instant how deeply Frederick abhorred his micromanaged childhood and the parents who had engineered it. At the age of five he resolved to find some way to put their patrician noses well and truly out of joint the moment that he came into full possession of the trust fund his grandfather had left him. Wisely averse to any act that would mortify his parents but harm himself in the process, Frederick could not take any of the more conventional paths to rebellion, such as substance abuse, sexual excess, decorating his skin with blobs of ink and globs of metal, or mail-ordering a ready-made polyester men's suit from Montgomery Ward. He was at what passed for his wit's end when he met Miss Scruggs and the angels sang.

They sang something by Patsy Cline, to be sure, something so down-home, simple, honest, and salt-of-the-earth as could not fail to send Frederick's parents into fits. Oh, how that thought left him gloating! Moreover, Miss Scruggs herself was so sweet, meek, and pleasing to the eye that it would be no great hardship for him to employ her as his bedmate as well as his implement of vengeance. He put the astonished girl through a whirlwind courtship, a hasty wedding flight to Las Vegas, and got her in the family way before my sister Katherine and Bryce came back from their honeymoon.

Alas for Frederick, he did not live to relish the fruits of his filial retaliation. He left his pregnant bride in their Central Park West pied-à-terre and was driving hell-for-finest-New-Zealand-lambskin-leather to Connecticut, to drop the proverbial bombshell on his parents, when his Mercedes lost an argument with a lawn furniture delivery truck somewhere east of Greenwich. Hilliard and Margot Austin-Cowles learned that they were childless, in-laws, and incipient grandparents at almost the same time that poor Nora found out she was a widow.

Of course The Club was soon buzzing with the details of what followed, to no one's surprise. The Club is a veritable beehive for rumor. My sister's last wedding, Frederick's ill-motivated pursuit of the unsuspecting Miss Scruggs, the new widow's genuine agony at the loss of her beloved young husband, all these juicy morsels of gossip quickly shriveled to mere dessicated jerky-bits of tittle-tattle on that crisp October evening when Preston Bedford came rushing into the bar and breathlessly announced:

"They've taken her in!"

And so they had, they being Frederick's parents and she being their pregnant daughter-in-law. This news was startling enough to anyone who knew the Austin-Cowleses' stringent outlook as to who was and was not socially acceptable. (They regarded the Pilgrim Fathers as pushy immigrants, the Johnny-Alden-come-lately embodiment of all that was dragging

241

America down into the populist mire.) But this was as nothing when compared to what followed, namely, the intense, immediate, and profound change we all observed in Margot and Hilliard the moment that little Wylda Serene was born.

She was a lovely child, for someone who had begun her existence as a means of petty payback. Her mother's reliable bread-and-butter comeliness had given a much-needed anchor to Wylda's father's frailer caviar-and-cabernet attractions. Her infant prettiness was but a faint harbinger of the glorious beauty she grew to be. Fiery red-gold hair, luminous skin, and eyes the color of newly unfurled leaves adorned a lithe and vibrant body of unquestionable appeal. She carried herself with the poise and elegance of a young gazelle, and her curves put the corniche at Monte Carlo to shame.

Her besotted grandparents gave her everything. Unlike their behavior toward their late son, every benefit they conferred upon his posthumous child was innocent of any agenda save her happiness. When she became an articulate being, she had but to voice a wish, however fanciful, and all the social and financial clout of the Austin-Cowles family would be brought into play for the sole purpose of fulfilling that desire.

Overindulgence of the young is a perilous thing. Children spoil more readily than oysters in July. Her grandparents' inexhaustible worship might have caused little Wylda's life to go very bad very quickly if she had entertained any unsuitable desires, but she had none, *none!* She accepted all the gifts and benefits with which her adoring grandparents showered her, doing so with a quiet graciousness fit to make the Queen of England look like a mule skinner by comparison, yet not one of these was ever her idea. She requested nothing.

Shame on that jaded soul who would leap to the cynical conclusion that Wylda's behavior was sly in the extreme, that she was mistress of the ancient art of acquisition through the Request Indirect. It was not so. She never dropped a hint, never sighed over high-ticket gewgaws, never wondered aloud how much was that doggie, dress, or Daimler in the window. She never so much as wrote a letter to Santa Claus.

If it is truly more blessed to give than to receive, young Wylda was sanctified in spades. Her grandparents gave her worldly gifts, but she gave them something infinitely more precious: the sincere, bone-deep docility that her father had died withholding.

She had not a single rebellious bone in her body, neither mutinous heart nor insubordinate mind.

In this she took after her mother. The Austin-Cowles manner of living was quite literally stunning to a woman of the former Miss Scruggs's social class. In the twenty-three years between Wylda's birth and wedding, the erstwhile florist's assistant dwelled in nigh-nunlike self-effacement in the shadow of her dynamic in-laws. Apart from the occasional command appearance at family functions, one would hardly guess she was there. This suited all parties concerned admirably.

I was in The Club bar discussing the finer points of bespoke golf balls with ten of my fellow members on that February day when Hilliard Austin-Cowles made the grand announcement. He drifted into our midst like a curl of bourbon-laced tobacco smoke, beckoned the barman, conveyed his desires in a whisper, then sat down in the leather armchair most removed from the rest of us. Within moments we knew that something was afoot, for through the bartender's particular sort of magic, there now appeared at our several elbows bottles of a buxom Veuve Clicquot champagne, served up in

The Club's best crystal flutes.

We maintained the silence proper to the occasion. When a gentleman sets drink of such quality before so many, it would be uncivil to rush him into an explanation. However, etiquette did not forbid us from sampling that effervescent nectar, and so we sipped and waited, waited and sipped. We knew that Hilliard was acutely aware of our painful curiosity and that, being human, he relished our mounting discomfort even more than we savored his champagne.

At last he spoke: "My friends, thank you for joining me in a modest drink. It's not every day that one's only grandchild becomes engaged to be married."

A politely muted clamor of congratulation went up from all our vintage-moistened lips. Bit by bit, we teased further details out of Hilliard's rock-ribbed old Yankee reticence. The name of the prospective bridegroom — one Miles Martial — was universally unfamiliar and, once uttered, required a fair portion of explication.

"Do you know, it was the strangest thing," Hilliard said. "At first our Wylda was abnormally secretive when Margot and I asked her how she met the gentleman. When we pressed her — we do have the right to know everything about our grandchild's life —

she became vague."

"Good heavens!" cried Middleton. He was not quite our Oldest Member, but well enough advanced in years. "Was there something unsavory in the man's background, or was some aspect of their introduction . . . improper? Hilliard, I'm astonished that you'd give your blessing to any of this."

A brief frown flittered across Hilliard's patrician features. "And I am astonished at your level of self-deception. Really, Cadby" — long acquaintance permitted him the employment of Middleton's Christian name — "your attraction to my granddaughter is common knowledge, as ill considered as it's ill concealed."

Middleton blushed and sputtered. "I resent your allegations deeply, Hilliard," he said. "Of course I'm fond of the child. I'm only concerned about her future happiness. If the circumstances surrounding her introduction to the man she intends to marry" — here he could not prevent his voice from breaking just a bit — "are so irregular that she withholds them even from you, perhaps you should stop this from going any farther. Purely for Wylda's sake, of course. She's young. With matters of the heart, the young tend to get . . . ideas, frivolous ones. In the long run, she'd benefit from the guidance of older, wiser heads."

"Tchah!" Thus Hilliard dismissed Middleton's clumsily veiled agenda. "My granddaughter hasn't had a frivolous idea in her life. As it happened, they met at a dog show last May. Martial's pedigreed mastiff, Champion Caesar Alexander's Philippi of Austerlitz-Manassas, took Best in Class. Her little school chum, Solana Winthrop, introduced her to Martial when Wylda remarked how much she would like to have a closer look at the winning canine. From that *most* proper introduction, mutual affection bloomed."

"Solana Winthrop . . ." I mused aloud upon the name. "How could she have been in attendance at a dog show last May? We were told that she would be studying art history in Paris from April through December."

"Er, yes," said Elwood Porter, who had married Solana's elder sister Meredith. "It turned out that her need to study art history was a false alarm."

"So you see, Wylda's reticence was motivated by discretion, not deception," Hilliard added. "Until Solana's family might find a tactful way to announce her reappearance in Society, Wylda chose to shield her friend.

Once there was no further need for confidentiality, she was suitably frank with her grandmother and me. Of course we also made our own inquiries. Miles Martial's bona fides are impeccable. He comes from an ancient family with unimpeachable connections in the worlds of finance, industry, and politics. The bulk of his fortune is derived from munitions, with prudent diversification in aviation technology, shipbuilding, and applied biochemical research."

"In other words, he's worth a mint," Hasbrook whispered in my ear. "And likely to stay so. You don't go broke catering wars."

"Have the happy couple set a date for the wedding?" Porter asked our host.

"As a matter of fact, our Wylda has decided on a June wedding."

Here Hilliard spared a moment to glare at us en masse, in case anyone would have the supremely bad taste to begin counting the months between now and June. A natural but unnecessary reaction on the part of that devoted grandparent: We had no need to resort to spiteful calculations in order to conclude that the girl was quite *out* of the family way. This was February. If Wylda had been in a condition delicate enough to oblige either marriage or the abrupt study of art history, a June wedding would display her indiscretion for all the world to see, even if she glided down the aisle in an oversized Empire-waisted bridal gown.

"Well, well, a June wedding!" Middleton affected a cheery air that fooled no one. "How nice to see that there are still some young people who value tradition. And where will the event take place?"

"Why, right here, of course," said Hilliard. "At The Club."

Elwood Porter gave a little cry of distress and dropped his champagne.

It was about a month later, as the caterer flies, that I was approached by Porter and Middleton on a matter of some delicacy. Rather than discuss the matter over drinks at The Club, they instead invited me to join them in New Haven for a private dinner at Morey's. There they laid matters on the table.

"You *must* speak with Hilliard," Middleton said. "You must make him see that what Wylda has in mind is out of the question. There must not be a wedding at The Club."

"Who knows what will happen if there is?" Porter shuddered and darted his eyes to left and right, as though the physical embodiment of Dire Consequences somehow had managed to procure a neighboring table.

(An impossibility, of course: Access to Morey's is reserved for carefully selected Yale men and — reluctantly I concede it — women. Dire Consequences and the Ivy League simply do not mix socially.)

"My friends," I said, "I understand your trepidation. I, too, feel somewhat less than sanguine at the prospect of such an event taking place at The Club, and with good cause: I have been a member since well before that dreadful day when Simpson turned our world upon its head."

"Ah yes," said Middleton, who had been a member of The Club for even longer than I. "Simpson." He pronounced the ill-starred name with the same intonation that medieval folk might have reserved for remarking, *Ah yes, the Black Death.*

To understand the enormity of harm that Simpson perpetrated upon The Club, it is best if first you comprehend The Club itself and all that it entails. Set amid the greenest of PGA-worthy golf courses, it is a monument to exquisite sophistication and understated luxury. It is blessed with a dining room whose innumerable perfections of cuisine send the most fastidious gourmets into gales of frustrated tears when they find absolutely nothing about which to complain. The wine cellar and the bar are stocked and tended by men who are more like high priests in the Holy Brotherhood of Grape and Grain rather than mere names on The Club payroll.

In the past, The Club had been the site of winter balls, summer dances, spring fêtes, autumn banquets, debutante cotillions, ladies' luncheons, gentlemen's smokers, high teas, and formal dinners to bewail or celebrate the outcome of The Game. (The *only* Game, that glorious struggle for gridiron supremacy between Yale and Harvard, beside which conflict the Hundred Years' War was a mere bagatelle, a historical hissy fit.) Indeed, as I have said already, The Club was the setting for the final chapter in my sister Katherine's matrimonial history.

Simpson changed all that.

He was one of that chancy yet unavoidable subgroup within The Club's membership, a Legacy. Had he applied for admission independent of his ancestors, his own character, attitude, and finances might not have permitted the Committee to accept him with open arms. As matters and the bylaws stood, they were obliged to do so.

Simpson was a rogue, a wild cannon, a smart aleck whose notion of an excellent jape tended to the exotic. It was this rather outré sense of humor that motivated him to bring back from his European travels a souvenir that changed both the fate and the face of The Club irrevocably.

It was a sphinx.

The sphinx in question was not of the Egyptian breed but Greek. Its leonine body did not stretch at ease upon the eternal desert sands but sat upright, winged like an eagle, poised for action. In retrospect, "it" is quite the wrong pronoun to apply to the beast, for it had a woman's head and pert, naked breasts. Moreover, lest you think that Simpson's sin against The Club was merely the donation of a somewhat vulgar statue, allow me to provide enlightenment: This sphinx was real.

None of us at The Club had any idea how Simpson managed to locate such a marvel, let alone transport her through Customs unmolested. We were too well-bred to ask, and Simpson was too much the slyboots to volunteer anything. He was one of those tedious people who believe that sitting on information like a broody hen upon the nest gives the sitter a mystical superiority over those *not* in the know.

Simpson's sphinx was named Oenone, and she had her breed's taste for blood and riddles. Tradition taught that the monster could not tear you to bloody bite-sized bits unless you failed to answer her sole riddle, so it was all rather sporting, in a ghastly way. Since everyone at The Club enjoyed the benefits of a Classical education, we all knew the answer to the sphinx's riddle from the story of Oedipus: What goes on four legs at dawn, two legs at noon, three legs at sunset? *Man.* Armed with this smug certainty, we agreed to Simpson's suggestion that Oenone be given prowling space on the back nine. It seemed wholly safe and somewhat piquant to permit her presence. It made The Club *different.*

"Different" is not an abiding synonym for "better," as we discovered to our grief on the day that Oenone learned some new riddles. That was when the disappearances began.

When we finally discovered why so many members were not returning from their appointed round of golf, Oenone took off for parts unknown. So did Simpson, but the damage was done: The sphinx's residence somehow had imbued our beloved Club with an otherworldly musk that attracted other mythic entities as capital gains draw tax vampires. These incursions made up for in ferocity what they lacked in frequency, for which we were as thankful as the circumstances allowed. How much comfort can one derive from the phrase *Why, yes, we* do *have bloodbaths here at The Club, but not really all that often?* The insecurity was almost as dire as the actual incidents: As with Democratic presidencies, we lived in constant fear, never knowing when the next one would occur.

This state of affairs tended to make most members think twice before engaging The Club as the setting for a grand-scale private affair like a wedding. Of what use the perfectly set table, the superbly prepared meal, if ultimately it would be befouled by an invasion of harpies? Moreover, mythology burgeoned with tales of weddings gone horribly wrong.

The battle of the Lapiths and the centaurs at the marriage of Theseus' bosom chum Perithoös occurred when the caterer neglected to note that creatures half man and half horse cannot hold their liquor in either half. A bit too much of the grape caused one centaur to confuse the bride with a wedding favor. He attempted to carry her off and the melee was on.

The Trojan War began at a wedding. Achilles' parents-to-be, the hero Pelias and the nymph Thetis, imagined they could avoid future marital unpleasantness by not inviting Eris to their nuptials. Eris was goddess of Discord, not Good Sportsmanship, and so took umbrage. Her umbrage in turn took the shape of a golden apple inscribed *For the Fairest,* which she tossed into the midst of the wedding reception. The beauty pageant brouhaha that ensued among the other goddesses led to the no-win Judgment of Paris, the abduction of Helen, the ten years' siege of Troy, and the eventual death of the aforementioned Achilles. To top off the ironic futility of it all, the marriage of Thetis and Pelias ended in divorce.

We all wanted better things for Wylda.

"I will speak to Hilliard," I said. "I will use all my powers of suasion, though for the life of me, I fail to see why this is necessary. The man is no newcomer to The Club. He knows our history. If I made no objection the very instant he declared Wylda's wedding plans, it was only because I was dumbfounded. What was he thinking?"

"He adores his granddaughter," Middleton reminded me. "Love is blind and blinding. Perhaps the sweet child has her heart set on a Club wedding and he didn't have the will to deny her wishes."

"Or the wish to terrify her by letting her know the reason why a Club wedding might not be the best idea," Porter added.

"True," I averred. "She has led a very

sheltered life. It is possible to visit The Club and never know the frightful things that happened there unless one is told."

"I suppose there is a chance that Wylda's wedding won't attract the attention of any mythical monsters," Porter ventured, ever the optimist. "She's such a charming girl; I'd hate to see her disappointed, and it *has* been far too long since The Club last enjoyed a celebration that wasn't spoiled by chaos, bloodshed, and forfeited security deposits."

"Are you suggesting that we risk so very much on the *chance* that nothing will happen? That we *gamble* with Wylda's wedding?" Middleton demanded, his snowy brows drawn together in an expression of the utmost severity. "I thought that you and I were in agreement, Porter: This marriage must not take place!"

"Don't you mean this *wedding?*" Porter ventured to correct the elder gentleman.

Middleton crimsoned, though it was impossible to determine whether it was with rage, embarrassment at his too-Freudian slip, or both. "Don't chop logic with me, sir!" he snapped. "None of *my* female relatives ever needed to go to Europe to study art history!"

I sorrow to report that at this instance

Porter felt compelled to defend the moral probity of his sister-in-law, which he did by seizing upon Middleton's autumnal passion for Wylda and flinging it in that man's venerable face. From there on, the dialogue between Porter and Middleton degenerated into personal remarks concerning the extended families of both men. The longer I sat there, the stronger grew my conviction that some people did not require the intervention of either gods or monsters to make an ugly hash of their lives. When at last I could bear to witness no more of such unsuitable sniping, I made my excuses and left the table, the establishment, and the city of New Haven. I have no idea when Porter or Middleton noticed that I was gone.

I made it my business to call upon the Austin-Cowles family within the week. I might have saved myself the trouble: Middleton was right.

"It was Wylda's idea," Margot told me as we sat taking tea together. She was attended by her husband and daughter-in-law, though the former Miss Scruggs might as well have been an umbrella stand for all the notice her in-laws paid her throughout my visit. "I wasn't happy with it, but she insisted: The wedding and the reception both will take place at The Club."

Hilliard confirmed this. "We both tried explaining the situation to her — Simpson, the sphinx, and the way things have been ever since. She thought we were joking."

A nostalgic look washed over Margot's elegant features. "Do you recall how it used to be, before that dreadful man and his bloodthirsty pet ruined everything?" she asked me. "The Club reception for your own dear sister's final wedding was one of the last *sane* events to be held there."

At the mention of my sister's nuptials, the former Miss Scruggs gave a deep, heartfelt sigh. "I remember that," she said, her face radiant, her eyes luminous with dreams, her voice so soft as to border on the inaudible. "I never saw anything so beautiful. It was the most wonderful day of my life. I still dream about it."

I was about to interject a polite remark in reply when Hilliard forged on as if his daughter-in-law had said nothing at all.

"It's lucky that The Club's budget is firmly founded on dues and the occasional bequest, or by now it would be bankrupt. No one engages The Club for personal events anymore. Even though *every* Club affair doesn't attract mythic undesirables, no one wants to play the odds."

"And yet, you are going to do just that, in three months' time," I pointed out.

Hilliard sighed. "If I could change the situation, I'd do it without a second thought."

Like any properly bred person of a certain social standing, I loathed to soil my lips by speaking of pecuniary matters — off the Trading Floor, that is — but in this case I felt compelled to inquire, "Have you not, then, taken the simple step of *refusing to pay* for the wedding unless it is held elsewhere?"

Margot blushed and for decency's sake averted her eyes from me the instant such mercantile words left my lips, nor could I blame her. Wylda's mother tensed visibly. Hilliard merely bowed his head.

"Of course I have," he said. "To no avail. For some reason she refuses to disclose, it's appallingly *vital* to our Wylda to have her wedding at The Club. After all these years, that sweet, docile child has become a veritable tiger on this one point. She's determined to have her wedding at The Club or not at all."

And there it was, my defeat. All further argument would be futile. There is no fortress more unassailable than the resolution of a heretofore submissive woman. Such creatures take all the willpower they have deferred during a lifetime of obedience, compliance, and meekness, gather it into one titanic mass, and focus it like a laser beam.

"She's always been such a *good* girl," Margot said plaintively. "She's never really wanted anything from us until now. How could we say no?"

They could not. We all knew it. The wedding would go on when and where Wylda decreed.

As for *how* it would go on . . . that remained to be seen.

As the date of Wylda's wedding drew nigh, The Club turned all atwitter. First there was the matter of the invitations. Those members who were included in the upcoming festivities wore satisfied smiles that were nonetheless somewhat wobbly at the corners. It was a privilege to be included at any fête hosted by that the Austin-Cowleses. No expense would be spared, no luxury be wanting. There would be lavishness without flash, sumptuousness tempered by sophistication.

And yet not a single mouthful of the best Sevruga caviar would pass the lips of any man or woman there without the passing shudder, the momentary frisson of trepidation, and the hasty, sidelong glance in the direction of the nearest exit. In short, my fellow invitees and myself would enjoy dear Wylda's wedding under a cloud, for who knew when or whether the beautiful display would be shattered?

Those members whose association with Margot and Hilliard was not close enough to procure them an invitation consoled themselves with many a goblet of Château des Sour Grapes: We wedding guests might dine on oysters, *pâté de foie gras, filet de boeuf,* and truffles, but our excluded brethren were certain that we would be gulping antacid tablets with every second mouthful.

I am convinced that the rumors concerning Wylda's fiancé originated with one of those embittered exiles from her approaching wedding. (It also might have been Middleton's doing. His unrequited ardor for young Wylda had festered badly. Melancholia possessed him, and each day seemed to sap a further measure of joy from his life. On the other hand, given his age, perhaps he simply had acid reflux.) Whoever began it, it spread rapidly. It was quite basic, as rumors go. No dark mutterings about the groom-to-be's latent vices, past debaucheries, ongoing addictions, or previous wives kept in fetters in the attic, merely this: "Why hasn't anyone *seen* this man?"

The obvious answer was, of course, that Miles Martial *had* been seen, and not solely by members of Wylda's immediate family. Had not Solana Winthrop introduced them?

But Solana Winthrop was only one soul, and a soul somewhat besmirched by the blot of unanticipated art history studies abroad. *What,* the vile whisperers in corners demanded, *what was* wrong *with the man, that kept him so shrouded in mystery?*

It was under these circumstances that I received a telephone call from Wylda's mother, the former Nora Scruggs, entreating me to bring Mr. Martial to The Club for dinner, or at least cocktails. To be frank, there were certain additional conditions in play at the time: My visit to the Austin-Cowles ménage had left me somewhat smitten by the physical attractions of Miss Scruggs, and as the lady was not averse, we struck up a relationship of mutual benefit soon thereafter.

"Please say you'll do it," my bourgeois beloved pleaded. "This would be the best way to smash those nasty rumors once and for all."

"Certainly, yes," I replied. "But would it

not be more appropriate for Hilliard to escort your daughter's betrothed?"

Nora gave a small, plaintive cry. "He *won't* do it. He said that an Austin-Cowles doesn't let a bunch of blabbermouth rumormongers *make* him do anything; it would be *surrendering.* I tried telling him that this isn't some stupid battle, but he wouldn't listen. Darling, you're my only hope."

My tender feelings for Nora restrained me from pointing out that the social niceties *are* a battle. It was easier to give her what she wanted.

I met Miles Martial at the train depot on a Saturday afternoon in late May. It was a traumatic encounter. Some people are blessed — if that is the proper word — with the ability to *invade* the space they occupy. I am not speaking of those theatrical individuals who flaunt, posture, and play to the cheap seats with every move they make. Anyone can draw attention to himself by making a scene.

Miles Martial belonged to a different breed, monumental without being melodramatic. He was a tall, brawny, well-built specimen of manhood, but as the polite lie goes, size is not everything. He was also handsome enough to dazzle. The sight of him, bronzed and blond, with steel blue eyes, perfect teeth, and a profile purloined from Michelangelo's *David,* filled my heart with a nauseating swirl of personal inadequacy and overpowering envy. In that moment I knew that no ordinary human being could ever *see* Miles Martial so much as *behold* him. There is a difference, as vast as it is subtle.

I also knew, in quick succession, that

1. I wanted to punch him in the face, for no other reason than because it was *there.*
2. Every man at The Club would share my feelings.
3. Were we fools enough to turn impulse into action, he would sidestep our blows easily and then, with insouciant grace, show us the way it should be done, i.e., accurately and painfully.
4. Every woman at The Club would behold Miles Martial and immediately desire the slaughter of dear, sweet, accursedly lucky little Wylda.
5. This was going to kill poor old Middleton.

Miles leaped into my car the instant that I pulled up at the depot, a grin in my direction his only greeting.

"Mr. Martial?" I said, just in case I might have picked up the wrong person by mistake. (Ah, fleeting hope, swiftly dashed!)

"Bingo," he said, pointing his index finger at me pistol-style and vocalizing a passable gunshot sound effect as he brought the thumb hammer down. He even went so far as to blow invisible smoke from his fingertip afterward.

My attempts to make light conversation during the drive to The Club met with mixed results. When I asked him whether the trip from New York City had been pleasant, he replied, "New York? Is that where I came from? Oh, right, right. Hey, buddy, you've gotta excuse me, I'm a little snafued these days. *Lots* of travel under the old belt. I just flew in from the Middle East yesterday and boy, are my arms tired." He filled my automobile with raw laughter.

It was a relief to rid myself of the man, even if only for the time it took to give my vehicle into the care of a parking valet. Miles Martial did not wait for me but bounded through the front doors and proceeded to take The Club by storm.

As it was a Saturday afternoon, the place swarmed with golfers and tennis players. His effect on the crowd was approximately what I had anticipated and yet, despite the amount of smoldering envy his physical perfections kindled, he somehow managed to create his own admiring bar-room coterie in the short time it took for me to rejoin him.

I should have been pleased to note how readily he had made his social conquests, but I could not do so with a whole heart: There was something vaguely disquieting about Wylda's beau. Although the tranquil surface of a pond reflects the silver beauty of the moon, that is no guarantee against it teeming with alligators. A smattering of caution would determine whether you came away from the encounter with a haiku or a bloody stump where your right hand used to be.

I regret to say that, at the moment, I did not express my uneasiness to anyone. I had done my duty by pleasing Nora; I needed to do no more.

There is something about weddings capable of thrilling the least romantic heart. Mine was no exception. By the day of her daughter's nuptials, the relationship between Nora Austin-Cowles (née Scruggs) and myself had reached a certain level of physical intimacy, but that signified little. Ordinary

266

alley cats can claim such amorous familiarity. When the lady demurely asked me to act as her escort, that was a truer gauge of my status in her eyes than a score of unclothed, oiled, and raucous hours spent together. It gave me sweet hope that I might yet see the light of matrimony at the end of the somber tunnel of bachelorhood.

The morning of Wylda's wedding dawned bright with sunshine tempered by an understandable miasma of anxiety. Many a guest's neck was wrenched painfully as high-strung souls strove to keep one eye on the nearest exit at all times.

Not everyone present was in an advanced state of nerves. Some were not merely tranquil but downright apathetic. Among these latter was Wylda's aged admirer, Middleton.

"Oh dear," said Nora. We were standing together at the door to the Oak Room, where the preceremony cocktail reception was taking place. "That's Mr. Middleton's *third* martini! I hope he knows what he's doing."

"He knows exactly what he is doing," I told her. "He is getting drunk."

"Drunk?" Nora's eyes went wide with shock, although there was the hint of a hotter emotion in her voice as she added: "At

my daughter's wedding?"

Being a gentleman, I could not reveal Middleton's motivation for seeking solace in liquor. I doubt it would have evoked Nora's sympathy. Instead, I offered her the weak consolation that excessive drink rendered Middleton melancholy and silent rather than loud and vulgar. His alcoholic excesses posed no threat to the smooth progress of Wylda's wedding.

Nora saw matters otherwise: "I don't care; he's still being a jerk. What if he gets ugly later on? This is just like something one of *my* relatives would pull. I grew up thinking that you couldn't have a wedding or a funeral or a baby shower or even *dinner* without someone making a scene. When your sister asked me to be her bridesmaid, and when I saw how *beautifully* you people behave, it was like a glimpse of heaven. No arguments, no fights, no cursing, nothing but dignity and refinement and *peace.* I only wish that Freddie and I could've had a wedding like that, here at The Club, but he was so insistent about eloping to Vegas . . . ! Well, maybe I didn't get the wedding of my dreams, but Wylda will."

Besotted as I was, I remained oblivious to the true sentiment underlying those words, namely: *Wylda will get the wedding of* my *dreams, and God help anyone who gets in the way.*

The preceremony reception ended and we progressed to the marriage rite itself, conducted in The Club rose garden. The setting was idyllic, the air perfumed, the flowers at that ideal point of maturity, blossoming but not yet blown. The guests sat in rows of white folding chairs decorated with snowy satin ribbons. As escort to the mother of the bride, I sat up front beside her, smiling like a sentimental ninny. A string quartet played a delicate air by Vivaldi to herald the groom. Miles Martial looked striking in his Prince Edward coat and trim gray trousers. As he took his place beside the minister from St. George's (who, at the Austin-Cowleses' behest, had consented to make a house call) his grin was brilliant enough to blind legions of paparazzi.

The lone bridesmaid, Solana Winthrop, walked down the aisle to a Mozart sonata, and then it was time for Wylda to make her entrance on her grandfather's arm. As the strings began to play Wagner's traditional tripe, we all rose on cue and turned to honor the bride.

"Stop the wedding!" A towering beautiful naked woman appeared out of nowhere and hip-checked Hilliard across the laps of the

269

guests in the back row. As chairs toppled like dominoes, she grabbed Wylda by the scruff of the neck and held the keen point of a foot-long golden projectile against the base of the girl's throat. "Nobody move! This is one of Eros's sharpest arrows, and I'm not afraid to use it!"

A communal gasp of fear and dread arose from all of us. The woman's extraordinary stature and splendor, her utter shamelessness, and her casual mention of Eros, the ancient Greek god of Love, left us no doubt that The Club had once more worked its undesired magic. Alas, this time we had been invaded by a creature more dire than any sphinx, harpy, gorgon, or minotaur, a being who commanded the most awesomely destructive power in the universe: Aphrodite, queen of Love and Beauty, had arrived.

She had not arrived alone.

"Way to go, Mom! *Work* that thing!" The vote of confidence came from one of a pair of tall, handsome young men who materialized beside the goddess. Their faces, hair, and clothing — tattered loincloths, nothing more — were all lavishly stained with smoke, ashes, gun oil, and blood.

"Don't call me that!" the naked woman snapped. "Just because I screwed your father doesn't make me your mom, Deimos!"

"So what does it make you now that you're *not* screwing him anymore?" the other one asked snidely.

"Don't worry, Phobos," the woman replied. "That's all about to change."

"Oh, my God!" Nora exclaimed, rising to her feet. "Doesn't this place have any security? You! Crazy naked lady! Get the hell away from my daughter!"

"*What* did you call me?" The goddess's eyes narrowed dangerously. She pressed the arrow point even closer to Wylda's flesh. The poor child's moans of terror sent the two ill-clad young men into ecstasies.

I clamped my hand across my beloved's mouth and dragged her back down into her seat. "If you value Wylda's life, be quiet," I whispered vehemently in her ear. "This is exactly what I feared might happen." Then, as swiftly and as succinctly as possible, I informed my delectably undereducated sweetheart as to the true nature of our uninvited guests.

For those who know the old Greek tales, there is a special irony to the catchphrase *Make love, not war.* Though Aphrodite was the wife of Hephaestus, weapons maker for the gods, the goddess of Love could not resist the potent attraction of Ares, god of War. Their adulterous union became, quite literally, the stuff of myth.

Now, for whatever reason, Ares apparently had tired of his divine ladylove. Like many another randy god — including his own sire, Zeus — Ares had disguised his true nature the better to conquer a comely mortal maiden.

"Unfortunately, it seems that Aphrodite is not the sort to deal well with rejection. What is worse, her rage is such that it has attracted Ares' sons, Deimos and Phobos, the gods of Fear and Terror. They are — *ow!*"

Nora had bitten my hand.

She fought free of my grasp and leaped back to her feet, bristling with fury. "Are you telling me that *my* baby's wedding is being spoiled because *that* two-bit toy soldier's been boinking *that* bimbo behind her husband's back for *how* long?"

"Hey!" There was nothing wrong with Nora's lungs or the gods' ears. Ares and Aphrodite heard her well enough and objected in chorus. The soi-disant Miles Martial strode forth to confront Nora. With each step, another facet of his mortal masquerade blew away like morning mist before the advent of the bronze helmet, breastplate, and greaves, the bloodred

loincloth, the shining spear, sword, and shield, and the iron-soled sandals of Ares. He ignored Aphrodite and Wylda, behaving as if his bride-to-be were not still in peril of her life at the hands of his mistress-that-was.

"What did you just say about me, woman?" he bawled in Nora's face. (Or rather, down upon it, for Ares had regained his divine stature and now towered over her by at least three feet.)

"Great, you're as dumb as she is." Nora jerked her thumb at Aphrodite. "Pay attention and take notes: You've got two minutes to ditch the bitch and the brats; then we're going to get this wedding back on track before the ice-sculpture swans melt, *or else.* Got it?"

"But Mommy, I don't *want* to marry him anymore," Wylda whimpered. "He lied to me, and he's got kids, and a girlfriend, and he's not even human, and —"

"Shut up!" Nora stamped her foot. "I spent the past twenty-three years of my life planning this day. You'll marry him and like it!"

"Wow," Phobos breathed, his eyes brimming with admiration as he gazed upon the wrath of Scruggs. "Now *that's* scary! I think I'm in love."

"I saw her first, loser!" Deimos yelled, and sprang upon his brother. The two of them vanished in a whirlwind of punches, kicks, and obscene name-calling. Fear and Terror might be potent forces in the short run, but they had very little staying power in civilized society.

"Don't you *dare* talk like that to the woman I love!" Thunder reverberated over our heads. However, it had nothing to do with the god of War, who had not so much as opened his mouth. The booming command had come from Middleton. The older man swept down upon Nora with a warrior's battle wrath. "If Wylda doesn't want to marry this scoundrel, she *won't.* She's a grown woman, not your dress-up bride doll, and it's about time you knew that!"

In spite of her stated yearning for sophistication, elegance, and peace, Nora's family heritage could not be suppressed or denied. She had been raised by people who never fled the field of battle except to fetch larger guns, and it showed.

"You're *drunk,*" she spat. "You're drunk and you're old and you'd like it just fine if my daughter were your *un*dress bride doll. Well, guess what, Grampa? *Not* gonna happen. This wedding is *go.*"

"Never!" Aphrodite protested. The goddess of Love was not used to being ignored and had decided to drag the spotlight back onto herself. "Ares doesn't *really* want to marry this little jellyfish. He started this whole stupid oooh-I'm-in-love-with-a-mortal thing because I haven't been paying enough attention to him lately. Just because a girl goes to a couple, nine Brad Pitt movies —"

"Who asked *you?*" Before the astonished eyes of gods and men, Nora stormed up to Aphrodite and slapped her face. The goddess was so startled that she dropped the golden arrow of Eros and lost her grip on Wylda. "Don't blame *my* baby if you don't know how to hold on to *your* man."

Aphrodite was still immobilized with shock as Nora grabbed Wylda by the wrist, hauled her down the aisle, and shoved her into Ares' arms. When Middleton tried to intervene, Nora laid him low with an impressive right cross.

Wylda witnessed her mother's summary treatment of the older gentleman and looked ready to burst into tears. The god of War kept darting nervous glances from his bride to his potential mother-in-law. His expression was that of a man firmly in the grip of second thoughts, his feet grown cold enough to bring on a new Ice Age.

"Was she always this big a control freak?" Ares asked his betrothed.

"Only since I told her we were getting married," Wylda said quietly. "I don't know why, but that started it. That was when Mommy . . . *changed.*" Wylda shivered at the awful memory. "She made me ask my grandparents for this huge, silly wedding as if it was all *my* idea, but I never wanted to get married at The Club."

"I'll tell you what you want and don't want!" Nora declared to her daughter.

"And what if *I* no longer wish this marriage to take place?" Ares brandished his sword in a menacing manner, but his attempt at last-minute intimidation was crushed the moment he looked Nora in the eye. The poor deity trembled so hard that his armor rattled. "Uhhh, forget I said anything," he said hastily sheathing the blade.

As I sat nursing my bitten hand and observing this heretofore unknown aspect of dear Nora's personality, I realized two things: one, that there are far worse fates than bachelorhood, and two, that while my beloved Club did attract monsters, alas, they did not all derive from Greek mythology. The tantrums of the most outrageous Bridezilla in the world are trifles beside the blazing chaos incarnate of the *Mother* of the Bridezilla.

Not that you could call sweet, timorous Wylda any sort of 'zilla. The poor thing seemed to be so thoroughly browbeaten by her monstrous mother that I wondered whether Wylda had a stick of striped sugar candy where her backbone should be.

I have since learned that it is possible to kill a man by stabbing him to death with a broken candy cane.

"You don't want to marry me?" Wylda asked her beau.

"Of course I do," Ares replied. But his eyes were still fixed nervously on Nora.

"No, you don't," Wylda stated. His mouth trembled. "You don't, and everyone here knows you don't, and the only reason you're saying you do is because Mommy's got you so terrified you're going to pee your pants."

"I am not!" Ares maintained. "I'm not wearing pants."

"And I'm not getting married." Wylda tore off her veil and flung it to the ground. "I quit."

Before Nora could reexert her imperious power over her daughter, the girl fled up the aisle. Aphrodite cheered. Nora took to her heels in hot pursuit of the wayward bride, but if she thought that simple escape was Wylda's intent, the girl quickly proved her wrong. At the head of the aisle, Wylda stooped suddenly and seized something from the grass, then whirled around just in time for her mother to collide with her head-on. The two women went cartwheeling over the lawn and fetched up in a thorny heap at the foot of a Mamie Eisenhower rosebush.

"Wylda, you get back to your groom *right this minute!*" Nora shrilled. "You're ruining my wedding."

"If you want this wedding so much, *you* have it," Wylda shot back, and stabbed her mother to the heart.

Nora looked down slowly at the slim, glittering shaft protruding from the center of her chest. She touched it lightly, and it crumbled to dust that blew away on the wind. There was no mark to show where it had been, no drop of blood, not the smallest tear in the bosom of her dress. She turned her head slowly from side to side as if she were awakening from a deep sleep with no idea at all of where she was or how she had come to be there.

Cadby Middleton was a gentleman of the old school. Although Wylda's mother had creased his jaw like a championship prizefighter, he could not allow a lady in an awkward public posture to remain unassisted. He stepped gingerly around Wylda — whom he now regarded not so much with love as apprehension — and approached the fallen Fury.

"May I?" he said calmly. Still dazed, Nora accepted the hand he proffered.

The sky rippled. The earth moved. The birds broke into hosannas of song. The roses exploded like fireworks, shooting fountains of fragrant petals everywhere. A halo of blinding silver light engulfed Middleton and the former Miss Scruggs, and when the flash faded they were locked in a kiss of such intensity that Aphrodite herself gave them a standing ovation.

It was a lovely wedding. Ares gave the bride away as quickly as he could, with Aphrodite as her maid of honor. Hilliard Austin-Cowles proposed the first toast at the reception. (It was less a toast than an announcement in which he declared he would see us all in hell before he paid for one second of this wedding. The happy groom promptly wrote out a check for the full amount, crumpled it up, and stuffed it in Hilliard's ear.)

Wylda Serene was unable to attend her mother's wedding reception. Ever the altruist, she instead volunteered to drive me to the hospital so that my bitten hand might be treated before infection set in.

We drove in silence until at last I remarked, "What a pleasant surprise to discover that a person of your generation is so familiar with Greek mythology. You knew that Love's own arrow would transform your mother's heart to the point where it would overrule her wedding-mad mind, and that the halo effect of Eros's power would enamor the first person with whom she came into physical contact. Brilliant."

"Not really," Wylda replied with becoming modesty. "I just wanted to kill her. But the way it all turned out was pretty good, too."

I arched one brow and gave the girl a speculative look. "It would appear that I have underestimated you, my dear. What other surprises are there beneath your façade of meekness and docility?"

"You're cute, for an older guy. Why don't we find out?" she responded with a smile, and reached over to pat my leg.

That is, I *presumed* she wished to pat my leg. As to which portion of my anatomy she *did* pat —

It was a long drive, but another lovely wedding at journey's end. A Las Vegas wedding, true, but at least the drag *artiste/* minister at the Church of Eternal Glitz was a Harvard man.

Nebula Award–winner ESTHER FRIESNER is the author of thirty-one novels and more than one hundred and fifty short stories, in addition to being the editor of seven popular anthologies. Her works have been published in the United States, the United Kingdom, Japan, Germany, Russia, France, Poland, and Italy. She is also a published poet, a produced playwright, and once wrote an advice column: "Ask Auntie Esther." Her articles on fiction writing have appeared in *Writer's Market* and *Writer's Digest* books.

Her latest publications are *Tempting Fate* from Dutton/Penguin and *Turn the Other Chick* from Baen Books; the fifth book in the popular Chicks in Chainmail series that she created and edits. She is married, the mother of two, harbors cats, and lives in Connecticut.

CHARMED BY THE
MOON

LORI HANDELAND

I awoke on the morning of my wedding with a big fat headache.

Most likely the result of too much wine at what we'd jokingly called the rehearsal dinner but had in truth been a security check complete with steaks and cabernet. Then again, maybe the pain in my brain was a reaction to the words "marriage," "wedding," and "Jessie McQuade" in the same sentence.

I'd lost my mind, but I wasn't exactly sure when.

Had it been the day I'd told Will I loved him? Or maybe the evening he'd asked me to marry him and I hadn't had the heart to say no again? I'd definitely been long gone when I'd agreed to a ceremony with all the froufrou nonsense that went with it.

Groaning, I levered myself out of bed and pulled back the curtain. Bright June sunlight shafted into my eyes like ice picks, and I let the drape fall over the glass.

"I still can't believe you agreed to go through with this."

I gave a little yelp and spun around, wincing at the movement, then putting my hand to my head so it wouldn't fall off.

"I told you not to drink that last gallon, but you wouldn't listen."

Leigh Tyler-Fitzgerald, one of my few friends left alive, stepped into the room. She appeared too tiny, blond, and cute for this early in the morning. She always did.

"Who the hell gave you a key?"

"Ah-ah-ah." Leigh waggled a Styrofoam cup. "Is that any way to speak to a woman bearing coffee?"

"Gimme."

I held out my hands like a child reaching for candy, and she took pity on me.

I suppose I should clarify why I'm short on friends. Not that I'd had all that many in the first place. Folks who hang around me tend to wind up dead. An occupational hazard. The same could be said of Leigh, which was probably why we'd bonded.

We're *Jäger-Suchers,* which translates to "hunter-searchers," for those of you who prefer English. We hunt things that prefer the night. Werewolves are our specialty.

Hey, I didn't believe it at first, either, but when you're staring death in the face and death has the eyes of someone you once loved, or at least knew, your belief system takes a big kick in the teeth.

The *Jäger-Suchers* are a select, secret group of operatives attempting to make the world safe, if not for democracy, at least for people who don't grow fur under the light of the moon. Unfortunately, the job is never ending. Werewolves not only like to kill; they also like to multiply — as do all their demonic cohorts.

I drank half the cup of coffee before coming up for air. My headache was still there, but it wasn't quite as bad.

"How long do I have until the wedding?"

"Long enough."

"I doubt it."

"You say that as if you're going to a funeral." Leigh sat on the bed. "What gives, Jessie? I've never seen anyone more in love than you and Will Cadotte."

Unless we were talking about her and her husband, Damien, but we weren't. At least not today.

"Love isn't the problem."

"What is?"

"I don't want to get married."

"Then why are you?"

I looked her straight in the eye. "I have no idea."

"You lost me."

"Will's been asking me to marry him for nearly a year."

I hadn't met William Cadotte under the most normal of circumstances. We were as unalike as two people could be. Will was a professor with a specialty in Native American totems. I was a cop — or at least I had been then. He was an Ojibwe, an activist, a glasses-wearing, tree-hugging book geek.

He was also hotter than hot. Women's heads nearly twisted off their necks when he walked by. He might like books, but he also liked to work out. He'd been practicing tai chi — a type of martial art that strengthened the mind as well as the body — for longer than I'd been carrying a gun. But what had gotten to me in the end was his sense of humor, if not the golden feather that swung from one ear.

I never had figured out what Will saw in me. Guys like him usually go for a girl like Leigh, but he'd never given her a second glance. I'd have thought he was gay if I hadn't enjoyed multiple evidence to the contrary.

I was a big girl — everywhere. My hair was neither brown nor blond, my eyes more shrewd than dreamy. I suppose I could have made myself presentable, if I'd cared, but I had better things to worry about.

I was tall, strong, in shape, because I had to be or die. I could drill a bullet through the eye of just about anything at a hundred yards. I had a job that I loved and a man I loved, too. Getting married . . . well, that hadn't been on my agenda.

Until the last time Will had asked me and I'd inexplicably said yes.

"I can't count how many people I've known who've gotten along just fine until they throw vows and rings and forever into the mix," I said. "Then *bam,* two months after the wedding they hate each other."

"That won't happen to you and Will. You'll be together forever."

"Forever isn't very long in our profession."

Understanding spread over Leigh's face. "Is that what's bugging you? That we might die tomorrow?"

"We might die tonight," I muttered.

One never knew.

"We're safe here."

"We aren't safe anywhere, Leigh, and you know it."

She shrugged. "*Safer* then. No one's going to sneak up on us in this place."

We'd rented out a lodge on Lake Superior in Minnesota. Will wanted to be married at the spirit tree, a twisted red cedar rumored to be three, four, even five hundred years old, depending upon whom you listened to. The tree was sacred to the Grand Portage Ojibwe, of which Will was one.

He'd grown up on the reservation, raised by his grandmother after his parents took off. When she'd died, he'd been passed to a succession of aunts and uncles. Now none of them were alive, either, but Will remembered this place with a great deal of fondness and the tree with a great deal of respect.

Since I had no strong feelings one way or another, Grand Portage was okeydokey with me.

"What if someone does sneak up on us?" I asked.

"Then we know they're werewolves and we blast them into the hell dimension. That's what we do, Jessie."

"I'd prefer we not be doing it at my wedding."

Hell, I'd prefer not to be having a wedding. So why was I?

Because I might be the roughest, toughest *Jäger-Sucher* around, but when it came to Will Cadotte, I had no guts at all. I didn't want to lose him. And wasn't that just the saddest, most pathetic admission of all?

One night he'd blindsided me with a silver

band and a moon-shaped diamond. With the bodies of wolves that weren't really wolves surrounding us, he'd pulled the thing from his pocket, slipped it onto my finger, and charmed me into marrying him.

Or maybe I'd just been charmed by the moon. Everyone else was.

"If Edward thinks we're safe, we are," Leigh said, and I knew she was right.

Our boss, Edward Mandenauer, was one spooky old man. But he was the best hunter on the planet. He knew how to set up a secure operation. If he said my wedding would be safe from werewolves, it would be, or he'd die trying to make it so. I trusted him with my life. More important, I trusted him with Will's.

Back in WW 2, Edward had been sent to obliterate Hitler's best-kept secret — a werewolf army. Too bad they'd escaped before Edward could complete his mission. Not to worry, he hadn't stopped trying.

"Want some food?" Leigh stood.

"Gack." I imitated throwing up.

"Lovely. I can see why Cadotte's so enamored of you."

"I can't."

Leigh tilted her head. "You don't think he loves you?"

"I know he loves me. And I love him."

"Then *what* is your problem?"

"Marriage is an outdated custom that's run its course."

"Oookay." Leigh twisted her wedding ring around her finger.

"No offense," I said.

"None taken."

I threw up my hands. "I can't figure out why I said yes."

"You're just having cold feet."

Hope lightened the weight in my chest. "Did you?"

"Well, no."

The hope died. There was something seriously lacking in me if I was unable to commit to the only man I'd ever loved. But I'd suspected that for a long time.

"Maybe you should talk to Will," Leigh ventured.

"I thought it was bad luck to see him before the wedding."

"It's worse luck to get married if you aren't really sure."

She was right, except —

"Every time I see him, I pretty much want to —"

"Do him. I can understand that."

I rolled my eyes. "I was going to say 'agree with anything he says.' "

Leigh frowned. "That's not like you."

"Exactly."

Nevertheless, I needed to make one final attempt to figure out why I was in northern Minnesota with a wedding gown in the closet and an appointment with a justice of the peace at the spirit tree at just after four this afternoon.

There'd been a small amount of trouble obtaining permission to have a wedding there, since the Grand Portage band had bought the tree a few years back. A sanctioned guide was required if you wanted to go anywhere near the place.

I'd suggested a shaman perform the wedding, but Will insisted the ceremony be legal, which was a first.

He'd been arrested for more protests than he'd bothered to count. His activism on the part of the Native American community had put him on more law enforcement watch lists than even I knew about. I'd always found his police record kind of arousing. An embarrassment for a woman who'd always played by the rules — at least until I'd met him.

In the end Will had managed to get permission for the ceremony on the grounds that he was a member of the Grand Portage band and therefore part owner of the tree. Sounded like bullshit to me, but Will had always been very good at it.

I brushed my teeth and threw on jeans and a T-shirt; then with a wave for Leigh, I padded down the hall and knocked on Will's door.

No one answered. Maybe he was in the shower.

I used my key, stuck my head in just a little, and murmured, "Will?"

I didn't hear water or anything else. Feeling kind of guilty, I stepped inside.

The bed had been slept in. His wedding clothes were laid out. No tuxedo for him. Instead Will would wear traditional Ojibwe dress — leggings, leather overskirt, a cotton blouse with beaded panels, and a pair of brightly beaded moccasins.

All of his things were here, but he wasn't, and I became uneasy. I wouldn't put it past one of the werewolves that had escaped — and a few always did — to kidnap Will in order to get to me.

I was a hunter, Will a professor. Sure he'd killed a few fanged and furry demons, but nowhere near what I had. Next to Edward and Leigh, I was the most feared *Jäger-Sucher.* There had to be bounties on my head, and those who'd put them there wouldn't flinch at murdering the man I loved.

Lycanthropy is a virus passed through the saliva while in wolf form. Until recently the only cure was a silver bullet, which wasn't really a cure, but you get my drift.

Once infected, humans can become wolves whenever the sun goes down. They live to kill, to destroy, to make others of their kind. Their selfishness, their evil, is what we refer to as the demon. It's as close a description as anything else.

There are hundreds, make that thousands, of the beasts roaming loose in this world, walking the streets as human as you and I, running through the night as monsters until dawn. Any one of them could have snatched Will in the hours I'd been asleep.

I hurried to the phone, intending to call Edward, get a search party started. But as I moved past the bed, I noticed an odd bulge in the pocket of Will's wedding shirt.

Being me, suspicious always, I pulled out what appeared to be a medicine bag, though I'd only seen one in a textbook. Some of the Ojibwe kept them, put all that was important inside, but I'd never known Will to have one.

I upended the bag. Herbs, seeds, a piece of cloth, tumbled onto the pristine white sheet. Nothing unusual there. What *was* unusual was the tiny wooden figurines carved into the shapes of a man and a woman, then tied together.

I'd seen talismans before. Twice now the werewolves had used them to try to rule the world. But those totems had been fashioned into wolves — one black, one white, equally magic.

I had no idea what this carved wooden man and woman might mean. That I'd found them on my wedding day couldn't be good.

I stirred the herbs and the seeds with one finger, then picked up the cloth. A chill whispered over my skin. The scrap appeared to be from my favorite pair of sweatpants. I'd had them since I was in technical school and took them everywhere I went.

Feeling naked without my weapons, I stuffed everything back into the bag and hurried to my room. I wanted to examine my sweatpants.

Leigh was gone, thank goodness. I didn't have time to explain anything now, even if I could.

I set the medicine bag on the nightstand, pulled a silver switchblade from between the mattress and the box spring, then unlocked my suitcase and withdrew my .44 Magnum.

I'd once had a boss who liked to quote

Clint Eastwood. An annoying trait, however, he *had* been right about the Magnum being the most powerful handgun in the world. I'd blown a lot of heads clean off. When dealing with werewolves, that was a good thing.

Suitably armed, I opened the closet and became distracted by the wedding gown I couldn't believe I'd bought.

The champagne shade of the satin sheath would make anyone resemble a princess. Even I looked spectacular in it. So why did the sight of the garment always make me want to punch something?

Just another mystery out of so many.

I left the dress in the closet, dragged out the sweats, then searched for a rip or a hole. The idea that some dickhead werewolf, or worse, had taken a chunk out of one of my favorite things was enough to make me want to kill something.

There. That was more like me.

I didn't find any telltale signs. No hack in the knee, no slash across the butt. How could anyone have obtained a swatch without leaving a clue?

I turned over the elastic band at the bottom of each leg and found a tiny notch in the excess fabric on the right side.

"Bingo," I murmured.

But what did it *mean?*

I had no idea, but I would find out. After I found Will.

I spun around and would have shrieked if I were the shrieking type at the sight of a man just inside the door. Instead I drew my gun.

Luckily I didn't follow *Jäger-Sucher* procedure and shoot first, worry about identity later, because the man was Will.

"What the hell are you doing here?" My chest hurt as my heart tried to thump its way out.

I was both thrilled to see him alive and annoyed he'd snuck up on me. He did that a lot.

"You left the door open."

"Oh."

His dark gaze lowered to my .44. "You know I love it when you point guns at me. Takes me right back to the night I first saw you."

As I'd said, we hadn't met under the most normal of circumstances.

"Ha-ha." I lowered the weapon. "Where have you been?"

"Doing tai chi."

Since he was wearing only loose cotton pants and nothing else — though he did have a shirt crumpled in one hand — I should have figured that out for myself.

His smooth, cinnamon skin gleamed with a light sheen of sweat that should have been unattractive but wasn't. The sheen only emphasized the ripples and curves of a well-honed body.

In the year we'd been together, he hadn't cut his hair, and it hung nearly to his shoulders, the blue-black strands playing hide-and-seek with that feather.

Maybe we could skip the wedding and head straight for the honeymoon.

He craned his neck. "Is that your dress?"

"Back off, Slick; you're not supposed to see."

Typically, he ignored me, kicking the door shut, then crossing the room, stopping so close I could have sworn I felt steam rising from his skin.

"I'm not supposed to see you wearing the dress until the wedding —"

"I don't think you're supposed to see *me,* either."

He brushed my hair from my cheek and whispered, "I couldn't stay away."

When he said things like that, I could deny the man nothing. Not my heart, my body, or my future.

At the moment, I wanted to promise Will everything all over again.

Sure marriage scared me, but so had the werewolves once. I'd gotten over it.

My panic attack was understandable given my upbringing. My father had taken off right about the time I'd started to talk — can't imagine why — and I hadn't seen him since. My mother had never really liked me.

Seriously. She hadn't. She'd waited until I turned eighteen, and then she'd taken off, too. Oh, she'd left a forwarding address, but she'd invested in caller ID and rarely picked up the phone on the few occasions I'd gotten drunk enough to call her. She hadn't bothered to respond when I'd left a message about my wedding.

Of course she was of the old school — Indians and whites did not mix; they certainly didn't match. That I was marrying one had probably gotten me taken off the speed dial, if I'd ever been on it in the first place. Which was just fine with me.

The only family I had was in Grand Portage with me now. The family I'd chosen, and that was as it should be.

"You're thinking too much again."

Will's hand slid around my neck. His lips brushed the frown line between my eyes, the tip of my nose, then settled against mine. I sighed and let him remind me of the only thing that mattered.

Us.

He pulled me closer. Our bodies aligned just right. They always had. He was tall enough so I could lay my head on his shoulder. Not too short that I couldn't wear high heels if I was of a mind to, not that I'd ever be *that* out of my mind. He was strong enough to pick me up, sling me around, kick my ass if I let him. Everything about Will was perfect, except his uncharacteristic desire for a wife.

He tasted like a winter wind in the middle of the summer heat. I gave myself up to the lust. From the beginning we'd wanted each other, and that desire had never weakened. Sometimes I wondered if we were truly in love or only dazzled by the sex. Then again, there were worse things to be dazzled by.

The backs of my knees hit the bed, and I tumbled onto the sheets, grunting when he landed on top of me. Something jabbed me in the shoulder. My wiggling only served to rub my T-shirt against my nipples. They hardened at the contact, poking against Will's bare chest.

If his low-voiced murmurs and the sudden thrust of his erection were any indication, Will believed the wiggling was encouragement.

I considered ignoring the pain, focusing

on the pleasure, until Will tugged at the button on my jeans. The resulting shift of his body weight made me say, "Ouch!"

Will's fingers stilled. "Ouch?"

"Get off a minute, will you?" Without question he rolled to the side.

I reached behind me and came up with the medicine bag. Before I could explain, he snatched it from my hand and leaped off the bed.

"Hey!" I protested, but he was already picking up his forgotten shirt from the floor and removing his glasses from the pocket, before pouring the contents into his palm.

For a minute, I was transfixed by him. Besides the earring, his glasses really did me in. That absentminded-professor thing always made me want to jump him.

"Love charm," he muttered. "Ojibwe."

"What does it do?"

"Uses magic to make one person love another."

"You believe that?"

He tilted his head. "Don't you?"

Something in his voice made my eyes narrow. "Wait just one damned minute. You think I made this? I don't know jack about Ojibwe love charms. Besides, smart guy, I found it in your shirt."

"Mine?" He patted his chest, realized he

wasn't wearing anything above the waist, and frowned. "Huh?"

"In your wedding outfit."

He froze. "You were in my room?"

He said it as if I'd stolen his diary and read the good parts on CNN.

"Is that a problem?" I asked. "You have something to hide?"

Although I was angry at his accusations, I was starting to get uneasy, too. Maybe Will *did* have something to hide. Like a love charm.

I'd wondered why I'd been so damn agreeable lately to everything he said. Sure I'd joked about being charmed by the moon, but I'd never considered a literal love charm. Really, I should have.

"If I'd concocted a love charm, I certainly wouldn't leave it around for you to find. I also wouldn't be studying it like I'd never seen one before. Which I haven't."

He was working up a good head of steam. Usually Cadotte was calm as still water, but when he got mad even I trembled.

"Sorry," I muttered. "I see your point."

"If this *were* my medicine bag," he continued, with deceptive tranquillity, "you shouldn't go rooting through it like you'd found my secret stash of Godiva chocolate."

"That was only once, and you said they

were for me anyway."

He ignored the excuse now as he had then. "In the old days the Ojibwe hung medicine bags outside in a tree for safety. Even children knew not to touch them. They're to be opened with great ceremony, only by the owner. They're never to be touched by a stranger."

"Stranger?" My voice had gone high and squeaky as my own anger — fueled by nerves and uncertainty — returned. "Do you *want* me to slug you?"

He sighed and looked away, slowly removing his glasses and setting them aside. His chest rose and fell in a rhythm I'd come to recognize. He was doing his tai chi breathing. Gee, I guess he wanted to slug me, too.

I'd consider that foreplay if I wasn't so furious.

"Let's just calm down," he murmured.

"You expect me to calm down when you accuse me of using a love charm to get you to marry me? You asked *me*, Slick. More than once."

"I know."

"I've been wondering why I said yes. Why I've been so damned easy to get along with lately."

He snorted. "You're a lot of things, Jess, but easy isn't one of them."

I jabbed a finger toward the closet. "I bought a dress for you. If that isn't the result of magic, I don't know what is."

"Wait a second." Will frowned at the herbs and seeds. "There should be a scrap from the clothing of the beloved."

"I found a piece of my gray sweatpants."

Will's eyebrows shot up. "Uh-oh."

He knew what those things meant to me.

Will dug a finger into the bag and came up with the fuzzy scrap. He carefully set all the items on the nightstand, then took me in his arms, leaning his forehead against mine.

"I swear I didn't do this. I want you to marry me because *you* want to, not because you're compelled to."

In his arms my anger left me. "I shouldn't have accused you."

"You had pretty damning evidence."

"I found the medicine bag, but then I couldn't find you. Considering the other talismans we've dealt with, I was afraid someone was up to no good again."

Will gently extricated himself from my arms and picked up the figurines. "If I didn't do this, and you didn't do this, who did?"

"Good question."

He stared at the tiny man and tiny woman.

"A better question might be, how long has the totem been in my pocket."

I blinked. "What?"

"I haven't worn my ceremonial dress since long before I met you."

The hair on my arms and the back of my neck tickled and I fought a shiver despite the rising heat of the summer day.

I'd wondered why he loved me. Maybe he never really had.

"Don't," Will murmured.

"Don't what?"

"Don't ever think I don't love you."

Sometimes I thought he knew me better than I knew myself. I tried to smile, but my heart wasn't in it.

"You might not, Will. Not really."

He tossed the talisman on the bed and grabbed me by the upper arms, his fingers digging into my skin almost desperately. "I know what I feel. I love you. I always will."

"I'm sure the feelings conjured by magic seem real."

"You're forgetting one thing, Jess."

"What's that?"

"Your clothing was in the bag; the bag was in my shirt."

I stared at him blankly.

"According to legend, that means the charm was for you. To make *you* love *me*."

"I do love you."

"You might not, Jess. Not really."

I scowled. "Don't tell me what I feel."

His hold gentled. "There's my girl."

I glanced at the clock on the nightstand. We had four hours before the wedding. "We can't get married until we're certain."

"Someone around here has to know something about love charms."

"Like what?"

His eyes met mine. "How to break them."

I left a message for Leigh on a notepad in my room. If she couldn't find me, she'd just use her key again. I didn't want to call her or see her at the moment, didn't want to explain what we were up to since I wasn't really sure.

Whatever Will and I had to do we had to do together. Leigh couldn't help me and neither could Edward. Besides, they had a habit of blasting first, questioning later, and right now we needed answers, not more dead bodies.

"Where are we going?" I asked, as Will turned the car onto the main road.

"The reservation."

Why hadn't I thought of that? Because I was a little preoccupied with my wedding day going to hell. Not that I hadn't expected it to, but as the result of a bloody werewolf attack, instead of a renegade love charm.

The Grand Portage Reservation extended for eighteen miles along some of the most beautiful shoreline of Lake Superior. I was surprised the government hadn't confiscated it yet. That seemed to be their habit as soon as Indian land showed any sort of profit.

Take the sacred Black Hills, which had been given to the Sioux, then snatched right back when gold was discovered there. Could you really blame them for kicking Custer's ass?

Then there was Indian Territory, where they'd set up reservations for the tribes yanked from their homeland. Until oil was found and suddenly we had Oklahoma.

Ever wonder where the plots came from for those Oklahoma Land Rushes? Two million acres smack-dab in the center of the Indian Territory.

At any rate, the powers that be must not have figured out how many condominiums they could build on the shores of the lake, or maybe the Ojibwe had found better lawyers. These days it was preferable to fight injustice with an attorney instead of a tomahawk. Although I kind of liked the old way better.

Will slowed when we reached the community of Grand Portage where the tribal buildings and most of the homes were congregated. Several old men lounged on the front porch of a weathered gray ranch. Will stopped the car and stepped out.

"Nimishoomis." Will addressed the man who appeared the oldest by the respectful title of "Grandfather." "I'm William Cadotte. I lived here as a boy. I am of the wolf clan."

In Ojibwe culture each family is believed to have descended from a clan animal. Those of the same clan are related, so even if a man was of the Grand Portage band and a woman of the Lac du Flambeau, if they're both wolf clan they're of the same blood and can't marry.

That Will was wolf clan and theoretically descended from the wolves I hunted had caused no small amount of trouble when the truth had been revealed. The memory of that trouble lay in the bullet-shaped scar on Will's arm.

"I have a question for your shaman," Will continued.

The man pointed, never saying a word. We followed the direction of his slightly crooked finger to a wigwam just visible past a brick house surrounded by towering evergreens.

"Thank you," Will said, and we headed in that direction.

"Did you see the wigwam when we drove up?" I murmured.

"Nope."

"Was it there?"

He slid a glance toward me, then away. "What do you think?"

"I hate it when you ask me that," I grumbled, and didn't bother to answer.

Had the wigwam materialized when we requested the shaman? A year ago I'd have laughed myself sick at the idea. Since then, I'd seen so much weird shit, nothing surprised me anymore.

Of course the day was young.

We stopped in front of the domed structure that measured about ten or twelve feet in diameter. The underlying branches were covered with birch bark, keeping the inhabitants dry during the summer rains and warm in the winter snows.

"Nimishoomis," Will called. "I'm Will Cadotte of the Grand Portage wolf clan. My *weedjiwagan* and I have a question."

"Your what?" I snapped.

"Partner in the path of life."

Well, that was true enough — at least until we discovered whether what we felt was real or manufactured. The idea that all we'd shared, all I'd believed, had been a lie made me want to commit violence, but then a lot of things did.

"Come in," called a voice from the other side of the leather flap that served as a door.

I shouldered Will aside and, with my hand on my gun, ducked into the surprisingly cool interior of the wigwam.

Light streamed through the smoke hole in the roof. The ground was bare except for the woven mats around a cold cooking fire.

On the opposite side of the structure sat a very old man. From the looks of him, he'd wandered the woods with this wigwam on his back in days long before the white men screwed everything up. Nevertheless, his eyes were clear, his gaze lucid.

White hair hung past his waist, braided and wrapped in cloth. He wore leggings and a buckskin tunic, the everyday dress of the old times. No beading, no porcupine quills, his moccasins, too, were plain.

The sense of having traveled back in time was so strong, I was tempted to step outside and make certain we hadn't been transported to another age along with the wigwam.

"You have trouble, my brother?"

The old man motioned for us to sit. I took the mat that allowed me to see both him and the door. Habits became habits for a reason.

He wasn't holding a weapon that I could see, but I didn't relax my guard. Monsters often lurked behind seemingly innocent faces.

"You're wolf clan?" Will asked.

"Yes."

Will quickly explained what we'd found and why we'd come. The shaman, who'd introduced himself as Thomas Bender, held out his hand. Will put the medicine bag into it. Instead of pouring everything out, Bender held the charm tightly and closed his eyes. "What is it you wish to know?"

"Who did this?" Will asked. "Why? How can we break the spell?"

"You want to break the spell?" Bender glanced back and forth between us. "But she is your *weedjiwagan*."

"Because of the charm, or because she truly is?"

"Does it matter?"

"Yes," I said.

The old man sighed. "The only way to know the truth is to ask the spirits."

"How?"

"Sit on the water beneath the spirit tree."

"Sit *on* the water?" I blurted. "Do I seem

like much of a walking-on-water type to you?"

Thomas Bender's gaze was bland. "Use a canoe."

"Oh."

Will laid a hand on my knee — his way of telling me to put a sock in it.

"Ask the spirits to reveal the truth."

"Thank you, Nimishoomis."

As we drove away, I glanced back. Where I'd thought the wigwam had been, instead there stood a white birch. I hadn't seen any birch trees when we'd arrived.

I faced front, muttering, "Must be the angle. Wigwam's just hidden by the house."

Will looked in the rearview mirror. "Sure it is."

We headed back the way we'd come. Will parked the car and together we climbed out, staring at the gnarled limbs of the spirit tree reaching toward the sky. By all rights the ancient icon should have tumbled off the stone ledge and into the water long ago. But magic trees so rarely did.

"You think it's going to speak to us?" I asked.

I had a sudden flash of the apple trees from *The Wizard of Oz*. They'd always scared the crap out of me — before I'd discovered so many better things to be afraid of.

"I have no idea," Will murmured.

The wind picked up; the branches swayed and creaked. What if the tree suddenly yanked up its roots and began to walk around like the ones from *Lord of the Rings?* I hadn't liked them, either.

I caught the scent of rain. Dark storm clouds tumbled across the western horizon.

"If we're going to do this," I said, "we'd better do it."

Will followed my gaze and frowned. "That's a thunderstorm."

"So?"

"We shouldn't be on the water if there's lightning."

"We shouldn't do a lot of things, Slick, but we always do."

For an instant I thought he'd refuse. Instead he shrugged. He knew me well. I'd only go alone if he wouldn't go with me.

"We'll need a canoe."

"You're sure we can't do . . . whatever from here."

"On the water means *on* the water, Jess."

"I thought Ojibwe ceremonies were vague."

"The legends are vague; the ceremonies are pretty specific. When an elder says sit on the water —"

"We sit on the water. Fine. The lodge rents

canoes."

Will followed me down a set of steps to a shack not far from the water.

The attendant, obviously a surfer wannabe — though why he was in Minnesota I have no idea; despite the ten thousand lakes, there aren't any waves worth riding — was tying down the canoes so they didn't fly off in a high wind.

"No more rentals until the storm passes."

Understandable. If a tornado could pick up a cow — and it could — a canoe, or twenty, would be no problem. Nevertheless . . .

"DNR." I pulled out my badge. "There's trouble on the lake, and I need a canoe. Now."

He snapped to. Must be from around here. Though the Department of Natural Resources — better known as the hunting and fishing police — was not well liked in the north woods, they were respected. The kid rented me a canoe.

As we glided onto the lake, the tourists raced in the other direction. By the time we'd paddled to the area just below the spirit tree, the water was deserted, the storm bearing down on us.

"Isn't rain on your wedding day good luck?" I asked.

"Sure," Will answered.

"Are you just saying that to shut me up or do you actually know?"

"To shut you up."

"That's what I thought."

Thunder rumbled. The clouds cast shadows across the water, disturbing the fish, making them dart about beneath the surface as if they were crazed. The wind whipped my hair into my face and made Will's earring dance madly. The lighting flashed and I shivered.

"You want to go inside?" Will asked. "We can do this tomorrow."

"Our wedding is today."

"We can postpone it."

"No. I can't go through another night without knowing."

Though it was awkward, Will leaned across the canoe and kissed me. "Then we won't."

The storm and the current had dragged us a few yards away from the tree. We paddled until we were in front of it again.

"Now what?"

"According to the shaman, we ask the tree for the truth."

"So ask."

Will shrugged. "Spirit tree, we seek the truth."

The wind howled. The tree bent and swayed. We got nothing.

"You try," Will said.

"You're the wolf clan dude."

"Which is irrelevant for once. The charm was made for you. Maybe you have to ask."

"Hey!" I shouted. "How about some truth!"

"Nice."

"That's me."

Once again, nothing happened.

"Maybe I need to hold the charm or something," I ventured.

Surprise spread across Will's face. "Good idea."

"Why are you so shocked? I'm not a complete magic moron."

I'd had too much on-the-job training.

Will pulled the medicine bag from his pocket. As I reached for it, the water sloshed, the canoe dipped, and our hands smacked together with the talisman in between.

A mighty flash and a thunderous crack were followed by the scent of brimstone. Flames shot toward the sky.

"Uh-oh," I muttered.

The tree had stood for centuries unharmed. One day near me and it was on fire.

"Did someone request the truth?"

The voice seemed to whisper on the wind, but I recognized it anyway, and my heart sank. Of all the possibilities in heaven and earth, the universe had to send her?

"Figures I'd smell hellfire just before *she* arrives."

"Jess," Will admonished. "Remember last time."

I remembered all right, which was why I wasn't too happy to see Cora Kopway standing on the ledge next to the flaming spirit tree.

A high-ranking member of the *midewiwin,* or the Grand Medicine Society, a secret religious fellowship devoted to healing through knowledge of the old ways, Cora Kopway had spent her life studying dusty texts and communing with the spirits in her visions.

She'd once taken away my voice with a mere flick of her wrist and some weird purple powder. The woman was quite powerful.

She was also quite dead. Had been for about six months now. That hadn't stopped her from sticking her nose into *Jäger-Sucher* business at least once.

Better make that twice.

Cora looked the same in death as she had

in life — tall, willowy, with flowing black hair that held only a trace of gray.

"For a dead old witch, she's surprisingly pretty," I mumbled.

Will gave me a glare that would have melted silver. I stared at Cora, who'd begun to walk . . . right across the water, stopping a few feet in front of the canoe.

"Isn't that blasphemous?" I asked.

Her eyes narrowed. "I silenced you once; I can do so again. Permanently."

The woman had a stick up her butt a mile wide, but since Will liked her, I did my best not to annoy Cora too much.

Unfortunately, my best was never good enough. I was a cop — or had been when I met her — a white girl, and a smart mouth. The top three sins on the Cora Kopway sin-o-meter.

"Why are you here, N'okomiss?" Will asked.

"I was enjoying my time in the Land of Souls."

Aka Ojibwe heaven.

"I would have preferred not to be torn out of it to help *you*." She wrinkled her nose in my direction. "But I had little choice."

"So head back to Deadville. If I'd known *you* were coming, I wouldn't have asked."

"We want the truth," Will snapped. "What

difference does it make where we get it?"

"Can we trust her?"

"She's never lied to us."

There *was* that. As annoying as Cora could be, she'd been truthful, as well as helpful. Alive or dead, she knew more about Ojibwe woo-woo than anyone.

"Fine," I muttered. "But I don't know why the spirit tree couldn't just tell us."

"That's not the way things work," Cora said. "You wanted the truth, and I'm the only one who knows it."

"How's that?"

"I made the talismans."

All I could do was blink at her.

Why on earth would Cora use magic to make me fall in love with Will? Unless she'd meant for me to love him, but he'd never love me back.

Ha! That had backfired on her ass.

The storm was coming in hard; whitecaps formed in the center of the lake. We needed to finish chatting and get off the water or we might just join her in the Land of Souls much sooner than we'd planned.

It probably seems odd that I believe in the afterlife. I admit that before I became a *Jäger-Sucher* I hadn't. However, I'd come to the conclusion that if there's evil, there's good; if there are demons, there are also

317

angels. And if Satan walks this earth — and he does, in the guise of more horrible beings than you can even dream of — then God has to be out there, too.

"I made the talismans," Cora said, "so you'd fall in love."

Hovering just above the swirling water, she wasn't transparent as a ghost should be. If not for the floating issue — and the DNA test that had identified her body — I'd think she was alive.

"Again, I gotta ask why?"

She made an exasperated sound and threw up her hands. "Haven't you learned anything?"

"Why don't you clue me in?"

"Love is stronger than hate, more powerful than evil. Together you're more than you could ever be apart."

Will and I exchanged glances, then returned our attention to Cora.

"Okay," I said. "Still don't get it."

"I knew your talent with weapons of destruction, combined with Will's intelligence, would make you a nearly invincible team. All you needed was something to bind you together forever. I gave it to you."

"But the charm was to make me love Will. How could you be certain he'd love me back?"

She frowned. "I said 'talismans.' Plural."

"Yeah." I held up the man and the woman. "Two of them."

She shook her head. "There is another."

"Have you been watching too much *Star Wars?*"

"In heaven? I don't think so."

"There's no *Star Wars* in heaven? I'm not going."

"I doubt you are." Cora sniffed. "But that's beside the point."

I scowled, and my fingers curled around the little man and woman.

"Take a big breath," Will murmured.

"You talk to her, Slick. I've had enough."

He sighed, though I wasn't sure if he was disappointed in me or in her — probably both of us.

"N'okomiss, you're saying there's another medicine bag?"

"One for each of you."

I couldn't speak, even without the magic powder. It had been bad enough wondering if I truly loved him, but to know that he didn't truly love me . . .

I felt lost, uncertain, alone, as if everything good in my life was a lie. Probably because it was.

"We found one medicine bag in my ceremonial dress."

"There's another in her makeup case."

Will did a double take. "You've got a makeup case?"

"Not that I use it or anything."

"Obviously," Cora drawled.

I ignored her because something else was bothering me and I couldn't quite get my mind around what it was. My focus had been shot to hell by an overwhelming sense of sadness, as if someone I loved had died.

My gaze wandered over Will's beloved face as the memories of all we'd shared filtered through my mind. The analogy was more apt than I cared for.

"You're saying you hid a medicine bag in each of our things to make us fall in love with each other?" I clarified.

"Yes."

I forced myself to concentrate, to isolate the kernel of information that was poking my brain like an annoying thistle in the thumb.

"We didn't meet you until *after* we fell in love."

My hope that this was all a big mistake, an April Fool's trick a few months too late, the Ojibwe idea of a practical joke, died at her shrug. "Time's not the same in the Land of Souls. We aren't on a linear plane."

"What the hell does that mean?"

"It means," Will interjected, "that she was able to go back to a time before we were in love and plant the talismans."

"Which makes no sense."

"You're looking at things with human eyes."

"That's all I got, Slick."

"And a human brain."

"Ditto."

"The other world follows different rules than this one."

"I'll take your word for it." I turned my attention to Cora. "How could you make the love charms if you're a ghost?"

"Who said I was a ghost?"

"What are you then?"

"Midewiwin."

Which was *so* helpful. Not.

"She was powerful in life, Jess. In death there's no telling what she can do."

Cora smiled, and the expression reminded me of a big snake watching a little mouse.

Terrific.

Lightning flashed again. Rain began to fall. The flames on the spirit tree hissed and sputtered. Cora glanced to the west as if someone had called her name. "I have to go."

"Ke-go-way-se-kah," Will murmured.

At my glare he translated, " 'You are going homeward.' We believe to the west lies the Che-ba-kun-ah, the road of souls."

AC/DC began to sing "Highway to Hell" inside my head. I stifled the music lest Cora could hear it, too. I wouldn't put it past her.

"One more question," I said. "How do we stop it?"

"Stop what?"

"The love spell."

"You want to make the magic go away?" Her forehead creased. "Isn't love better than hate?"

"Yes. But truth is better than a lie."

She tilted her head and contemplated me with a bemused expression. "Maybe I've been too hard on you."

"You think?"

Her eyes narrowed as her be-ringed fingers stroked the pocket of the same colorful skirt where she'd once kept that silencing purple powder.

"Leave well enough alone, would you?" Will muttered.

I tightened my lips and refrained, barely, from slapping my hands over my mouth for good measure.

"The choice is yours," Cora said. "If you wish to live in the world the way it would be if I hadn't interfered, all you need do is crush the icons beneath your feet."

"That's all?" Will asked.

"That is all."

Thunder crashed. I blinked, and she was gone. Will stared at the place where she'd been.

"Did I flip out and see something I shouldn't?"

"Cora was here," Will said. "Or as here as a dead woman gets."

Lightning split the sky directly above us. We put our paddles to the water and headed for the shore as warm summer rain tumbled down.

After turning the canoe over to surfer dude, we climbed into the car. Luckily the seats were leather, because we were both dripping.

Will slowed to a crawl as we reached the spirit tree; then he stopped completely. We both peered through the windshield.

No smoke, no blackened limbs, there wasn't a sign of the flames we'd witnessed from the lake. The tree was exactly as it had been when we'd left, except for being as wet as we were.

I was beginning to doubt everything I'd seen. What else was new?

"The tree was on fire, right?"

"Right." Will put the car into gear and drove the rest of the way to the lodge.

Leigh wasn't in my room. Neither was Edward. There wasn't any note, and no voice mail, either. Apparently, no one had noticed we were gone.

"You're cold," Will murmured.

I hadn't realized I was shivering.

"Why don't you get out of those wet clothes? Take a shower?"

I opened my mouth to invite him to join me — he was shivering, too — then snapped it shut again. If we shared water, we'd share a lot more. We always did.

I couldn't bear to make love to him now and find out it had only been sex later. Even if all the love of the past year turned out to be nothing but lust, and maybe not even that much, I wasn't going to compound the pain by adding more of the same.

"Let's just get this done," I said, and yanked my makeup case from the closet.

Shiny pink vinyl. I'd torn off the Barbie emblem only last week. I'm not sure why I'd kept the ghastly bag, except it was one of the few things my mother had given me besides an inferiority complex. I remembered very clearly how she'd come home from work one bright summer day when I was twelve and handed me the gift.

"Try being a girl," she'd ordered.

I'd tried, but I'd never been very good at

it. After one pathetic attempt to use the powders and potions inside, I'd picked up my pellet gun and gone squirrel hunting. Gotta stick with your strengths.

"That's awful small," Will observed. "How could you have missed seeing a medicine bag in there?"

"I never open the thing. I only brought it along because . . ."

I shrugged, not wanting to admit I'd planned to dazzle him on our wedding day. A dress, jewelry, makeup, and a hairdo. He wouldn't have known what hit him. He probably wouldn't have known me.

I yanked on the zipper and upended the bag on the bed. Two lipsticks, one blush, mascara, and a trial tube of base tumbled out along with a second medicine bag. Inside were figurines that matched the others, the same herbs, similar seeds, and a tiny swatch of stone-washed denim.

Will fingered the cloth. "I wondered how I put a hole in those pants."

"Ready?" I asked.

Grim determination came over his face, and he gave a sharp nod. I stuffed the figurines, cloth, and other items into the bag, then tossed it onto the floor and lifted my foot.

"Wait."

Will dropped his talisman next to mine, then grabbed me around the waist. His lips were soft, his hands hard, and as always, when he touched me I could think of nothing but him.

From the beginning we'd felt more for each other than two people should so quickly. I'd shoved aside the unease, convincing myself we'd been under stress, fighting for our lives. We'd almost died. Of course what we felt was intense beyond all reason.

Once the danger was over — or as over as it got for *Jäger-Suchers* — I'd continued to delude myself, rationalizing that we were lucky to have found each other, thereby avoiding the whisper in my head that insisted *I* was the lucky one. I shouldn't question or probe because Will might come to his senses and see that he could do so much better than me.

In a few minutes he *would* come to his senses, and while I couldn't bring myself to get naked with him one last time, I also couldn't deny myself one last kiss.

He lifted his head, brushed his thumb across my cheek. He was so beautiful he made my eyes ache. What *had* he ever seen in me? Nothing that hadn't been put there by magic.

"We'll destroy the talismans," he murmured. "But I'll still feel the same."

I smiled softly and took his hand, then touched my lips to his knuckles. "I doubt that, Will."

His eyes flickered. I so rarely used his first name. When I did, life was about to get serious.

I moved toward the talismans. He held on tight. "Let's throw them in the lake."

"What?"

"I love you. You love me. Cora was right. Love is stronger than hate. We're better together than apart. I don't want to lose you, Jess."

"You don't want to be with someone you don't really love." I took a deep breath. "I know I don't."

"We'll love each other even without the magic."

"Then it won't hurt to destroy the talismans."

Silence fell between us as he considered my statement.

"Okay," he said at last. "If that's what you want."

What I wanted was him and me together forever. I saw that clearly now; I couldn't believe I'd doubted it before. Why do we always have to lose something to know how much it means to us?

Oh yeah, human nature.

I took another deep breath. "It's what I want."

"All right," he said. "On three. One, two —"

We lifted our feet.

"Three."

And brought them down on the medicine bags. The little wooden people crunched beneath the sole of my hiking boot. I winced at the sound, like tiny bones breaking.

The earth rumbled, lightning flickered, and a chill wind swept through the room, ruffling my hair, making Will's earring twirl.

I glanced at the window. Not only was it shut, but the sun was shining. I waited for a sense that something had changed inside of me.

Our gazes met, and I realized that something had. I loved him even more.

I held my breath, terrified Cora had wreaked her last vengeance, leaving me to desperately love a man who couldn't abide the sight of me.

"Jess," Will said, and in his voice I heard everything I'd ever dreamed of.

Or at least I thought I did. Being me, I had to make sure.

"How's the heart, Slick? Any changes in it?"

"Not a one."

Was that good or bad? My confusion must have shown on my face, because he tugged me into his arms and held on. His lips brushed my temple. I hate to admit it, but I clung.

My eyes were drawn to the window again as a shaft of sunlight beat down on the spirit tree, turning the arching dark limbs a burnished gold.

"Look," I whispered.

"I think that's an omen," Will murmured. "Don't you?"

I'd always known that the love of my life was Will, but I hadn't truly believed the opposite was true. I did now.

"Yes," I answered.

From his smile he understood I was saying yes to more than just that question.

"How do you feel about kids?" he asked.

I choked.

Ah, hell. Kids were *not* an option. Not in a world where anyone could turn into a monster at any time and everyone we loved was considered wolf bait. Will could take care of himself, but a child —

I couldn't do it.

"If you want kids, Slick, you're gonna

need a bigger charm."

"My thoughts exactly."

"You don't want children?"

"Not in our world, Jess. I wanted to make sure you didn't."

"Can you see me as a mother?"

"Actually I can, or I wouldn't have asked."

I shook my head, amazed. "You always think more of me than I could ever be."

"No, I don't."

Another reason I loved him.

He tugged on my hair. "We can skip the wedding if you like."

"I thought you were set on making an honest woman of me."

"You're the most honest woman I know."

A definite compliment from an Indian. They'd been lied to enough.

"Besides," he continued, "for the Ojibwe, living together for a year is as good as a marriage license."

My eyes narrowed in mock fury. "You couldn't tell me this before I bought a thousand-dollar gown?"

He shrugged sheepishly. "We don't need the wedding. In my heart we've been married from the first day we met."

"You are so full of it."

"I know." He took my hand again. "But I only want this if you do."

"A hundred werewolves couldn't keep me away," I whispered.

I put on the dress, the shoes, even the makeup. I let a stranger do something frou-frou with my hair; then I walked out of the lodge and into the sunlight.

I let an ancient wolf hunter walk me down a gravel-strewn path to the spirit tree, and put my hand into the hand of an Ojibwe wolf clan member. Hard to believe, but then most things in my life were.

"You will take care of her," Edward said.

"I can take care of myself," I snapped.

"Then what are you marrying him for?"

I stared into Will's eyes. "I can't help myself."

Edward snorted and joined the others — hunters all. My wedding looked like an armory had exploded, weapons, weapons everywhere, and silver bullets, too.

The justice of the peace we'd hired from Duluth appeared nervous in the midst of all the guns and ammo, but he managed.

"I now pronounce you man and wife."

Funny, that didn't sound right.

"We're *weedjiwagan*," I said.

And Will answered, "Partners in the path of life."

LORI HANDELAND is the author of the bestselling Nightcreature novels. The first in the series, *Blue Moon,* won the RITA Award from the Romance Writers of America for Best Paranormal of 2004. Lori lives in Wisconsin with her husband, two teenage sons, and a yellow lab named Elwood. She can be reached through her Web site: www.lori handeland.com.

TACKY

CHARLAINE HARRIS

"I'm going because I can't believe I've lived to see it," Dahlia said. "Also, I'm a bridesmaid, which is an honor. I have an obligation." She widened her eyes at her companion, to emphasize the point. She had big green eyes, so it was a vivid effect.

Glenda Shore choked on her sip of synthetic blood. "You're kidding," she said faintly. "You think this is an honor? Well, bite me. Being a bridesmaid means we have to mingle with the nasty things. Like that party tonight, at the Were bar. Taffy called me specially, but I put her off. I won't do it! It's bad enough, all the teasing I've gotten. Maisie called me 'Fur Lover'; Thomas Pickens gives wolf howls whenever he sees me. It's just humiliating."

Dahlia gave her head a practiced toss to flip her long wavy black hair back over her shoulders. She glanced down to make sure her strapless burgundy cocktail dress was still in place. There was a line between being adorably provocative and simply tacky. Dahlia was an expert at treading that line.

"I've known Taffy for maybe a couple hundred years," Dahlia said quietly. "I feel that I have to go through with this." She kept her voice casual; she didn't want to sound smugly superior. Glenda hadn't even been alive that long — or dead, rather. Neither had the other two females Taffy had asked to act as bridesmaids.

Glenda was a very young vampire, a flat-chested flapper who'd been turned during the Al Capone era in Chicago. To Dahlia's distaste, Glenda still liked wearing clothes reminiscent of the ones she'd worn while she was living. Tonight she was wearing a cloche hat. Conspicuous.

Oh, sure, it was legal to be a vampire now that the synthetic blood marketed by the Japanese had proven to satisfy the nutritional needs of the undead. But there was more to surviving as a vamp than slugging down TrueBlood or Red Stuff in all-night bars that catered strictly to vamps, like this one. There were pockets of humans who snatched vamps off the streets and drained their blood to sell on the black market.

There were other cults who simply wanted vamps dead because they'd decided vamps were evil blood-sucking fiends.

You had to learn discretion.

Besides various fringe groups of humans, you had to add to the list of vampire haters the Werewolves, whose ongoing feud with the undead occasionally flared into out-and-out war. Thinking of Weres brought Dahlia back to the subject at hand, her friend Taffy's wedding.

"Taffy and I nested together for a decade in Mexico," Dahlia said. "We were quite close. We went through the War of 1812 together; nothing cements a relationship like going through a war. And we've nested together at Cedric's for the past, oh, twenty years?"

"Where could Taffy have met such a creature?" Glenda asked, fingering the long, long string of pearls that dangled to her waist. Her eyes glinted with relish. This was as much fun as discussing a previously un-encountered sexual perversion.

Dahlia beckoned to the bartender. "Taffy was always . . . adventurous. She lived with a regular human for ten years, once."

Glenda looked pleasurably horrified. "Do you think she'll wear white?" Glenda asked. "And our bridesmaid dresses . . . I bet we'll have pink ruffles."

"Why would it be pink ruffles?" Dahlia's

mouth was suddenly pressed in a grim line. Dahlia took her clothes very, very, seriously.

"You know what they say about bridesmaid dresses!" Glenda laughed out loud.

"I do not," said Dahlia, her voice cold enough to goose an icicle. "I was turned before there was such a thing as a designated attendant for the bride."

"Oh, my goodness!" The younger vampire was shocked. And then delighted at the prospect of introducing her superior friend to the certainty of an unpleasant ordeal. "Then let's go find a church and watch a wedding. Well, maybe not a church," she added nervously. Glenda had been a Christian in life, and churches made her mighty twitchy. "Maybe we'll check out a country club, or find a garden wedding."

Glenda actually had a sensible idea, Dahlia decided. It would help to know the worst. And though all the bridesmaids were due at a party in honor of the happy couple, if she and Glenda hurried, they wouldn't be late.

"The big mansions on the lakeside," she suggested. "It's a June weekend. Isn't that a prime time for weddings in America?" Dahlia had a vague recollection of seeing bridal magazines on the shelves at newspaper kiosks when she'd been buying her monthly copy of *Fang*.

"That's a keen idea. Let's go!" Glenda was eager. The worst enemy of a vampire was ennui. Any new diversion was worth its weight in gold.

Since they were both gifted with flight (not all vampires possessed this skill), the two were able to reach the most imposing mansions in the city quickly. Glenda and Dahlia hovered over them to detect an outside celebration that might prove to be a wedding. At the VanTreeve place, they struck nuptial pay dirt. Tiffany VanTreeve was marrying Brendan Blaine Buffington that very night. The two vamps landed unobtrusively behind a tent set up on the grounds.

Dahlia eyed the scene critically, taking mental notes. The vampire sheriff of her area in the city of Rhodes, Cedric Deeming, was worried about giving a proper wedding in such a hurry. Though lazy and lax in many respects, Cedric was a stickler for protocol. He'd urged all the vampires who nested with him to bring home details of modern wedding proceedings.

Dahlia obediently began making mental notes. Close to the house, there were two long tables loaded with food and a huge cake, though the food was discreetly covered with drapes for the moment. There was a cage full of doves, with an attendant in coveralls. Perhaps these were intended for a ritual sacrifice? There were two phalanxes of white chairs on the lawn, arranged facing a large white dais adorned with banks of pink flowers. A long red carpet ran between the two sections of chairs, right up the steps of the dais, where a minister in a sober black robe stood waiting.

Note to self: Find some kind of priest. Wasn't Harry Oakheart some kind of Druid? Maybe he knew a ceremony.

A string quartet was playing Handel. (*Note to self: Find musicians*) Not only were all the seats full, but there was a standing crowd at the back.

"What a swell spread," Glenda whispered, eyeing the buffet tables. "I guess the wolves'll need food. Looks like we're expected to feed them. The sheriff won't like that. You know what a tightwad he is. At least Cedric won't have to provide food for half the guests." She winked at Dahlia, as if it were very funny that vampires didn't eat food. "And we'll need liquor for the Weres, and we'll need a big stock of blood. Maybe we could nip off the guests?"

Dahlia looked daggers at Glenda. "Don't even say it as a joke," she told the younger

338

vampire. "You know what'll happen if we even suggest that to a breather. Follow the rules. Only from a willing adult!"

"Spoilsport," Glenda muttered.

"Cedric has already hired a caterer, a man who says he can do the whole thing, flowers and all. Cedric is so cheap, he took the lowest bid. No sit-down dinner, just . . . finger food." Even Dahlia could not suppress her smile at the term, and Glenda laughed out loud. A few of the guests turned to see who was so being so boisterous, and Dahlia slammed Glenda in the ribs with a sharp elbow. Everyone else present was being properly solemn. "But we have to do it properly," Dahlia said, in a whisper inaudible to the humans around her. "We can't be found wanting. It would shame Taffy, and the nest."

Glenda gave it as her opinion that the Weres should be grateful they were even being allowed in Cedric's mansion. "I'm surprised Cedric will acknowledge the wedding," she said.

The music gave a final flourish, and the guests rustled expectantly.

The two vampires watched the ceremony unfold: Glenda with a sentimental tear or two (tinged red) and Dahlia with fascinated horror. The groom, looking as though he'd been hit over the head with something large, took his place in front of the minister and stared down the strip of red carpet rolling between the two fields of white chairs. His groomsmen lined up on his side of the dais. At a signal that was invisible to Dahlia, who was stretching up on her tiptoes to see, the traditional music began.

"Here's the most interesting part," Glenda whispered.

One by one, the bridesmaids emerged from the white tent. Some were tall and some were small; some were buxom and some were slim as reeds. But the seven girls were all united in costume. Dahlia, the most elegant and particular of women, closed her eyes in appalled horror.

All the bridesmaids were wearing matching floor-length lime green silk sheaths. *If you could strip the dress down to its basic essentials, it wouldn't be too bad,* Dahlia thought. But the dresses were accessorized with lace gloves and tiny veiled hats pinned to each lacquered head. Worst of all, there was a gigantic bow perched atop each girlish butt. The waggle of each passing lime green rear end made Dahlia feel like weeping, too, along with some of the female guests — though Dahlia assumed they were crying for a different reason.

Glenda gave an audible snigger, and Dahlia despaired of ever teaching the girl manners. Dahlia herself was maintaining an appropriately pleasant wedding guest face despite the dreadful possibility that she'd have to wear such a monstrous ensemble. Though the prospect was a blow, Dahlia conscientiously remained to note the entire procedure. She was disappointed when the doves were simply released into the sky at the climax of the ceremony.

Long after Glenda had lost interest, Dahlia traced all the events of the wedding back to their human director, who was hovering at the rear of the gathering. Though the poor wedding planner was quite busy, Dahlia was ruthless (in a charming way) in getting the answers to several astute questions. She garnered information that made her feel that (if it had been beating at all) her heart would now burst.

"The groomsmen — those men up there on the husband's side — they'll be from among the groom's friends," Dahlia said, her hand gripping Glenda's shoulder.

"Well, sure, Dally," Glenda said. "Really, you! Didn't you know that?"

Dahlia shook her raven head back and forth. "Werewolves," she moaned. "They'll all be Werewolves."

"Ewww," said Glenda. "We'll have to let one *touch* us, Dally. Did you see that each bridesmaid took the arm of a groomsman on their way out of the . . . the . . . designated wedding area?"

And for the first time in her long, long life, Dahlia Lynley-Chivers said, "Ewww."

To cover her shame, she added quickly, "If you call me Dally again, I'll tear your throat out."

When Dahlia said something like that, it was smart to assume she meant it. Glenda said, "Well, I'm sure not going to any stupid Were party with you *now*."

Dahlia had to back down, something she was unused to doing. "Glenda," she said stiffly, "neither Cassie nor Fortunata will go, and I was relying on you. It's your duty as a bridesmaid to attend this party. Taffy said so."

"If you think we'll be greeted with open arms by a bunch of stupid Weres, you can think again, Miss Perfect. Open *jaws* is what they'll have." Glenda disappeared behind the tent to conceal her liftoff, and Dahlia watched her companion disappear. No doubt, Glenda would describe the bridesmaid dresses to any vamp who would listen.

With her little jaw set grimly, Dahlia Lynley-Chivers made her way to a part of

Rhodes she seldom visited. This time, she took a cab. Humans became very upset when they saw her fly, and she was determined to do her best by her friend Taffy. Taffy had been born Taphronia, daughter of Leonidas, centuries ago. She'd been calling herself Taffy for the past forty years. Taffy and her fiancé, Don Swiftfoot (of course that was his pack name — his human name was Don Swinton), were celebrating their forthcoming nuptials at a bar in the Werewolf part of town. The whole wedding party would be there; at least, the whole wedding party was supposed to be there. Since the other bridesmaids had dropped the baton, Dahlia feared she'd be the only vampire in attendance. She had a wide range of curses at her disposal since she'd lived so long, and she voiced a few of them on the drive through the city. Luckily, the cabdriver spoke none of the languages she used.

Dahlia got out of the cab a block away from the bar. This area of Rhodes was a bit run-down, a bit seedy. The sidewalks were crowded, even this late at night, with bar-hopping humans, who didn't realize they were just on the safe side of the moon cycle. Of course, no one who lived in Rhodes realized they were partying in an area that had a high concentration of Werewolves.

Humans didn't know about Werewolves yet. The two-natured had to retain their human faces on their nights out.

The bar, called Moonshine, was practically buzzing with energy and magic. Any humans who wandered in uninvited developed severe headaches and went home early, as a rule. Moonshine was closed three nights out of the month.

Dahlia made sure her cocktail dress was smooth over her hips. Since she was representing her nest, she put on a little lipstick and brushed her rippling hair before she entered the bar. It was marked by a blinking neon sign formed in a white circle — representing the moon, if you had a lot of imagination.

"Tacky," Dahlia muttered. She read the notice taped to the door: *Closed tonight for private party.* Because she was a little anxious about entering a Werewolf-infested bar, she stood a little straighter on her spike heels — which brought her height all the way up to five foot one — held her head proudly, tucked her tiny flat purse under her bare arm, and marched inside, her haughtiest expression fixed on her heart-shaped face.

A chorus of so-called wolf whistles met her entrance. Of course, in their wolf forms, these guys couldn't whistle for diddly-squat;

but they managed just fine in their human guise. Dahlia pretended to be deaf as she scanned the tiny bar for Taffy.

Really, you can't expect any better, she told herself. After all, true Weres were generally guys and gals with a keen interest in motorcycles and monster trucks. All the Weres in this bar were pure Weres, with two full-blooded parents. (Even Taffy wouldn't expose her friends to mongrels.)

Dahlia couldn't spy Taffy among the people, mostly male, crowding the bar, so she began to make her way to the only doorway not marked: *Restroom.*

A very tall and very athletically built male stepped in front of her. "Sorry, lady, this bar is closed tonight for a private party."

"Yes, I read the sign on the door."

"Then you're pretty slow taking a hint."

Dahlia looked up (and up) at the bright blue eyes in the broad face. This Were had thick, curling brown hair pulled back into a ponytail, and he was clean-shaven. He was wearing gold-rimmed glasses, a bit to her surprise, and a tight T-shirt and jeans . . . the jeans, now that she came to take a look, were pretty damn tight, too. And boots. He had on big boots.

Dahlia shook herself (mentally, of course). The rude jerk was waiting for her reply. "I am here seeking my friend Taffy," she said coldly, meeting his eyes squarely.

They stood stock-still for a long minute.

"A *vamp*," he said, loathing replacing the admiration in his voice. "Damn, I knew we shoulda put some new lightbulbs in this place. Then I woulda noticed how pale you are. What do you want with Taff? You gonna try to talk her out of marrying Don, too?"

If it was possible to get any stiffer, Dahlia did. "I am going to . . . actually, what I want with Taffy is none of your business, Were. I require an audience with her." Dahlia was so rattled by the Were's anger that she became colder and stiffer and caught herself reverting to former speech patterns.

"Oh yeah, and we're supposed to bow and scrape for the little madam?" he said. "You should get that stick out of your ass and behave more like Taffy. She doesn't act so snooty and superior. After all, what you got on us? We live longer than humans, and we're stronger than humans, and we can do all kinds of things that humans can't do."

"Excuse me," Dahlia said frigidly. "I am *so* not interested."

"I'll show you interested," the huge monster growled, reaching down as if he was actually going to pick Dahlia up and give her a shake. The next instant, he was looking up at her from the floor and his friends had leaped to their feet, their eyes glowing. Snarls issued from several male throats, and one or two female ones.

"No," called the man from the floor, just as Dahlia prepared to free her hands for fighting by tucking her tiny evening purse into the gartered top of her hose (a process that distracted the males for a few long seconds), "she's in the right, guys."

"What?" asked a blond man built like a fire hydrant. "You gonna let a vamp get away with putting you on the floor?"

"Yeah, Richie," said the man, getting up. "She did it fair and square after I provoked her."

The rest of the Weres seemed disconcerted, but they backed away a foot or two. Dahlia felt a mixture of relief and regret. Her fangs had extended as she readied to fight, and she would have enjoyed relieving the tension by ripping off a few limbs.

"Come on, little highness," Brown Ponytail said. "I'll take you to Taffy."

She nodded curtly. He turned to lead the way, and she followed right behind him. The crowd parted along the way rather reluctantly.

"Cold-blooded creep," said one Were woman. She was built like an Amazon, broad shouldered. Dahlia would have loved to flash out a hand and bury it in the Were's abdomen, but ladies didn't do such things — not if they wanted the truce to hold.

Dahlia was proud of herself when she didn't meet the woman's eyes in challenge. Instead, Dahlia kept her gaze focused forward. *Which is no hardship,* she had to admit to herself, as she examined the curve of the butt moving in front of her. It certainly was a prime one, packed into the worn Levi's in a most attractive way.

Dahlia winced, realizing that she'd actually caught herself admiring a Were.

Her guide stepped aside, and Dahlia was relieved beyond measure to see Taffy sitting in a padded booth behind a round table with Don cuddling close to her right and another Were to her left. Dahlia barely kept her upper lip from drawing back in distaste. It was like seeing a racehorse cavorting with zebras.

"Dahlia!" shrieked Taffy. Her auburn curls were piled up on top of her head, and she was wearing a halter top and blue jeans, as far as Dahlia could tell. Oh, *really,* Dahlia thought, exasperated, remembering the care she'd taken to dress correctly. *Taffy looks like a real human.* Probably trying to blend in. As if she could.

"Taffy," Dahlia said, thrown seriously off track, "can we have a talk?" She didn't even want to acknowledge Don. He was as red-headed as Taffy, but his hair was short and rough looking, like the coat of a terrier.

"Hey, beautiful!" Don said expansively.

Dahlia gave Don a stiff nod of greeting. She was no barbarian.

Don had a beard, and bright filaments of red stuck out from the neck of his golf shirt. Dahlia shuddered. She was glad to look back at Taffy.

"You still got that cold bitch thing goin' on," Don observed. "Doesn't she, Todd?"

"She's got it down pat," agreed her guide. "Didn't even bother to introduce herself." Dahlia realized, with a pang, that the Were was correct. "She's a brave little thing, though," the Were went on. "Knocked me ass-backward."

Don grinned approvingly. "People should do that more often, Todd. It seems to soften you up."

While Dahlia tried to estimate how long it would take her to kill them all, Taffy was extricating herself from the booth, which seemed to involve a lot of unnecessary brushing against Don, with wriggling and kisses strewn in for good measure. This was the source of many teasing comments and much laughter from the assembled Weres.

I seem to be the only one who's in a bad mood, Dahlia thought, and then without meaning to, her eyes met the tall Were's again. Nope, Todd was less than happy, too. Dahlia wondered whether it was the engagement between Don and Taffy or her own intrusion that had triggered Todd's irritation.

"This is my friend Dahlia Lynley-Chivers," Taffy announced to the crowd of Weres. "She's my maid of honor."

There was a smattering of polite response. Dahlia inclined her head civilly. She couldn't force a smile.

"Snotty-nose bitch," muttered the other Were sitting in the booth. He had dark curly hair and a pugnacious attitude. "Having one in the bar at a time is enough."

Dahlia's tiny hand darted out and dug into the Were's throat.

He gagged, his eyes going wide with shock and fear, and the atmosphere of the bar went into high gear.

"Dahlia!" said Taffy. "He didn't know what he was saying, Dahlia. Please, for me."

Dahlia released the dark-haired Were, and he collapsed against the wood of the booth, breathing heavily. There was an uneasy stirring among the denizens of the crowded bar.

"Thanks, honey," Taffy murmured. "Let's take this out on the sidewalk, okay?"

Her back as straight and her head as high as ever, Dahlia followed Taffy out of the bar, looking neither to the right nor to the left, ignoring the growing chorus of growls that surged in her wake.

"Smooth move, Dahlia," Taffy said, the words bursting out as soon as they were on the sidewalk.

"You were the one who invited me! If you weren't the one engaged to that . . . that dog man . . . do you think I'd go inside such a place?"

"Where are the others?" Taffy lost her anger and looked a bit lost. Maybe she hadn't been quite as comfortable as she'd seemed, being the only vamp in a crowd of Weres.

"Ah, they couldn't make it." Dahlia couldn't think of any way to cushion the rudeness of Taffy's other bridesmaids and her sheriff, Cedric.

Taffy sighed. "I didn't think it was too much to ask, coming to a party in our honor to wish me well." Dahlia's cheeks would have flushed if they could have; she was embarrassed at the poor manners of her sisters. "I guess it's a measure of our friend-ship that you came inside to see me," Taffy admitted. "I know we're buddies. Please, help me get through this wedding with peace between our people. I want you there on my wedding day, and I want my other friends there, too, and the last thing I want is a bloodbath between the two tribes, us and the Weres, right there in Cedric's garden."

Cedric had offered the garden of his mansion as the locale for the wedding, to everyone's surprise. Cedric had told Dahlia, in his languid way, that he had been sure Taffy would cry off before the day actually arrived. Now that the wedding was fast approaching and still a reality, the notably lazy Cedric was scrambling to get the grounds ready and also calling in markers in an effort to assemble some of the more level-headed vamps to act as security for the big night, which was shaping up to be *the* scandalous social event of the season in the supernatural world.

Ignoring the Weres who were peering out of the bar, Dahlia and Taffy began to stroll down the street, arm in arm, an old-fashioned habit that drew a few stares.

"Taffy, I'm worried."

"What about, Dahlia?" Taffy asked gently.

"You know that Cedric's mansion is in a turmoil of preparation," Dahlia began, trying to think of the best way to voice her concerns without sounding like a complete alarmist.

"I heard." Taffy laughed, her throat tilted back. "That old bastard! Serves Cedric right for making a promise he had no intention of keeping."

"Taffy, you've been with the Weres too much. Don't disrespect the sheriff so boldly."

"You're right," Taffy said, sobering quickly enough to satisfy even the worried Dahlia. "So, Cedric's in an uproar. What of it?"

"The Weres and the vampires aren't the only ones who may have heard of this wedding," Dahlia said. She was voicing something she'd not told anyone else, and her voice wasn't completely steady. "Since the Weres haven't come out yet, to the world it must look as though you're illegally marrying a human."

Vampires didn't have the legal right to marry in the United States, not yet anyway. Dahlia couldn't have cared less about her legal rights, since she knew how transitory governments were, but there was no denying it was sweet to be able to walk the streets openly, admitting her true nature, and to know that if she was killed, her death would be state-avenged.

Well, maybe, under certain circumstances.

The point was, society was moving in the right direction, and the backlash from this affair might knock all of them sideways.

"Who in the mundane world knows?"

"It won't make a difference if humans know it afterward; we can explain it wasn't a true wedding at all. Cedric can get reporters to believe anything. But if it becomes common knowledge beforehand, there'll be human reporters all over the place, and protesters, and who knows what else."

"Cedric's gardeners are human," Taffy said slowly. "The florist is human." Her face was utterly serious now, and she looked like a true vampire. They turned back to return to the bar.

Dahlia nodded, silently, knowing her point had been taken. She was thrilled to see Taffy looking like her former self, until she realized that though the familiar calculation had returned to Taffy's face, something had been taken away: the lighthearted joy that made the ancient vampire look so renewed.

"So, you're saying that we might need more security than Cedric's thinking of providing," Taffy continued.

Dahlia cursed inside. Her point had been that Taffy should call off this insane ceremony. But Taffy had simply not considered it for a moment. "Sister," Dahlia said, calling on the bond of the nest-mate. "You must not go through with this wedding. It will bring trouble on the nest, and . . . and . . ." Dahlia had a flash of inspiration. "It may bring the Weres out into the open before they are ready to be known," Dahlia said, confident she was playing a trump card.

"This is a big secret," Taffy whispered, and not even a gnat could have heard her whisper, "but in the next month, the Weres are voting at their council about that very issue."

It had taken years of worldwide secret negotiations to pick the moment for the vampires: months of coordination, selection, and a carefully composed text that had been translated into a myriad of languages. The Weres would probably slouch in front of the television cameras with beers in their paws and dare the world to deny them citizenship.

"Then delay the wedding until then," Dahlia urged, trying to ignore all these side issues and stick to the main point.

"Sorry, no can do," Taffy said.

It took Dahlia a minute to grasp the meaning of Taffy's words. "Why not?" she asked. She made her lips manufacture a smile. "I know you're not pregnant." Dead bodies, however animated they looked, could not produce live children.

"No, but Don's ex is." Taffy's face was grim as she looked down at Dahlia's stunned face. "We have to get hitched before she has the baby, or she can appear before the Were council and demand they reinstate her marriage. Don hasn't had a child with anyone else, and you know how the Weres are about the purebloods reproducing with each other."

Dahlia could not do something so gauche as gape, but she came close. "I've never heard of such a thing," she said weakly.

"None of us knows much about the Were culture," Taffy said. "Our arrogance keeps us ignorant." The two stepped off the curb to cross the mouth of the alley. The bright lights of the bar were only half a block away.

Dahlia brightened. "I'll kill her," she said. There, she'd solved the problem. "Then you can hold off on your marriage, or cancel it altogether. No need to get married, right? What does this bitch look like?"

"Like this," said a sweet voice from the shadows, and a young woman leaped out, the knife in her hand glinting in the streetlight. But as fast as the Were stabbed at Taffy, Dahlia jumped to intercept it. She deflected it with her bare hands, but not quickly enough. It lodged between Dahlia's ribs, and the strong Were woman began to twist the blade. Just in time, Dahlia gripped the Were's wrist, and neatly broke it before the gesture could be completed.

The woman's screams drew an outrush of Weres from the bar. They circled Dahlia, growling and snapping, sure that the vampire had attacked first. Dahlia herself was standing very still, trying to keep from shrieking. That would have been unseemly, in Dahlia's opinion, and she was a vampire who lived by a code.

Taffy was so shocked that she didn't react with the speed one expected of a vampire. Between trying to explain to her fiancé what had happened and positioning herself to slap away the hands that would have struck Dahlia, Taffy was too occupied to evaluate Dahlia's plight. Oddly enough, it was Todd who calmed things down by silencing the crowd with a yell that was perilously close to a howl.

Into the hush he said, "Keep all humans away, first of all." There was a flurry of activity as the few humans who'd been drawn by the ruckus were hustled off, diverted with some story that would hardly make sense when it was reconsidered.

"What happened?" Don asked Taffy. Several female Weres were kneeling on the ground around the moaning ex-wife. The Amazonian Were called, "The vamp bitch attacked Amber and broke her arm!" A chorus of growls swelled the throats of the werewolves.

Dahlia concentrated on her breathing. Though vamps healed with amazing speed, the initial injury hurt just as much as it would any other being. The blood dripped from her hands, but it was slowing. She held them out in the light, and the crowd murmured. Taffy exclaimed, "She did this for me!" and then became quite still. Her voice shaking with a very unvamplike quiver, Taffy said, "Dahlia protected me with her life. Not exactly in the bridesmaid description."

Don was clearly conflicted between the woman on the ground (whom Dahlia could see now was what she thought of as medium pregnant), his distraught fiancée, and Dahlia.

"Dahlia, what do you say?" he asked harshly.

"I say, the fucking bitch stabbed me," Dahlia said clearly. "And would someone please pull out this damn knife before I heal around it? I mean, just any old time will do, unless you want to moan some more over

Little Miss Homicide there." It was convenient that none of them had heard Dahlia offer to take care of Don's ex a few moments earlier. It gave her the definite moral high ground. Pregnant women, after all, were revered by almost everyone, both supernatural and human, and Dahlia needed all the leverage she could get. Without moving, because the pain was so intense she might fall down, Dahlia scanned the ring of Weres blocking the group from the view of passersby. "Todd, would you do the honors?" she asked, biting her lips with the pain. "You might even enjoy it."

Todd looked like there was nothing he'd enjoy less.

He bent down to look into Dahlia's green eyes, narrowed with the effort of sustaining her dignity. "I salute your courage," he said, and then he put one hand against her abdomen and yanked out the knife with the other.

Dahlia would have collapsed to her knees (terribly embarrassing) if the big Were hadn't caught her.

The next few minutes were a dim blur for Dahlia. She heard Don's stern voice, even deeper than usual, ordering Amber to tell the truth. Amber, a medium-sized blonde with a large bosom, wept copious tears and told her own jumbled version of events. In this version, she just happened to have a knife with her, in fact, ready in her hand, when Dahlia had jumped her. As to why Amber happened to be there in the first place, she whined that she'd just wanted to catch a glimpse of Don. Even the Weres didn't believe that.

"An attack on the packmaster's wife is an attack on the packmaster himself," Todd said.

"Then this vampire is as much at fault for breaking Amber's arm as Amber is for trying to kill Taffy," said the Amazon, trying very hard not to smile. "Since Amber is Don's wife."

"*Was* Don's wife," the packmaster himself corrected. "Before the state and the pack, I divorced Amber. Her attack on Taffy counts as an attack against me."

"Does not," argued the Amazon. "You haven't married Taffy, yet."

"Oh, for goodness' sake," Dahlia muttered. "Bore me to death, why don't you."

She felt Todd's chest shaking, and realized he was laughing silently. The wound in her side was almost healed, but she took her time pushing away from the Were's support. He was warm, and he smelled good.

She looked down at herself, taking stock.

Her dress was ruined. Ruined! And she'd just paid off her credit card bill! "My dress," she said sadly. "At least make her pay for my dress. Did blood get on my shoes?" She hobbled over to a streetlight and held out a foot in an attempt to survey the damage. "Yes!" she said, going from grief to outrage in an undead minute. The shoes were brand-new and had cost more than the dress. "Okay, that does it." Her head snapped up and she glared at Don. "Amber pays for my dress and my shoes, and she doesn't come within five miles of Taffy for a year."

She was speaking into a chasm of silence. At the sound of her crisp voice, all conversation had ceased. Everyone was staring at her, even the whimpering Amber.

Don blinked. "Ah, that sounds fair," he said. "Honey?"

There was another embarrassing moment when both Amber and Taffy believed this appellation referred to them and began to respond simultaneously. Don gave Amber a look of withering contempt, which prompted a fresh burst of noisy tears.

Taffy said, "That seems a very moderate sentence, to me."

Dahlia knew from her friend's mild tone that Taffy thought Amber should be drawn and quartered, no matter what her condition.

"Amber, do you agree?" Don asked.

"What about her paying my hospital bill? I have to get this wrist set, after all."

"That's stupid, even for you," Todd said, into the general silence. "Amber, one more offense and the whole pack will abjure you."

Dahlia didn't know what being abjured consisted of, but the mere threat was an effective deterrent. Amber was shocked silent.

Two of the Were women loaded Amber into a car and headed off, presumably for the hospital. The rest of the crowd dispersed, leaving Todd, Dahlia, Don, and Taffy on the sidewalk.

Dahlia held up a hand to examine in the light. The slash across the palm had completely healed, and when she touched the wound in her ribs, she only felt a slight tenderness. "I'll take my leave," she said. She wanted to divest herself of her ruined clothes, shower, and knock back a few pints of synthetic blood before dawn.

"I'll walk you home," Todd said. It would be hard to say who in the little crowd was the most surprised by this statement.

"That's not necessary," Dahlia said, after a second's recovery.

"I know you can carry me over your

shoulder like a sack of potatoes," Todd said. He looked down at Dahlia. "And I'm not saying I'm happy about my packleader marrying a vamp, legal or not. But I'm gonna walk you home, unless you fly away."

Dahlia's brows drew together.

"After all," he said, "I'm in charge of security for the wedding, and I'm the best man. Since you're the maid of honor, I understand, you'll be responsible for security on your side? We should talk."

Dahlia turned to Don and Taffy, who were standing hand in hand, looking shell-shocked. "I will see you tomorrow night, Taffy," the vampire said formally. "Don." She nodded at the packleader, still not able to think of a formal pleasantry that would suit the unsuitable alliance.

The big Were and the little vampire walked side by side for a few blocks. Everyone they met stepped off the sidewalk to give them room, and the odd pair never even noticed.

"You're quite articulate for a Were." Dahlia's voice was cool and steady.

"Hey, some of us have even graduated from high school," he said easily. "Myself, I made it through college without tearing up one single coed."

"I shared my brother's tutor until my parents decided that, as a girl, I didn't need to learn any more," Dahlia said, to her own surprise. To cover her confession, Dahlia launched into a discussion of the security measures for the wedding. The vampires would guard the doors to the mansion; the only people on the premises should be the invited guests and the catering staff.

"Are all the vampires living in the mansion invited to the wedding?" Todd asked, trying to sound casual.

"Yes," Dahlia said, after a moment's consideration. "We're all nest-mates, after all."

"How's that work?"

"Well, we live together under Cedric's rule, since he's the sheriff of this area. As long as we're nest-mates, we protect each other and come to each other's aid."

"And contribute to Cedric's purse?"

"Well, yes. If we stayed in a hotel, we'd pay for lodging, so that's fair."

"And do his bidding?"

"Yes, that, too."

"A lot like the pack does for the pack-leader."

"I had assumed so. What part will the Weres play in security?" Dahlia asked. Todd was asking entirely too many questions.

"There should be a Were at every door, too, along with a vamp. We need to make sure that one or the other knows everyone who comes into the mansion that day. This wedding isn't popular with anyone, vamps or Weres, and though Don is totally not worried, I am."

"None of the vampires are worried, except me," Dahlia confessed. They'd arrived at a side door to the huge house on a street in the heart of the haughtiest section of the city. Cedric had had centuries of savings to use in purchasing this prime piece of Rhodes real estate, and though having a vampire among them hadn't made the wealthy neighbors happy, the city's Freedom of Housing ordinance had reinforced the vampires' right to live where they chose.

Todd said, "Good night, dead lady."

"Good night, hairball," she said. But just before the door closed behind her, she turned to smile at him.

The day of the wedding closed clear and warm, ideal for the outside ceremony. Acting uneasily in tandem, the Were and vamp security teams had admitted the catering staff, scanning their ID cards quickly. The teams paid more careful attention to the invitations presented by their own kind.

When Dahlia checked out the garden, the fountain of synthetic blood was flowing beautifully, champagne glasses arranged in a tier on a table beside it. It was a pretty touch, and Dahlia was proud she'd arranged it with the caterer, along with a groaning buffet for the Weres and a bar with drinks both alcoholic and nonalcoholic. Dahlia walked down the buffet, checking the stainless-steel eating utensils and the napkins and heated containers full of food. It seemed sufficient, though Dahlia was not much of a judge. The two servers stood stiffly behind the buffet, eyeing her passage with unhappy eyes. Every human on the catering staff was tense. *They've never served vampires,* she thought, *and maybe the Weres are giving off some kind of vibration, too.*

She wasn't a bit surprised to encounter Todd, who was making a circuit of the high brick wall that guarded the large backyard of the mansion.

"Where's your dress?" he asked. "I'm panting to see it." Dahlia was in a black robe, modestly tied at her waist. Todd was already in his tuxedo. Dahlia had to blink.

"You look good," she said, her voice almost as calm as usual, though her fangs were sliding out. "Good" was a definite understatement. "Like a life-size Ken doll."

"I can't believe you even know what a Ken

366

doll is," he said, laughing. "If I'm a big Ken, you're a miniature vampire Barbie."

She'd been called worse things. She'd always admired Barbie's wardrobe and fashion sense.

"See you in a few minutes," she said, and went to get dressed.

Hanging over the door to the closet in Dahlia's little room was the bridesmaid dress. After a prolonged struggle with Taffy, Dahlia had talked her out of ordering pale pink with ruffles or pale blue with artificial roses sewn across the bodice. And no big bow on the butt. And no hat with veil. In fact, her nest-mate Fortunata came in just as Dahlia shimmied into the gown. Fortunata smiled at Dahlia's cautious look down the length of her body.

Taffy, despite her strange lack of judgment about this marriage, had finally had the sense to realize vampires would look ridiculous in innocent ruffles, girlish flounces, and insipid colors. The bridesmaids, four of them, were wearing dark blue square-necked long dresses that were form-fitting but not sleazily tight, and the spaghetti straps ensured that no one would lose whatever modesty she might possess. There were a few glittery sequins strewn across the chest to give the dress a little sparkle, and they were all wearing black high heels and carrying bouquets of pale pink and creamy white roses. Fortunata had just come from adding a little extra item to the bouquets, at Dahlia's request.

"Mission accomplished. Now I'm ready to fix your hair," Fortunata said, finding Dahlia's brush in the clutter on the dressing table. Fortunata had had a way with hair for centuries, and she brushed and pulled and twisted until Dahlia's black tresses were a model of sophisticated simplicity, with a couple of ringlets trailing here and there carelessly, to add just that touch of sensuous abandon.

"Not too shabby," was Fortunata's verdict when she and Dahlia stood side by side, and Dahlia had to agree. She felt a pleasurable tingle when she thought of Todd seeing her in the complete ensemble, and she hurriedly suppressed the reaction. Every time she viewed herself in a mirror, she felt a thrill of pleasure that the old canard about vamps having no reflection simply wasn't true.

The two bridesmaids united with the rest of the bride's side of the wedding party in the large common room at the back of the mansion. Taffy was in full wedding regalia, a pale redhead dripping in ivory lace. "She looks like a big white cake covered in icing," Fortunata muttered, and Dahlia, who actually agreed, said, "Hush. She looks beautiful." The long sleeves, the lace, the veil, the coronet of pearls . . . "We're lucky we're bridesmaids," Dahlia muttered. She drifted across the enormous, opulent room to gaze out the French doors at the scene outside. The French doors led out onto the flagstoned terrace, and from the terrace down onto the lawn. The scene looked very familiar, with white chairs in two groups of orderly lines, with a red carpet bisecting the groups. Either the catering company Cedric had hired was the same one that had had the concession at the wedding Dahlia attended a couple of weeks before or the arrangement was standard operating procedure. Dahlia had dispensed with the doves, fearing some of the Weres would eat the birds before they could be released.

A fairy or two mingled with the crowd, carefully staying over on the groom's side. Fairies were notoriously delicious to vampires, and though everyone was sure to be on his or her best behavior, not every vamp had the same threshold of self-control. Dahlia recognized a goblin or two that Cedric did business with and assorted shape-shifters, including one dark exotic who changed into a cobra. (That had been a memorable sight on a memorable night. Dahlia smiled reminiscently.)

Just then, a chorus of howls outside announced the arrival of the groomsmen, all decked out in their tuxes. Dahlia could distinguish Todd even at a distance. His burnished head was shining in the torches that had been set at intervals up and down the lawn. His glasses glinted. Dahlia sighed.

The music, provided by a Were rock band that was a favorite of the groom's, was surprisingly pleasant. The lead singer had a wonderfully tender voice that wrapped itself around love songs in an affecting way. He began to sing a number that she knew was called simply "The Wedding Song," because Taffy had dragged her along when she picked out the music.

Of course, the words weren't altogether pertinent since the subjects getting married weren't human. Don wasn't going to leave his mother, and Taffy wasn't going to leave her home. Taffy's home had slid into the ocean a couple of centuries before, and Don's mother was now pregnant by another member of the pack. But the sentiment, that the two would cleave together, was timely.

Just as Dahlia's eyes began to feel a little watery, Cedric appeared to give Taffy away.

This was his right as sheriff, and Dahlia was proud that Cedric had stirred himself enough to be fitted for a traditional tuxedo. (He'd threatened to appear in an elaboration of his court costume from the time of Henry VIII.) The scene outside seemed to be boiling with activity, lots of the caterer's minions milling around. They needed to be more unobtrusive, Dahlia thought, and frowned.

The music changed, and Dahlia recognized the signal. She snapped her fingers. The bridesmaids grew still, and Taffy stared around her, looking as though she was going to panic. Cedric was searching around in his pocket for a handkerchief, since he was prone to tears at weddings, he'd said. Though he was perhaps a foot shorter than Taffy, he looked quite dapper in his black-and-white. His gleaming skin and dark Vandyke beard and mustache made him appear quite distinguished, and if it hadn't been for a few niggling worries, Dahlia would have been very satisfied with the showing the vampires were providing. Cedric might not be a ball of energy, but he was handsome and had a polished turn of phrase that would come in handy at the wedding banquet.

"What's happening out there?" Taffy

371

asked. "Do I look all right?"

"Don has come to stand by his friend the minister," Dahlia reported. She had to stand on her tiptoes, even though she was at a slight elevation, to see what was happening. Don's friend, who'd been chosen over Harry the Druid, was a mail-order minister who happened to have a wonderfully solemn voice and an appropriate black robe. The marriage wouldn't exactly be legal anyway, so appearance was more important than religious preference. "He's looking toward the house, waiting for you!" Dahlia tried her best to sound excited, and the other bridesmaids twittered obligingly.

"Here's Todd, coming for me," she said, making sure she sounded quite emotionless. This was the way they'd agreed to do it, each bridesmaid going down the aisle paired with a Were, echoing the bridal couple. "That sucks," Glenda had said frankly, but Dahlia had given the other bridesmaids her big-eyed gaze, and they'd buckled.

Dahlia held her bouquet in the correct grip, and as Fortunata opened the door, Dahlia stepped out to meet the approaching Todd, who offered his arm at the right moment. The assembled guests gasped and murmured in a gratifying way at Dahlia's beauty, but Dahlia wanted to record only one reaction. Todd's eyes flared wide in the response Dahlia had long recognized as signaling sure attraction. Dahlia suppressed a grin and tried her best to look sweet and demure as she reached up to take Todd's brawny arm.

He bent down to tell her something confidential, and she waited with the faintest of smiles as they walked slowly down the red carpet.

"The caterers," he whispered. "There are too many of them."

"I wondered," she said, keeping her face arranged in a smile with some effort. "How'd they get in?"

"The caterer's in on it. They all had ID cards."

"This may be more fun that we'd counted on," she said, looking up at him for the first time. He caught his breath. "Woman, you stir my blood," he said sincerely.

She put her own feelings into her eyes and felt his pulse quicken in response. She murmured, "Armed?"

"Don't think we need to be," he said. "Tomorrow night's the full moon. We can change tonight, if we throw ourselves into it."

"When do you think it'll happen?"

"When the bride comes out," he said.

"Of course." The fanatics would want Taffy most of all. What a triumph for them if they could destroy the dead thing that wanted to marry a living man!

"If you change . . . there can't be any survivors," she observed, her soft voice audible only to his sharp ears.

He smiled down at her. "Not a problem."

They'd reached the front of the assemblage now. Dahlia was close enough to notice that the waiting groom was trembling with nerves, though Todd's arm under her hand felt rock-steady. They were due to split up here, Dahlia going to the bride's side and Todd to the groom's. "Don't separate," she said at the last minute, and they turned to face the guests together, but no longer arm in arm. The pair following in their wake, Fortunata and the stubby blond Were named Richie, were quick enough on the uptake to follow suit, as did the other two couples.

Now they formed a wall in front of the groom, and all Dahlia's hopes for her friend's safety depended on Taffy getting down the aisle and gaining safety behind the phalanx formed by the wedding party.

The men and women in white jackets — who'd been setting up tables and ferrying food from the kitchen and setting up the blood bar and the alcohol bar — were now trying to subtly position themselves in a loose circle around the guests and the wedding party.

All Dahlia's suspicions were confirmed.

It didn't take the crowd long to smell something odd. A confused murmur had just begun to spread through the guests when an apparently unsuspecting Taffy stepped out of the French doors. Cedric followed right behind her, giving her room to emerge in her full bridal splendor.

The caterers drew their weapons from under their white jackets and opened fire. Lots of the bullets were aimed at the bride.

But Taffy wasn't there. She had jumped five feet up in the air, and she was hurling her bridal bouquet at the nearest shooter hard enough to knock him down. Her eyes were blazing. Her red hair came loose from its elaborate arrangement, and she looked magnificent, every inch a vampire: a vampire totally pissed off that her wedding plans were being ruined.

Dahlia was proud enough to burst. But there wasn't any time to revel in her pleasure, because just as Todd bent to the ground and began to turn furry, Richie's chest exploded in a spray of red and Fortunata gasped with pain as a shot penetrated her arm.

From her own bouquet Dahlia extracted the wicked dagger she'd gotten Fortunata to conceal in its center, and with a bloodcurdling battle yell, she laid into the nearest server, a pie-faced young woman who hadn't mastered the art of close combat.

Dahlia and the other vamps mowed through the white-coated gunslingers like scythes, and the huge bronze wolf by her side was just as effective.

Though they may have been heavily briefed on the evil and vicious nature of vampires, the attackers certainly hadn't counted on such an instantaneous and drastic counterattack. And they didn't know anything about Werewolves. The shock value of seeing many of the guests turn into animals rendered some of the gun toters simply paralytic with astonishment, during which moment the wolves rendered them — well, literally rendered them.

One fanatical young man faced Dahlia's approach and held open his arms to either side, proclaiming, "I am ready to die for my faith!"

"Good," Dahlia said, somewhat startled that he was being so obliging. She separated him from his head with a quick swipe of the knife.

When the fighting was over, Dahlia and Todd found themselves back-to-back on a pile of rather objectionable corpses, looking around for any further opposition. But the only live people around them were those of their own kind. Dahlia turned to her companion. "It appears there are no more objections to the marriage," she said.

From the expression on his muzzle Dahlia could tell that she'd never looked so beautiful to the big Were — even covered in blood, her dress ruined. Todd changed from a wolf into an equally blood-dappled man wearing no clothes at all. "Oh," Dahlia said, happily. "Oh, *bravo!*"

Dahlia had paused to take some gulps of the real thing (to hell with the synthetic blood fountain) during the slaughter, and now she was rosy cheeked and feeling quite invigorated.

"The knives were your idea, weren't they?" Todd said admiringly.

Dahlia nodded, trying to look shy.

"It's a human tradition that the best man and the maid of honor have a fling at the wedding," Todd said.

"Is that right?" Dahlia looked up at him. "But you know, there hasn't been a wedding yet."

They looked around them as they made

their way to the terrace. Cedric and Glenda were sipping from cups they'd filled with blood that wasn't synthetic at all. Ever the gracious host, Cedric had uncorked some champagne and offered the bottle to Don. Taffy, hanging on to Don's bare arm, was laughing breathlessly. Her pearl coronet was still straight, but her dress was ripped in several places. She didn't seem to care.

Richie, the sole serious casualty on the supernatural side, was being tended ably by a little doctor who looked suspiciously like a hobbit.

"I now pronounce you man and wife!" called the Were friend who'd been the "minister" at the ceremony. He was as naked as Todd. He had his arms wrapped around the Amazonian Were woman, who was equally bereft of clothing. They seemed quite happy, but not as happy as Don and Taffy as they kissed each other.

The wedding was pronounced a great success. In fact, though it had been termed scandalous before it occurred, Taffy and Don's wedding turned out to be *the* social event of the Rhodes summer season, in certain supernatural circles.

The disappearance of the Lucky Caterer's entire staff was a nine-day wonder in Rhodes law enforcement circles. Luckily for the vampires and the Weres, owner Lucky Jones had kept the wedding off the books because she expected the humans would kill all the guests.

And it's true that, as Dahlia had told Glenda, going through a war together breeds comradeship; less than a year later, the same Were minister was officiating at Todd and Dahlia's nuptials.

The couple wisely opted to have a less formal wedding — in fact, a potluck. Dahlia had decided that, contrary to all social indicators, caterers were simply tacky.

CHARLAINE HARRIS, who has been writing books for twenty-five years, is a native of Mississippi. She has written the lighthearted Aurora Teagarden books and the much edgier Lily Bard series. Now she's working on a series about a lightning-struck young woman named Harper Connelly, and the Sookie Stackhouse books, which blend mystery, humor, romance, and the supernatural. The Sookie books are also being read in Japan, Spain, Greece, Great Britain, Germany, Thailand, Russia, and France.

In addition to her work as a writer, Harris is married and the mother of three. A former weight lifter and karate student, she is an avid reader and cinemaphile. Harris is a member of the Mystery Writers of America and the American Crime Writers League. She has served on the board of Sisters in Crime, and alternates with Joan Hess as president of the Arkansas Mystery Writers Alliance.

A Hard Day's
Night-Searcher

SHERRILYN KENYON

1

"Isn't it great?"

Rafael Santiago wasn't a religious man in any sense of the word, but as he read the short story Jeff Brinks had published in the SF magazine in his hands, he felt a deep need to cross himself. . . .

Or at the very least, club the college student over the head until he lost all consciousness.

Keeping his expression carefully blank, Rafael slowly closed the magazine and met his Squire's eager look. At twenty-three, Jeff was tall and lean, with dark brown hair and brown eyes. He'd only been a Squire to Rafael for the last couple of months, since Jeff's father had retired. An eager young man, Jeff had been good enough at remembering to pay bills on time, run Rafael's business, and help to protect his immortal status from the unknowing humans. But the

one thing Jeff had wanted more than anything else was to publish one of the stories
he was always scribbling on.

Now he had. . . .

Rafael tried to remember a time when
he'd had dreams of grandeur, too. A time
when he'd been human and had wanted to
leave his mark on the world.

And just like him, Jeff's dreams were
about to get the boy killed. "Have you
shown this to anyone else?"

Damn, but Jeff reminded Rafael of a
cocker spaniel puppy wanting someone to
pet his head even though he'd just unknow-
ingly pissed all over his owner's best shoes.
"Not yet, why?"

"Oh, I don't know," Rafael said, stretching the words out and trying to mitigate
some of the sarcasm in his tone. "I'm thinking the Night-Searcher series you're starting might be a really bad idea."

Jeff's face fell instantly. "You didn't like
the story?"

"Not a question of liking it really. More a
question of getting your ass kicked for spill-
ing our secrets."

Jeff furrowed his brow, and by his baffled
look it was obvious the boy had no idea
what Rafael was talking about. "How do
you mean?"

This time there was no way to keep the venom out of his voice. "I know they say to write what you know, but damn, Jeff . . . Ralph St. James? Night-Searchers? You've written the whole Dark-Hunter/Apollite vampire legend, and I really resent your making me a Taye Diggs clone. Nothing against the man, but other than the occasional bald head, the color of our skin, and a diamond stud in the left ear, we have nothing in common."

Jeff took the magazine from Raphael's hands, flipped to his story, and skimmed a few lines. "I don't understand what you're talking about, Rafael. This isn't about you or the Dark-Hunters. The only thing they have in common is that the Night-Searchers hunt down cursed vampires like the Dark-Hunters do. That's it."

Uh-huh. Rafael looked back at the story again, and even with the magazine upside down his eyes fell straight to the scene. "What about this, where the Taye Diggs look-alike Dark-Hunter is confronting a Daimon who's just stolen a human soul to elongate his life?"

Jeff made a sound of disgust. "That's a Night-Searcher who found a vampire to kill. It has nothing to do with the Dark-Hunters."

Yeah, right. "A vampire who just happens to steal human souls to elongate his life as opposed to the normal Hollywood variety where they live forever on blood?"

"Well, that's just cliché. It's so much better to have vampires who have really short lives and are then compelled, against their wills, and by a hatred fired by envy, to lash out at the human race. Makes it so much more interesting, don't you think?"

Not really. Especially since he was one of the people caught up in that battle. "That is also the reality we live in, Jeff. What you just described is a Daimon, not a vampire."

"Well maybe I borrowed from the Daimons a little, but the rest is all mine."

Rafael flipped to the next page. "Let's see. What about the cursed Tyber race that pissed off the Norse god Odin and is now damned to live only twenty-seven years unless they turn vampire and steal human souls. Substitute 'Apollite' for 'Tyber' and 'Apollo' for 'Odin' and again you have the story of the Apollite race who turn Daimon."

Sighing, Jeff crossed his arms over his chest. He shook his head in denial.

"And what about this part here where the Night-Searchers sell their souls to the Norse goddess Freya, who is a vibrant redheaded femme fatale dressed all in white, to get revenge on whoever caused them to die?"

"No one is going to figure out that Artemis is Freya."

Rafael growled at him. "For the record, unlike Artemis, Freya happens to be a strawberry blonde. But you were right about one thing. She is gorgeous and highly seductive. Definitely hard to say no to her."

"Oh." Deepening his scowl, Jeff looked up. "How do you know all that?"

Rafael grew quiet as he remembered the night he'd met the Norse goddess and she had tempted him well. That had definitely been one hell of a day. . . . "Freya's the goddess who hand selects warriors for Valhalla. Or in the case of myself, she wanted to take me off with her to her own hall and add me to her harem."

Jeff gaped. "And you chose to fight for Artemis instead, what kind of stupid are you?"

There were times when the kid could be eerily astute. "Yeah, well, in retrospect it was a bad bargain on my part. But at the time Artemis was offering me vengeance on my enemies it seemed so much more appealing than being Freya's love slave . . . which gets back to Freya being Artemis in your story."

"But you just said she's not Artemis and she comes after warriors, too. So it could happen. She could make a bargain like the one I wrote about in my story."

And icicles could grow on the sun. Freya collected warriors, she didn't send them back to the mortal plane to fight Daimons/vampires. Artemis did that. But not willing to argue the point anymore when it was obvious Jeff didn't see it, Rafael moved on to the next similarity. "And what about this? Ralph — Jesus, boy, couldn't you come up with something better than a bodily function to name me — was a Caribbean pirate, son of an Ethiopian slave and Brazilian merchant. . . ." He glanced down to read the description: "At six six, Ralph was one to intimidate anyone who saw him. With his shaved head that was tattooed with African tribal symbols given to him by a Shaman he'd met in his travels, he walked the earth as if he owned it. But more than that, the black tattoos blended at times with his dark brown flesh, making the two of them seem indistinguishable from each other as if he bore some kind of alien skin."

Unable to read another word of the description that was so eerily close to himself that it made him want to choke his Squire, Rafael let out a disgusted breath. "While

I'm both flattered and highly offended, I can assure you, this won't win you a Hugo or Nebula nomination."

Jeff pulled the magazine out of his hands again in a high-handed manner. "I resent that. It's a great story. And you don't exactly have those tattoos, either, now do you?"

Rafael's right eye started twitching from the aggravation. "I have intricate scroll work tattooed up my neck to the base of my skull and like *Ralph*" — he growled the word — "I have them on both arms. They're close enough to what you describe. No matter how you disguise this trite bullshit, it's my life, Jeff. Penned in an awkward manner. It's things I didn't want to see in black-and-white print. You're lucky after three hundred years that I've mellowed. In my human days, I'd have slit your throat, pulled your tongue through the opening, and left you tied to a tree for the wolves to eat."

"Ew!"

"Yes," he said, taking a step toward the overgrown adolescent, "and effective. Trust me, no one betrayed me twice."

"What about the guy who killed you?"

Rafael's eyes flared as he fought his urge to kill the boy. It was a damn good thing that he liked Jeff's father and the man had served him well for over twenty years.

Otherwise Jeff would be meeting with an "accident" right about . . . oh, now.

Taking a deep breath, Rafael asked in a tone that belied his anger, "I only have one more question. What's the circulation on this rag?"

Jeff shrugged. "I don't know. About one hundred and fifty thousand worldwide, I think."

"You are so dead."

"Oh, come on," Jeff said, dismissing the very real danger he was facing. "You're overreacting. No one is going to care." The best place to hide is out in the open. Haven't you ever heard that? Step out of the Dark Ages, Rafe. Everywhere you look there are vampires and a whole counterculture dedicated to them. Open your mouth to a woman, show her your fangs, and she'll beg you to bite her. Trust me. I have a fake set I wear to parties and use frequently. Nowadays being undead doesn't get you killed. It just makes it easier to get laid."

Rafael shook his head. "That argument has reached a whole new level of lame."

"Please, spare me that, old wise one. There's a whole new school of thought going around about how best to protect and hide you guys. If we start telling people about the Dark-Hunters, but make them think it's a book series or some urban fantasy thing, when they actually meet one of you, they'll just think you're either actors or roleplayers. Or at the very worst, they'll think you're insane, but never will they believe you're real."

He was seriously considering getting Jeff a CAT scan to make sure the kid still had a brain. "What Einstein came up with this?"

"Well . . . originally it was Nick Gautier."

"And the poor man is now dead. Shouldn't you guys be following someone else's ideas?"

"No. It makes perfect sense. Get out of the basement, Rafe, and hang with the new generation. We know the 911."

Rafael snorted. "It's 411, Jeff, and you don't know shit. But you are going to need 911 once the Council learns about this."

"I'll be fine, trust me. Nick and I aren't the only ones who think like this these days."

Those words had no sooner left his mouth than Rafael's cell phone started ringing. He checked the ID to see "Ephani." An ancient Amazon who'd crossed over almost three thousand years ago, she was definitely an acquired taste. But even so, he liked her a great deal. Pulling the phone off his belt, he answered it.

"What's up, Amazon?" he asked, stepping

away from Jeff while his Squire continued to admire his story in the magazine.

The kid had no sense of self-preservation.

"Hey, Rafe. I-um . . . I'm not sure how to break this to you, but do you know what your Squire's been up to lately?"

Deciding to play it cool, Rafael cut a glare at Jeff. "Writing the great American novel, what else?"

"Uh-huh. Have you ever read one of those novels he's been working on?"

"Not until today. Why?"

She let out a long sigh. "I'm assuming you have a copy of the *Escape Velocity* magazine with his story in it, right?"

"I do."

"Good, then it won't come as a shock to you to know that my Squire just left and she's heading over to your house to have a *talk* with Jeff. If I were you —"

"Say no more. He's leaving the country even as we speak. Thanks for the call, Eph."

"No problem, amigo."

Hanging up the phone, he narrowed his eyes on Jeff. "That was Ephani warning me that you're about twenty minutes from dying."

Jeff's face turned stone white. "What?"

He nodded. "Her Squire, Celena, Ms. Blood Rite, I-kill-anything-that-breaks-

390

formation, is on her way over here to have a word with you. Since Celena isn't real big on conversation, I'm taking that as a euphemism for 'kick your ass.' "

Rafael paused as those words conjured one hell of an image in his mind — Celena kicking *his* ass in that pair of stiletto corset boots she often wore. And in his mind she was wearing nothing but a thong. . . . Yeah . . . that was something he definitely wouldn't mind.

A native of Trinidad, Celena had the most perfect mocha complexion he'd ever seen. It was so smooth and inviting that it begged a man to taste it.

And her lips . . .

Angelina Jolie had nothing on her. She moved slow and seductive like a cat and he'd spent more than his fair share of time wanting her to rub that lean, curvy body of hers up against his.

But unfortunately, she was a Squire and he was a Dark-Hunter. By the rules of their world, she was off limits to him, and though Rafael didn't give two shits about most rules, Celena lived for them.

It was a crime against nature in his opinion that a woman that fine couldn't be corrupted.

"What do I do?" Jeff asked.

"Well, not to insult a man who looks like a rocket scientist in comparison to you, but . . . *run, Forrest, run.*"

"But I didn't do anything wrong. It's a new era where —"

"Do you really want to argue that point while someone, who is only a few minutes away, is speeding over here to most likely kill you?"

Jeff paused for a single heartbeat before common sense finally seized him. "Where should I hide?"

If it wasn't for the fact that as a Dark-Hunter Rafael was impervious to illness, he'd swear a migraine was starting right behind his left eye. "Get to the basement and hide there. Don't make a peep and don't leave until I tell you it's safe."

Jeff nodded before he ran for the door. Two seconds later he was back. Rafael watched him with a frown as he searched around the room until he located the baseball bat he'd used yesterday at the batting cages. He picked it up and cradled it to his chest before he headed back toward the basement.

"What are you doing?" Rafael asked.

"Protection."

Yeah, right. Celena was highly trained and deadly. A whack with the bat would only piss her off an instant before she jerked it out of Jeff's hands and beat him with it, but far be it from him to tell Gomer that.

"Hide well," Rafael said, exaggerating his voice.

Jeff nodded again before he dashed down to where Rafael's bedroom and living area were.

Pressing the heel of his hand against his brow where the imagined pain seemed to be located, Rafael glanced around the parlor of his Victorian house to make sure that Jeff hadn't left anything like his underwear lying about. The boy was a good Squire in that he kept up the appearance that someone lived in the house who actually aged but seriously sucked when it came to general housekeeping.

At least for once the place was decent. Except for the Xbox that Jeff had left stretched from the plasma TV to the leather sofa. Rafael had just turned the game off and put it away when he heard a fierce knock on his front door.

Rafael straightened his shirt before he sauntered over to answer it. He could already see Celena's curvy outline though the frosting on the glass. The porch light highlighted her medium brown hair that she wore pulled back from her face to trail in a ponytail of small braids from the crown of her head.

Her lips were perfect and outlined in dark red glossy lipstick. She had catlike almond-shaped eyes and an attractive mole right above the left arch of those lips.

Damn, she was the finest-looking woman he'd ever seen. Opening the door, he gave her the sexiest smile he could. "Hi, Celena."

But she was all business. Her dark brown eyes didn't even glance his way. They went straight past him, into the house.

"Where's Jeff?"

"Don't know."

That finally succeeded in getting her to look at him, but then she quickly glanced away and continued to search the house with her gaze. "What do you mean, you don't know? After dark, a Dark-Hunter is always supposed to know the whereabouts of his or her Squire."

"Ah, c'mon," he teased. "You don't really tell Ephani every place you go after dark, do you?"

"Of course I do."

She tried to step past him, but he quickly blocked her way and kept her outside on the porch.

"So what do you want with Jeff?" he asked in a nonchalant tone.

"That's Squires' business."

"Really? I thought anything that concerned a Hunter's Squire also concerned the Hunter, since he's my partner, in a purely platonic sense."

The edges of her lips twitched as if she found something funny about his words.

He couldn't explain it, but he really wanted to see a full-blown smile from this woman. "What?"

One corner of her mouth lifted into an attractive grin, but it still wasn't the smile he wanted to see from her. The kind that would light up her eyes and make her laugh. "I was just thinking about Rum, Sodomy, and the Lash — the pirate's credo."

He laughed at that even though he should have been offended. "Jeff is too hairy for my tastes. I much prefer a woman's smooth skin . . . the softness of a female body. I never was one to cuddle a porcupine."

Celena swallowed at the seductive tone in Rafael's deep voice. The sound of it had always reminded her of James Earl Jones, except Rafael's was marked by a heavy Brazilian accent. One that sent a chill down her spine.

She knew she had no business even looking at him with anything remotely similar to lust, and yet the man set her hormones on fire. Especially that wicked scent of masculine power tinged with Brut aftershave. It was a deadly combination.

Not to mention the fact that he was wearing a tight black V-neck sweater that only emphasized how perfectly formed he was. It clung to every dip and bulge of the muscles on his body. How was a woman supposed to keep her mind straight when a man like this was in front of her?

Clearing her throat, she forced her thoughts back to business. "Where is he?"

A devilish glint taunted her from the midnight depths of his eyes. "Tell me what you want with him and I might tell you where he is."

Narrowing her gaze, she found it difficult to maintain her outraged anger while he looked at her with that playful air. And that seriously annoyed her. "I'm here to take him into custody and deliver him to the Council."

"Well, that sucks." Even though his tone was sincere, she could tell he was mocking the Council and their orders. "Bank robbery, handing out the passwords for the Dark-Hunter Web site, carjacking, mugging, cats mixing with dogs, and now this . . . writing a short story. High crimes all. You get the rope and we'll hang him for it. God forbid the whole twelve subscribers of that magazine should actually read a fictional story and think it real."

She glared at him. How dare he make light of this. "It has a *substantial* readership."

"And Jeff used a pseudonym for not only us but himself as well. As the kid says, what better place to hide than under people's noses?" Even as he said that, he couldn't believe he was backing Jeff's story. But then that was what friends should do for each other. "It's nothing to worry over."

"Nothing?" She was aghast at his light tone. How could he write this off as if it were nothing more than a simple hangnail that bothered them? "He's exposed us."

"No, Talon getting filmed in the middle of a hissy fit in New Orleans exposed us. Zarek getting caught on tape exposed us. This is minor. I mean, damn, Acheron was able to cover up all the others with little incidence. This, too, shall pass."

Not bloody likely. "This is entirely different."

"I agree. Jeff is mortal and only has a handful of years left to him, whereas Talon and Zarek have an eternity to continue being stupid. Let's not shorten the kid's life any more than we have to, shall we?"

He did have a point, but she hated to

admit that. Besides, that didn't matter. She was here to do her job. Rafael didn't control her. She was a representative of the Council. "What happens to him isn't my decision. It's the Council's. I'm merely here to collect him."

"He's just a kid."

"He's only two years younger than I am and he's certainly old enough to know to keep his mouth shut."

"Haven't you ever done something you knew you shouldn't and then regretted it?"

She didn't hesitate with her answer. "No."

"No?" he asked incredulously. "You've never once broken a rule, lied, or got away with anything?"

"Only once in junior high when my sister came home late, because I didn't want to get her into trouble. Then one week later, she did it again and was injured in a car wreck, trying to get home before dawn, which taught me the value of lying to help someone. Since then I've never told another one and I don't intend to start now. I have integrity."

"Wow. You have one boring life."

"I resent that."

Those dark eyes teased and tormented her with a mixture of amusement and pity. "Resent all you want, but it's true. How have you managed to live such a perfect life?"

And that she resented even more. "It's not perfect. It has moments of . . ." She paused as she realized what she'd almost let slip. There were times when she really hated how uptight she was. But every time she'd ever tried to do something that was even remotely fun or even the least bit dishonest, she'd paid for it in the worst sort of way.

Like the time in high school when her sister had talked her into skipping school. They'd no more than driven down the street when her sister had plowed into the side of a Mercedes. Or the one time Celena had cut a man off in traffic only to get a flat tire immediately.

She had bad karma, which kept her perpetually toeing the line. If she'd been Jeff, the moment they published that story she'd have probably died of ink poisoning or something equally as bizarre.

But this wasn't about her. It was about a man who'd broken his Squire's oath, and he needed to be reprimanded.

Rafael tilted his head as he waited for her to finish her sentence. She was thinking of something, and from the darkness of her eyes and the furrow of her brow he could tell it was painful for her. "Of?"

Her expression turned blank. "Nothing."

Rafael gave her his best smile as he considered a way to save Jeff and to get him the one thing he wanted most . . . more time with a woman who tempted him.

"C'mon, Celena. Learn to live a little."

"I have rules to follow and a job to do. Surely even you can appreciate that."

"But don't you want to break free and have some fun just once in your life?"

She didn't answer, but by the look on her face he could tell that he was getting to her.

"Look," he said, trying to weaken her even more, "let's make a deal. Give me a week and if I can't get you to break one single Squire's rule, I'll hand Jeff over and let you hang him. . . . Hell, I'll even buy the rope. But if I do get you to break a rule . . . one teensy little rule, you'll let him go."

She shook her head. "It'll never work. The Council won't wait a week."

"Sure they will. Tell them you can't find him and that you're looking for him."

Her face hardened. "I can't do that. It's a lie."

She was a tough one. He'd never met anyone with so much resolve to do the right thing before. But then again, he'd been a pirate in his mortal life and high moral fiber wasn't exactly something they had a plethora of. In fact, those possessed of that madness usually found themselves killed off fairly quickly.

It was part of what he found so fascinating about her. How could someone live her life as she did? He didn't understand it, and a strange part of himself wanted to.

It was the same part of himself that wanted to know more about this woman other than the fact that she looked edible in those black jeans and crop top.

"You know," he said playfully, "it's not a lie. You really don't know where he is, and I can make sure that he runs from you for eternity."

She let out a tired breath as if she were suddenly tired of fighting him. "Why are you doing this?"

For once, Rafael was honest. "Because as stupid as he is, Jeff is a friend of mine, and I'm not going to hang him out to dry."

Celena had to admire that. Many Dark-Hunters could care less what happened to their Squires. To them a Squire was a servant, plain and simple.

"C'mon, Celena." He gave her a wink. "It's the only shot you have at getting him."

"And if I don't break a rule in a week's time?"

"I'll hand him over."

She cocked her head as she considered that. Rafael wasn't exactly known for keeping his word. "You swear?"

"Every day."

She hissed at him. "That's not what I mean and you know it."

For the first time, his handsome face turned completely serious. "On my word as a pirate who died defending his crew, absolutely."

He said it with such conviction that she found herself actually believing it. Besides, he was right. If he wanted to hide Jeff, there wasn't much they could do to reclaim him. And knowing the two of them, Jeff and Rafael would probably rub all their noses in it, too.

"Okay. I'm going to trust you. In seven days, I'll be back to collect him. Have him here and waiting."

She turned to leave only to find Rafael's hand on her arm, pulling her to a stop.

"Whoa, wait a sec, love. You don't think it's that easy, do you?"

"How do you mean?"

That devilish gleam returned to his midnight eyes. "There can be no faith without doubt. No strength without temptation. In order for this bargain to stand, you have to be *here* so that I can oversee your behavior myself."

She stiffened at his implication. "My word is gold."

"And usually mine is pyrite. At the moment, though, to see this through, I want you here to serve me. It's only fair anyway, since you're the reason I'm being deprived of Jeff's service, such as it is."

"Who will look after Ephani?"

"Call in a substitute. That's what you would've had to do to find him anyway, right?"

Celena was beginning to hate this man. "You can't be serious."

"Quite. Now is it a deal, or not? Think quickly before I change the terms again."

And he probably would, too, just to annoy her. "Fine, it's a deal." And yet even as she said those words, she had the sneaking suspicion that she'd just signed her soul away to the devil.

2

As soon as Rafael had Celena out of his house, he rushed to the basement only to find Jeff lying back on his black leather sofa, feet up on the coffee table, playing his PSP as if he didn't have a care in the world. It was so unbelievable that Rafael stood in the doorway for a full minute, staring with a slackened jaw.

Jeff was the kind of man that as pirates they'd have buried alive in the sand and left to rot. Why? Because people like him really were too stupid to live. It was a public service to speed them to their graves.

Honestly, the temptation to kill him was there and it was strong. Damn strong.

Yet again, Jeff was lucky Rafael had mellowed tremendously over the centuries. Not to mention the small fact that Rafael wanted an opportunity to break at least one more major rule before one of them died.

Jeff had no idea that he owed his life right now to the fact that Celena had the most tempting lips this side of paradise and if Rafael wanted a taste of them, he had to get Jeff out of here before she returned.

Rafael grabbed the tiny remote from the table to his left and turned the PSP off.

"Hey!" Jeff snapped, looking up. "I was on level four and I didn't save it."

"Screw level four. I need you to get out of here, pronto."

"And go where?"

"My boat in the marina."

Jeff curled his lip in distaste. "And do what?"

"Live through the night, which is more than you're going to get to do if you don't

404

stop lipping off. Now get up and get started. I've bought you some time, kid, but it's finite. You have to go lie low for a week."

While Jeff made juvenile noises of discontent, Rafael's attention fell to his laptop, which was on the table at Jeff's feet — that should do to keep him occupied and out of trouble.

At least until the poor bastard published something again.

Picking the laptop up, Rafael handed it off to Jeff. "Go write your great American novel, but for God's sake, do what everyone else does and make the whole story up."

Jeff grimaced at him. "You know I get seasick."

"You'll survive seasickness. Lead poisoning's another matter. There's enough staples and such on board that you should be fine. Keep your ass below deck and if you so much as look at the helm, I'll cut your head off myself. You're not to go joyriding or anything else on my boat — it really is worth more to me than your life. Do not leave the lower deck under any circumstances barring fire, and whatever you do, keep a bucket nearby and don't puke on anything."

Jeff screwed his face up as if that were the most sickening thought he'd ever had. "But

I want to stay here."

"And people in hell want ice water and if you don't go to the boat, you'll probably be able to take it to them in person in about twenty minutes. Get out, Jeff. Now."

Jeff started to grumble as he got up, then caught himself. "Can I take the PSP?"

"If it will speed you on your way."

"You got any more games for it?"

Raphael growled low in his throat as he picked the small black game case off the coffee table and chucked it at him. "Anything else?"

"A hooker would be nice."

"Jeff . . ."

"I'm going; I'm going."

The pain in Rafael's skull returned as Jeff made his way back upstairs at a pace that would make a slug proud. Oh yeah, they'd have sacrificed him on the main deck ten seconds after boarding.

"Could you pick up the pace, Jeff? We only have another eight or nine hours until daybreak."

He cast a grimace at Rafael over his shoulder. "You're such a bossy asshole."

"Comes with being a pirate captain . . . which my father was, too, by the way. He wasn't a merchant like you have in your story. He ate those for breakfast."

Jeff actually stopped on the stairs. "Really?"

"Jeff!" he snapped. "Up. The. Stairs."

Mocking his words, Jeff finally managed to make it up to the door. It took about fifteen minutes to get him packed and out of the house, along with more warnings about what Rafael would do if Jeff so much as scuffed a board on his boat.

Jeff had only been gone at most five minutes before Celena returned. Rafael had to force himself not to glance down the street after Jeff, since it was obvious the two of them must have passed each other on the road. But unlike Jeff, Celena was quick on the uptake and would realize why Rafael was looking north.

No doubt she'd catch the snail and salt him well.

"Welcome back, my lady," Rafael said as Celena adjusted the black backpack on her shoulder as she neared his door.

She only grumbled in response as she stepped past him and entered his house. "I can't believe I have to do this," she said under her breath.

He was a bit stung by her words until he realized she still wasn't looking at him. In fact, she avoided it with such determination that it made him smile. No woman did that unless she was interested and was trying to fight it.

"Let me show you where to bunk."

Celena stepped back so that Raphael could lead her toward the mahogany stairs in the middle of the house. She really did hate being here. How could she serve a man who distracted her so much? And as he headed up the stairs and she had an unobstructed view of that tight, perfectly formed butt, it was all she could do not to reach out and grope it.

This was wrong on so many levels. How had she allowed him to talk her into this?

It's the only way to get Jeff. Or was that just an excuse so that she could be here with him? Not wanting to even consider that thought, she forced herself back to business. She'd have to keep her thoughts on her work and not on how good Rafael looked while dressed all in black. . . .

Or more to the point, wonder what he'd look like without those clothes on.

He took her to the first room on the left. "This is the guest room, not that I ever have guests, except for . . ." He glanced at her and winked. "We won't go into that, but it's clean and well kept."

"Thanks," she said, stepping inside to find a room that was decorated in Victorian antiques. It was actually quite lovely, with heavy burgundy drapes and gold brocade Chippendale chairs. The Victorian tester bed held a matching burgundy and gold bedspread that looked lush and inviting.

Not half as inviting as it would be with a naked Rafael in it, but what could she do?

Ask him to join you?

Yeah. Shaking her head at her errant thoughts, she set her backpack on the mattress, then turned to look at Rafael, who cut a tempting pose in the doorway. With him dressed in black pleated pants and a black sweater that clung to his body, it was hard to think straight. Which meant she needed to get him out of here before she lost all sense of her duties and succumbed to the idea of stripping him bare.

"Shouldn't you be out patrolling?" she asked.

"Still too early. Besides, there hasn't been much Daimon activity lately." He crossed himself. "Since Danger died, it's been unnaturally quiet."

"Yeah, that's what Ephani says, too. It's like they've moved on, which is weird. You'd think killing a Dark-Hunter would have invigorated them."

Without commenting, he moved closer to her . . . so close that the scent of him invaded her senses. More than that, it warmed her completely. There was something calming about that scent of Brut and man. Something tempting and sinful.

It kept her spellbound as he paused right beside her and lifted his hand to brush a stray braid from her shoulder. Her heart racing, she couldn't move. All she wanted was to feel him touching her.

A small smile hovered on the edges of his lips as he dipped his head toward hers. She knew he was going to kiss her and still she couldn't move.

Not until his lips parted and she glimpsed his fangs.

He's a Dark-Hunter.

That jolted her enough that she could take three steps back. "We should reorganize your house while I'm here so that it's more efficient."

Rafael bit back a foul curse. One more second and he would have had her. "House is fine."

"No. No, it's not. Do you even have an evacuation plan for what to do if it were to catch fire during the daylight? You know you could roast and die quite easily, then you'd be a soulless Shade and screwed for eternity."

That went over him like a cold shower.

Now there was something he'd never thought about before, and he was pretty good at putting together disaster plans.

"It happens a lot with these older homes," she continued. "What with their faulty wiring and all. I heard of one Dark-Hunter who died like that just last year."

"Who?"

"I can't remember the name, but it was one of the Dark-Hunters in England. Total barbecue. You can check it on the Web site."

He'd really rather not. No Dark-Hunter liked to read about the death of another one. It brought home that even though they were technically immortal, there were still things out there that could kill them. And having died already, it wasn't something Rafael wanted to experience again.

Still, she didn't relent. "You should contact a friend of mine. He specializes in fireproofing underground bunkers for Dark-Hunters. He can put in a sprinkler system and —"

"You're rambling."

"No, I'm not. Dark-Hunter safety is a Squire's number one priority. In fact, I'll call Leonard first thing in the morning and see when he can come out for an estimate. We should also make sure that you have a roll bar in your car in case you flip over in a wreck. Oh, and a steel bar shield on the driver's side in the event you run up under something, so that you can't be decapitated."

Without conscious thought, Rafael's hand went to his throat. Damn, the woman gave paranoia a whole new meaning.

"We should also look into the history of this house and make sure that it was never used as a bed-and-breakfast."

"Why?"

"If property has ever been used as a community place such as a boardinghouse, restaurant, or anything open to the public, then the Daimons can enter without an invitation. You don't want them barging in on you and killing you, now do you?"

"Not really."

"Then we need to do a property search. Unless your last Squire did that."

"No."

She tsked. "I need a piece of paper. This is going to take a while."

And by the time she fished that paper out of her backpack and started making a list, Rafael felt ill. The woman should work as a Codes Inspector. Jeez. She thought of dangers that had never occurred to him.

She even went outside and inspected the grade of his basement, which wasn't high enough, in her estimation. After all, according to her, a foundation shift could cause a crack that could theoretically expose him to daylight.

Not bloody likely, but she seemed determined to ferret out any possible — heavy emphasis on the "possible" — threat.

By the time ten o'clock rolled around, he was more than ready to begin his patrol. He came up from the basement to find an arsenal on the table.

Two daggers, three stakes because two could break in a fight, a Daimon tracker that he'd always profaned using, a Kevlar jacket, his cell phone, and a watch were all laid out for him.

When she lifted the Kevlar to help him into it, he merely stared at her. "Bullets can't kill me."

"No, but they do hurt. The Daimons could, in theory, shoot you until you're too weakened to fight them and then behead you."

He shook his head at her as he again declined to put on the jacket. She was perturbed as she set it aside while he hid the daggers in his boots.

"Want to put a cone around my head like a dog to make sure that they can't decapitate me while we're at it?" he asked sarcastically.

"I would," she said to his instant incredulous dismay, "but Ephani got really angry when I tried that with her, so I learned that it's more important for you to blend in than protect the neck. But I do have this." She pulled a thick black steel collar from her pocket. "If you wear it under a turtleneck, it's not so obvious. Kind of medievally looking."

He had no response to that. It was the most ludicrous thing he'd ever heard. In fact, as he tucked the stakes away, he had to force himself not to use them on his latest menace. . . .

Her.

She handed him the watch. "I double-checked the sunrise on weather.com and cross-checked it with the meteorological society and my friend who's an astronomer to be sure it was accurate. It's at six fifty-nine a.m. sharp. I've already set the alarm to give you a twenty-minute warning." Next, she held out a piece of paper. "Here's a list of how long it will take you from various parts of the tri-city area to get back here. I'll keep an eye on your tracers to make sure that you have adequate time to make it back home without threat or harm."

Then she handed him a folded-up black body bag. "And in the event you can't make it back, zip yourself up in this and press the panic alarm I added to your key chain. Then I can come get you home before the daylight makes you burst into flames."

Again, he was speechless.

She picked up his cell phone. "I preprogrammed my number in on the speed dial under one and Acheron under two. Did you know you didn't have any numbers listed as 'ICE'? You should always have an In Case of Emergency contact number. So I put mine in for that, too."

"What about Jeff?"

"Since he won't be with us much longer, I didn't bother."

This was madness. No wonder Ephani hadn't fought him on having Celena replaced for a week. Jesus, Mary, and Joseph, the woman was insane.

"Anything else, Mom?" he asked.

"Yes. Play nice with the other kids and don't let the Daimons get the drop on you. Use the tracer so that you know where they are at all times."

Raphael couldn't get out of his house fast enough. So much for his thoughts about trying to seduce her. He'd rather face the Daimon horde blindfolded and with both hands tied behind his back.

More than that, he'd rather go babysit

Jeff. If anyone had ever told him that he'd prefer the lazy, lackadaisical boy to the hot Caribbean sex goddess, he'd have laughed in their face.

Now he could appreciate Jeff's laid-back nature.

Maybe it's just a ploy of hers. . . .

He paused at that thought. Maybe she was just doing this to drive him away. It was possible.

Very possible.

Oh yeah, he was on to her now. It made total sense.

Fine then. Two could play this game.

Getting into his car, he smiled. *"En garde, ma petite."* They were about to go to war, and at the end of this, he was going to win.

3

Rafael wasn't winning his war. He was losing it miserably and not even with style. No matter what he tried, Celena circumvented his best efforts. The woman was a machine, and after forty-eight hours of having her in his house, he'd had enough.

Sitting on his couch in the basement an hour after sunset — because, quite frankly, if he went upstairs, he might kill her — he

416

called Ephani, who answered on the third ring.

"Come get your Squire," he said without preamble.

Her tone was dry and snide. "Hi to you, too, Rafael. Nice to hear from you."

"Cut the crap, Eph, and come get her before I kill her."

"She making you crazy?" He could hear the humor in her voice.

"You think? How do you stand it night in and night out and not lose your mind?"

"She's a little obsessive, but —"

"A *little?*" he asked incredulously. "The woman makes a serial stalker look like a Boy Scout."

Ephani snorted. "She's not that bad."

"Oh yes, she is. Trust me. I almost lost my head to a Daimon the first night she was here."

"How so?"

He clenched his teeth at the memory. "Picture this. There I am in the alleyway, sneaking up on a group of Daimons who have this college kid trapped between them. Just as I go to make my move to save the kid, the phone rings with Ms. I-have-no-purpose-save-to-make-you-crazy calling to tell me that according to the tracer she has on me it's time for me to head home so that

I won't get caught out in daylight."

Ephani was laughing so hard that he wanted to reach through the phone and choke her.

"It's not funny."

She kept laughing.

Rafael let out a disgusted sigh. "Did she reorganize your kitchen and fill it up with wheat germ and shit? I tried to explain the whole I'm-immortal-I-live-forever to her, but she doesn't get it. She said that even immortals need to eat healthy foods."

Still Ephani was laughing.

And still Rafael wanted to kill the Amazon as well as Celena. "This really isn't funny, Eph."

"Oh yeah, it is. Gah, Rafe. You're such a man."

"And I'm going to take that as a compliment."

Clearing her throat, Ephani finally sobered. "There's a few things you need to understand about Celena."

"You mean something other than she's nuts?"

Ephani tsked at him over the phone. "She's not nuts."

He glanced up to the ceiling. No doubt Celena was up there right now doing something extremely odd in order to protect *him,* the immortal warrior. "I think I'll reserve my opinion."

"Trust me, Blackbeard. She's not nuts."

"Then what is she?"

"Scared." The word surprised him. Celena certainly didn't act that way. "Have you tried to ask her anything about her family?"

"A couple of times, but she won't talk about them."

"That's right and do you know why?"

"She's nuts?" This time he said it with a little less enthusiasm.

"No . . . she's scared."

But that didn't make sense to him. "Of what?"

"Of losing the people she loves, so she tries to keep up walls to protect herself. If she doesn't talk about people, then they can't be close to her. But it's a crock. I know this because when her father died a year ago, it almost killed her. She still cries about him in the middle of the day when she thinks I'm sleeping."

The news floored him. That was so opposite of the hard-nosed woman upstairs. There was nothing vulnerable about her, and honestly, he couldn't imagine her crying about anything. "Celena?"

"Yes, Celena. And do you know why she's so anal about her duties?"

"She's nuts?" He was back to being convinced. Anyone who executed their duties to such an nth degree wasn't normal.

"No," Ephani said in an irritated tone. "Like Jeff, she's from a Squire family. The Dark-Hunter she grew up with was killed eight years ago because he was cornered by a group of Daimons and executed. If that wasn't bad enough, the first Dark-Hunter she was assigned to died because she couldn't make it back before sunup. Celena tried to get to her in time, but there was no place for her to hide, so she turned into toast minutes before Celena got there. The Council warned me when they sent her over that she was a bit . . . traumatized by the event. Hell, if you think she's bad now, you should have seen her when she first came to work for me."

If she was worse, then he was grateful he hadn't met her then. But all that actually explained a great deal about her psychosis.

"And she must really like you to be so paranoid that she's calling you all the time to make sure you get back home in time. She's not that bad even with me." Then she added under her breath, "Then again, I always follow her patrol plans and get back before she freaks."

Rafael was quiet for a second as he considered Ephani's words. "That puts a lot of perspective on her, doesn't it?"

"Yeah."

"Okay," he said with a sigh, "I won't kill her tonight."

"Please don't. All in all, I'm rather fond of her, and I have to say I much prefer her to the one I'm dealing with right now. This one's kind of lazy. She even balked at making my scrambled eggs with cheese and onions in them."

Rafael laughed at that. "I guess it's what you're used to."

"I guess. But send Celena home soon. I miss her."

He shook his head. "By the way, thanks, Eph."

"No prob. Just take care of my girl."

"Will do." Rafael hung up the phone and tucked it back in his pants pocket. His mind whirling with what he'd learned, he headed upstairs to find his "breakfast" waiting.

Grabbing a piece of bacon, he had to admit that this was the one thing he liked about having Celena around. Unlike Jeff, she was up all night with him and made sure that he had plenty of food prepared. She even packed him a snack bag to take with him. Of course it was full of wholesome foods that he poked at like an alien life-form, but it was a nice thought.

"Hi."

He swallowed his bacon as she brought him a glass of orange juice. "Hi."

After he took the glass, she lifted a notebook up from the table. "I've made notes on your patrolling patterns. I've noticed that you tend to stay here in Columbus around campus until about midnight and then you head over to Starkville. I was thinking that —"

He took the pad from her hand and set it aside. "I like *my* pattern, Celena."

"But it would be safer for you to patrol Starkville first and then head back this way."

"And I was a pirate who laughed as he died and spat in the face of my killer. Safety's not my concern."

"It should be," she insisted.

"Why?"

Her brow creased by worry, her face held a very faint hysterical note in it. "Because you could die and become a Shade, wandering the earth with no body and no soul, in constant pain and misery. Wanting food. Wanting someone to hear you. Wanting someone to just touch you and having no one able to see you. To —"

He stopped her words by laying his fingers on her lips. Personally, he didn't like the

422

gruesome image she painted with her words. "It's okay, Celena. I'm not going to die."

But he could see the pain and fear in her eyes. "That's why you should rethink your pattern."

Moving his fingers from her soft lips, Rafael dipped his head down to capture her mouth only to have her retreat from him again.

He let out a tired breath. "Don't you ever date?"

"Not anymore. To bring an outsider in could threaten the safety of Ephani. What if I were on a date and she needed me?"

"What if a meteorite fell through the house right now and flattened us both?"

She actually glanced up at the ceiling.

If it wasn't so serious, he'd laugh. "Celena, you can't go through your entire life worrying about what *might* happen." He closed the distance between them. "Any more than you can go through life alone. Trust me on this one. It's lonely as hell."

"You live that way."

"Not always. I do reach out to someone from time to time."

Instead of comforting her, those words brought out her anger. "And I'm not your one-night stand. We both have duties to attend to. Oaths to uphold."

"I would kiss you anyway, but I have a feeling that if I tried —"

"I'd kick you in the nuts and tear your ear off." There was no mistaking the sincerity of her angry tone.

"That would hurt."

"That's the idea."

Rafael shook his head at her. She was saucy, and as she walked away from him he couldn't help the heat that flooded his body. Everything about her appealed to him on a primal level.

Honestly, he was losing his mind being this close to something that tempted him while unable to touch it. No wonder the Council preferred to assign only Squires who were the opposite sex of what a Dark-Hunter lusted for.

I can't take it. He needed some distance from her.

"I'm going to kill Daimons now."

"But it's early."

"I know. But I have a feeling they're out already and I need to patrol." Or stay here with the hard-on from hell until he lost what little sanity he had left. As Oscar Wilde once said, he could resist anything except temptation.

Before Rafael could make it to the door, his phone rang. Without looking at the ID, he answered it.

"Rafe?" It was Jeff whispering in a panicked tone.

"Yeah?"

"There's a group of Daimons here at the marina."

"It's too early for them to be out."

"Tell *them* that!"

"Calm down and tell me what's going on."

"It's spooky as hell. There's some kind of party going on at the houseboat next door that started at sundown and I just saw six of them heading for it."

"All right. Lie low and I'll be there in a few minutes."

Celena frowned at the concern in Rafael's voice. "Is there a problem?"

"Major Daimon alert."

Before she could ask anything else, he was gone, but his words rang in her ears. Major Daimon alert . . .

This could be bad.

You're a Squire. Her place was at home, especially after dark. And then she saw Eamon's face in her mind. His smiling face as he teased her about not eating peas.

"Did ya do yer homework, lass?"

God, how she'd loved that man. He was like an older brother, a best friend, and a father all rolled into one. And in one heartbeat, the Daimons had killed him.

Let's face it, with the exception of Ephani, you've had a bad run with Dark-Hunters. The more she cared for them, the more horrible their deaths.

And she loved Rafael. She'd loved him since the first moment she'd met him after she moved to West Point, Mississippi. He was intelligent, smart, and he had a wicked sense of humor.

Now he was going to fight the Daimons. Alone.

A thousand scenarios went through her head, with all of them coming to one single conclusion.

Rafael dead. Panic set her heart to beating furiously as she looked about his home. She couldn't pack up another Dark-Hunter's home. She couldn't hold another vigil service to pay respect to someone she loved.

She couldn't.

And before she could stop herself, she grabbed the tracer off the table and her keys.

4

When Jeff had said that there was a group of Daimons heading for a party, Rafael had taken that to mean that there were only six Daimons at a *human* party. You know — a regular party with teenaged or college-aged

426

humans groping each other while drinking heavily. The kind of party that he normally crashed so that he could protect the humans from the Daimons who wanted to feast on their souls.

What the rocket scientist had failed to mention to Rafael was the small fact that the Daimons were headed into an *Apollite* wedding reception. Something he, himself, hadn't realized until he'd walked onto the boat that was filled with tall, gorgeous pale *blond* preternatural people.

Oh yeah, the six-foot-six bald black man dressed all in black leather really didn't blend into the overdressed crowd of Nordic vampires. And Rafael had to admit that right now looking at the Apollites and Daimons who were staring angrily at him made him feel like the last steak in the Kennel Club.

It was so silent, the only sound he could hear, even with heightened hearing, was his own heart beating. Though there was blood in their goblets — he could smell it — there didn't appear to be any humans around who needed saving.

Except for, maybe, him.

One of the Apollites closest to him arched a brow before he spoke. "Bride's side or groom's?"

"I'm with catering," Rafael said in a flat tone.

A Daimon stepped forward to give him a cold, feral once-over. "Yeah, you look like food to me."

The Daimon female beside him smiled, showing off her fangs. "We can't really eat him, since his blood is poisonous to us, but killing him should have some entertainment value. What do you think?"

Yeah, he'd walked right into the lion's den. There were at least twelve Daimons that he could sense. And another twenty Apollites. Normally Apollites didn't fight against Dark-Hunters, since Dark-Hunters were forbidden to touch them until they stopped feasting on fellow Apollites and began feasting on human souls, thereby becoming Daimons. Then it was open warfare between them.

However, this group didn't seem too concerned with keeping the unspoken truce between Dark-Hunters and Apollites. They truly were bloodthirsty.

And now they were attacking.

Reaching under his coat, Rafael grabbed his steel stake and plunged it into the heart of the first Daimon to reach him. With an anguished cry, the Daimon exploded into dust. Two more came at him. He caught the first one a quick hit that sent him flying backward, into the arms of another Daimon, while he flipped the second one over and stabbed him straight in the chest.

Before he could straighten up from the kill, the Daimons overran him like ants over a sugar cube. He hit the ground face-first as they clawed at him. He could feel something biting into his back that felt like a knife wound, but it was hard to tell as he struggled to get them off him.

Celena knew she was breaking the rules, but Rafael didn't have to know it. All she was going to do was make sure he was okay, then head back to his house. No one would ever know what she'd done. No one.

She parked her car as close to the docks as she could before she took off running toward where the tracer in her hand said Rafael was. A thousand fears shredded her as she relived the night Sara had died. Celena had been trying to get to her. They'd been on the cell phone together as she raced to make it in time.

The last sound she'd heard had been Sara screaming as she burst into flames.

Grief threatened to overwhelm Celena. She couldn't lose another Dark-Hunter. And especially not Rafael. She'd loved him far too long to let him die.

With no clear thought of what she had in mind to do to help him if he was in trouble, she ran onto the boat, then skidded to a stop.

It was total chaos.

But more than that, there was no sign of Rafael anywhere. He appeared to be buried by the large stack of Daimons and Apollites in the center of the boat.

Her eyes welling with tears, she met the gaze of a woman in a wedding dress for only an instant before she pulled a stake out of her coat.

"Rafael?" Celena cried, heading for the fray.

A Daimon turned on her then. Celena kicked him back and kept going toward the largest group of them. She knew that was where Rafael had to be.

She couldn't see anything as she pushed, kicked, and fought until she finally saw what she'd come for. Rafael knocked a Daimon off him while another was trying to pin him to the ground. But what made her panic swell most was the Daimon coming toward them with an ax.

If they managed to cut off Rafael's head, it was over.

The Daimons pulled back as someone

grabbed her from behind. Reacting on pure instinct, Celena head-butted her assailant with the back of her head and launched herself at Rafael who still lay on the ground. From the corner of her eye, she saw the ax falling.

She curled herself around Rafael's head and waited for the pain of the ax slicing through her.

It never came.

There was a sudden silence that rang out as everything seemed to freeze into place. Her heart racing, Celena opened her eyes to see the Apollites and Daimons staring above her. She rolled over to find the Daimon who'd held the ax. Only now the ax was gone.

It was in the hands of the groom who stared not at them but at the others with a stern glare. "Enough!" he roared. "This is supposed to be my wedding!" He looked over at the bride, whose face was pale, her delicate lips trembling. "And you're upsetting Chloe. I've only got five more years with her before I die and the last thing I want is to have what few memories I have left ruined by a bunch of bloodthirsty assholes." He picked out with his gaze the ones who must be Daimons. "No more bloodshed!"

The Daimon next to Celena curled his lip. "He killed my brother."

The groom snarled. "Your brother was a dickhead and he's lucky I didn't kill him. I told all of you that you weren't to cause any problems tonight, didn't I?"

The Daimon turned sheepish.

The groom tossed the ax overboard before he approached them. To Celena's complete shock, he held his hand out to her.

She exchanged an uncertain look with Rafael before she reached out, clasped the groom's hand, and allowed him to pull her to her feet.

"You can't let him go," another Daimon sneered.

"It's my wedding. I can do what I please. This is supposed to be a night of celebration —"

"Then let's celebrate by killing a Dark-Hunter."

The groom looked disgusted. "Someone stake that bastard, please, and for the sake of the gods, dust Benny off the table by the fountain. That powder's disgusting and it's getting into the blood." He helped Rafael up. "Don't worry. It's not human blood. It's ours."

Rafael wasn't sure what to think as he faced the Apollite in front of him. They could have killed him and Celena both. He was having a hard time believing that they would just let him go.

"Why are you doing this?" Rafael asked.

The groom looked back at his bride. "Because life's too short to spend it fighting when you could be holding the one you love. And love's too rare to squander it with petty concerns." He took his wife's hand in his and held it tight. "I'm lucky I have Chloe and I have no intention of letting a war I didn't start rob me of one second of my time with her. Go in peace, Dark-Hunter."

Rafael was surprised by his words, but even more so by his charity. "You're a good man."

The Apollite scoffed. "I guess we'll see in about five years, huh? If I die peacefully, then I'm good. If not, then we'll face each other again as predators." He indicated the ramp with a jerk of his chin. "Now go before I change my mind."

Deciding not to press his luck, Rafael draped his arm around Celena and held her close to him to protect her as they made their way off the boat. He didn't stop walking until they'd made their way over to the dock by his boat. He paused at the prow to turn back and see the Apollites and Daimons resuming their party.

"That was flipping amazing!" He looked up to see Jeff in the shadows.

He reminded Rafael of a kid who'd just got away with something. "I thought you were dead. Man, I was in the process of calling Acheron for help when I saw the two of you leaving. How did you manage it?"

Instead of removing his arm from around Celena, Rafael leaned his head against hers. "Luck . . . which I'll take over skill any day."

Jeff's face sobered as he realized Celena was there. He actually gulped. "I'm dead, aren't I?"

Rafael held his breath as he met Celena's speculative gaze. He expected her to shove him away from her and go after Jeff.

Instead, she wrapped her arm around Rafael's hips. "I made a deal with Rafael, and it seems you're safe from me."

A small smile hovered at the edges of Rafael's lips as he stared at her in the moonlight. "Go home, Jeff."

"Okay, let me pack and —"

"No," he said sternly. "Go home right now and don't stop until you're safe in your room. You can get your stuff later."

He could tell Jeff wanted to argue, but luckily for his Squire, the man caught the tone of his voice and immediately left. And as soon as he did, Rafael did what he'd been dying to do. He finally kissed Celena.

Celena moaned at the taste of Rafael as his tongue swept against hers. He cupped her face in his hands as she inhaled the sharp scent of his skin and aftershave. It was a breathtaking combination, and all she wanted to do was peel his clothes off him and lick every inch of his body.

She knew she had no business with him, and for once she didn't care about rules. The Apollite had been right. There were some things more important than something so trivial.

Rafael pulled back from the kiss. "Why did you come for me?"

"I was afraid you were in danger."

He shook his head at her. "You know that was amazingly stupid of you. I'm rancid meat to them, but you . . . you're a buffet. You're damn lucky they let you go."

She smiled up at him before she repeated her earlier words. "Yeah, well, I'll take luck over skill any day."

He laughed before he kissed her again. "And that still doesn't tell me why you came after me. You broke a dozen rules by following me tonight."

And for some reason that didn't bother her. Nothing had mattered to her except seeing him safe. "I know, but I couldn't let you die."

"Why?"

She bit her lip as the reasonable side of her brain begged her not to say anything else. But all the years of her hiding her emotions for this man rushed to the forefront, and after being with him for this last week, she couldn't hide it anymore. "Because I love you."

Rafael couldn't have been more stunned had she stabbed him. He stood there in complete shock as he watched her eyes dilate ever so slightly. In all the centuries he'd lived, only one other woman had ever said those words to him . . .

And she had died in his arms on their wedding night under the assault of his enemies.

He'd never had the chance to taste her. Never had a chance to show her just how much he loved her.

He wasn't going to take that chance with Celena. His body burning, he scooped her up in his arms and carried her on board his boat.

"What are you doing?" she asked as she wrapped her arms around his neck.

"Carpe noctem. I'm seizing the night. But most of all, I'm seizing the woman in my arms."

Celena didn't say another word as he took her below the deck. As soon as they were out of the sight of any passersby, she literally ripped the shirt from his back so that she could finally touch the body that had haunted her dreams for the last few years.

Her career as a Squire was over, but she didn't care. The only thing that mattered right then was being with Rafael. She shivered as he pulled her shirt over her head and cupped her breast through her bra.

Closing her eyes, she savored the heat of his hand as he pushed the satin aside to touch her flesh. She captured his lips with hers as she feverishly opened his fly, then dipped her hand down to touch him. He hissed in response, making her soar in satisfaction.

"Boy," he whispered against her lips, "When you break the rules, you seriously break the rules."

Celena didn't respond as he pulled her pants down her legs. She sucked her breath in sharply between her teeth as she saw him kneeling on the ground at her feet. Lifting her foot, she let him remove her shoes, which he tossed over his shoulder before he undressed her.

His dark eyes flashed an instant before he reached up to remove her panties. Her entire body burned as he bared her to his hungry gaze. Reaching down, she traced the outline of his lips as he gently tongued her fingertips. She'd dreamed of this moment a thousand times.

He was the main reason she'd never really dated. After she'd met him, other men never seemed to compare. They weren't as handsome. Weren't as dangerous.

Weren't as forbidden.

And now she was finally going to know what it felt like to hold him. . . .

Rafael couldn't breathe as he slowly rose to his feet. He still couldn't believe that Celena was here with him. That she who lived for rules and regulations was willing to sacrifice her Squire's oath.

His heart pounding, he reached down to brush his hand against the softness of her abdomen, then lower to the short, crisp hairs until he found what he sought. He groaned at the sensation of her wet heat against his fingers while she stroked him with her hand.

Unable to stand it anymore, he pinned her back against the wall and kissed her passionately.

Celena clung to him as she lifted one leg to wrap it around his hips. Taking the invitation, he drove himself deep inside her.

Rafael's head spun as an unimagined ecstasy tore through him. Celena had almost died to protect him. No woman had ever done such a thing for him before. Her strength, her courage . . .

It was unlike anything he'd ever known.

And now she met him stroke for stroke as they made love furiously. He smiled as each thrust was punctuated by the sound of the beads on the ends of her braids scraping against the wall.

Celena buried her lips against Rafael's throat as she forced herself not to think about what was going to happen tomorrow. She couldn't stay with him. She knew it. He was a Dark-Hunter. But here for the moment, he was hers, and that was all that mattered.

Arching her back, she cried out with every powerful thrust of him inside her as she clutched him to her. He dipped his head down to capture her breast and tongue it in time to his strokes. She cradled his head to her as her body was overwhelmed by pleasure. With every stroke it increased until she finally couldn't stand it anymore. Her body burst into a thousand tendrils of ecstasy.

Rafael growled as he felt Celena climaxing. Wanting to give her even more, he quickened his strokes and watched as she threw her head back and moaned.

His smile faded as he lost himself to his own orgasm. Burying himself deep inside her, he shook with the force of it. Her breathing ragged in his ear, she gently stroked his back as he slowly drifted back into himself. This was one of the most amazing moments in his life. Not because of the sex, but because he was being held by a woman who was willing to sacrifice herself for him. A woman who was willing to break the rules. . . .

Most of all, a woman who loved him.

He kissed her tenderly on the lips. "Don't leave, Celena."

"I'll be here until morning."

"No," he said, his voice thick with the emotions that were churning inside him. "I mean don't leave. Ever."

Her mouth opened ever so slightly. "What are you saying, Rafael?"

"I love you."

She couldn't believe her ears. It was more than she'd ever hoped for. "You don't have to say that."

"It's not that I'm saying it. It's that I'm feeling it."

Thrilled by his words, she squeezed him tight. "So what's to become of us now?"

"Looks like I'll be joining the human race again."

"Are you sure?"

Rafael grew quiet as he considered it. If he continued being a Dark-Hunter, he'd have to let her go.

The Apollite's words rang in Rafael's head. He'd been alone for all these centuries. Not once in all this time had any woman ever made him feel his emotions more strongly than Celena. She made him crazy, angry, happy. . . .

But most of all, she made him feel like he could fly.

He didn't want to live without this. Without her.

"Yeah, I'm sure. That is, if you're willing to take Artemis's test."

"For you, my pirate, I'd walk through the fires of hell."

EPILOGUE

Two Months Later

Celena stared at Acheron, the Dark-Hunter leader, as he explained that in order to free Rafael from Artemis's service she would have to kill him. "You've got to be kidding me."

"Do I look like I'm joking?"

She raked her gaze from the top of his

long black hair to the tips of his custom-made Goth biker boots with bat buckles. And at six foot eight there was a lot of him to rake, too, but every bit of his long, lean frame was deadly sincere, which made her sick to her stomach.

How could she kill the man she loved? What kind of psycho had instituted that policy?

Then she looked to Rafael, who was standing behind Acheron, in the hallway. His handsome face betrayed nothing but trust. His black eyes were kind and gentle, encouraging, and that made the love she felt for him swell.

"I can't kill him."

Acheron let out a patient breath. "He won't be dead long. You simply stop his heart from beating, then you hold the stone against his bow and arrow tattoo. His soul will leave the stone and return to his body."

"You can do it, baby," Rafael said with that decadent accent of his. "You told me just last night that you wanted to choke the life out of me."

Instead of smiling, she grimaced at him. "That was for hogging the remote, and I wasn't serious. This is entirely different."

Acheron shrugged. "Fine then, he continues being a Dark-Hunter, and the Council will reassign you away from him."

Her heart stopped at the mere thought of not seeing him anymore. "You can't let them do that."

"I control the Dark-Hunters. The Squires are their concern, not mine. I have no jurisdiction there, which is why Jeff is now cooling his heels in Squire jail for writing that story. I personally thought it was funny, but the Council doesn't really have a sense of humor, do they?"

Frustrated, Celena wanted to argue, but she knew better. If she and Rafael were to ever have a normal life, he would have to be human again.

Right now, the Council knew nothing about their relationship, but sooner or later they were bound to find out and then there would be hell for her to pay.

Unless she and Rafael were already married. Then there was nothing the Council could do. There was no law prohibiting her from marrying a human male. It was the only loophole they could hope for.

"Okay," she said with a determined sigh. "I can do this."

This time it was Acheron who hesitated. "There's one more thing you need to know."

She gave Acheron a peeved stare. "And that would be?"

"The stone with his soul in it will burn your skin the minute you touch it, and it won't stop until his soul has returned to his body. If you drop the stone before that time, he'll be a Shade."

Oh, that was a pleasant thought. In freeing him, she could very well be damning him to an eternity of hell. Shades couldn't eat, couldn't be seen or heard. It was a fate far worse than death.

And she could be the one to gift him with that oh, so not pleasant existence.

Still Rafael's gaze burned into her. "I want to be with you, Celena. As a man."

How could she argue with that? What's more, she wanted it, too. So long as he remained a Dark-Hunter, they couldn't have children. But if she freed him . . .

They could have a family. They could be married and grow old together. It was all she wanted.

"Okay," she breathed. "Tell me what to do."

Acheron pulled a long, evil-looking dagger from his boot and handed it to her. "Pierce his heart and leave the dagger in until he goes limp." He shrugged his black backpack off his shoulder and took out a black box that was about the size of a softball. He opened the lid to show her a vibrant blue stone that was chiseled with intricate markings. It was a strange, compelling object that seemed to hum with life.

She reached for it only to have Acheron move it away.

"Remember, it burns. I'll hand it to you and then you press it to Artemis's mark."

She gulped as she stared at the stone. It was hard to fathom that was Rafael's human soul in there. "Are you sure this works?"

"Kyrian, Talon, Valerius —"

"Okay," she said as Acheron listed off the Dark-Hunters she knew had gone free. "Let's do it."

Rafael pulled his shirt off so that she could see the double bow and arrow mark on his left shoulder.

Her heart pounding, she gripped the dagger tight in her hand and met his obsidian gaze. The love there scorched her.

"You can do it," he whispered. "Just pretend I'm Jeff."

She wanted to laugh at his joke, but she couldn't even muster it. Instead, she ground her teeth and did the hardest thing she'd ever done in her life.

She tried to stab him, but the dagger didn't so much as pierce his skin. Stunned, she tried harder, but still it wouldn't budge.

"What's wrong?" she asked.

Acheron grimaced. "Damn. We forgot to drain his Dark-Hunter powers out of him. You can't kill him while he's immortal . . . at least not and leave his body whole."

"Then what do we do?"

Acheron scratched the back of his neck. "I'm not supposed to interfere, but what the hell? For you two, I'll make an exception."

He took the dagger from her hand and plunged it into Rafael's heart, up to its hilt.

Rafael staggered back before he slid slowly to the floor.

"Oh God," she cried, horrified by what Acheron had done, as she knelt down beside him.

Rafael's face was contorted by pain as a small trickle of blood left the corner of his mouth.

Instinctively, she reached for the dagger to pull it out.

"Not yet," Acheron said, pulling her back. "He has to die or he can't go free."

Tears filled her eyes as she panted along with Rafael. He cupped her cheek in his palm as he offered her a small smile. "It's okay, Celena."

She only hoped he was right.

Covering his hand with hers, she held it

tight as she watched the light fade from his eyes. And she gave a small cry as the last breath was expelled from his body.

Acheron took the stone from the box and held it out to her. His swirling silver eyes bore into hers. "Don't drop it."

Nodding, she took it from him only to scream out as a furious pain seared her skin. It burned worse than any imaginable fire and it was all she could do to maintain her hold. The only thing that kept her from releasing it was the knowledge that Rafael would die if she did.

She ground her teeth as Acheron helped her place the stone over the mark. Tears flowed down her cheeks from the pain and fear as she waited for Rafael to open his eyes.

It seemed an eternity had passed before Acheron pulled the dagger out of his chest.

An instant later, Rafael took a deep breath and blinked his eyes open to look at her.

Celena laughed in giddiness as she saw eyes that were no longer black. Now his eyes were a light amber brown that sparkled with human life. He was even more handsome than he'd been before.

Biting her lip, she pulled him into her arms and held him close.

Acheron moved away and returned the

dagger to his boot.

"Thanks, boss," Rafael said as he pushed himself to his feet.

Acheron gave him a kind grin. "I'm not your boss anymore, Rafael. *She* is."

Rafael laughed. "That doesn't bother me."

Acheron snorted. "Yeah, be glad you're human now. Nothing like answering to one single woman for eleven thousand years to make you wish for the end of time."

Celena laughed again. "Thank you, Acheron."

He inclined his head to them. "You kids have fun."

Rafael looked down at the woman in his arms and tightened his hold on her. "Trust me, we will."

And as soon as Acheron was gone, Celena pulled him down for a fierce kiss. Rafael's head swam at the taste of her. It was a taste he would now spend the rest of his life savoring.

New York Times bestselling author SHERRI-LYN KENYON has more than six million copies of her books in print, in twenty-four countries. She is the author of the Dark-Hunter novels, which have an international cult following and have appeared on the top-ten lists of *The New York Times, The Globe and Mail*

(Toronto), *Publishers Weekly,* and *USA Today.* Writing as both Sherrilyn Kenyon and Kinley MacGregor, she is the author of several other series, including Brotherhood of the Sword, Lords of Avalon, and BAD.

Near Nashville, Tennessee, Sherrilyn Kenyon lives a life of extraordinary danger . . . as does any woman with three sons, a husband, a menagerie of pets, and a collection of swords on which all of the above have a major fixation.

Visit her Web sites at www.sherrilynkenyon .com and www.Dark-Hunter.com.

". . . Or Forever Hold Your Peace" A Kit and Olivia Adventure

SUSAN KRINARD

Author's note: This story is set in an alternate Victorian England, Albion, where magical talents, like land and titles of the peerage, are inherited or "entailed" among the Albian aristocracy. Commoners may sometimes manifest "knacks" or minor Residual Talents.

". . . Into which holy estate these two persons present come now to be joined. Therefore if any man can show any just cause why they may not lawfully be joined together, let him now speak, or else hereafter for ever hold his —"

"I have cause!"

The bishop's mouth dropped open, showing a full set of crooked teeth. The congregation in the pews twisted around with like expressions of shock, and a deadly hush fell over St. Bertram's-in-the-Fens.

The man who had spoken stood at the rear of the church, fists clenched in defi-

450

ance. Though he wore respectable-enough clothing and his hair was neatly combed, his accent was that of the Eirish commons, and it was immediately clear to Lady Olivia Dowling that he did not belong in this exalted company of Albion's most noble patricians. Lord Edward Parish, still kneeling at the altar, glared at the intruder with such ire that he seemed very apt to display his Luciferian powers and start a fire right then and there.

"Who are you?" he demanded.

The unwelcome guest faltered beneath several score hostile, unwavering stares and then gathered his courage. "My name does not matter," he said, his voice booming up to the buttresses. He looked directly at Lady Emma, bride-to-be and daughter of the Earl of Wakefield. "If only you had told me the truth. I would have understood. I —"

He broke off, his ruddy skin going pale. Olivia frowned and studied him more carefully, sinking deep into her Talent as an Anatomist. The man's body betrayed him. His heart had begun to beat very fast, his palms to sweat, his eyes to widen with violent alarm. Olivia glanced again at Edward, who still stood at the altar. Lady Emma swayed, and Edward caught her against him.

The bishop finally found his voice. "Who are you?" he echoed. "You have interrupted a most solemn ceremony. What have you to say?"

When it was over, Olivia could not have said precisely what she had felt before the man bolted. It was rather as if she heard something through his ears, an eerie wail that could not have come from a mortal throat. She knew that the stranger was consumed by such dreadful fear that it seemed that his heart must burst from his body.

He spun about, fell to one knee, scrambled to his feet, and charged for the doors, keening in despair.

A woman screamed. Everyone rose in a rustle of long skirts and the shuffle of polished shoes, and a trio of guests at the rear of the nave pursued the intruder out into the watery London sunshine. Olivia heard a rough, masculine cry of sheer terror, and then silence. A moment later one of the guests returned, his expression set and grim. He started for the altar, where Lady Emma trembled in Edward's arms.

"I beg your pardon," Olivia said to her nearest neighbors as she squeezed past them out of the aisle. She looked about for Kit and, not seeing him, strode for the doors.

A flood of wedding guests poured out of the church, crowding about Olivia as she paused at the top of the steps. A woman at Olivia's elbow gasped, and a gentleman cursed under his breath.

The stranger lay at the bottom of the steps, his body twisted, his head bent at an improbable angle. One of the guests crouched by his side. Christopher Meredith — "Kit" to his dearest friends — was particularly handsome today in his wedding clothes, his unruly black hair tamed into a semblance of order and no whiff of the Black Dog about him, though he wore his smoke-lensed spectacles to hide the crimson glint in his eyes.

Olivia remembered the third guest who had followed the unfortunate stranger and searched the crowd of gawkers that had gathered in the square to point and gossip. She caught a glimpse of a gentleman's well-cut suit, an impression of aristocratic features, just before the man turned and vanished into the mob.

Olivia lifted her skirts and rushed down the steps with indecorous haste. Kit looked up as she joined him.

"Lady Olivia," he said, inclining his head with grave formality. "I'm afraid he has passed on."

Olivia knelt beside him, calling upon her fickle Residual gift and praying that this time it would obey her summons. In an instant she knew that Kit's diagnosis was correct.

"He appears to have died of a broken neck," she murmured. "What do you suppose he was running away from?"

"Probably thought better of his dashed interruption in a church filled to the rafters with Talent and a bridegroom capable of frying him in his boots."

Olivia clucked. "This is no time for levity, Kit. He was terrified before he fled the church, as if he'd seen a . . ."

A what? she asked herself. Unless one of the guests was an Illusionist or an extremely rare Conjuror, it was highly unlikely that the man could have seen an apparition invisible to the guests. And yet . . .

"There's a stink of magic in the air," Kit said more seriously, "but I can't identify it. It isn't human, that's certain."

"Then he was driven to his death by supernatural means."

Kit frowned. "It's possible. But just as I arrived, I saw a man in wedding clothes departing the scene. It wouldn't be difficult to trip someone fleeing down the stairs in a state of mortal terror."

"And if this man was murdered . . ." She bit her lip. "Who would want to silence a man with objections to a marriage?"

She and Kit exchanged glances. The motives were obvious when one wished to protect the reputation of one's daughter . . . or fiancée.

"Lord Wakefield wouldn't stoop to such an act, even if he anticipated this disturbance in time to arrange the murder," Olivia protested. "And as for Edward . . ."

"Impossible," Kit agreed. "But whatever or whoever contributed to this man's end, the devil's in it now. The police are on their way, although I'm sure that Lord Wakefield will arrange to keep the matter quiet. The bishop will call a halt to the proceedings pending an investigation . . . and as the subject is dead . . ."

"Poor Emma. What an odious thing to happen on one's wedding day." She shook her head. "Will you see Edward?"

"Yes. He'll be distraught, but Emma . . ." He sighed. "You should go to her, Livvy. Her mother will be having a fit of the vapors, and her other relations won't help in the least."

"Of course." She touched Kit's arm. "I'll see you later, then."

She hurried back up the stairs and continued on through the nave to the vestry, where Emma sat surrounded by her family and a most agitated clergyman. Emma's sister was weeping, Lord Wakefield was pacing furiously, his wife the countess lay prostrate on a settee, and Edward was nowhere to be seen.

Olivia went straight to Emma and took her icy hands. "Are you all right, my dear?" she asked gently.

Emma met Olivia's gaze, her eyes great wells of misery. "Edward is furious," she whispered. "The wedding must be postponed. And I hear that the young man is dead. . . ."

"Hush." Olivia stroked a loose strand of hair away from Emma's face. "Don't trouble yourself about that now. I want to help you, Emma. Can you answer a few questions?"

"I . . . believe so."

"Good girl. Have you ever seen that man before?"

Olivia felt Emma's heart jump, but her answer was swift and vehement. "No."

"He is of Eirish descent. You know no one from that country?"

"Only servants, and they would have no cause —" She broke off and raised her handkerchief to her mouth, stifling a sob.

She was clearly in no state to cooperate in

any investigation, so Olivia comforted the thwarted bride with every reassurance she could muster. "Don't worry, my dear. I will do whatever I can to help you."

Emma sniffed but didn't answer. Olivia took her leave and went back outside, where the guests were finally beginning to disperse. The police had come and gone, taking the body with them.

"Any luck?" Kit asked, coming up beside her.

"None. Apparently Emma didn't know the man, although . . ."

Kit arched a brow. "Although what?"

"There is something very peculiar about the entire situation."

"And you naturally wish to get to the bottom of it."

"Naturally. Emma is in a great deal of distress. If the investigators determine that the stranger was in fact made to fall, suspicion could descend upon Emma's family. This could be a scandal of epic proportions —"

"And you could never contain your curiosity in any case."

Olivia wrinkled her nose. "Don't tell me that you have not resolved to take action yourself."

"But of course. I am Edward's friend,

457

after all." Kit offered his arm, and they walked in the direction of Olivia's waiting carriage. "But I would never dream of doing so without you at my side."

"Or you at mine." They smiled at each other, content in the perfect understanding of a long and durable friendship.

"Emma is gone."

"Gone?"

"Is my speech as incomprehensible as all that, Mr. Meredith?" Olivia said irritably, pausing to instruct the coachman to deliver her to her hotel. "The countess says that Emma must have departed before dawn this morning — crept out without so much as waking her maid — and left only a brief note that said nothing of her reasons save that she had no choice but to go. She took only one small bag . . . scarcely enough for a lady of her breeding, even for a single day."

"Not all ladies of breeding feel compelled to carry their entire wardrobe wherever they travel," Kit said, giving Olivia a pointed glance. "Perhaps Lady Emma is more like you than most of these simpering society damsels."

"Don't be foolish, Kit. Even if that were so, why should she run off, and without a decent word to her family? Surely she can't be so ashamed of yesterday's incident —"

Unless she has something to do with the death, Olivia thought, but Kit suggested a slightly more palatable explanation.

"It's quite possible that she knows there is some substance to the stranger's objection, which she has failed to admit to her interrogators" — he cast Olivia another piercing look — "and she fears to have her secret exposed."

Olivia folded her arms across her chest. "What 'secret' do you suggest? That Emma is already married, or that she and Edward are within the proscribed degree of blood relation?" She snorted. "That is ridiculous, and you know it."

"I admit that it does seem unlikely. But it's no coincidence that she left within a day of the interrupted wedding."

"No. And Emma's family have not been able to locate her, though they have had servants, police, and Finders looking for her since she was first discovered missing."

Kit examined a cracked fingernail. "Are you still committed to solving this mystery, Livvy?"

"More than ever."

"Then we shall have to summon Old Shuck."

Olivia rolled her eyes at the quaint old

East Anglian name Kit gave his other half. "You know I'm as fond of dogs as any good Albian, but —"

"Old Shuck is no mere dog," Kit said with feigned affront. "Really, Livvy. If even Finders can't locate Lady Emma, then she has well and truly disappeared. A Residual Talent, perhaps?"

Olivia thought of her own vexingly unreliable ability as an Anatomist — one who could literally see into the human body, which was only a tiny part of the power she would receive once her grandmother chose to bestow her magical inheritance. Primogeniture declared that nonmagical assets such as land and title were almost always passed on from peer to eldest son, leaving younger sons and daughters with lesser property or modest annuities.

With Talents it was different. Each bearer of Talent in a Great Family, male *and* female, respectively, selected a boy and girl of the next generation to inherit that line's magic. Inheritance was not dependent upon the matrimonial state of the heir. When the elder died or chose to surrender his or her powers, the younger successor received the Talent in full measure.

Emma was almost certainly Lady Wakefield's chosen heir. She might possess some

Residual form of her mother's gift.

"Have you heard anything of her maternal line's Talent?" Kit persisted. "Edward has never mentioned it, which leads me to believe that Lady Wakefield's line is one that prefers to keep the nature of its magic hidden from the world."

Rather like Kit himself, whose Wild Magic would not be considered quite acceptable in good society. It carried the stigma of illegitimacy and the Cymry and Eirish rebellions, of dark ceremonies chanted over ancient altars in the black of night.

A Talented family only concealed the form of its magic when said gift either was embarrassingly trivial, like a commoner's Residual knack, or carried darker implications. Such concealment was considered somewhat bad form, and could arouse suspicion . . . but the countess's secret had certainly not prevented the Earl of Wakefield from marrying her, or obtaining an excellent match for their daughter.

"Emma has never spoken of it, either," Olivia said. "I always assumed it was a minor and useless ability, like calling up an unpleasant odor." Her eyes narrowed. "Do you think the Eirishman's objection had something to do with her family Talent?"

"I can't imagine any Talent that would

provide a real obstacle to the marriage."

"Nor can I. Well, once we find Emma, we shall simply have to persuade her to speak."

On that note they reached Olivia's hotel, where she alighted to pack her belongings while Kit made his own arrangements. Though the rules of strict propriety dictated that Olivia should take her maid on any excursion with a bachelor, the situation was not precisely conducive to propriety. It required the utmost discretion. And though Alice was far from unfamiliar with the workings of Great Family magic, she would return to Waveney Hall the next morning.

At sunset, just as Olivia was setting down her book on the life of Elizabeth III, she heard the expected knock at her door. Alice answered it and showed Kit into the room.

"I've found her trail," he said, grinning as he removed his spectacles. His eyes still burned with the Black Dog's crimson light. "She took the Oxford road."

Olivia dismissed Alice and offered Kit a glass of his favorite whiskey. "How was she traveling?"

"By carriage, or I might not have located her." He downed the whiskey in one swallow. "She must have hired a Residual to cover her tracks, but it wasn't enough to draw me off the scent."

"How far did you follow her?"

"Not far. I came back for you." He glanced about the small sitting room. "Are you ready?"

"Of course. I —"

Another loud rapping came at the door, and with scarcely a pause Edward burst through.

"Kit!" he said. "I hoped I'd find you here." He bowed stiffly to Olivia. "Lady Olivia. I am sorry to disturb you, but . . ." He blew out his cheeks, looked straight at the whiskey carafe, and charged for the sideboard. "May I?"

"Of course." Olivia poured for him, judging that he was in no state to drink more than a little of the potent stuff. "You have heard nothing from Lady Emma?"

"Nothing." He drained the snifter and set it down with a trembling hand. "It's intolerable. There's no telling what predicament she has —" His voice thickened, and he swallowed. "I've come to ask for your help, Meredith. No one can seem to locate Emma, but I know that you . . ." He cleared his throat, peering with fascination into Kit's red-tinted eyes. "You have certain —"

"Shadowy abilities?" Kit offered wryly. "Wild Magic?"

Edward flushed, and the long-dead ashes

463

in the grate suddenly began to spark. "I beg your pardon. I assume that Lady Olivia knows . . ."

"Oh yes," Olivia said, striving to inject a little lightness into the conversation. "I've known since we were children."

"And it's hardly a secret anymore," Kit added, "at least not from my friends, though I'd prefer that it *remain* among friends."

"Naturally," Edward said, looking relieved. "Can you help me?"

"*We* shall help you," Olivia said. "Kit has discovered the way she took out of London, and now it is only a matter of —"

"Bless you," Edward said, seizing her hands. He noticed the bags standing alongside the sofa. "But you are leaving . . ."

"Only to find Emma," Olivia said. "I won't advertise that I am traveling alone with two unmarried gentlemen if you will not."

"I shall defend your honor with my life . . . as I will defend Emma's."

"You are not troubled by the mysterious objection?"

"It is obvious to me that my fiancée is in some sort of trouble," he said fiercely, "and I shall do whatever is necessary to get her out of it."

"No matter what our investigation may

uncover?" Kit asked.

"You haven't known Emma long," he said to his friend. "She has changed immeasurably since she returned from the Continent. Our marriage was desired by both our families, and we were engaged before she went away for her health." He stared at the carpet. "I confess that I did not love her then. I found her spoiled and more than a little arrogant, but I was prepared to do my duty. I was not prepared for the woman who came home to Albion."

"I did not know her well in those days, either," Olivia confessed. "We are distant cousins but had few occasions to meet. Now it seems that everyone wishes to be near her."

"Yes," Edward said, "and with good reason. Generosity and love of life have replaced vanity and overindulgence." His voice softened. "She seems almost a different person."

"You love her very much," Olivia said, glancing shyly at Kit.

"More than life itself." He glared at the coals in the grate, which gave up their feeble attempts to blaze with a gasp of gray smoke. "That is why I cannot bear . . . might we leave soon?"

"Immediately." She hesitated. "Is there

anyone you wish to inform?"

"No. Better by far that Emma's family know nothing of this until . . . until we have found her."

"Very well. Give me a moment to speak with my maid."

Olivia hurried into the bedroom to consult with Alice and returned to find that the men had already taken up her baggage and were champing at the bit. Olivia's own coachman was waiting on the street, and the three of them climbed into the carriage as the last of the light faded from the overcast London sky.

Once they had reached the western outskirts of the city, Kit disappeared and made his transformation. The Black Dog burst from a thick patch of shrubbery, his great shaggy coat exuding steam, his red eyes burning with eagerness to begin the hunt. With a booming *woof* he bounded away, setting off on the Oxford road.

"What happened to his clothes?" Edward asked as the carriage set off after Kit. "Surely he didn't leave them in a pile behind the shrubbery."

Olivia laughed. "Hardly. He 'takes' his clothing with him . . . though what actually becomes of it I have no notion. It's magic."

"Of course." Edward sighed. "And I suppose he is tireless and can run for hundreds of miles without stopping?"

"Wild Magic is often that way, though it also possesses its share of disadvantages. I have reminded Kit that we are not quite so resilient. He knows we'll have to make frequent stops to change horses and take meals, though in Black Dog form he can be rather impatient."

True to her assertions, Kit ranged far ahead and returned frequently to eye his human companions with crimson glares of disapproval. At High Wycombe the coachman and his passengers paused to change horses and share a quick meal. The moon had risen, and Edward supplemented its light with a ball of fire — a miniature sun that he held in place above the carriage. His magical strength was nearly spent by the time Kit finally came to a halt at Oxford's city limits.

"This is as far as my nose takes me," Kit said, emerging from behind a byre at the town's edge. He adjusted his spectacles. "There is a large train station here. It seems likely that she boarded once she was confident that no one followed her."

Edward, pale with exhaustion and fear for Emma, flung himself into a bout of furious pacing. "Can you track her on a train?"

"I fear not. But you mustn't give up hope, old man."

"And there must be some in town who saw her," Olivia said, "at least in the vicinity of the train station. We shall go at once."

"In the middle of the night?" Edward asked.

"There will still be people at the station," she said. "I doubt that any of us can sleep. I certainly could not."

The men agreed, and so they went on to the station, where — after an impatient attempt by Edward to intimidate the ticket seller — Olivia insisted upon asking the questions. Though she used all her charm, it soon became evident that the fellow was not being entirely forthcoming. His heartbeat was much too fast, and sweat flooded from his pores.

"He's lying," Kit said. "I could smell it from here."

"I'll get the truth out of him," Edward snarled, snapping a flame to life between his fingers.

Olivia winced. The last thing they needed was a hotheaded Lucifer getting out of hand. She placed her fingertips on Edward's arm.

"We shall learn the truth," she promised. "Why don't you and Kit wait here while I learn who else might have seen Emma."

With much grumbling and his friend's encouragement — for Kit well knew that Olivia could take care of herself — Edward consented. Olivia made the rounds of the station, finding a few employees and a handful of passengers waiting for the next train. None of them admitted to seeing a dark-haired, pretty young woman traveling alone.

At last Olivia returned to the one man she knew had something to hide. The ticket seller was just as stubbornly uncooperative as before, and Olivia finally resorted to bringing Kit along for motivation. One glance at Old Shuck convinced the terrified agent that he was best served by honesty.

"They said they'd pay me well if I kept me mouth shut," he said, mopping his forehead with a damp handkerchief. "They also said they'd be . . . most unhappy if I said aught about —"

"Who are 'they'?" Kit demanded.

"I don't know." The man squeezed his eyes closed. "Important toffs, they was, but they didn't want nobody to recognize 'em. I saw when they met the lady . . . just like the one you described, ma'am."

"She did not go willingly?"

"Not as I could see. They carried her off to their carriage, and —"

469

A streak of fire shot narrowly past Olivia's head, slipped through the window of the ticket booth, and dropped to the ground at the agent's feet. He yelped and danced wildly to put it out.

"Where did they go?" Edward said in a dangerously soft voice.

The man shrank in on himself, trembling. "East. 'at's all I know. All I know."

"He's telling the truth," Olivia said. "Kit, we'll require your services again."

Fortunately, there was only one road leading east out of town. Once they had changed horses again and collected a hasty dawn breakfast of bread, cheese, and freshly picked berries, the Black Dog sniffed out the trail without undue difficulty. It led them to Cheltenham and another set of fresh horses . . . as well as an innkeeper who reluctantly admitted to having seen a number of "rough characters" with a lovely young woman headed east.

Edward was nearly beside himself, but Olivia managed to calm him before he set the inn afire. On they traveled through the morning, skirting Gloucester and Hereford. Inevitably the road branched into any number of smaller lanes, and at each one Kit sat on his massive haunches, pricked his long, silky ears, and sucked air through his broad, black nose until he had isolated the desired scent.

It was by such winding back roads — and after making several stops throughout the long day — that they came to the river Wye, which led at last to the border of Cymru. The hilly country was interlaced with pockets of dense woodland, secret valleys, and isolated farmsteads, any one of which could have concealed an abducted young woman and her captors.

Kit never gave up. He made clear that the others were to wait with the carriage while he ranged ahead. Olivia, Edward, and the coachman shared the last of their luncheon of sausage and meat pies and nursed the bumps and bruises of the long and difficult ride. Olivia kept up a steady patter of soothing conversation to distract Edward, who smoldered like a peat fire barely contained under the earth.

The Black Dog returned with the setting of the sun. He quickly changed and approached Edward with very sensible wariness.

"I've found her," he said. Edward leaped up. Kit gripped his friend's shoulder. "Steady, my lad. She's in the hands of several very competent-looking fellows, and there are guards outside the byre where they're keeping her."

"Is she hurt?"

"I was only able to catch a glimpse through a window, but she seems un-harmed," Kit said. "She is bound, however, and they appear to be questioning her."

Edward rattled off a string of obscenities, hardly remembering to beg Olivia's pardon. "By God," he rasped. "I'll . . . I'll . . ."

"You'll remain calm, and we shall approach this as rational beings, not children," Olivia chided. She met Kit's gaze. "How many men did you say?"

"Ten, at most, including the guards."

"And we are three."

"I won't have the law involved in this," Edward said.

"No need," Kit said. "One of the Black Dog's most useful skills is the ability to arouse fright in most men . . . especially since he is often a harbinger of death in myth and legend." He grinned. "Let me handle the guards. You and Livvy wait until I give the signal, and then we'll deal with the rest" — he pinned Olivia with a particu-larly meaningful stare — "when it's *safe* to do so."

Grim-faced, Edward pulled a gun from his coat pocket and checked it over care-fully. Olivia shuddered, loathing the thought of violence and yet knowing it might not be possible to avoid it. She had no useful weapon like the men; she was no Puppet-master to actually influence the workings of the human body. But she did have the element of surprise.

Kit set out again. Olivia found a patch of soft bracken where she could rest her weary head and jarred body for a few regrettably brief moments. When she woke, Edward had disappeared.

Her own store of imprecations was considerably larger than even Kit would have believed. She spoke briefly to the coachman, instructing him to stay with the horses in readiness for a hasty flight, and made her way by moonlight in the direction Kit had gone. A mile of stumbling over pebbles the size of boulders, and collecting a forest's worth of twigs and leaves in her skirts, brought her to an escarpment overlooking a scattering of farmstead buildings, many collapsed and all dark save for faint illumination streaming from the byre. Olivia scrambled down the steep and rocky incline, landing on a very welcome patch of soft grass.

It was not difficult to tell where Edward had gone. Even as she made her way cautiously toward the byre, a hot light blossomed at one corner of the byre. Alarmed voices rose in the distance. Olivia ran.

She arrived to a scene of utter chaos. Men were fleeing the byre in all directions as the fire, spreading rapidly, consumed half-rotted timbers and thatch. The Black Dog bounded this way and that, his thunderous voice shaking the ground beneath Olivia's feet.

Olivia could think only of Emma, trapped somewhere within that raging conflagration. She darted for the byre's open door, dodged the wall of searing heat, and peered through the choking swirls of smoke.

Two figures crouched in the center, one male and one female. Just as Olivia was plotting her path to reach them, the man rose with the woman in his arms and raced for the door. Olivia retreated, and the three of them collapsed in a coughing, soot-stained heap.

A warm, wet tongue slurped across Olivia's face.

"Ugh. Kit, do you mind . . ."

The Black Dog grinned, showing massive white teeth, and trotted away. A moment later Kit returned.

"The men are gone. Are you all right?" he asked, including Edward and Emma in his glance.

Olivia dragged her hand across her face.

"I am fine," she said. "Emma?"

The young woman looked up, blinking, her dazed eyes catching the reflection of the suddenly dying fire. "Where . . . where am I?"

Edward held her in his arms, his cheek pressed to her hair. "She doesn't seem to know how she got here," he murmured.

"Her captors were certainly treated to a glorious announcement of our arrival," Olivia said crossly. "Could you not control yourself?"

Edward flushed. "I saw her through the window, and I couldn't bear —"

"Edward?" Emma turned in his arms. "Edward, are you really here?"

"Yes, darling. You're safe now. Those brigands won't bother you again."

Olivia knelt before Emma. "You aren't hurt?"

"I . . . no." She glanced up at Kit. "Did you all come after me?"

"You simply disappeared," Edward said, his voice growing stern. "What did you expect? That I would not take an interest?"

"Oh, Edward." She covered her face with her hands. "I've made such a mess of things. If only you'd stayed away . . ."

"I'm sure we all have much to discuss," Kit interrupted, "but it would be best if we leave this place, as the fire is very likely to attract attention, and the men may return with reinforcements."

"An inn is out of the question —" Edward began.

"But I have another suggestion. When he died, my father left me a cottage not far from here. It is extremely modest, but it should serve to provide us with shelter and a bed tonight."

"A cottage?" Olivia said. "I never heard of it."

"I've scarcely ever been there, and not in many years," Kit said with a diffident air. "There may be a an elderly caretaker in residence, but no servants. I wish I could offer you better. . . ."

"I'm sure it will suffice," Edward said. "Lead on, my friend."

They hurried back to the carriage as fast as bruises and aching muscles would allow, only to find that Olivia's coachman had deserted them. Edward admitted to some skill in driving, but since Kit knew the way, he took the ribbons while the others climbed into the seats and resigned themselves to another fast and uncomfortable ride.

"Who were those men, Emma?" Olivia asked once they were well on their way. "Can you tell us why they abducted you?"

Emma took a deep breath, and Olivia could see that she was considering prevarication.

"You'd better tell us the truth," she said. "Nothing less will do, I fear."

"Yes." Emma fixed her gaze on Olivia. "I don't know who they were, as they always wore hoods or low hats, but one was an Inquisitor. He was the man I saw most often."

"An Inquisitor?" Edward said. "Why were they questioning you, Emma? Has this to do with what happened at the wedding?"

Emma pulled away from Edward and wrapped her arms about her chest. "These men . . . and quite possibly the man in the church . . . must have known that I have spent the past several years working for the War Office as a confidential agent at the Burgundian Court. My captors are almost certainly the enemies of Albion."

Edward paled. "A confidential agent? You?"

"Good Lord," Olivia murmured. "The mist begins to clear."

The tale spilled out of Emma as though she had no means or will to stop it. With every revelation Edward lost a little more color. Yet when it was finished and Edward recognized the extent to which his bride had

477

deceived him, he forgave her with all his generous heart.

"My poor darling," he said. "What you must have endured, risking your life for Albion!"

Emma looked away, refusing to meet his eyes.

As Kit had warned them, the cottage was an unprepossessing affair — a single-story house surrounded by an overgrown garden amid a few acres of rough land — yet it was certainly no laborer's hovel. Olivia supposed that it might have been used as a hunting lodge, or a country residence for men who desired to take holiday without their womenfolk. Kit went inside while Edward stabled the horses in a small byre adjacent to the house. Kit reemerged with a grim expression.

"It's somewhat the worse for wear," he admitted. "Old Dafydd, the caretaker, isn't here at the moment, but at least he left the place reasonably clean." Kit's cheeks took on a tinge of pink. "I can draw a bath for the ladies and prepare a meal of sorts. I do apologize for my poor hospitality."

"Don't be ridiculous, Kit," Olivia said. "Anything remotely civilized will be welcome under the circumstances."

Once they were inside, Olivia could see that the place had been long neglected in spite of its resident caretaker. Of course she knew a little about Kit's father . . . he'd been one of the old nobility and also a clandestine member of the Rebellion, which had exhausted his fortune and eventually compelled him to flee Cymru and settle in East Anglia. There he had met and married Sarah Brasnett, a viscount's daughter of exceptionally good breeding, who had lost something of her reputation by joining her name to a man whose family blood ran hot with Wild Magic. In fact, the couple had lived and raised Kit in a condition of genteel poverty.

But Kit had always known he was loved, and nothing could take that certainty away from him.

He, however, was clearly out of sorts, and spurned Olivia's efforts to engage him in conversation while he prepared rooms for his female guests.

What has come between us, my friend? she thought. *We have always been the best of co-conspirators. Something troubles you, and it is far more than the state of this house.*

She never found the right moment to ask him, for shortly he announced that the yellow and blue bedchambers were ready for occupation. Once Olivia had seen to Emma's comfort, she retired to her own room, where she made a hasty toilette at the washstand and was glad enough to close her eyes after a night and day of rattling about in a coach, no matter how well sprung.

She woke to heavy silence and the aroma of brewing coffee. Buttoning up her gown, she went down to join Kit and Edward in the tiny sitting room. They broke off their conversation at once. It was still the wee hours of the morning, a time for secrets, and Kit had a vaguely guilty look about him. Olivia vowed that she would not allow herself to be hurt by Kit's behavior.

"I smell coffee," she said brightly. "I would dearly love a cup."

"You detest the stuff," Kit protested with a slight smile.

"I will have some, nonetheless."

She had barely taken her first sip when a bloodcurdling scream rent the air.

Edward shot to his feet. Kit dashed for the stairs, Olivia at his heels. She rushed ahead and blocked the way into Emma's room.

"Let me go in," she said. "If I require assistance, I will let you know."

"She needs me!" Edward protested. He lunged for the door, but Kit intercepted him, holding on with stubborn strength. Olivia went into the room and closed the door.

Emma was sitting upright in bed, her face streaked with tears. Her gaze was focused on some point above Olivia's head.

"Did you see it?" she asked in a whisper.

Olivia looked up at the wall. "See what, Emma?"

The young woman swiped her sleeve across her face. "I couldn't have imagined it. It was real. Just as real as . . ." She paused, her eyes acknowledging Olivia with guarded defiance. "You will think me mad."

"Not at all." Olivia sat on the edge of the bed and took Emma's hand. "You have been through a great deal. What is it you saw?"

Emma shuddered. "A spirit. A particular kind of apparition that . . . that my maid, Kate, used to speak of."

Kate O'Brennan, as Olivia well knew, was the young woman who had met an untimely end on the Continent while she was serving Emma. Her tragic and unexpected demise had brought Emma home to Albion, but Kate's body had been left behind, lost in the Loire River.

"You saw a ghost?" Olivia asked gently.

"Not a ghost. A banshee."

"A banshee? The creatures that are supposed to appear when . . . when someone is about to —"

"— die. Yes." Emma shivered. "It is not the first time I have seen one, Olivia. The first time was at St. Bertram's . . . just before the young Eirishman fell down the steps and broke his neck."

Kit grunted as he pulled the massive book from the dusty library shelf and began to thumb the dog-eared pages.

" 'Banshee,' " he muttered. " 'Bean-sidhe. Eirish folklore. A spirit or fairy who presages a death by wailing.' "

"Do you mean that this 'bean-sidhe' killed the man in the church?" Olivia asked.

"Not at all. They don't kill . . . they only warn of impending death." He looked up with a frown. "That much is common knowledge to any student of magic. But from what I understand, they only appear to those of Eirish descent, particularly those of noble or royal blood."

"Emma isn't Eirish," Edward said.

"Some prefer not to advertise such connections," Olivia said dryly, stirring her cold coffee with a bent silver spoon. "There are but three possibilities: Either Emma imagined this apparition —"

"I don't believe it," Edward interjected.

"— there is hidden Eirish blood in either the Denholme or Brightwell lines, or this bean-sidhe is behaving very much out of character."

"And there is a further complication," Kit said, setting the book down on a side table. "The bean-sidhe is only supposed to appear when a loved one or member of the family is about to die."

"And Emma said that she saw the spirit in the church just before the stranger met his untimely end," Olivia said.

Edward sat up in his chair. "She had nothing to do with his death!"

"I was not implying that she did. She denies ever having seen his face."

Edward remained stiff as a poker. "She has no family in this house," he said, "But depending upon the definition of 'loved one' . . ."

"We gain nothing by such cheerless speculation." Olivia tapped the spoon against her lip. "Only Emma can make sense of this, and evidently she is not prepared to tell everything she knows."

"Are you suggesting —"

"If she was a spy for the War Office, there are doubtless many things she isn't permitted to reveal," Olivia said. "As soon as she is recovered, we must get her back to civilization and under the protection of the Crown."

"If that is what she wishes," Kit said. "She tried to escape before. Apparently she doesn't believe that the War Office can protect her."

"There's no telling how many enemies she has, even here in Albion," Edward said. "I'll get her out of the country. We'll go to the Colonies if we must."

"I doubt that the War Office will simply allow her to leave," Kit said, "particularly once they've learned that she was abducted and questioned. If she has knowledge of state secrets —" He stopped, jerked up his head, and swung toward the door to the hall. Olivia could almost see the hair stand straight up on the back of his neck.

"Someone is approaching the house," he said. "Several men, from the sound of it."

Edward snatched the gun that he had left on a side table. Kit growled deep in his throat.

"I should have sensed them if they followed us," he said. "Unless one of them is a Dissembler. . . ."

"They are the same men?" Olivia asked, peering between the faded curtains.

"Stay away from the window, Livvy." He flared his nostrils. "I can't quite make out the scent." He glanced at Edward and then toward the stairs. "You stay with the women, and I'll go out and meet them."

"You should stay, Christopher. I can raise a firewall if they don't listen to reason."

Emma's Talent might conceivably be of some use about now, Olivia thought, *if only she would reveal it.* Olivia coughed behind her hand. "Gentlemen . . . though I am not well versed in the matter of fisticuffs or firearms, I do have a small skill that should free you both. I can set wards across the doorways, so that no stranger can enter without triggering an uproar."

Edward looked at her curiously. "But warding is a form of witchcraft, isn't it?"

Olivia blushed. "My great-aunt was a hedge-witch. She was considered the black sheep in the family, but there was a time . . . when I thought I might follow in her footsteps."

"I never heard anything of this," Kit said, his voice strained.

Olivia looked away. "I suggest that one of you go out the back door and the other the front, and I shall set the wards."

With a doubtful grumble, Edward headed for the front door. Kit slipped out the back. Olivia stilled her mind and drew upon everything she had learned from Great-

Aunt Celia. The spell came with surprising ease, reminding Olivia of what she had chosen to give up for the sake of familial duty.

She had no sooner completed her work than the wards chimed, indicating that a friend was attempting to pass. Edward gingerly stepped over the threshold, bolting the door behind him.

"It's the local constable," he said. "He has a dozen men with him, and he says he's come to arrest Emma."

"Arrest her! Why?"

"It's preposterous. They claim that she murdered Kate O'Brennan!"

"I did not do it," Emma said, jaw set and eyes bright with rebellion.

She sat erect on the edge of her chair, her hands clasped in her lap, every inch the earl's daughter and disciplined agent. Edward sat beside her, clearly frustrated by her refusal to let him touch or comfort her. It was as if she had pushed him away both mentally and physically . . . as if they were complete strangers who had barely escaped the dreadful mistake of holy wedlock.

Edward had begun to entertain his own doubts. He had confessed as much to Kit, who in turn had warned Olivia of the strain developing between them. But that seemed the least of their worries, given that the constable and his men were lined up directly on the other side of Edward's firewall, waiting for Edward's strength — and his magic — to fail. Kit had not yet returned.

"We believe you, my dear," Olivia said. "However, it is evident that something has led the authorities to judge you a suspect. If ever there was a time for frankness, it is now." She sighed at Emma's stubborn expression. "Were you aware that there were questions surrounding Kate's death? Was this the objection the Eirishman was about to raise at the wedding? And what of the men who abducted you? Can you tell us no more about them?"

"I remember nothing of the questions they asked me, and little of the men themselves. I have told you all I know."

"All you are permitted to say . . . is that it?" Edward asked. "Darling, your future, possibly your life, is at stake. Whatever it is, I will understand —"

Emma cut him off with shockingly cold precision. "Even if — as Edward believes — this constable is genuine, the timing of his arrest cannot be coincidence."

"I had reached a similar conclusion," Olivia said. "But why are these men so eager to take you, Emma? If they are Albion's enemies and foreign agents, how can they be so blatant in their approach, even in a place as isolated as this?"

"They must be using Talent to disguise their purpose from any who might interfere," Edward said, "just as they used it to cloud Emma's memory of her interrogation. Some among them must be highly placed, in Albion or abroad. Their confidence suggests that they have the advantage on their side."

"I fear you may be right," Olivia said. "Whoever they are, they surely won't wait forever." She glanced toward the window. "What can be keeping Kit?"

Edward touched her shoulder. "Christopher can take care of himself."

Perhaps he could, Olivia reflected, but he also had a wild streak that even she could not predict. She muttered something about finding tea in the kitchen, armed herself with a poker from the hearth, and ventured out the back door.

Edward's firewall still stood unbreached, though Olivia knew that Kit must have found a way to pass through it unharmed . . . another peculiar and occasionally useful Black Doggish talent, no doubt. To her eyes and ears it rose as a solid wall of flame, perhaps four feet in width, its upper edge licking at shoulder-height. It would burn most men and women, Talented or not, as effectively as a real fire, though this one made no sound and relied on no solid fuel that Olivia could detect. It would falter when Edward had exhausted his magical strength.

She made her way around the house just inside the wall. At the front of the cottage clustered a group of men. Olivia took a firmer grip on her poker and approached the fire.

"You," she called. "Constable. I am Lady Olivia Dowling."

A stout, thickset man broke away from the others and strode toward her, pausing only when the heat grew too intense for him to bear. He shielded his face with one broad hand and peered through the leaping flames.

"Lady Olivia," he said. "It would be best for everyone if you would encourage your companions to give themselves up. Lady Emma is assured of a fair trial under the law."

Olivia smiled. "I'm certain that Lady Emma would be more inclined to cooperate if she had not already been kidnapped and questioned by persons unknown." She cocked her head. "Yours is an honest face,

Constable. I'm sure you have no knowledge of such activities."

"I do not, my lady." He glanced behind him. "Can you name the men who committed this alleged act?"

"Unfortunately, I cannot, and Lady Emma was subjected to a Talent which impaired her memory of the event. You can see why she is not keen to trust anyone at the moment."

"Nevertheless, I am the duly appointed representative of the Crown, and I —" He stopped as a man came up to join him, and bent his head to listen to the other's low-voiced words. He straightened. "Under the law, I am permitted to take any action necessary to serve my warrant, and . . ."

Olivia didn't hear the rest of his speech. Her attention was riveted on the man who had spoken to the constable . . . a man whose face was hidden under a low-brimmed hat and high collar, a man who walked with a slight limp that no one but an Anatomist might remark. She released her breath and allowed her Residual gift to take command of her senses.

She scanned down the length of the man's right leg and found the healed fracture, the peculiar pattern of the break, and the thickness of long-healed tissue where the bone had penetrated flesh. She remembered when the accident had happened. She had been there, along with her father, on the day that the dashing Sir Valentine Crowley — for whom she had nurtured a devastating childhood infatuation — had tumbled from his horse at a flying gallop.

She made her decision in an instant. "Sir Valentine," she called.

He stopped in the act of turning away, his heartbeat reaching a furious velocity. She felt the blood surge into his muscles.

"Sir Valentine. Do you not remember me? Olivia Dowling?"

He faced her slowly under the constable's curious eye. "Lady Olivia," he said without inflection.

"Sir Valentine?" the constable said, clearly surprised. "When you came to me about Lady Emma, I'd no idea who you —"

"It would have been better if you hadn't recognized me, Olivia," Valentine said, "but I didn't know your grandmother had died."

"She hasn't," Olivia said, bewildered. "I seem to have obtained some of her Talent Residually. It is a mixed blessing. . . ." She trailed off, well aware that something was badly amiss. "Why should I not have recognized you?"

He sighed, his shoulders rising and fall-

491

ing, and tipped the brim of his hat. "What do you want, Livvy?"

"An explanation. Why have charges been brought against Lady Emma? How are you involved in this?"

Silence. Then the constable made a low, startled sound, and Olivia saw the gun pointed at his chest.

"I had hoped it wouldn't come to this," Sir Valentine said, "but it seems there is no help for it now." He met Olivia's gaze through the fire. "Tell Lady Emma, Lord Edward, and your friend Mr. Meredith that we will not be going away until she gives herself up. We have the numbers and the Talent. We —"

His sentence ended in a soft *oomph* as the constable lunged for the gun. The weapon's report boomed and echoed. A body sprawled on the earth, and it was not Sir Valentine's.

"A pity," he said. "But you must understand that we will have Lady Emma sooner or later, and it will go easier with her if you surrender."

Sickness clutched at Olivia's stomach. Her blood turned to ice, and she clenched her fists in impotent fury. "Who are you, Crowley? What are you? Did you abduct Lady Emma?"

"The less you know, the better for you."

But of course she could already guess. *"My captors are almost certainly the enemies of Albion,"* Emma had said. And here was one of them in the flesh.

"If you will kill a man in cold blood," Olivia said, "murder him . . . why should we believe you will not do the same to us?"

"Because you have no choice." He raised the gun. "Lord Edward's firewall may hinder a man, but it will not halt a bullet."

Olivia stared at the gun, her mouth gone dry. "The others must know I am gone by now. They will have heard the first shot. Edward and Emma are both resourceful; they'll get away —"

Sir Valentine gestured to the henchmen gathering at his back. "Even if my men fail to catch them," he said, "your friends are sure to submit when I inform them that you will bleed to death if I do not send for a physician immediately." He took careful aim. "It won't kill you, my dear. There will be time —"

A mass of black fur and muscle soared out of the air on the other side of the firewall, crashing into Crowley with a roar like an oncoming locomotive. A chorus of yells and snarls beat against Olivia's ears.

"Kit!" she cried.

The huge head swung toward her, and Crowley's gun cracked. The Black Dog's growls snapped off in a shriek of pain. Sir Valentine's underlings summoned their courage and began to close in. Sir Valentine heaved himself up, face and neck streaked with blood, eyes wild. He aimed at the crouching canine.

Olivia had no thought for herself, no doubts about what she could and could not do. She closed her eyes and envisioned Sir Valentine's body . . . his heart pumping the fluid of life, his stomach busy with digestion, his muscles tensed to kill. A strange darkness overwhelmed her, a bitter new knowledge that bubbled to the surface of her consciousness like some noxious gas beneath still, dark waters.

She gave a little twist to the image in her mind, shifting molecules with the force of her will. Crowley's agonized cry was more terrible than anything Olivia could have anticipated. Sir Valentine dropped the gun and doubled over, clutching at his belly. The henchmen stared from him to Olivia, blanched as one, and fled.

The strength drained out of Olivia's legs like hot air from an aerostat. She struck the ground with enough force to empty her lungs, and as she struggled to breathe she took in the bizarre tableau of a gibbering Sir Valentine, a bloodied and limping Old Shuck, and an unnamed constable rising from the dead.

"There, now," the lawman's voice floated through the firewall. "You'll be fine, my lady."

Olivia got to her knees. "But you . . . I saw you —"

"I thought it best to play dead," the constable said, relieving Crowley of his gun. "He only nicked me on the shoulder. Not as good a shot as he believes. And as for your friend, here . . ." He regarded the Black Dog with wary respect. "He is your friend, I take it?"

"Indeed." Olivia still felt a spot of nausea, and a distant horror at what she had done, but there would be time to deal with that at a more suitable moment. "Kit! Can you come over to me?"

The Dog growled, plunged through the firewall, and abruptly vanished. Kit stood in his place, his clothing only slightly askew. Blood welled from a wound in his right leg, rapidly soaking the black wool of his trousers.

"It's nothing," he said gruffly. "It didn't hit anything important." He felt for the spectacles that no longer sat on his nose.

"Blast it, I lost them. Pardon, Livvy."

He sounded immeasurably weary and hurting, but he was alive. "We must get you inside at once," Olivia said. "And your arm must also be seen to, Constable."

"It's Greaves, my lady," he said. "At your service. I'll secure Sir Valentine while you lower the firewall. And we'll need reinforcements to round up Sir Valentine's lackeys." He squinted at her thoughtfully. "Begging your pardon, but why did Sir Valentine conceal his true identity when he presented me with the warrant for Lady Emma's arrest? Why does he want her so badly that he'd shoot us to take her?"

"I suspect I know only part of the story, Greaves." She told him of her belief that Sir Valentine had abducted Emma once, and that he or one of his men was an Inquisitor intent on gaining some coveted information that only she possessed. "The rest may be beyond my province to explain, but we shall have answers eventually."

She tore off a wide strip of her petticoat and bandaged Kit's leg while Greaves handcuffed the weeping Crowley. She and Kit plodded back toward the house, where Edward met them.

"Thank god!" he cried, extinguishing the firewall with a twitch of his fingers. "We heard the shots, but Emma fainted just when I was about to look for you." He offered Kit his shoulder. "What the hell is going on?"

Olivia explained as best she could, finishing as Greaves joined them. The constable deposited Sir Valentine in the pantry and braced the door closed with the heavy kitchen table. Greaves remained behind while Kit, Edward, and Olivia entered the sitting room to find Emma perched on the edge of the settee, her lips curled in a mocking smile.

"What have we here?" she asked. "Two dogs and a bitch limping in with their bedraggled prey. You timed your rescue exquisitely well, Eddie dear."

"Emma?" Edward said, leaving Kit in an overstuffed armchair. "Are you all right?"

"Better than I've been in months." She stretched her arms high above her head. "So well, in fact, that I have no intention of going back."

"Going back?" Olivia echoed. "Emma, we have the man who abducted you, and the others have fled. You're safe —"

"Safe." She laughed. "If it were left up to Eddie, I'd be dead. Fortunately, I have the competence he has always lacked." She smiled at her stunned fiancé. "Did you think

I'd willingly marry you for anything but your money, Eddie dear?"

Olivia approached Emma as she might a mad dog. "What is wrong with you, Emma?" She narrowed her eyes, aware of a raging turmoil inside the other woman, a battle every bit as ferocious as the one that had taken place outside. "No," she whispered. "It isn't . . ."

"What's the matter, darling? Cat got your tongue?"

"Who *are* you?"

"That is what I wondered for some time." Greaves stood in the doorway, Sir Valentine's gun in his hand. "Fortunately, Lady Emma was happy to tell me once we were alone." He grinned. "Now perhaps we can finish our interrupted conversation."

"Greaves?" Edward said. "What nonsense is this?"

Kit stirred in his chair, and the pistol swung toward him. "No nonsense," he said grimly. "But I think we have made a serious error in judgment."

Emma stared at Greaves. "You fool," she breathed. "We could have been allies, if only you'd been patient and not let your fears of exposure overwhelm you."

"Exposure," Olivia said. "Then Greaves is . . . both he and Sir Valentine —"

"Are Burgundian agents," Emma finished. "They made fools of you all."

"Sir Valentine has run off, the filthy coward," Greaves said. He gestured with the gun. "All of you, over there with Lady Emma."

"She isn't Lady Emma," Olivia said.

"You're wrong," Emma said. "The one who occupied my body was the imposter." She glared at Edward. "The one *you* almost married. The one who tried and failed to kill me."

Edward's mouth dropped open in shock. Kit growled. A great many things began to make sense to Olivia.

"It was Kate," Emma said. "Kate who seized my body when her own was dying."

Greaves clucked reprovingly. "But it isn't that simple, my dear, and you know it." He turned to his captive audience. "You see, dear Emma was indeed a very skillful Albian agent at the Burgundian court . . . and also my lover. I had been a confidential agent for Burgundy working in Albion until a year ago, and it was her task to discover what Albian intelligence I had collected during my time here. But she forgot her sense of objectivity and became infatuated with the subject of her observation. She was persuaded to transfer her allegiance to

Mother Burgundy. Quite a coup for me —"

"Liar," Emma hissed. "I have never seen you before yesterday."

As Olivia watched in amazement, Greaves's face melted into a completely different visage, and his stout body lengthened to aristocratic lines. Emma gasped.

"Serge," she said.

"You are not the only one with a useful Talent, my dear."

"He's a Pretender," Kit muttered.

Serge bowed. "That is my particular skill, as Emma's is —" He gave a grunt of surprise, and his body began to shake. The gun twisted in his hand as if it had developed a life of its own.

Olivia glanced at Emma. She was smiling in bitter triumph, and there was no further doubt in Olivia's mind.

"Puppetmaster," Olivia said. "You are a Puppetmaster!"

"Very astute of you," Emma said. "While Serge's Talent may be dramatic, mine is ultimately more useful . . . particularly when I need to rid myself of witnesses who might interfere with the new life I shall make for myself in Albion." She stroked her lower lip. "Who shall I start with first? The big Dog?"

Slowly, fighting her silent commands with rigid muscle and clenched jaw, Greaves turned his pistol on Kit.

"No!" Olivia cried. "Kate!" She stepped in front of Kit, who tried to shove her out of the way. He lost his balance and stumbled. Greaves aimed anew.

"No!"

The voice was both strange and familiar. Emma closed her eyes, and when she opened them they shone with blessed sanity.

"It's all right, Lady Olivia," she said. "I have control again." She stared at Serge. "Tell them the whole story, Beaumarchais, or I shall let Emma shoot you."

The Burgundian's mouth worked, but his face was pale with relief. "Oui," he said hoarsely. He looked at Olivia. "All I said before was true, but I . . ." He swallowed. "Lady Emma did plan to defect to Burgundy but her scheme was uncovered by her maid and fellow agent, Kate O'Brennan . . . a very skilled Eirish commoner with several Residual knacks of use in our profession. Emma well knew that Kate would try to stop her, and so she resolved to kill the girl."

"Go on," Kate said coldly.

"However, when Emma wielded her Puppetmaster talent in an effort to murder Kate, the maid showed remarkable strength and will for one of her station. Emma lost control of her own Talent. At the instant of Kate's death, a bizarre transference occurred."

"Their souls," Olivia said. "Their spirits . . . changed places."

"Not entirely," Kate said, her voice heavy with memory. "My body died, but I fought for survival. And I did survive . . . in Emma's body."

"I did not know at the time," Serge said, gazing at the gun that had so easily turned against him. "Kate played her part so well that I never suspected that Emma existed only as a shadow in her own body. She asked for my help in disposing of Kate's body, and we threw it in the Loire. But when Emma changed her mind about defecting, I knew something was wrong." He sucked in a deep breath. "I followed her to Albion, knowing she might have been playing the double agent all along. My Albian sources revealed that she resigned from the War Office immediately upon her arrival. But as long as she remained at large, her intentions unknown, she was a threat to any Burgundian agent in Albion."

"And that is why you abducted her," Kit said. "But why did you wait so long after she returned to Albion?"

"Because I did not realize how complicated matters had become until a former lover of Kate's, one Eamonn Lyons, visited Emma at her father's estate to question her about Kate's death. My informant there overheard the interview — an informant who is now safely back in Burgundy." He smiled bitterly. "Lyons was himself an ex-agent, and a man of considerable gifts. He recognized some unique mannerism that convinced him of 'Lady Emma's' true identity, and he accused her of a cruel deception."

"Lyons is the man who objected at the wedding!" Olivia said.

"Oui. He believed that Lord Edward was about to marry an imposter. This knowledge inspired us to act when the opportunity presented itself, as it did when Lady Emma fled London. And so I learned the singular facts of the case."

"Were you the one who 'assisted' Lyons in falling down the church steps?" Kit asked.

"You may lay that death at the feet of Sir Valentine. He did not wish any outside interference until we had properly interrogated Lady Emma."

"Oh god," Edward groaned. "I cannot believe any of this."

"It is true," Kate said. She met his gaze

bravely. "I had intended to explain as soon as I returned to Albion . . . but when I met Emma's parents, I couldn't bear to tell them the truth about their daughter. And then . . . I met you. And I grew to love you so dearly that I could not . . . I couldn't bear —" She bowed her head. "I know it's over between us. I can only hope that one day, you'll —"

She stiffened, and her eyes glazed with shock. "Forgive her," she said in that other voice, and laughed. "No need for such extreme measures, Eddie. Kate didn't quite kill me when she took my body, but I was too weak to fight for it . . . until Serge's interrogation set me free. Now I'll keep what's mine."

Once again the gun wavered in Serge's trembling hand.

"Fight her, Kate!" Olivia commanded. "If you were strong enough to endure once before, you can do so again."

"Her previous victory was a mere stroke of luck," Emma snarled, but Olivia saw that her forehead was beaded with perspiration and her jaw worked with effort.

Olivia moved closer. "Kate," she said, "whatever guilt you may feel, whatever horror at taking Emma's body, remember it was not you who attempted murder —"

"Silence!" Emma shouted.

"— and would just as willingly murder everyone in this room," Olivia finished.

The gun in Beaumarchais's hand pointed toward Olivia. "You bitch," Emma hissed. "That is exactly what I shall do."

"Not this time. *Kate!*"

"I —" Kate-Emma made a strangled sound. "I cannot —"

"She cares too much," Emma said. "That is why she, and all of you, will die."

With growing despair, Olivia realized that Emma was winning the battle. Her will was too strong, too ruthless. And no one but Kate could defeat her.

"Good-bye," Kate whispered. "Forgive . . ."

"*No*" Edward said, standing to face her. "Don't you dare leave me."

Her eyes opened wide, reflecting the ferocity of the struggle for survival. "Edward . . . I love . . ."

"I love you more than life. I will not let you go, do you hear? Come back to me!"

Tears spilled down Emma's cheeks. She half-rose, shaking violently. "You . . . love me . . ."

"With all my heart."

Emma's body jerked like an Animator's mannequin and collapsed to the carpet. Kit sprang to take the gun from Serge's limp fingers. Edward rushed to Kate's side.

"Kate! Kate, do you hear me?"

The limp form stirred. "Edward?"

He stroked her cheek with his fingers. "My love . . . is it you?"

"Emma is gone," she whispered. "I am Kate. Kate O'Brennan."

"I didn't know why I fell in love when . . . when you returned from the Continent," Edward said, clasping Kate's hands in his, "but it was real. As real as you are now. I love you, Kate . . . if you will still have me."

Kate wiped the tears from the corners of her eyes. "If you can forgive such a terrible deception. . . ."

He took her in his arms. "It is you I loved — *your* soul, *your* brave and generous spirit — never Emma."

"But your family . . . I'm a commoner, of Eirish blood —"

"And that," Olivia said to Kit as she abandoned her eavesdropping, "explains in part why she saw the bean-sidhe."

"But only in part," Kit said. "Something badly frightened Eamon Lyons in St. Bertram's. He, too, must have seen the banshee. Remember, it's supposed that only the Eirish of noble blood can detect them."

"Then perhaps Kate has even more secrets than we have guessed." Olivia sighed. "The girl will have a great deal to sort out, especially since she has resolved to tell the full story to the War Office and Emma's family. Sir Valentine and his allies must be apprehended. And Kate doubtless bears some guilt for the death of her Eirish friend in St. Bertram's."

"But it wasn't she or the bean-sidhe that caused his death."

"No, but if she'd told him the truth, he might not have died at all."

"Perhaps. Or perhaps it was simply his time." He frowned. "And what of the bean-sidhe she saw here at the cottage? Whose death did that portend?"

"Don't you see, Kit?" Olivia asked. "It was Emma's demise the bean-sidhe foretold . . . the end of the murderess who lingered on to corrupt Kate's new life. *That* was justice indeed."

". . . if any man can show any just cause why they may not lawfully be joined together, let him now speak, or else hereafter for ever hold his peace."

An expectant, almost painful hush descended over the nave of St. Bertram's-in-the-Fens. Kate and Edward, kneeling at the altar, did not move a muscle. No one spoke.

The bishop released a gusty breath and rushed through the remainder of the ceremony at record speed.

"With this ring I thee worship," Edward intoned, his face radiant with happiness. "With my body I thee worship, and with all my worldly goods I thee endow."

The congregation bowed its collective head in prayer. As the final hymn reached its conclusion, Olivia took Kit's hand.

"I think very well of Edward for putting love above every other consideration," she said. "In the end, he brought his family to see things his way. And now it is done, all right and proper."

"I doubt very much," Kit said wryly, "that those two are contemplating propriety at the moment."

"Why, Kit!" Olivia smiled, noting the twinkle in his eye. "I never knew one could have such unseemly thoughts."

"Oh, I have them often enough." He cleared his throat. "The world would be a much happier place if love could overcome every obstacle in its path."

"But it can, my dear. Who should know that better than the world's most formidable canine?"

"Woof," he said with a grin.

"Woof," she said, taking his hand.

SUSAN KRINARD is the author of fourteen fantasy romance novels, several novellas, and two epic fantasy novels. Susan graduated from the California College of Arts and Crafts with the intention of becoming a science fiction cover artist, but fate led her in another direction when her first manuscript was acquired by a major publisher. Born and raised in the California Bay Area, Susan now makes her home in the "Land of Enchantment," New Mexico, with her husband, three mixed-breed dogs, and a cat named Jefferson.